WASTE IS A TERRIBLE THING TO MINE

A land yacht was cutting straight for Brax across the Fresh Kills Minimum-Security Landfill, throwing up a wake of red dust. Brax turned and ran blindly. He didn't realize until too late that he'd blundered onto a working mine face—an exposed hillside of garbage. He lost his footing and hurtled down, slewing and thrashing.

He bodysurfed through coffee grounds, vegetable trimmings, and decaying meat, crud-coated plastic bags and bottles, lawn cuttings and tuna-fish tins, scabby Band-Aids and wadded Kleenexes—flushing rats and other things before him.

And all the time, his main terror was not death by laceration or concussion but rather that he would lose momentum, would sink, would drown in garbage . . .

By Jack McKinney
Published by Ballantine Books:

THE ROBOTECH™ SERIES:

THE SENTINELS™ SERIES:

KADUNA MEMORIES

THE BLACK HOLE TRAVEL AGENCY:

FREE RADICALS

Book Three of
The Black Hole Travel Agency

Jack McKinney

A Del Rey Book
BALLANTINE BOOKS • NEW YORK

A Del Rey Book
Published by Ballantine Books

Copyright © 1992 by Jack McKinney

All rights reserved under International and Pan-American Copyright Conventions. Published in the United States of America by Ballantine Books, a division of Random House, Inc., New York, and simultaneously in Canada by Random House of Canada Limited, Toronto.

Library of Congress Catalog Card Number: 91-93165

ISBN 0-345-37078-3

Manufactured in the United States of America

First Edition: May 1992

Cover Art by Dorian Vallejo

for Paul Geiman

good man and good neighbor,
who much enjoyed a good laugh

What gives value to travel is fear.

Albert Camus
Notebooks 1935–1942

. . . the entire world was increasingly described by the metaphor of a theme park.

Michael Crichton
Jurassic Park

Thanks to Dori Stibolt for her wise
counsel on women's field hockey
and Ginny Stibolt for
expert advice on matters botanical

My gratitude to the Kahlúa Kid for her
enlightenment regarding the nation and
people of Japan, and to Barbara Smith
for the L. A. breakdown

PART ONE

Though Hell Should Bar the Way

ONE

Chapter 37: Sex Crimes of the Gods

IN DELIVERING THE coup de grace *to Washington, D.C., alien invasion had beaten out Japanese and EC bill collectors—though it was close there for a while.*

As the young rebel commander watched in horror through the wreckage of the Oval Office windows, the merciless XT artillery barrage walked inexorably from the flattened rubble of the Washington Monument, gleefully hurling flame and annihilation high. Volley upon volley advanced, turning Constitution Avenue into wasteland.

Congress's Graham-Rudman-Hollings debt reduction package had nothing on the Sirians.

The wall of holocaust explosions came rolling across the Ellipse, straight for the Rose Garden beneath the window—closer, ever closer, making the very earth frisson in terror.

A rasped breath escaped Lance Killdare and his square, smoke-darkened jaw clenched with fury. It looked like this would be all she wrote for the U.S.A., not to mention the gently bobbing R. Rugosas below the window. "Damn this war." *The words struggled to escape his muscular throat.*

The "incoming mail" was being expressed by refitted South African G-15 surface-effect artillery pieces—the 200-millimeter howitzer model with the phased-radar array fire control suite, reactive armor upgrades, biowarfare package, and three-speed, self-defrosting windshield wipers. Powerful war machines, and the pollution-loving Sirian androids who were about to become unchallenged overlords of the planet no doubt reveled in the armored behemoths' shitty mileage.

The G-15s had already bombarded the Jefferson Memorial into a scattering of marble granola and blasted the Washington

3

Monument to moth flakes. Now they lobbed in a virtual typhoon of the strange Sirian-style incendiary rounds, which exploded in bizarre vortices of color, and antipersonnel shells which produced the aliens' fiendish "smart shrapnel." The hallowed Oval Office, this very room in which the moral rectitude of liberty, democracy, and profit-motive government had been affirmed over and over, would in seconds exist no more.

"Stinking, sicko little mutoid cheeseheads," Lance snarled through white, even teeth.

Suddenly, behind him, a figure sprawled on the floor tossed back a magnificent mane of hair the color of 24-carat gold, albeit now begrimed with soot and plaster dust. "L-Lance?" A tear caught in the corner of her left eye could be seen to glisten in the hellish twilight.

"Velma! My god! You're alive!"

Killdare rushed to her side, laying down the Colt-Schmeisser 3.35mm submachine gun with its belt-fed grenade launcher, dopplering ×40 nightscope, auto-comped bipod, and redial feature. As he knelt to catch her up in his embrace, the swelling of gleaming thews shone through the tatters of his shirtsleeves. Their mouths locked together, the interplay of their tongues against their concave cheeks catching orange-yellow highlights.

When the exchange ended at last, she gazed up at him adoringly. "Oh, Lance! Is that the impact of enemy munitions or just the pounding of my heart?"

The valiant youth couldn't stifle an admiring chuckle. "For the vice-president of the United States you're some kisser, Velma."

But there was a strange glint in her eyes, one that not even the approach of the alien artillery Götterdämmerung could account for. "I'm a lot more than that, my love . . . my human love! If we are to die, let us die with no deceptions between us!"

With that, Velma's hands clutched at the base of her smooth throat. Without warning the flesh there bunched, crinkled, and came away with a hideous, sucking sound. Before Lance could regain his mental equipoise, the thing before him had peeled away the disguise—bullion-bright tresses and all—and cast it aside. The features beneath betrayed an otherworldly physiognomy the dauntless young firebrand knew well.

"Franz!"

The Morphean espionage agent threw his single-nostriled

head back and laughed bitterly, the Velma-breasts swelling suggestively against the watered silk of his once-impeccable blouse.

"Yes, it is I! Why else did you think you were spared at, and escaped so fortuitously from, our Grand Morphean auto da fé?"

Lance had fallen back with a wrenching cry, and now the being from another world rose to face him. "Lance, my dear, you have avowed your love for me—for Velma—and yet well do I know that a love between you and Franz the Morphean cannot be, so let it all end here!"

The being swept a grand gesture at the detonations that were already ripping up by far the biggest divots ever bashed from the turf of South Executive Place, even counting Gerald Ford's administration. "Better this than what the Androids have prepared for us! Better this than the acid rays of the diabolical White Dwarves of the Sirian Mind Police!"

Panting, Lance measured the distance between himself and his weapon, evaluating his chances, playing for time. "Well, I've got to hand it to you: no vice-president's ever played out such a scene in the Oval Office!"

Franz/Velma laughed again, more caustically. "Ah, think you so indeed? How ignorant you Americans are, Lance, of your own history! Would that I had the time to tell you of the one you Earthlings call 'Dan Quayle.' And would that I had the time to tell you the story of the Trough, the Adits between worlds, and the conspiracy known as Black Hole!"

"Whoa!" Lucky Junknowitz breathed to himself, taking another look at the paperback's cover. Adits? Black Hole? Ol' Bixby Santiago was really outing some serious conspiracy, there. A helluva passage to run across here on planet Confabulon.

He could sense that someone—or something—hovering off to one side of him at the swap shelf was craning for a look at the tattered book he'd been skimming, *Edge of Space*. But in an uncharacteristic act of assertiveness Lucky turned more shoulder toward whoever it was. The book was a lot more than just a chance-found bit of Earth nostalgia to latch onto, out here hell-and-gone in the Trough.

He had picked up the novel while rummaging around in the swap corner's shelves, stasis pigeonholes, and so on; he'd been more interested in the wondrous clutter of interstellar castoffs there for the taking. Pearlescent data crystals lay heaped by luminous cyber nodes, and there appeared to be a glut on the market for indestructible metallic slug-fiches. Delicate fan-shapes of icy lace, rainbow-beautiful, might be some inhuman species' racial saga or possibly insurance brochures.

The tall, pyramidal swap shelf made him think of some fantastic offworld Christmas tree. Even so, it gave him a jolt of nostalgia, remembering the way more mundane versions he'd seen in hostels, inns, flops, and campgrounds from the Mc-Murdo Sound Ramada to the Admiral Byrd Caravanserai. He was only in his mid-twenties and looked it—lanky, with a boyish grin, cowlick, sleepy eyes, snub nose, and rather large ears—but he'd gotten around. Especially if you counted the last few weeks and the parsecs in between Adits.

Lucky had picked up the book with only passing interest; it wasn't the first time he'd come across proof that other Ter-rans had preceded him into the Trough. He'd thumbed the novel idly, meaning to investigate more enigmatic shelfware instead. Then he'd realized he was holding *Edge of Space*—the book in which author Bixby Santiago had tried to lay it on the line about the Black Hole Travel Agency's plot against Earth. Bixby Santiago had tried to make clear that beings from other worlds not only existed and were visiting the planet via naked-singularity Adits, but were planning to take it over and exploit it ruinously. He had been terribly punished for what he'd tried to write and his message muti-lated with purple prose and drastic editorial revisions. And here was a copy of that pivotal novel, floating around the Trough.

Lucky checked the cover again. The illo was a real schmeer, featuring crashing space dreadnoughts, insectile-armored alien warriors, burning Terran landmark structures, and lightly clad centerfold femmes. There was no sign of the Lance-Franz contretemps—perhaps so that the younger buyers could slip the purchase past Mom and Dad.

The title, along with the notation *Worlds Abound #32*, was in raised foil letters that had half peeled over the years since its publication by Sony-Neuhaus. The book was dog-eared and flaccid with surrender, yellowed pages smelling of self-destructing acid-based paper, its spine gray-veined with the stresses of much passing around. How it had gotten a jillion parsecs or whatever from Earth to Confabulon was one more riddle of the Trough.

Clasping the book close to him, Lucky looked back to the shelf where he'd found it. He could see no other Terran books, but back behind where *Edge of Space* had lain gleamed something round and shiny. Lucky pocketed the paperback absently and reached for it, his mouth suddenly dry. The artifact was solid but surprisingly light, with the texture of plastic and an equatorial banding something like the grooves on a pre-Turn phonograph record.

As he drew the sphere toward him Lucky could see that one arc of it had been lopped off, perhaps to serve as a base. He turned the flattened part toward him and found that it was a darkened bull's-eye. Rotating it in both hands now, he found some sort of symbol, black on white, on the point opposite the bull's-eye.

He puzzled over it: two crop-cornered black rectangles standing on their short ends side by side, touching one another. Lucky thought of the infinite meanings this alien character might have, the near-impossibility of bringing to light what it might represent. But somehow the artifact had cast a spell over him, and he had the deep-seated conviction that he must know more about it.

Then it came to him that his thumb was covering most of a smaller feature, a little golden oval with black hieroglyphs on it, to one side of the white disk. He stared at the symbols that spoke of the impenetrable secrets of space and time, he—

"Hey! Wait a sec."

—he turned it so that he could read the English letters on the little oval sticker: "IDEAL: Made in China."

Looking down, he realized that the symbol on the white disk was a large number eight. Which Lucky—raised by toy-loving hippie parents—knew had to mean that, that . . .

"It's a *Magic 8 Ball*!"

He rolled it back to gaze down into the bull's-eye window. Up through the blue fluid floated the words YOU MAY RELY ON IT.

Operant paranoia took hold for a moment, Lucky shooting nervous glances in every direction for Black Hole Security's White Dwarves. The conviction had hit him like an audit notice that they'd set up this whole *Edge of Space* 8 Ball thing just for a bit of a giggle at his expense before they hung him upside down and shoved an enema nozzle down his nostril, or whatever the Trough equivalent was—acid rays, for all he knew.

Lucky was still at a loss about most of the finer points of Trough life.

His free-floating twitchiness had been building ever since he left Earth, determined to rescue Harley Paradise and Sheena Hec'k, who'd been abducted by Black Hole. The late Rashad Tittle had told Lucky that two women had been taken to the Agency's interrogation center and gulag on al-Reem, and it was to that dreaded world that Lucky had to make his way somehow or other, against all odds. One possibility had brought him to Confabulon, but there was the ever-present danger that Black Hole was laying for him. So nervousness was to be expected; he was one lone tertiary-planet hick up against the shadowy powers that ruled the Trough.

Despite premonitions of doom, Lucky couldn't see anything immediately menacing or suspicious in the foyer of Pension Panache—just the comings and goings of guests who'd faded to planet Confabulon for the travel-industry trade fair.

As far as he could tell, he blended in. He'd left in his overnight bag the dashing cape, cummerbund, gaucho pants, and kneeboots Sheena Hec'k had foisted on him back on Edri—a tad spitefully, no two ways about it—as "all the rage in the Trough." Instead he was turned out in a roomy and durable suit of intricately patterned fabric, sporting high-gloss lapels, that made him look a little like he earned his living showing people to their seats with a flashlight.

That didn't bother Lucky much. On the plus side, by getting the two-headed salesbeing into an argument with itself he had gotten it to throw in a pair of individually fitted ankle boots that were airy, comfortable, gave great support, and seemed weightless. Better than any Terran high-tech hiking gear. Best of all, there were a lot of humanoids strolling around town in the same getup or one in a similar vein; avoiding attention was just what he'd wanted.

It was with that in mind that he was carrying in an inner pocket, rather than wearing around his neck, the strange disk with the interlocking eight-rings logo, which he'd had made into a medallion. The disk had careened into him out of—so it appeared at the time—midair on Earth months before. The eight-ring pattern got weird reactions from Trough types, but he'd never been able to find out exactly why. At any rate, Lucky wasn't out to attract notice today and felt he was doing a pretty good job.

Thus it came as a surprise when something squirmy touched him tentatively on the right thigh.

Lucky was still in the air a foot or so when the XT added peremptorily, "I say there, Thing, but if you're through examining that rather quaint-looking whatsit, I should like to take a glance at it."

A fellow guest at the Panache, Lucky concluded. The being suggested nothing so much as a clam on two L-shaped, comic-strip legs. The shell was tilted back and slightly open so that two round, large-pupiled eyes could stare up at Lucky from far back in its depths. As he watched, a rather short, skinny arm with three mutually opposable digits emerged from the darkness of the clam's interior and made wholly inadequate reaching motions. The limb looked fairly rigid and had skin like amber Naugahyde—nothing like whatever squiggly bit had touched Lucky's leg.

"Who ya calling 'Thing' . . . Mussels?" Lucky shot back snappily, holding the Magic 8 Ball over his head keepaway style. "I saw it first."

The critter was making awkward little upsurges that proved it hadn't evolved for volleyball or steeplechase events. "What sort of deranged moral reasoning is that? Especially since my interest in alien cultures makes that sphere of doubtless greater interest and benefit to me?"

Lucky didn't want to attract attention, but another glance around the Panache assured him no one was watching. What with the wild assortment of races and subspecies thronging through the Adits between worlds, misunderstandings were all too common a hazard. A naive traveler might slap out the flames on a fellow pilgrim's posterior brachs only to find out he'd interrupted a beauty treatment or holy sacrament. Thus, a studied disinterest was often the best course. And so the giraffe-like guest continued perusing the tours advertised for offworld visitors; a couple resembling Disney's ice-skating *Fantasia* pixies went on feeling each other up while light-footing it for the lift tube; and a passing gleamer wearing a HOSPITALITY BATTALION brassard on its alloy chest trundled an unconscious Nall to his room in an antigrav wheelbarrow.

"How about possession being nine-tenths of the law?" Lucky riposted. "Besides, got my own reasons for hanging onto *agghh!*"

He shook like St. Vitus had filled out his dance card as a surge of electricity raced up his leg to set off fireworks behind his eyeballs. The 8 Ball slipped from his spastic fingers.

The zapping subsided. Gasping for breath, he saw that the creature had caught the contested toy in the three-digit limb and was retracting into its shell's interior a flexible organ or member that looked like nothing so much as the upper part of a bamboo fly-casting rod. Lucky thought about reaching for the 8 Ball but decided against risking more shell-shock. He wondered how many other kinds of extremity the being had.

"Ninety per cent of your law being in my favor now," the 8 Ball's new possessor said, "I trust you will concede the legality of my ownership." It examined the toy closely, its eyes up very close to the opening of the darkened shell now.

"Why, ya little *putz*!" But in spite of his anger, Lucky kept his distance. Maybe if he could have laid hands on some rubber long johns it would've been worth a go. But there wasn't time for all that, and besides, he was late for his new job.

He had to get going over to the convention center, where he was to begin a five-day gig working for one Supervisor Undershort. Lucky himself would be using the alias Salty Waters, which had been thrust on him along with his cover story by a dying Rashad Tittle. Much as he needed to get moving, though, he couldn't bear to leave without the 8 Ball.

"Look, bro, that artifact's of great, ah, religious significance to me."

The thing stopped its dexterous turning of the 8 Ball. "Is that so? Religious?"

He wasn't sure if he'd caught a trace of sympathy or not, but it was the only card he had to play right now. "Y-yeah." He couldn't tell if the damned bemmie was buying the tremor in his voice—if its translation nanites were even picking up the emotional connotation—but it was worth a shot.

He did his best to work up tears; it wasn't hard, after all he'd been through. "Y-you see, mister, if I can't get guidance from it I'm going to make bonehead theological errors and, no question about it, bad career moves. I'll end up in hell for sure." He snuffled a bit for effect and discovered he'd actually gotten his nose to run.

The being leaned back fastidiously, eyes withdrawing far into its shell. "Kindly do not secrete those substances in my direction."

"Sorry." Lucky swallowed, fished out a pocket handkerchief he'd improvised from an Yggdraasian battle pennon, and dabbed at his cheeks and snout theatrically, playing pathos.

The clam considered him intently. "You mean your species regards such objects as means of divination? Suppliers of auguries? And deprivation of its enigmatic connection with the Cosmic All will cause you to discorporate?"

"That's about it, mister," Lucky said sorrowfully.

It leaned forward eagerly. "Do you mind if I watch? And perhaps tape the more interesting parts?"

"You typical fucking *tourist!*" Lucky screamed. Even in the Trough you couldn't get away from them. *Especially* in the Trough. Lucky was resolutely nonviolent, but being thus abused by a tourist stripped him of all higher impulses—and perhaps the strange attraction the 8 Ball exerted on him had something to do with it. Still mindful of the clam's high-amp defense, he reached for a weapon.

The closest serviceable object was several shelves below the one from which the paperback and 8 Ball had come; he snatched it automatically—some big, weighty oblong with a moderately shiny black finish. "Gimme my oracle or I'll smash in your head. That is, I'll smash in your shell, or, I mean, that is, you *know* what I mean—"

But the XT had already dropped the 8 Ball, holding up the three-fingered limb in a way that looked placating. "Easy there, Thing. E-e-easy! You may *have* your holy oracle, see? Only *do not damage that obelisk you hold!*"

At least Lucky's nanite translators rendered the word as *obelisk.* He froze in dread, expecting to hear a little of *Thus Spake Zarathustra* and then disappear in a lightning bolt. Events in the Trough often seemed a fun-house-mirror reflection of those on Earth—real and imagined—and so getting gigawatted by some big-time monolith makers was not by any means out of the question.

But no Jovian bolt came, so he gingerly lowered the black obelisk, cringing a bit. As it came level with his eyes, he saw golden letters on it: GIDEON BIBLE.

"Gently, now, Thing!" The XT was kibitzing. "You mustn't damage it!"

Mama hadn't raised no fools. "Well now, little buddy, that all kinda depends on what's in it for *me,* doesn't it?"

The creature was hopping from one foot to the other. "But can't you sense the aura of religious importance all about it?

Can't you see its inestimable value? Behold the skins of wild
beasts with which it is mounted! The precious metals with
which the holy symbols are inscribed, and the pages edged!''
He was almost weeping. "How barbaric! Surely it is unique,
one of a kind!''

Don't get around much, do you, shorty? Lucky thought as he
rubbed his numb thigh. He retrieved the 8 Ball and curled his
lip at the being at the same time. "A lot *you* know about it,
castanet face,'' he blurted before considering that that might
not be wise from a negotiating standpoint.

But the creature placed its fingertips on its shell dramatically, looking somehow offended and self-righteous. "I beg to
differ! I have made quite some study of Earth, where that
volume originated, although, I admit, I haven't yet achieved a
comprehensive—''

"Wait, wha? Ear—'' Lucky brought himself up short before
he could yell the name; maybe it was an ambush after all.

But the lobby was still quiet. "Why are you studying, um,
you-know-where?''

The life-form stood even taller, attenuating its legs somewhat. "I've been dispatched to Confabulon to promote Earth
tourism on behalf of my employer, the Black Hole Travel
Agency. My card.''

Though Lucky heard "card,'' he was offered a slimy, vit-
reous bead produced from somewhere in his new acquaintance's interior. He didn't want to accept what might for all he
knew be a kidney stone, but felt that under the circumstances
he'd better. As soon as he touched it, the glassy pellet sent out
a ray that formed a swirling holofield in midair.

"Allow me to introduce myself,'' the being said. "Undershort's the name.''

Lucky was used to his tongue twisters and other implants
rendering alien languages in eccentric, even loony ways; it was
somewhat understandable, since he'd been salted with nanites
intended for the Terran semiotics scholar Dr. Miles Vanderloop—whose badge Lucky had had the misfortune to be wearing at PhenomiCon, thus getting himself kidnapped by a
bungling Black Hole Peer Group.

The frigging nanites went scavenging and noodling around
in odd corners of Lucky's gray matter and came up with the
damnedest renderings. In a certain sense, *he* was coming up
with these expressions, and he didn't quite know what to think

of that. He suspected those mighty mites were having a jolly old yuck at his expense.

All that aside, though, it was still a profound shock to hear the little geek's name. "Um, really? Undershort?"

The being drew itself up to all three feet or so of its height. "And what conceivable reason, pray tell, would I have to lie? Did you not read my card?"

Lucky glanced back sharply to the holofield. Sure enough, there it was in the wormcrawl alien script:

Ozwaldo Undershort
(Planet Dyllos IV—"Root Canal")
Supervisor, Earth Tourism Promotional Delegation
InterTrough Travel Expo for
Singularity Flings
a leisure-time division of
THE BLACK HOLE TRAVEL AGENCY

A projection of the being in question struck what Lucky presumed to be a suitably dignified and replike pose—shell held at a noble cant and two of the three-digit arms placed akimbo.

Lucky looked back to Supervisor Undershort with a weak attempt at his "What—me worry?" grin. "Nice to meet you, sir. You see, I'm your creative consultant, administrative support staff, and, uh, faithful native Earth guide. Yep, I'm your man." Literally. "Here, have a Gideon Bible."

Supervisor Undershort accepted the book reverently. "I see. And you are—"

"Salty Waters, at your service." Lucky saluted loyally.

TWO

HIS NAME WAS Zastro Lint and he was not expecting the eerie bath of radiation that hit him as he came through the door.

He was Internal Revenue Service agent number 2309, subgroup 2, of East Coast Collection Section 6797, and the ambush took him by surprise because the man who had ushered him into the room was an NYPD captain from Midtown South named Randy Barnes. Barnes and Lint were working on the same delightfully convoluted case: the matter of Lucky Junknowitz and the Gordian tangle of people and events surrounding him.

Lint was forty-nine years old, five foot eight, a hundred and fifty pounds, with yellow-brown skin tone, a receding gray hairline, and plans for early retirement in Baja California. He had been under the impression he'd been invited by Barnes to a council of war. Not a man of action, he'd been excited over teaming up with the much-decorated veteran cop.

At the moment he was a vacant-eyed, malleable zombie, swaying on his feet, who had stepped under a camouflaged emitter in the basement of an undisclosed location about an infield throw from City Hall. As Randy Barnes half supported him and another man perfunctorily loosened his tie, a remote bit of Zastro Lint's brain told him life as he knew it was over.

He'd started his career the same way the IRS started out, when you got right down to it: with the honorable idea that everybody should pay their fair share. Both Lint and his agency had been warped by the immutable fact that most people didn't want to do that but demanded it of everybody else. He might have resigned in disillusionment, but in the upheavals of the Turn that would have put him out on the street—in the middle of the worldwide dislocations of the planet's reordering—he

14

chose instead to apply himself to his job with an uncompromising adherence to rules and regulations.

In a bureaucracy where knowledge of minutiae replaced wisdom and dogged pursuit of technicalities substituted for justice, Lint's name had become a byword for tenacity. He'd been making the noises about retirement largely because they were expected; secretly, he was at a loss as to how he would occupy all that unstructured time. Lint was an IRS homing missile, uncomfortable with the idea of being disarmed and made obsolete. And this time out, the target signature he'd locked in on belonged to Junknowitz.

"Let's get you in the mindbender, sport." As if he were handling a sleepwalker, Barnes eased Lint down into a twenty-fifth-century dentist's chair kind of thing that squirmed, reconformed under him, and held him fast. Lint waited dizzily for some sinister brain-sucking device to fasten itself to his skull, but instead he just lay there surrounded by a spacious, padded headrest cowling.

"Can you hear me?" Barnes asked, drawing up a chair. Lint was vaguely aware of other people moving around the room.

"Yes," he answered, but it was as if someone else were doing it for him.

"The mindbender's online," somebody out of sight reported matter-of-factly.

Barnes studied Lint's face. "Agent Lint, I want you to relax. Nobody's going to hurt you. In fact, we've brought you here to help you. You want to find Lucky Junknowitz, isn't that right?"

"Yes," Lint answered a little dreamily. "That's my assignment."

"Will you accept our help in doing that?"

"Whose help?" Lint asked automatically. "I'm not allowed to violate procedure. All fieldwork has to conform to Service regulations."

Barnes was nodding. "Oh, don't worry. We got your regs covered. What I want to know is, how badly do you want Junknowitz?"

Distantly Lint thought that over. "He's my case," he responded at last.

Barnes was wearing a thin, bleak smile. "And you never give up on a case until you've settled it according to the, uh, regs. Right?"

"I never have," Lint replied in all honesty.

"Good. Okay, just lie still for a while."

Lint wanted to ask why, but all at once his head was aswim with images and ghostly voices, with paragraphs of IRS doctrine he didn't recognize scrolling by at astounding speed—and yet he knew each word, each citation.

There were other things going on, things being done to him by pintle-mounted instruments, by glowing devices deployed on mechanical arms. He couldn't keep track of the passage of time; intermittently, he became aware of the movements and conversations of Barnes and others in the background, only to lose track of them again.

At one point he picked up the thread of that indifferent third party's remarks for a few moments: "—should be any better than Agency hunters, or even free-lancers?"

"Because Lint is an Earthman, and he knows how we think," Lint heard Barnes respond. "And he's the right—oh, I forget the buzzword. This is what Lint *does*, it's what he *is*. The mindbender will target him on Junknowitz."

"The special probability isolate should bring the two together, ineluctably. Lint will be one tough little Earther, too, when we're done with him. Yes, it could work."

"And what the hell," Barnes reflected, "ours is not to reason why. Light Trap's curious to see what'll happen. If Lint doesn't work out, we'll try—"

Lint's attention drifted elsewhere like an aimless camera pan in an art film. Then there was an indefinite period of drifting in restful clouds of pink, gold, and purple.

"Bugger all!" One of the Intubi clan glowered as the golden flying craft's occupant hopped out. "It's that whingeing pommie bastard again!"

Gipper Beidjie stared at the approaching Englishman and wondered, What in bloody hell does that sticky-beak want with us, and how's he keep finding us? Might's well see. The old man leaned on the spears he held in his right hand, cocking his left leg up and resting its horny sole against his right kneecap. He wasn't in the best of moods anyway, having been unable to locate the bull-roarer that young Bluesy had left behind several aditz back; he suspected that one of the ersatz "ancestral messengers" or someone working with them had found it.

One of the staunchest traditions of his people had been that they not trade away anything of their own or let their possessions fall into others' hands, nor acknowledge a need for anything that they hadn't provided for themselves. Even the early Brit and Euro explorers of Australia had remarked on it. It was very important to Gipper that the old ways be observed again; whitefellas and those like them used money dreaming, business dreaming, to steal control of things and of people.

The genteel Englishman wasn't the only one to step from the silent VTOL frisbee craft. Two of the bulldog-faced, armor-plated ockers called Yggdraasians—whom the Intubis had taken to calling "bunyips" after the mythical Australian yetis—lumbered out after him.

Gipper reckoned they were the ones the Intubis had met earlier, because this time they were smart enough to keep their distance. Funnybook popguns or no, the bunyips had learned not to come throwing their weight around—not now that the Aborigines' powers were reawakening on their walkabout under alien suns.

Gipper had seen right off, from their vigilance and nervousness, that the bunyips and the Englishman with the funny name weren't mates with the tall poppies who ran this Trough maze. So when the pom, Vanderloop, showed up a few "aditz" back with a lot of foolish questions, wanting the Intubis to accompany him someplace, then whingeing when Gipper said no, the Intubis had shot through an aditz Gipper had sung up—after they had dealt the Yggdraasians a king hit or two. After all, Gipper wasn't leading his people along these alien songlines on school holiday; there was work to be done.

"Now what's that galah want with us?" Bluesy muttered.

"Oh, I don't know; I think he's a spunk, a real beauty," comely Saddie New opined. Bluesy shot her a dark look; everybody knew he was mad about Saddie.

Vanderloop, clad in vaguely Elizabethan heavy-metal Trough finery, gave them a small wave. "Let 'im come; maybe he can tell us the way through to home," someone added. Gipper's frown deepened.

"Bloody poofter," Bluesy spat.

Miles Vanderloop checked himself from running full tilt at the Aborigines; he feared he'd see them disappear around a tree or vanish into a cave once more, departing for another point in the Trough without benefit of Adit technology.

Since he'd lost them on Rooom's Choice, trying to pick up the Intubis again had been a study in frustration. The only saving grace of the whole business was that he'd come to like playing the part of his cover identity, a free-lance voice coach

from Aart's World by the name of Leonardo Welt—except that
the fashion statement was a bit much.

First there'd been the problem of finding out about verified
sightings, Ka Shamok's rebel intelligence system being hit-or-
miss in some areas. Then there was the difficulty of reaching
the place in question via Adit and then, as here on Roto, getting
from the Adit to the clan's actual location. Overtaking a group
that passed among the worlds with no more difficulty than
walking among the houses of a town had proven a devilish
task.

Not that Vanderloop had for a moment considered giving up.
The mission would have possessed him even if Ka Shamok
hadn't more or less ordered him to do it and later assigned the
Yggdraasian bone-breakers to see that he persevered. And to
insure that he didn't desert? Vanderloop had a growing conviction that such was the case, not that it mattered for the time
being. Besides, the Yggs had been more subdued since the
Intubis had handed them that drubbing on Rooom's Choice.

Events surrounding the Englishman's own disappearance
into the Trough, and even the existence of the Trough itself,
paled before this fantastic phenomenon: low-tech Terran aboriginals using their belief system, or power of mind—or whatever you will—to physically transport themselves from place to
place. Or manipulate *everybody's* perception of reality so that
it came out to the same thing. Or whatever.

This time, on Roto, he'd caught up with them at last. They
were on a lush hillside where tall orange fronds bunched like
feather dusters and sparse, low scrub clustered like black jack-
straws. Roto's sun shone reddish overhead, and the air, smelling like some chemical pine gum, carried wafting things that
suggested the monocellular organisms Vanderloop had watched
through his microscope as a lad.

He knew he had to make good on this contact; he might well
never get another. He slowed now, approaching with a smile
on his face. "Hello there. We meet again."

In other places and times his boyish grin had served him
well—though he hated playing off his good looks, and for that
reason had become a faceless scholar accessible only by computer link or disguised VirtNet persona. The winning smile
wasn't having much success on Roto, however: dark faces of
amazing dignity and reserve stared back at him without com-
ment.

Except for one lithe young lovely in denim skirt and epauletted khaki shirt with the arms torn off. "Oh, this one's a beauty, too right," she laughed, giving the other women a sly wink.

"Ah, belt up!" a fellow of twenty or so growled at her, but instead of being intimidated she gave him an airy look and a blithe chuckle, which some of the other women took up.

One of the elders—Vanderloop recognized him as the leader, Gipper—glared the women to silence. He was a medium-height, unstooped old fellow without an excess ounce of flesh to him, white-haired and sporting a white, bifurcate beard. His skin was the lusterless black of some stealth plane or moonless, starless night. He wore nothing but a pair of venerable shorts and what looked to be a tartan headband, and carried digging stick, spears, and nulla-nulla spear-thrower. He wore a dilly bag in which bulked what had to be his sacred tjuringa—an oval wooden plaque that was both songline score sheet and avatar of a revered Ancestor, as well as an Aborigine's embodiment of soul, talisman of power.

Gipper pointed one gnarled old finger at Vanderloop. "Right, mate: wherever you came from, you just piss off right back."

Vanderloop stood his ground, a not-negligible act of courage, given the circumstances. "Mr. Beidjie, I'm trying to help you."

That sent the man's thick white eyebrows up. "Y'know me name, eh? Wull, help me by buggerin' off!"

"Why not hear him out?" one of the women asked. "Maybe he can point us the right way through."

Gipper knew he had to be careful. He had no intention of taking his clan back to Papunya Reserve yet, but didn't want them thinking too hard about that. "Take the pom's advice, is it? And end up with more cackser-handed escorts leadin' us round by the nose?"

That got them. Nobody wanted to be back with the keepers who claimed to be envoys of the revered Ancestors. The boss fellas of the Trough had sent them to corral the Intubi and waltz them around the aditz, but Gipper had tired of the patronizing treatment, the lies; with his old-time songline powers renewed and somehow multiplied by this walkabout among the worlds, he'd sung open portals of his own and led his clan away from captivity. His enhanced abilities had even let him reach out to contact a faraway emu-cousin, the telly-dreamer Ziggy, in New York City. The clan had seen the strength of his songs and let him make the decisions for the time being; ostensibly, he was to lead them home.

But Papunya would have to wait until the Intubis were ready. The *julubidi,* the heritage of law from the Dreamtime, had to be made strong in them first; what Gipper had it in mind to do on Earth, he couldn't do alone. So far no one had challenged his authority to any great extent, but their own abilities were beginning to manifest themselves, which had Gipper both elated and worried.

"Wait, now," Vanderloop broke in. "These things that've happened to you and that you're doing—they need to be understood."

"Just doin' a bit o' California Dreamin' is all." Gipper chortled, some of the other Intubis joining in. The pre-Turn song title had always tickled him, and had become a standing joke between himself and Bluesy, meaning a sort of pointless sightseeing walkabout to the Never-Never. Only, though Gipper was keeping it to himself, this current walkabout had a very special purpose indeed.

"Perhaps you don't need anybody's help," Vanderloop conceded, "but there are people who need yours, need it rather badly."

They were starting to listen to him, Gipper saw. He debated pointing the bone at the Englishman or otherwise eliminating him, but to do so without provocation would certainly bring dissent out into the open.

Just about the time he had made up his mind that he'd risk it—the pommie was still rattling on about black holes and rebels—Gipper heard a rumbling. With no more warning than that, immense blockish flying machines hove into view at all points of the compass, their golden surfaces crackling with red bolts of electricity. The bolts licked from one to the other until the stupendous floating cubes formed a fence around the hills and began closing in.

"So they sent you to catch us out, eh, whacker?" Gipper squinted balefully at Vanderloop, but secretly was pleased. There would be no more talk of throwing in with rebels or pommie experiments.

"No, I—" Vanderloop was looking back toward his escorts, but the Yggs had piled into the gilt frisbee and were lifting off in a hurry. "You must believe me, I knew nothing about this!" He had no idea whether this was some betrayal by Ka Shamok or a rogue operation mounted by some impatient faction within the resistance.

"Bonzer!" Gipper yelled back, motioning for the Intubis to follow him. "Then, why'n't you go spank 'em on the pee-pee?"

No, I don't think that's going to happen, Vanderloop told himself. The encircling cubes spat and crackled, crimson discharges breaking from one to the other and from all to the ground. In a panic he ran toward the spot where the airship had set him down, but all at once the ground came alive with a red radiance that shot agony through him, making him windmill back. Spikes in the radiant effect—higher in the direction of the closing ships, much lower at the center of their circle—made it clear that the attack was a wolf hunt. Prey was being driven to the middle of the pattern, but to what end?

As Vanderloop backpedaled away from the energy net he tripped, fell full length with the wind knocked out of him, and lay there hearing a sound that didn't fit in, a rhythmic, almost buzzing human vocalization that was somehow rising above the cacophony of the energy ground-beating. Spitting out orange frond, he rolled over and saw Gipper and the other Intubis heading toward the wall of radiance. They were walking in single file, seventeen ragtag figures of assorted ages, carrying spears, digging sticks, and other artifacts so low-tech that most primary- and secondary-world Trough dwellers would have laughed at them. The rest of the clan had taken up the songline Gipper had set them. Vanderloop was no expert, but he'd done a bit of research and he was prepared to swear it was unlike any songline sung on Earth.

In any case there was a sinkhole partway down the hill, and it was in this direction the Intubis were bound. Their insistent singing seemed to have set up some dissonance with the energy net closing in on them, because all at once the crimson spikes were jumping and pulsing aimlessly. There seemed to be some kind of feedback problem, irregular red spasms of energy bursting on the sides of the cubes themselves, jolting and rocking them.

The Yggdraasians' golden saucer, shooting straight upward in a dash for safety, abruptly ran into a webwork of coruscating megavoltage; the craft lurched, went into a sideways slip, and plowed edge-first into the ground, crumpling like aluminum foil and then detonating with such violence that it nearly knocked Vanderloop off his feet again. He turned and sprinted as hard as he could for the Intubis, whose songline still sounded over the crashing artificial lightning. Behind him, orange fronds were aflame.

Lower on the hillside where the Aborigines were headed, the fronds grew higher and, in the lashing of the heated air, bent and bowed together. One particularly tall stand had formed a living tunnel, and it was for this that the Intubis were making.

And beyond that overhang tunnel, Vanderloop could see that *the landscape had altered.*

Instead of orange fronds and the reddish sunlight of Roto the light had a distinctly blue tint, shining down on what seemed to be a flatland of fragmented gray chert. The Intubis jogged toward it unhurriedly, and had already passed through when Vanderloop pounded into the overhanging passageway, smelling a spore-laden ozone. He cast one last look over his shoulder and saw that the encircling storm of red lightning had devolved into a general chaos of raving energy—he felt ground-shaking eruptions, as if the cube-ships were blowing up—and the scene itself was defocusing, fading from sight. It was as much a mental phenomenon as a visual one, and it didn't feel at all like stepping through an Adit; the country behind him had gone away as new country was sung up.

He'd run as fast as he could—and Vanderloop had won his share of trophies in track—but the Intubis were somehow much farther ahead of him than they had seemed, and picking up his stride to the utmost made no difference. It was as if the land were conveying them along.

He sensed that he was falling behind the Intubis' sphere of influence. He could see no structures, vehicles, or other signs of civilization in any direction. If Gipper got too far ahead of him and Vanderloop was left behind the area affected by the songline, he would be marooned, perhaps even killed right away by some adverse environmental factor that the singing staved off.

Lowering his head a bit and making himself breathe more evenly, Vanderloop settled into his best long-distance pace and grimly took up the challenge of keeping up with the clan from Papunya Reserve.

ROBOTECH: THE END OF THE CIRCLE #18

THREE

TAKUMA TANABE GAZED out over an unreal Japan but
meditated upon the real.

He was on the roof of a modern office complex, but he might
have been gazing through a time machine rather than Nikon-
Zeiss binoculars. The sounds of trickling water and tinkling
wind chimes and the smells of the garden around him reinforced the illusion. Tanabe slowly surveyed the five-hundred-
odd acres of the theme park he had created, World Nihon,
where travelers from near and far would supposedly see the
many sides of the real Japan.

He was also thinking back on a story—an image, really—
that had been handed down in his family for a century and more
and stayed vivid within him always.

It concerned a Mr. Sugimoto, once a renowned samurai and
head of a noble clan, who'd fallen on hard times in the wake
of the Meiji restoration. In the headlong scramble to emulate
the West, to do away with all things old-fashioned and embrace
foreign ways, Japan had turned her back on Mr. Sugimoto and
his caste.

By the early nineteen-hundreds—disarmed, alone, impoverished, and thwarted by the new age in every attempt, from
teaching go to painting signs, to make his way in the world—
the old man had been forced to eke out a living as a doorman
at one of the new office buildings in Edo, by then known as
Tokyo.

So there he had stood, unfailingly a man of the most dignified mien despite the absurd, braided occidental jacket and hat
he was obliged to wear. Mr. Sugimoto manned his last post in
a life of service—never quite losing the subtle droop of the left

23

shoulder that forever singled out a man who'd worn in his sash the two swords of the samurai.

With magisterial bearing Mr. Sugimoto opened the door for arrogant young Japanese clerks in Western finery who frequently swept past him without so much as a nod of thanks—a feature of the new foreign demeanor embraced by "progressive" young people. The old fighting man suffered all this with a slight smile, perhaps thinking upon the irony that, not so very long before, those same callow youths would have knelt, trembling, with heads to the ground while Mr. Sugimoto galloped by—that, or lose those heads.

In a way, Japan herself was like Mr. Sugimoto, Tanabe had come to think. Except that rather than pass away as a mortal human must she'd endured her humiliation and recovered, rebounded—contending in the Western arena with undilutedly Japanese mettle, discipline, and determination to win.

A shoji screen barely whispered as it slid open behind him. When he turned, Miss Sato bobbed a kowtow to him. This because they were in business attire now, in an office situation, even though the penthouse was a painstakingly re-created piece of the feudal world.

Had they been in traditional costume she'd have bowed her way into the room to kneel in *seiza* posture on a tatami mat. She would have sat at right angles to him, her face in semi-profile so that he, as her superior, could watch her while her eyes remained fixed elsewhere.

Instead she stood meeting his gaze, hands clasped lightly before her. "All is in readiness for your inspection, Tanabe-san," she singsonged in formal and deferential Japanese. "Your son and his companion await your pleasure, and the—other *special personage* is expected shortly, ETA twenty-seven minutes."

Tanabe grunted in brusque acknowledgment. He didn't doubt that his son and Mickey Formica had been brought. But it was very unlikely that they saw themselves as awaiting his pleasure.

"And your *jonin* and his personnel are on-site," Miss Sato added.

Tanabe acknowledged curtly, "Uhss-ss." He wanted his top ninja upper man, his *jonin,* to supervise this matter personally. And as for that other, the *special personage* who was due . . . "Very good." As at all such times in business surroundings, his form of address was emphatically lordly. "I will see my most honored guest, the personage, shortly, at the *o-furo*. In the meantime, have my son and his companion brought to me at *Tengu Mountain*.''

If she had any reaction to mention of the place, Miss Sato concealed it with the skill of long practice, though she was only in her mid-twenties. Tanabe had known she would, and yet he watched her closely; there could be no relaxation or unwariness, no tolerance of error or sloth, especially now.

Miss Sato was the only woman in his coterie of advisers and liege men. Her presence there shocked many in the closed and tradition-bound circles in which he moved, and she had to perform flawlessly in all things or Tanabe himself would lose face. Though she'd reached her *tekireiki,* the suitable age for marriage, Miss Sato had made it clear to Tanabe that conventional marriage and family plans were not her aspirations.

Miss Sato had retreated to a corner to speak softly into the button mike concealed in a palm dermal, looking as if she might be clearing her throat daintily. Tanabe was already on the move, and Miss Sato fell in behind him, as did the almost facelessly bland Mr. Natsuki, Tanabe's most trusted man, who'd been posted in the hall. Others would already be scurrying, accommodating themselves to Tanabe's sudden shift into motion. The three descended in the vitrex-paned external elevator mounted on the northern face of the complex, its transparent, sandwiched-composite sides allowing a sweeping view of the theme park while protecting the occupants against any weapon short of an armor-piercing round.

The August sun burned brutally hot, throwing harsh light on the shrines and temples, shops and houses and fortified places of *Land of Yamato*, the historic section of World Nihon. Many of the structures had been disassembled at their original locations and transported to the theme park.

When originals were too cumbersome or sacrosanct to move, reproductions had been fashioned with meticulous precision out of authentic materials. Tanabe looked with particular satisfaction at the three-quarter-scale replica of fabulous Crow Castle, the full-size torii copied exactly from the one at Miyajima, and Kyoto's Golden Temple.

Other attractions were new, like the purposely inaccurate and improbable Ninja Stronghold with its bewildering secret panels and passageways, spectacular death traps and similar movie and *manga* contrivances, far more elaborate than any real appointments in Iga, Takayama, or Koga. In addition,

World Nihon's buildings displayed more and brighter colors than in classical Japan; motivational and ad consultants on the park's creative team had persuaded him on that point.

The thought of ninjas struck craftily at Tanabe's calm with the image of his son the would-be *shinobi*. A child could be the most terrible trial of all. Tanabe wondered what one of his own Harvard Business School classmates would have said about it all. Perhaps falling back on an outmoded phrase, "Payback's a bitch"?

He betrayed none of his discomfiture over Nikkei, of course. When the elevator doors opened he walked confidently but unhurriedly to his personal a-cell touring cart. A dozen or so senior officers and their aides, plus a mixed handful of other VIPs, piled aboard four following carts. There were at least two plainclothes bodyguards in all four, and many more watching from various vantage points on the premises.

Among the guests was Justin Duplex, star of *Zone Defense* and a number of other box-office nukes, one arm around the succulent Brigit Miner, his current costar and main squeeze. They were scheduled to appear at opening-day festivities the following week and had been brought in for photo opportunities and a familiarization tour. Idols of the multitudes, Duplex and Miner nevertheless hurried like all the rest to keep up with Tanabe.

Tanabe had grown used to the feeling of people hastening in the background to make all things agreeable to him and put all matters in accord with his will—and, closer to him, in a tranquil and dignified zone like the eye of a typhoon, he was used to the respect and deference of those many who owed him their total and unquestioning loyalty. *That* was how things got done—the only reliable way.

The convoy reached the boundary of *Land of Yamato* and a cleverly disguised section of sloped stone wall slid aside to let them into the park proper. They emerged on a street of scrubbed paving stones, passing between the regal beauty of the Noh theater and the bannered martial ferocity of the *Budokan*. The Noh would undoubtedly prove too tedious for most Western visitors—and a lot of Japanese as well—but elsewhere there were Kabuki and Bunraku. Over in *Planet Now* there'd be kinostatic multimedia chaoticists, neo-*Butoh* dancers, and every sort of unwarehoused modern performing art. Tanabe was perfectly happy to present the Noh at a loss, just so long as his theater was the best in the world.

As for the *Budokan,* it wasn't the largest, but would offer every conceivable kind of contest—Brahmin *Vajra-Musti* wrestling from India, American cowboy rope-pull matches, and Heidelberg-style saber duels, as well as karate, kendo, *naginata,* and the rest.

The a-cell carts were so quiet that the hissing of the tires was clearly audible along with murmured exclamations from the visitors. The course selected by Tanabe took them past the artisans' district, the Temple of Amateratsu with its historical dioramas and S/FX wonders, and the *Amah* section of the expansive *Sea of Japan* area, where visitors could either watch lovely female pearl divers both above and below the waves, or accompany them on a dive. Out across the water Godzilla, Mothra, and the rest of the mechanical colossi waited to terrify visitors to Monster Island.

The various other park subsections would offer kiddie rides, participation games like *Shuriken*-Throw and Yoshitsune's Gauntlet, photo areas for mingling with costumed themers, and top-end thrill rides. His guests gulped, gaping up at the *Fujiyama Flail,* a pewlike seating stage big enough for eighty riders side by side. Suspended from counter-rotating swing arms on sixty-foot-high towers, it was already the talk of the wild-eyed ride-rush junkie underground.

There were also costume-rental stations for visitors who craved complete themer involvement. Carefully integrated into the park's attractions, and not missed by any of the business reps on the tour, were omnipresent souvenir shops, refreshment stands, restaurants, boutiques, franchise-item outlets, and theme bars—both *karaoke* and not.

World Nihon would be opening ahead of schedule and under budget: that was how Tanabe liked things.

Three reenactment performers—a basket-hat priest, a wandering mountebank, and an elegant *tayu,* a courtesan of the first rank—all kowtowed to him. Tanabe made a polite, minimal response. But as he seated himself on the cart he dictated a memo to Miss Sato. "Since *tayu* would never be seen unaccompanied, such themers must never be seen by the public without proper attendants."

Miss Sato inclined her head obediently. *"Hai!"* The oversight would be taken care of at once and never reoccur. His cart whisking toward the demon mountain, Tanabe took in every detail around him, giving Miss Sato more notes but reserving other matters to his own memory.

For all the work and treasure that had gone into it, World Nihon wasn't as big a dollar investment as some of Tanabe's other responsibilities—most notably projects with Nagoya Aerospace and Matsuya/Genentech Bio-Med. But of all the projects under his authority the park gave Tanabe the greatest satisfaction, as well as the most sobering preoccupation.

Demographics suggested that, once the place was open, World Nihon would trounce Disney's per-visitor profit figures by three percent or more. And—Tanabe savored the thought—that was without the demographers knowing what *real* surprises the park held in store.

Then again, what the future would bring when Black Hole's hidden schemes became common knowledge on Earth—and Tanabe's secret plans went into a high gear of their own—no one could say for sure.

Charlie Cola was sitting in the back-room office of his Bronx convenience store, the area Quick Fix franchise—and, until recently, interstellar Adit location—thinking about sealing his fate by the flip of a coin.

Why not? It was about as good a decision support system as any, with things as far down the crapper as they'd plunged. Heads he hunkered down, made do with the parts of his life he had left—cut all losses, ran the store, and hoped things took a turn for the better soon.

Tails?

Well, tails would maybe be that he fought back against the adversaries and adversities ganging up on him from all sides, but that didn't hold much promise. Most of his resources had evaporated. His father Patsy had bequeathed him a going business and a minuscule nibble at a galactic enterprise; all Charlie had accomplished in almost fifty years of life—the way he saw it today—was let it slip through his fingers.

A short time before, his personal star had been ascendant within Black Hole's local operation. Then inquiries had started coming down about irregularities in how he ran his shop, auditors from Black Hole faded in from offworld, and teleportation operations had been shifted to the mobile Adit aboard the cruise ship *Crystal Harmonic*. Charlie had been prepared to believe he would get his tush in a crack over the skimming he'd done over the years, but not that upper management would relocate the Adit because of it; that just wasn't cost-effective.

Besides, although the cooked account books he'd shown

offworld auditors Tal'Asper and Rouge weren't masterpieces of the art, there'd been no charges brought against him as far as he knew. No, something else was going on within Black Hole.

Charlie didn't doubt that it had something to do with the astoundingly snarled events surrounding the bollixed Vanderloop kidnapping, including Lucky Junknowitz and his eccentric clique of unguided human missiles. But nothing seemed to parse out rationally—not surprisingly since he had only some of the facts. And no one, old friends included, could or would enlighten him. Even Sierra Pit Boss Mussh Kunwar, a well-placed source and a helluva good joe for a Nall, had been no help.

Among other mysteries, newscasts had carried scenes of the bloody Rodeo East murder of a walk-in from the Trough Charlie knew as Gaspar de Torque, but nobody in the organization would discuss it.

Longtime ally Dante Bhang was keeping so low a profile that he was unreachable; he'd badly overstepped his authority in sanctioning the grab on Sheena Hec'k, then had presided over a botched job to boot, inadvertently netting Harley Paradise as well. Or at least it *seemed* to be ineptitude on Bhang's part that had put Charlie in vile odor with Black Hole; Charlie hated to consider any alternative. Bhang's henchmen Mickey Formica and Nikkei Tanabe had by all accounts ceased to exist after being summoned to account to the elder Tanabe for their bungling.

Worse yet, the reward money offered throughout the Trough for the capture of Sheena Hec'k had, through some kind of fine print in his contract, been denied Charlie and his franchise as well as all other participants.

Trough and Adits biggie Llesh Llerrudz, who, with scalpel-flanged gleamer amanuensis Barb Steel, had been standing in Charlie's very office when Dante lugged in the twin-packed women, was in all likelihood still on the *Crystal Harmonic*. He wasn't returning Charlie's calls, either. Nor were any of the Phoenix Enterprises Twenty-Ones who'd been so warm to Charlie only a few weeks before.

Asked what the future held for him back then, Charlie would have said there was no limit; a major position in one of Black Hole's new Earth enterprises and a comfortable retirement on the luxury planet of his choice were in the category of virtual cinch.

These days his wife, Didi, finally comprehending the precarious spot in which Charlie and everyone connected to him was caught, was holed up in their Westhampton beachfront mansion—so rattled that she'd given up nagging him for home improvements, new clothes, a more opulent life-style. He heaved a long sigh, considering suicide.

"Dad?"

Charlie straightened antique, steel-rimmed bifocals and looked up at his adopted sons Labib Ismael and Jesus Powell, who stood in the office doorway. "Dad," Labib said again, "the stock's put up; we're gonna see if we can get the—are you all right?"

He nodded, running hands through his balding hair. "Well, of course I'm all right. Just a little tired because *some* people around here always need someone to clean up after their sloppy work."

The two rolled their eyes, taking up Charlie's pretense that their old man was on their case, business as usual. Actually, tension in the former Adit as Quick Fixers waited for the other shoe to hit the floor was almost palpable. But Charlie had been abruptly and poignantly reminded of why he couldn't just give up. People were depending on him—the boys and Didi, counter clerk Sanpol Amsat, and, yes, even Molly, daughter of his late father's partner Jacob Riddle.

All right, maybe Charlie was somehow guilty for things having come to this pass—though for the life of him he couldn't fathom how. If so, he was that much more responsible for setting them to rights again, for getting his little band through dangerous times.

He slipped the coin back into his pocket, forgetting about heads or tails. "And I thought the soy processor was going to be back up and running by midnight?"

Labib and Jesus, retreating, swore there were good reasons they were behind schedule. Charlie knew that they were telling the truth, but didn't give it away—they needed to be kept busy, spared the misgivings and dread devouring Charlie Cola.

FOUR

THE WANTED-POSTER HOLOGRAMS were common enough to make Lucky think mirrors had become universal decor on Confabulon. There was his face, holoed forth at every public information booth and governmental installation—among others, it was true, but clearly he was one of those with whom the Black Hole Travel Agency most urgently wished to interface.

Fortunately, he no longer looked like the images of himself that loomed around the city; he'd had a Face Scrub—cosmetic alteration for ID-change purposes—en route. The black hair, green eyes, freckle-concealing skin tint, and other alterations were now more durable than Earthly techniques could make them. Life-forms who could differentiate among humanoids would see he didn't resemble his mug shot; life-forms who couldn't were no problem. His Wise-Guise nanite would protect him—he hoped—from magic-marker scanners and such.

He saw a Wanted-poster holo of the gleamer Silvercup, whom he'd met under her then-current alias, Metallica. She'd looked slightly different in a high-hemmed medtech's shift; the naked gleaming metalflesh female in the Wanted-poster holo, her body so conforming to human anatomy and yet so unlike it, was at once troubling and divine.

Silvercup's Wanted posters and Harley Paradise's ubiquitous travel ads promoting Earth tourism—Lucky doubted he could walk a hundred feet in any way station or Adit stop in the galaxy without seeing them. And now his face was up there with theirs.

No one had connected him with his poster, though, not even Undershort. Lucky trudged along feeling, although blessed in that he knew them and Sheena Hec'k, horribly and illogically

31

guilty for Black Hole's malice toward them. He already had
one of Harley's holo posters, in projector-chip format, as a
pinup. He supposed he would add Silvercup to his collection,
but the increase only depressed him.

"What troubles me, Waters," Supervisor Undershort said as
he and Lucky made their way down the hundred-yard-wide
parkland strip of a vast boulevard, "is that you were wasting
accommodation time."

Lucky thought that one over cagily as they hurried along, the
Root Canalian moving in a kind of rapid goose step. It was
hard to read the delegation leader's mood through his shell.
The boulevard's surface was a mossy red sward soft as cotton.
It was pleasantly but not dramatically landscaped; the archi-
tecture of the city had the same clean but dull feeling. For
Lucky's money, the skyline could have been upended chem-
class glassware drying on a rack.

The real eye-catchers in the urbanscape were the
advertisements—rooftop holos, window-display flash panels,
football-field-sized strobe signs and such—that promoted the
various expo participants. About the only thing that wasn't
ballyhooed was any competing trade-fair or convention locale;
the Confabulonians weren't dumb.

Lucky had fallen into an intermediate hiking stride to keep
up with Undershort's businesslike goose step. Since the convention center was only half a mile away, the supervisor had
decreed that they would walk to save travel expenses.

The two had already straightened out the fact that Undershort had come to the Pension Panache specifically to find his
assistant, having been informed by Black Hole that Salty Waters would be staying there. The unpleasantness at the swap
shelf had been put behind them with some embarrassment on
both sides, and they were on their way to the convention center
to set up their display area and open for business.

But now, out of left field, this accommodation stuff.
"Waste, boss? I don't getcha. I came downstairs a little early
to meet you, and I was just waiting around when we, uh,
you—"

"If you require less sleep than is provided in your rental
arrangement," the creature broke in, "why did you not secure
some sort of pro-rated refund? Egad! The Black Hole Travel
Agency is paying for an empty bed!"

Lucky's accommodations at the Panache amounted to a hor-
izontal sleeping capsule about the size of an Earthside coffin

hotel. He would've objected that Undershort was going over-board with corporate loyalty, but it turned out that the super-visor's digs consisted of a kind of capsule filled with plant sap, barely big enough for the occupant, racked with various other XT canisters like a cube in an ice tray in a place that catered to nonhumanoids. Undershort was paying on a use basis, in ap-proximately two-minute increments.

"It's a human thing," Lucky finally mumbled. "You wouldn't understand."

"*You* are a human Thing, Waters," the Root Canalian shot back. "And I understand that we are obliged to minimize our employer's expenses and optimize the bottom line."

Lucky decided some distraction was in order. "Well, you couldn't ask for a nicer day, could you?"

His supervisor angled his shell back to inspect the sky. "A not unpleasant tang of acidity and ozone in the air, true," he allowed. "And a passable violet tint to the sky, if one goes in for such. But after all, that *is* Weather Control's job."

"And no clouds," Lucky observed. "Haven't seen but one or two since I got here."

"Well, I should hope not! Inclement weather might impede the flow of visitors to and from the expo, render difficult some business meeting, or complicate commerce-related recreational events."

Lucky already knew all about that from asking around the Panache. Confabulon had been picked to host the tourism expo for the same reasons it was suitable for many Trough-wide biz meets: it offered a conducive level of comfort, novelty and diversion, but not *too* much; not so much as to distract from the central reason for being there, which was the pushing of prod-ucts, trumpeting of investments, or hyping of other enterprises. In short, business. So coming to Confabulon was a little like attending a Terran business conference at an airport hotel far from town. A calculated narrowing of distractions, even a restriction of sensory stimuli, was felt to be good for goal achievement.

Confabulon was an unremarkable moonless planet with broad temperate zones, stable in orbit and lacking in axial tilt, located in a stellar system with nothing extraordinary to draw visitors off on explorations. There were a few modest mountain ranges, some tepid seas, a number of moderately interesting underground cave systems—but nothing worth faxing home about. Thus the attention of travel agents, group-tour organizers, junket pushers, and the rest would, it was hoped, focus on the expo and the attractions offered by hundreds of *other* worlds.

The whole place was carefully unobtrusive and understated, and the ocher sward they now marched along was meticulously groomed. Nearby Lucky spied a huddle of green individuals a yard tall, who put him in mind of moles, crouched around a translucently radiant console the size and shape of a two-foot-high roulette wheel. They were arguing about a big section of the redsward marked by floating, luminous blue ribbon to keep civilians from blundering into the work area.

The touchpads on the roulette wheel glowed in various colors. Whenever a mole pressed a few, tones sounded and in response to them some section of the nearby turf ballooned, subsided, or subtly changed shades of red, in areas ranging in size from a doormat to half a basketball court. These stimulated sections of smart turf quavered, humped, or rippled in intricate waves, taking on a wide assortment of new conformations. There were a few airborne lackey remotes—recording or controlling, it was hard to tell which—floating around like despondent, dim-witted beetles.

The landscapers seemed to be experimenting, too, with a system of subsurface, turf-nurturing horticultural servos that rose up to dispense water, nutrients, vermicides, and diet-balancers to the moss-grass. As Lucky looked on the workers summoned up low hunches of putting-green-quality lawn with the intent of, who knew? Putting in lawn flamingos, perhaps. One of them pressed a glowing golden touchpad square, and from the radiant console came a whistle like a birdsong riff. Up from the ground rose complicated lampposts whose silhouettes suggested airport control towers. They'd been discreetly concealed, their lids covered with wigs of scarlet sod.

"Egad!" Undershort had to jump sideways to avoid being painfully elevated upon the moss toupee of one of the lawn towers, which was spinning around and back, extending nozzles and servos in what looked like a quick set of mechanical calisthenics. As quickly as they'd arisen, the devices retracted their extremities and lowered back down into the turf again, either successful in their test or awaiting another.

Among the roly-poly landscapers bitter argument had broken out. It seemed to bear on the fact that the tower that had nearly caught Undershort, had come up outside the work zone designated by the warning ribbon, as had a few others.

Lucky wanted to give his boss a steadying hand but wasn't sure how it would be received. "You all right, chief?"

The Root Canalian clashed his shell once or twice but looked otherwise unharmed. "Yes, I believe so."

The green moles were going through a major falling-out, the one with the most belly actually leaping up and down, swinging four-fingered fists in circles over his head. A less corpulent one stood glowering back. "You petal-pushing twit!" the angry one railed. "Do you want to launch those guests into orbit and land us all in the subaqueation chambers?"

The smaller mole lost restraint and shrieked back, "You can't talk to me that way, you artless *weed whacker!*"

At those fighting words the bigger one let go a wordless scream and tried to hurl himself on the other, but the rest of the moles leapt in to keep the two apart. All of them were jabbering, and many were punching at the roulette wheel touch surfaces, generating all kinds of tonal commands as they argued. Everybody took a hand in it. The contested turf humped and dipped; the subsurface emplacements rose and fell and shot up again as the argument went on.

"Let's get out of here before they decide we'd look good in mulch," Lucky urged Undershort.

The pair went on. It became apparent to Lucky that various trade delegations and tourism councils were manically, perhaps desperately, on the make promotion-wise. It all underscored Undershort's observations about how rough the fight for travel profits was becoming. Eyeing the tasteful customer-information terminals, the light-and-sound-show brochure dispensers, the handbill-plying automata and bioform hawkers, Lucky began to understand just how intense the competition was.

Or so he thought.

As the two wended their way between two soaring violet flexinia trees whose branches stood straight up, undulating slowly like a seaweed forest, Lucky's eyes fell on a pulsating cube of ethereal fire. Slowly rotating and tumbling in the faint shimmerfog of a suspension field, it wafted a few yards farther along the footpath. Each of its six-foot-square facets displayed a different image—it was a huge version of a snapshot display block, only the images were moving in three dimensions. The cube was playing lilting music and each side was a window into another world.

A hale, attractive humanoid couple dressed in transparent

shrinkwrap was repulsor-skiing over a wintry landscape of surreal beauty; some kind of antigrav sailboat floated across an
effervescently green-white sea. Gorgeous, laughing beings of
diverse species conversed and danced and made poetically salacious overtures to one another on a mountaintop pavilion
with a spectacular view of virgin countryside, under a sky filled
with coruscating nebulae, blazing meteors, racing, multicolored moons, and a gem-hoard of stars. Some moron shot down
an unoffending herbivore from behind with a weapon that
packed the wallop of a supercollider, then posed proudly next
to the corpse.

A sultry voice-over beckoned, "Tired of your dull routine?
Longing for an escape from the population pressures, the leg-
islated sameness, the banality of life on your overcrowded
homeworld?"

Lucky had already escaped his homeworld, not to mention
the time he'd been kidnapped from it, when all this Trough
madness had started. But there was something mesmerizing
about the pulsating scenes, the flow of illumination. In fact,
except for the hunting part it looked pretty nice.

"Then come to Nu-Topia, *the* exciting new concept in
leisure-world time-sharing! Explore the awesome beauty of the
trackless outlands! Brave the luminous deeps of the Diamond
Sea! Find new companions in the Tactile Grotto!"

Sounded pretty good to Lucky. Especially a little groping in
the Grotto with that steamy-looking, purple-skinned wench
wearing nothing but a flimsy cincture of many-colored blossoms who was beckoning to him now with the long forefinger
of one webbed hand. He walked along without looking where
he was going, ignoring Undershort, who was nattering on about
the need for cost containment, demographic precision, infrastructure max-utilization, and market penetration.

"Make contact now for your free weekend trial vacation on
glorious Nu-Topia," the merwoman in the cube bade him hus-
kily. "As a guest of Nu-Topia Shares Incorporated, your
travel, lodging, and all incidental costs will be billed to us,
with no obligation to you! Think of it! Three days and three
nights on the Trough's newest and most glamorous getaway
planet! Plus a valuable free gift that will be yours just for
coming."

Which was what Lucky felt like he was about to do. It
seemed to him a little downtime would be just the thing. Something in the back of his brain was yelling for attention, but an

invisible force emanating from the cube, and the vistas it was showing him, made it easy to ignore distractions. He liked the way she puckered her lips.

And when, as he drew close, the Lorelei cube repeated, "Make contact . . . *now-www!*" in a loving whisper, it extruded the upper torso of the merwoman, back arched, head thrown back ecstatically, deep purple hair floating all around him and buoyant breasts presented for his caress. Lucky, slack-jawed, reached out reverently, tenderly, hand conforming adoringly to the shape of it—dimly surprised to feel not fleshy contact, but rather a sizzling play of energies.

"Stop! What are you doing!" Lucky only faintly heard the screech of dismay from Undershort, but he got excellent reception on the jolt of lightning that shot up his leg for the second time that day.

"*WWW-owwch!*" The wash of bioelectricity broke the cube's spell and sent Lucky leaping back, stuttering a Maori cussword he hadn't used in years. "What'd you do *that* for?"

For a change Undershort sounded more alarmed than angry. "Are you addled? Loop-worn? Making contact with a time-share Boob-Cube?"

"No—but she, I mean *it*—"

Undershort was making chivying gestures with two of his triple-digit hands. "Go, quickly! It is imperative that we absent ourselves from this spot before—"

He stopped as a sudden humming noise grew louder overhead and something swooshed through the air toward them. A pewter egg the size of a delivery truck descended to hover an inch or two above the mossy carpet; then a thick hatch dropped open with a clang. Lucky gulped, peering into the darkness within.

Out skipped a flashily dressed little guy who struck Lucky as a cross between Jiminy Cricket and a game-show host. He was wearing a nacreous dress suit of sorts, cut for his strangely articulated hind legs, with a high stiff collar and a big cravat. Finishing off the outfit was a soft, blue top hat. He was talking on the move. "Hello, there! Congratulations on your fine judgment and perception in reaching out and touching Nu-Topian Time-shares, Mr.—ahh—"

He looked to a darting remote that reminded Lucky of a Christmas-tree star, which whirled down close to his tiny toadstool-like ear and appeared to speak into it.

"—Waters!" he finished. Lucky knew an instant's relief

that at least his Wise-Guise was conning all the local ID systems.

The salesman rattled on. "Yessir, I am Coordinator Tadwallader, here to conduct you to your free, all-expenses-paid trial vacation *and* your valuable free gift." He gave Lucky a dazzling smile and batted improbably long lashes. "Now, kindly climb aboard at once, please; we're running on a rather tight schedule."

"Um, there's been some mistake," Lucky mumbled. "I just, um, wanted more information." Grotto gropes or no, he couldn't just duck out on the trade fair, since he was counting on it to give him some means of reaching al-Reem. Moreover, Undershort's distress and Tadwallader's impatience had the hair on the back of his neck standing up.

At Lucky's reply the Christmas-star remote gave an electronic squeal, then zipped out of the way as if to avoid the line of fire. Tadwallader asked, with exaggerated sweetness, "But you fondled the Boob-Cube, did you not?"

He turned to the floating cube, which was still showing Nu-Topian vacation scenes though the sound function had gone mute. "Did he not?"

The merwoman's upper half protruded momentarily from the Boob-Cube for a moment to testify in a businesslike way, "Affirmative, Glooey. DNA scan is now on file, constituting conclusive evidence."

Which made Lucky a boob indeed. His voice cracked. "This is a con game! Count me out!"

Tadwallader's cartoon expression took on a nasty glower. "Oh, a welsher, eh? Listen, rube, when you felt up that advert-projection you entered into a contract, anybody but some ignorant tertiary-world imbecile knows that. You agreed to go to Nu-Topia for three days and three nights and that's just what you're going to do!"

He turned and whistled over his shoulder, adding, "Hey, boys! We've got a deadbeat here!"

The hovering egg shifted a little on its antigrav field as something weighty moved in the darkness. Lucky looked desperately to Undershort for some help or hint. The little Black Hole rep was standing his ground; evidently it was too late to run.

Out of the egg stepped three hulking bruisers who put Lucky in mind of Yggdraasians—immensely muscled things in heavy-gauge vanity plate. Two had already unholstered heavy hand weapons that looked to Lucky like cordless drills big enough to ream out fencepost holes. The third dragged an electronet and cut the air with a long energy prod, orange discharges crackling around the tip.

"Which one's the chiseler, Glooey?" one of them asked Tadwallader. His voice had the timbre of dire tritone organ music played on an empty subway platform.

Tadwallader pointed to Lucky, adding with a malicious wink to the victim, "There ain't no such thing as a free feel, primate!"

As the hulking enforcers advanced on Lucky he looked imploringly at Undershort—although he was uncertain Undershort even understood what an imploring look was. But the little Root Canalian stood transfixed. The polelike electroprod member had edged into sight through his minimally open shell—reflexively, Lucky got the impression—but only a little. For very understandable reasons the supervisor didn't appear to want to get involved.

Lucky was sorry about that but hip-bumped the Root Canalian from behind anyway. Undershort lurched forward and the rod touched one stooge right on his alloy-clad kneecap. There was a snapping, writhing burst of electricity and the ogre stumbled back into his companions.

Lucky tried to feint, but the armored behemoths regrouped and countered a lot faster than their looks had implied. Undershort had skipped out of the way with a startled little bleep, for which Lucky didn't blame him. Few employees were worth a dustup with three big squarefoots only slightly larger than telephone booths.

Lucky's immediate path of retreat was blocked by a spiky snarl of hawser-thick barbed vine with thorns that glistened in oily, poisonous colors. Trying another direction, he jinked one way, then the other, panting hard. The squarefoots weren't faked out at all but hemmed him in closer, the one with the electronet whirling it over his head now, *retarius* style, for the cast.

Surely there was some kinda Captain Kirk move Lucky could use to good effect here, he thought wildly. *Hey, Bud, yer spaceboot's demagnetizing!* But leisurely TV judo chops didn't seem to hold much promise; indeed, his assessment was that it'd be much like throwing a haymaker at the main armor belt of the U.S.S. *Havana*. This was a job for his brother Sean—

Sean with his street-kido moves, his Army-programmed killquick reflexes, his *capoeira* dance-of-death footwork.

Only nobody was yelling "Cut!" so they could send in the stunt double.

The twirling electronet passed close, its field making the hair on Lucky's head stand up. The fuzz on his neck and arms was already at attention. Okay; he was no *mano-a-mano* space-hound. Lucky Junknowitz was only an incredibly misplaced themer and theme-park troubleshooter, and the goliaths closing in on him now bore no resemblance to lovable character-suiters in the Magic Kingdoms, the animatronic Lands of the Living Cuckoo Clocks—*wait a second!*

Even before the PhenomiCon kidnapping, he'd noticed that much as he loathed and avoided violence, when it came his way he could clear his mind and mobilize what resources he had to cope with it. No doubt the nanites deserved part of the credit for the fact that he could still do that in the insanity of the Trough—that he wasn't a catatonic or an upholstered-room case.

Lucky felt mental focus ring him around like soundproofing curtains. It was the incidental image of a cuckoo popping out of a clock that had put the plan in his head. Lucky puckered his lips and blew, hoping his memory hadn't failed him. The Nu-Topia goons paused in surprise, hearing the run of trilled notes, then moved in again.

But as the net came lofting overhead to bag him, it was snagged in the air by something that shot up from the ground, showering multicolored sparks. The net holder was pulled off balance, dropping his neural prod. Another of the lawn-care poles had risen almost into the face of the second creature. Furious at being made to flinch, he stopped and smashed at it with the butt of his pistol.

The last enforcer was resuming his approach, urged on by a howling Tadwallader. The *retarius* was getting his net disentangled. The first goon had just about finished smashing the bejesus out of the pole that had surprised him. Looking around wildly, Lucky saw still another of the servo periscopes rising up—over by the tangle of bayonet-thorned vine.

He took a running start at it, three long steps, vaguely aware of yelling at the top of his lungs. He wasn't kidding himself about having any Batman moves, but it was amazing what adrenaline was doing for his willingness to give any viable possibility a shot.

The ankleboots gave him terrific traction. He leapt, coming down on the rising column's little wig of redblades with both soles as it passed the four-foot mark and kept on ascending. Using it as a springboard, he launched himself in a thrashing dive, with no idea how wide the spiky barrier was or what lay on the other side.

In that instant his senses were preternaturally keen. Confabulon seemed to move down rather than he up. The thorn wall fell away beneath him and he felt a fleeting instant of triumph—even as he was doing a fair impression of a crashing helicopter, even as he was waiting for the shot from behind, the impalement on poisoned thorns, the enraged tiger or its XT equivalent on the other side of the thicket that would spell the end of him.

Maybe it was something cellular, this living for the moment. But his survival instincts—and perhaps the nanites as well—kept him from exulting for very long.

Like a bonus miracle, the thorns were only hedge-thick. On the other hand, under the heading of drawbacks, the ground fell away sharply on the other side. Down Lucky hurtled, bitterly sorry that he hadn't thought to wear some kind of impact-bag feature, or bat wings—or at least a propeller beanie.

As he descended, spinning and flailing, it was tough to get a good look at what was below. No jagged, glass-edged rocks, from what he could see, though; no automated combine machine. There seemed to be more of the ocher lawn and a medium-sized gray puddle.

But the puddle was moving, moving along the ground in an undulating motion, and it was growing bigger fast because he was headed straight for it.

Maybe if he had done some high diving or trampoline work or bungee-jumping he'd have been able to alter his reentry arc, but as it was Lucky could only let go a wordless yell, partly in warning, and recall too late that he probably ought to tuck or something.

As he dropped at the gray surface like a brick he had the distinct impression that a horned, blank visage swiveled up to look at him. He hit whatever it was and sank into it, the object soaking up the force of his fall and stopping him gradually all in a fraction of a second. Not that it was by any means gentle; it felt more like he'd flung himself onto a mound of cement bags. And whatever he'd landed on was still moving, making him feel as if he were on a water bed filled with warm tar.

"Young man, just what is it that you think you're about?"

Lucky was staring upside down into a face like a boxing glove with two questing tentacular protrusions on either side, the superior pair featuring soulful eyes. His nanites had rendered the voice as female—dowagerlike, in fact—and so when he regained a little breath he got out, "Ma'am, I've gotta admit that's been puzzling me for some time now. But I'm very, very sorry for, you know, landing on you and all. Are you okay?"

The slug dowager drew herself up a bit, jostling Lucky. "Well, I should *hope* I am undamaged, in light of your diminutive stature! I *am* a direct-line descendant of the Primogenitors, after all! But that hardly answers my question, does it? And by way of an aside, are *you* quite all right?"

It wasn't the first time Lucky had felt this down-the-rabbit-hole sensation. "Yes, thanks."

"Then perhaps I'd better let you down." Her body undulated grandly, and Lucky was deposited on the redsward by her side. "I am Dame Snarynxx, by the by."

She'd said it with a hint of pique, and Lucky, scrambling to his feet, made haste to repair his gaffe. "I apologize for not introducing myself sooner! Luc—that is, Salty Waters, here. Nice to meet you."

That was the truth, but even so, he was looking for a good escape vector. Before he could spot one he heard Tadwallader's voice behind him. "There he is!"

Dame Snarynxx hemmed in Lucky in one direction, the thorn hedge in another, and the approach of Tadwallader and his action figures closed off most of the remaining alternatives. The electronet whirled and the spike fists clenched. But as the Nu-Topia squad drew closer, Lucky found that a shadow had fallen across him.

"That will be quite enough of that!" Dame Snarynxx, sounding like the Queen of England speaking through outdoor concert amplifiers, reared so high that the lummox closest to her fell over backward trying to keep her horned head in view. There was no way of telling exactly what retribution she could inflict, but no one wanted to be the first to find out.

"Cease and desist!" Supervisor Undershort had arrived on the scene. While the goons were looking to Tadwallader for new instructions, Undershort interposed himself between them and Lucky, holding out an ID badge. "This entity is an employee of the Black Hole Travel Agency and, as such, entitled to expo perks!"

"What of it?" Tadwallader asked with a sneer that had lost

some of its conviction. "He goes to Nu-Topia just like any other boob."

Undershort clashed his shell at Tadwallader for emphasis. "If so, then with *professional discounts!* And I have reviewed the ones Nu-Topia has offered for the expo."

Tadwallader let out a mournful cry and threw his hat on the ground. Then he whirled on Lucky in blind fury. "What are you, Waters, a saboteur? To reach out and touch a Boob-Cube and solicit hard-sell tactics when you know we'll be obliged to feed and keep you and then actually *let you leave?* Is this some kind of sneaky new intermarket warfare, hmmmm?"

"More like a mistake," Lucky began, still eyeing the squarefoots and wondering if he should take off running now that he saw an opening. Then again, he felt a lot safer there in the lee of Dame Snarynxx.

"Our Mr. Waters here is certainly not as devious and foolish as his looks might lead you to believe," Undershort put in primly. "He merely, ah—"

"—had a religious experience, fellas," Lucky supplied, thinking back on the mermaid damsel. "Guess yer Boob-Cube mistakenly keyed into that. Purely involuntary and unintentional."

"Wha-aat?" Tadwallader snarled, but Lucky's nanites picked up a note of uncertainty. Reaching into a chitinous pouch that might have been either natural or artificial, the salesbeing produced a little instrument that could for all the world have been a three-quarter-inch galvanized floor flange. Tadwallader's spiny digits manipulated it in a blur and it hoaloed a field of incomprehensible alphanumerics. "What religion? *I* don't find any record of such a belief system."

"It's a human thing," Undershort maintained stoutly. "You wouldn't understand. He's from Adit Navel, you see."

Tadwallader looked back to Lucky. "You're an Earther?"

Lucky almost nodded, but he'd learned in the Trough that a gesture didn't always mean what one intended, and even his nanites' general-information banks couldn't catch every error. So he said aloud, "Yes. But I'd rather not talk about it."

One of the squarefoot goons gargled a harsh laugh. "I *bet* you don't you little geek. Earth, haw!" He spat into the ocher turf.

"Okay, Waters, I'll cut you a break this one time," Tadwallader decided. "but keep your hands off our handouts and quit feeling up our Boob-Cubes! Let's go, boys."

As soon as the press-gang had departed, Lucky muttered, "Thanks, boss."

"I wouldn't have compromised myself in that fashion except that I require your expertise to carry out this assignment," the supervisor sniffed. "And don't call me boss!"

They realized that Dame Snarynxx was still regarding them with eyes, horns, and unreadable physiognomy. Lucky muttered to Undershort. "B—sir, d'you have another business card?"

The supervisor passed it to him and Lucky presented the radiating bead to the dowager slug with a flourish. "Please call on us for all your travel needs!"

A pseudopod came out of her side, took the bead, and drew it into her flesh. "I shall consider it, Salty Waters."

"And thanks for the happy landing, ma'am," Lucky added.

"You are a disorganized, non-energy-efficient, and possibly crazed individual," the dowager observed. "So nice of you to drop in."

FIVE

BARNES, GLANCING OVER the tech's shoulder, surmised that the mindbender readings all looked good.

The tech was on temporary duty directly from Light Trap and the hasty job the support people there had done hadn't left him looking or smelling Terran enough to suit Barnes, who had had to keep him indoors and under wraps.

For that matter, a lot of things about this Lint business were irritating. But as a Black Hole resident operative—a coopted indig—Barnes didn't dare even consider refusing a direct order from Light Trap. Barnes's investigation on Earth had indicated that somehow Junknowitz had gotten back into the Trough, and that was regarded as very troubling up-Trap, where dwelt the powers that be. Formerly, they had been wary of moving against the probability node that was Junknowitz; now they wanted him found so that active measures could be taken.

"Very well," the tech said. "Now comes the interesting part." That was one way to put it. Barnes lost no time in getting out the door, putting the portable shielding between himself and the irradiator deployed over Lint's supine body.

"Will he feel anything?" Barnes asked.

The tech shook his head. "Not really. That's why Junknowitz never realized he'd been exposed."

"But this isn't the same brand of probability shit, or whatever you're calling it?"

"Right. It's a variation keyed to the isolate that hit Junknowitz—and in this case a very, very limited exposure. It will make Lint an iron filing to Junknowitz's magnet."

When Lint opened his eyes again he was sitting in an office chair and the only other person in the room was Barnes, sitting across a steel desk from him. "You awake?"

45

"Quite," Lint shot back curtly. He wasn't inclined to chit-chat; time was passing and his prey might be getting farther and farther away.

Barnes was not altogether convinced. "You understand you'll have to go into the Trough to find Jun—"

"It doesn't matter where Junknowitz is or what he's doing." Lint sounded brittle. He mentally reviewed the unconventional, detached-duty orders under which he was now operating. Not like any assignment he'd ever heard of before.

This teleporting business seemed to conflict with basic IRS premises and rules, but since reawakening Zastro Lint had had no doubt about what was most important to him. "Junknowitz is a taxpayer, just like everybody else. I'll find him."

"Good," Barnes said slowly. Though Lint thought he was on detached duty, arrangements had been made to have his early retirement put through. No one down at the IRS would be expecting to see his face again. "You'll be needing this," Barnes added. He placed on the desk a briefcase, marvelously crafted, the rich red-brown hue of an old-time Technicolor cowboy's saddle. It had fittings of some black alloy and a handle mounted with what appeared to be sharkskin.

"New type of field equipment," Barnes explained. He glanced to the briefcase—and addressed it. "You're imprinted on your user?"

"What do I look like, a *stupe?*" the case snarled back at him in a voice like that of a cartoon mouse. "C'mon, c'mon, meatbrain—let's get this turkey in the oven. Zastro and me've got things to do."

Barnes seemed on the verge of ripping the case into shreds with his bare hands, then regained control of himself. "Off-world technology," he explained to Lint, scowling darkly at the attaché. "The adaptation was a rush job, so there may be some glitches. Still, this is your most important tool on this assignment, understand? It's got all the, oh, the doctrine and regs you'll need to follow."

Lint was feeling alive, revitalized, eager to be on the case. "What is it?"

Barnes stood up. "Smart luggage. But don't ever forget, you're the one in charge of this assignment and if you screw it up, it's *your* ass, Lint. Let's get a move on."

Lint stood up, too, ignoring the half-veiled threat. He was used to upper echelon bureaucrats trying to cover their panic by acting tough.

"Where are we going?" Lint knew in a depersonalized way that he had to enter the interstellar transit system known as the Trough but he was a little fuzzy on details. Besides, his attention was focused on Lucky Junknowitz.

"A plane ride, Zas," Barnes answered casually. "Then a helo connection to a tasty little tub called the *Crystal Harmonic,* and from there you go on alone."

Lint had caught a note of unease in Barnes's voice. So, somewhere down deep, Barnes the big tough policeman was terrified of leaving Earth, of having all familiar points of reference whisked away. Well, Lint wasn't. Not if it meant catching up with Junknowitz.

"Drop yer puds and grab yer duds!" the smart briefcase shrilled at them. "Junknowitz, here we come!"

Lint and the Light Trap tech left together, bound for the *Crystal Harmonic* and her Adit. Barnes was taking care of some details when he realized he wasn't alone. "What're you doing here?"

Dante Bhang, looking very GQ, took the seat vacated by Lint. "I was curious about this hush-hush task they delegated to you. Very amusing, this Lint gambit."

"You hear me good, Bhang. You're working for me. You step out of line one time and I cancel your witness-protection status and send you up for about the next forty years."

Bhang's aplomb was unshakable. Not surprising, as he was an unsentimental realist who had abandoned Charlie Cola after the mistaken abduction at Rodeo East and hitched his wagon to Randy Barnes, NYPD. "Captain Barnes, I've always admired your competence; that was why I suggested cooperating. With the Phoenix Enterprises members vying for the uppermost hand and Black Hole getting ready to open Earth, there are unlimited possibilities for the likes of us. But if we're to profit together from this situation—"

"We ain't partners!" Barnes's face was flushed. "I *own* you!"

"So? And who also owns that numbered bank account in Chile? Who's falsified evidence in investigations and perjured himself on the witness stand? Who's keeping that rather fetching little mistress in Yorkville and supplying her with fantazine—"

Barnes's hand had slid under his jacket. "I could kill you right here, shithead, and nobody'd ever know."

"Yes, they would; I've arranged for that. Then where would you run, the Trough? No, you don't want to go there any more than I."

Barnes's face had lost a lot of its color now, but he was listening. Bhang went on. "Nor am I interested in conflict. Captain, we can work together to our mutual benefit—serve our own interests as well as the Agency.

"We can become Black Hole's new capos."

"See that all three prisoners are prepped for a fade to End Zone," The Awesome Vogonskiy trumpeted like the showman he was. "The fun's only begun."

Being dragged across the bridge deck helipad of the tour ship *Crystal Harmonic,* Sean Junknowitz tried groggily to marshal himself for one—just one!—try at Vogonskiy. Not that Sean expected to be able to kill the alien illusionist; Black Hole held too many of the cards.

That didn't change the fact that the elder Junknowitz brother wanted to get something back for all his pain, for the exertion and investment of inner resources needed to mount the disastrous attack on the XT party boat. Sean also wanted to do some damage on behalf of the late Bullets Strayhand, whom Vogonskiy's delayed-reaction death-dap had sent to an early grave in appallingly short order.

Today wasn't Sean's day, however; not many had been in recent years. He blinked away blood that had seeped from the gash in his forehead, suffered when the *Crystal Harmonic* used some kind of invisible force field to pluck the attackers' swift-boat out of the water, slam it back down, then hoist it and dump it ignominiously on the helipad—where it sat now, tipped to port and shedding seawater. The war-surplus smart mine that Sean's former Tiger Team buddies had procured had been dealt with even more contemptuously.

Somebody had slapped a dermal patch behind Sean's ear and now he felt as weak as a wrung rag. A lolling look around told him that Eddie Ensign and Willy Ninja, somewhat unwilling collaborators in the disastrous swiftboat assault, were no better off: dazed, injured, and well in hand. Besides, a number of uniformed crew members had him covered, as did a few ostensible "alien themers" pointing daunting-looking special-effects gizmos. Their cover story—that they were humans wearing clever disguises as part of a worldwide promo tour—had let the XTs roam the planet at will.

Also worsening Sean's odds was a jostling throng of on-lookers still heartily enjoying the light sport Vogonskiy's Trough-tech magic and tongue-in-cheek voice-over had made of the assault on the *Harmonic*. There were plenty of fangs, claws, stingers, and barbed tentacles among them.

Nope, not much chance of taking Vogonskiy off the roster today, nor that purplish homunculus familiar of his, Tumi, sneering at Sean just now around the massive magician's hefty starboard buttock.

As far as Sean could tell, neither his three Tiger Team buddies nor the two piratical Filipinos who'd owned and crewed the boat had been taken. Whether that made them more fortunate than him, Eddie, and Willy was problematical just at the moment. The nearest land was miles away and he doubted Skeeter Robyn, and the rest had even managed to get into lifevests; but on the other hand Sean, Eddie, and Willy were headed for "End Zone," whatever that was.

Sean looked to Vogonskiy, still standing to one side after his gloating narration of the "performance" he had dubbed Sneak Attack. "I'm not through with you yet, you tub a' shit," Sean slurred. He was vaguely hoping to get the bastard mad enough to come at him. All right, maybe high-tech had been the wrong way to go, but that still left the unarmed mayhem Sean knew so well how to deal out—and other, more arcane assaults as well. This preening XT was everything Sean hated and re-sented, a phony and a liar, a hypocrite and double-crosser; worse yet, he had treated Sean with condescension and con-tempt.

Vogonskiy only roared with laughter, his full beard bobbing, hands splayed across his immense belly. Then, from his full six-foot-eight-inch height, he glowered down at Sean. "Well, little man, I am as yet not through with *you*, either."

Leaving the passengers to the excitement of what many of them still believed to be a staged performance, Vogonskiy led the way to the ladderwell. Eddie groaned. "Way to go, Sean. Cop us a plea."

"Shut up," Sean could just about focus sufficiently to an-swer. Whatever Vogonskiy and Black Hole had planned for the three, there'd been no possibility of a reprieve or lessening of the sentence anyway.

Sean was prepared to accept that—so long as he could clear his head, get a little closer to Vogonskiy, show him he wasn't the only one with a little evil mojo on tap. So he did *ki-*

gathering drills and yogic concentration exercises as he and his brother's former roommates were dragged belowdecks. Passengers ignored the procession the way sheltered, well-heeled Twenty-Ones would no doubt turn away from the sight of a sneak thief being lugged out of some Third-World five-star hotel. Just more of those shiftless, heathen indigs, making trouble.

The next deck down had an industrial look to it, and guards made way for the group. Eddie's derm must've had him out of it a little, because Sean distinctly heard him giggle. "Finished redecorating, huh?"

Sean knew that meant they were close to where the movable Adit, one of the first of its kind, had been mounted. Eddie had seen its upper section more than a week before, while sneaking around on deck with Lucky. Down here the Adit area looked like a reactor containment housing. The three captives were hustled through an elaborately secured lock, and a moment later Sean had his first look at a Black Hole Travel Agency Adit.

As Lucky had once put it, an Adit was impressive but nothing a good Hollywood set crew couldn't knock together. Maybe it was the fact that it all looked so utilitarian, including the Pit Boss plugged and jacked and skull-ported into his horseshoe of instruments, that sent Sean's hackles up. Everything was so matter-of-fact.

Lucky had said the design of the Adits varied. This one was centered on a raised octagon like a small bandstand, under a dome of neon Bucky Fuller monkey bars. There was already an energetic hum building in the place; Sean knew he didn't have time to waste. He focused himself, his mind fixed on a pinpoint of cosmic light three inches before his eyes, moved like lightning—

But Vogonskiy wasn't where he'd been standing. Roaring with that maddening laughter, he had left one foot out and Sean went sprawling over it. The guards had moved well back.

Vogonskiy made a two-handed shoving motion, as though rolling a small car at Sean. From nowhere, dark smoke with a nauseating tinge appeared, swirling at Sean. Like trick cinematography, it blew into him—high, low, and in between. Sean hadn't let anybody hear a sound of pain out of him since the war, but now he cried aloud. It was as if needles were being shoved through every cell of him—but worse, he felt as if something inhuman and hungry were moving into him, making itself at home, licking its chops and examining the goodies.

Sean, vision gone, heard Eddie scream, then Willy—and knew they'd gotten the treatment, too. The activation sounds coming from the Adit had built, and now there was a crackling of static from somewhere. His equilibrium gone, he knew he was being muscled around again but couldn't coordinate any defense. There was a brief feeling of free-fall from which he slid directly into a timeless, sensationless void.

"Ugh! Get the fuck away from me!"

Sean had been slowly coming awake to a low grunting sound and had only just begun to realize that he was the one making it when Eddie's yell brought him all the way back in a second or two. Old combat reflexes helped him prioritize the things vying for his attention, so he didn't stop to reflect on the peculiarly light feeling of his body despite sharp pain, or the fact that he didn't know where he was or how he'd gotten there.

He knew at once that he was outdoors, in a place filled with alarming and sickening smells he couldn't identify; that he was unarmed and maybe ill or drugged; that it was the voice of a friendly he'd heard. There was also a lot of chuffing, slurping, oinking—whatever. He'd been lying facedown in what felt like sodden, rotting leaves; now he was rolling to rise in a defensive crouch, the kind of move he'd made thousands of times.

Only this time his body felt full of broken glass, grinding away at his flesh and bones. This time there was a reservoir of something inert and malignly painful in his midsection; this time lasers of agony bounced around in his head trying to fry his eyeballs.

He only completed the move to his feet because he had driven into himself the disciplines of working onward through pain. Even so, he wasn't sure it was something he could do twice in a row. He was weaving on his feet, on guard, in a forest of what looked like decaying biopsies strewn over rotting bones. He had no time to inspect the sickly undergrowth, the tobacco-cud ground underfoot, the doleful flying things wheeling overhead, instead watched the circle of creatures backing away from him now; and away from Willy—who'd struggled into a sitting position—and Eddie, who lay moaning and panting for breath nearby.

"I don't think they tried to hurt us," Willy grated. "Picking us over for what they could steal, more likely."

"Seeing if we'd make a good meal's more likely," Sean scoffed. But he had to agree that the motley gang of scavengers didn't look any too formidable. They all appeared to be in various advanced stages of starvation and disease. From the tattered clothing, worn-out footwear, empty equipment loops, and the like, he took it that they were survivors of some misfortune—castaways? Or purposely stranded?

Perhaps the latter, because they all showed the signs of some malady. Lesions, running sores, abscesses; necrotic skin and tissue eaten away to show internal structures; edemas and what looked like gas-gangrene ulcerations. Then there were the growths and afflictions for which earthly medicine had no word, like the one poor son of a bitch whose head was about to be enveloped by a coral reef of calciferous stuff that emerged from his own cranial openings.

Sean thought he recognized some species from Lucky and Sheena's stories: Nalls and Shaks and Yggs. And there were others to which he could put no name, creatures of fantasy— except that each was suffering from some repulsive affliction. Yeah, he supposed they weren't much threat.

Bits of what had happened to him in the attack and onboard the *Crystal Harmonic* were reassembling themselves. So Vogonskiy had pitched them onto some kind of Devil's Island, huh? Maybe to come hunt down Sean and his companions at leisure? Well, Lardass the Magnificent was in for a surprise.

Sean had been a Tiger Team member, so good that he and a few others like him were used to test the SEALs, Rangers, Pathfinders, and their ilk. More than that, he'd danced with the Guaranis and been adopted by the Lacandón, learned the tricks of the Inuit and Masai. There was no trap he couldn't make or outwit, no trail he couldn't follow or tracker he couldn't shake. Just the materials he could see from where he stood would give him deadly weapons enough to deal with anything that lived.

He laughed harshly, though the effort smarted some. "So this is the worst Vogonskiy could throw at us, huh? Eddie, Willy, on your feet." Willy the half-Cherokee musician and Eddie the laid-back celeb taper: not much raw material for a takeover, but they'd do—Sean would *make* them do. "C'mon, this place is about to come under new management."

"You fucking idiot!" Eddie said straining between clenched teeth. "Don't you get it? Vogonskiy didn't throw us into End Zone for revenge; he *threw his revenge into us!*"

As he said it he sat up and for the first time Sean saw the dark lesions on Eddie's face and neck, the cloudy gray cataracts that had appeared in Willy's eyes. And for the first time Sean let himself truly feel the pain in his gut, palpate his swollen, tender midsection a bit. His own touch made him gasp and cough and wheeze; his mouth filled with sputum and he wiped blood from his lips.

Then he understood. There would be no night stalking, no Malayan tiger traps or woodcraft triumphs.

Eddie saw it in his eyes and nodded, looking as pale as Sean felt. "That's right, GI. Vogonskiy's not playing a 'Most Dangerous Game,' he's playing a *new* game. Welcome to the leper colony."

SIX

THE CARTS SWUNG past the carefully groomed battle-
field area and down the Street of the Armorers. From there it
was possible to see the higher parts of attractions in World
Nihon's other areas. The sprawling acreage offered *Launchpad
Earth*, complete with a gimballed mock-up/adaptation of the
Shimuzu corp orbital luxury hotel; the *Biosphere* eco-domain;
and the requisite *IMagicNation* 'toon fairyland. Even more
promising for the bottom line was the opulent shopping mall.

But *Land of Yamato*, feudal Japan, was the place Tanabe
loved best. The mounted archers' lists were all ready, as were
the other *bugei* exhibition areas. Over where the forty-seven
ronin would muster for their epic attack and dreadfully bloody
revenge—six shows daily—all was prepared. And the Ghost-
Fox Train was nearly ready to roll.

Tengu Mountain reared up before them, an alp of synthetics
and ferrocrete and quarried stone—a craggy, spooky scarp,
which the tech staff had switched on for the VIPs' benefit and
a full-dress check. Hideous long-nosed or -beaked *tengu* demons of various descriptions leapt from hiding places or
swooped down on beating wings to shriek at passersby; witches
hissed from their jackstraw thatch huts while ghosts wafted
above them, moaning appallingly; shape-shifting spirits beckoned or threatened; a dragon belched fire from a cave of ice and
a sea serpent reared up from fiery waters at the mountain's
base. As always, Tanabe felt just the slightest twinge at those
shape-shifters, one he'd never felt when he was younger. One
he'd never felt before he'd discovered there were such things.

A camouflaged door in the rear of *Tengu Mountain* opened
for Tanabe's cart, which rolled toward a subsurface garage
while the rest of the convoy continued on a tour that would end

in *Launchpad Earth*, where he would presently rejoin it. Justin Duplex gave him a wave and yelled, "Take a bow, dude!" Tanabe reflected upon what hundreds of millions of fans would say if they learned Duplex wasn't human, or ever got a look at what lay under his elaborate disguise.

Behind-the-scenes staffers in brown uniforms, *jikatabi* boots, yellow safety helmets, and white gloves lined up to kowtow to the CEO as he disembarked, followed by Miss Sato and Mr. Natsuki. As another elevator bore him upward, Tanabe considered *Launchpad Earth*.

It was amazing and sad—though not so sad that he and others hadn't taken good advantage of the fact—that it had taken the American people so long to face the truth: *Japan, not the U.S., was the template for the twenty-first century.*

Not the U.S. with its frontier mentality and its fallacies of unlimited space, boundless resources, endless new beginnings and fresh starts. Those led to unchecked splurging, unconscionable waste, insane shortsightedness, rampant irresponsibility—and turned the country from the world's premier power to a fractious, semiliterate debt addict.

No, it was Japan that understood the twenty-first century, was best positioned for it. Japan had the new millennium's problems bred in the bone: population pressure, scarcity of resources, the need for cooperation, diligence, sacrifice. Japan could bring to bear national reverence for education, thrift, patience, self-denial, sense of duty and obligation.

Strangest of all, Tanabe mused, the Americans never seemed—except for the brightest and most alienated of them—to realize the source of the problem. Or perhaps they simply didn't want to confront it. The few times he'd pointed it out at school his American friends had either ignored him, taken offense, or made ineffective rebuttal.

Tanabe suspected the Founding Fathers, those astoundingly wise and capable men, had missed the fatal flaw utterly. Jefferson and the rest were hard workers—energetic, often Renaissance men driven to achieve. They had perhaps been blind to the danger that there would arise in their glorious republic a species of *career candidate* who would do little or nothing in life but court votes. Nearly all American failures and vulnerabilities came from the simple fact that the need to win elections and reelections swept aside morals, conscience, convictions, and truth. Politicians who were willing to lie could usually put to rout those who weren't, or who lied less well—

because Americans were accustomed, like spoiled babies, to being given or at least promised whatever they desired and spared bad news.

Wall Street had helped, its investors expecting not the slow and sure increase of their monies but rather the jackpot, like the drunks Tanabe had seen at Atlantic City slot machines. And the bean counters were all too eager to slice up the U.S. infrastructure for the sake of the next quarter's profit.

The elevator slowed three-quarters of the way up the interior of *Tengu Mountain*. Tanabe broke his distraction. Like the old samurai Mr. Sugimoto enduring the comical doorman's outfit, Japan had suffered her adversities with stoic dignity and unswerving commitment to her own values. Japan's time had come around again by dint of sheer hard work—and, he would've admitted in a moment of introspection, classic American self-deception.

Which brought him back to the subject of his son.

The elevator doors *swish*ed open on a hellish scene and Tanabe walked forward into it. His *jonin*, Mr. Kamimura, stepped forward to bow crisply. He wore the same uniform, safety helmet, and gloves as thousands of park employees but also had a white sanitary mask on his face—the kind worn in many places by those who were ill or wished to avoid contracting a cold. "This way, Tanabe-san." Miss Sato and Mr. Natsuki fell in behind.

The *tengu*—literally, "heavenly dogs"—of traditional myth tended to be tricksters and mischief-makers rather than malevolent fiends, and so most of the mountain was an ultimate fun house. Holo and animatronic *tengu* could pull a huge variety of scary but harmless pranks on visitors. But here in the nether region a place had been prepared for those ticket-buyers determined to visit the Abyss.

The ninja upper man led them through billows of special nontoxic smoke. A frightful Emma-O, judge of the underworld, waited to pass harsh sentences. Ghouls gnawed flesh from pieces of bone and specters wailed in pain and despair. All around were the baths of flaming lava, the torture instruments of ice and stone and bloodstained iron, the fiery pits and brimstone cauldrons and the rest of the appurtenances the visitors would expect. The costumed themers who would man the place and do the actual torturing were absent; today, security was all-important.

Tanabe was shown to a chair near the foot of the great

Emma-O's judgment seat. A nod from him and Kamimura gave a subtle signal. A large metal airline cargo module was wheeled in by anonymous employees in the same nondescript clothing their *jonin* wore.

Two of them cracked the module doors and stepped back. Several seconds passed in silence, then Nikkei Tanabe and Mickey Formica eased out into the sinister light. Both of them looked much the worse for wear: glassy-eyed and unsteady on their feet, unkempt, unfed, and stinking. Nikkei's chunkiness had been starved down to a shrunken-bellied muscularity; taller, sinewy Mickey looked like an HIVirus victim except for the alertness and fierce resentment in his eyes. The minor gunshot wound on Mickey's right wrist, the one Sean Junknowitz had given him in New York City's The Dreamy Lotus restaurant, was now a pink scar under layers of dirt. But both young men had plenty of new wounds and injuries albeit nothing disabling.

There was one surprise, a silent commentary prepared by Nikkei. Somewhere he'd gotten red stain—a grease pencil or marker he'd copped, perhaps—and crudely reddened his cheeks. The act was at once a mockery of classic samurai sensibility and an adherence to it; the samurai's blend of macho swagger and effete refinement dictated a warrior's cheeks be rouged when he met death—that they not suffer a vulgar loss of color. More than anything, Tanabe knew, the rouge was an act of defiance. Nikkei was well aware that his father had long vacillated between the *giri* of duty and the *ninjo* of paternal feelings in debating whether or not to exact death from his son. Now Nikkei was daring him.

Aside from that, their condition was as Tanabe had intended it to be. Since they'd surrendered themselves to Tanabe's handlers in the wake of the botched kidnapping of Harley Paradise and Sheena Hec'k, they had been held in a variety of places, told nothing, moved without warning, and given treatment that veered between near-decency and torture. They'd made a number of surprisingly resourceful attempts to escape but had gotten nowhere against Kamimura's people. Tanabe saw with grudging approval that they'd come through their trials with a measure of morale intact—but of course they hadn't been tested to the fullest.

Having received periodic surveillance reports on his son ever since their devastating estrangement several years earlier, Tanabe knew Nikkei and Mickey had operated more or less as equals in their asinine endeavors as mercenary *genin*—lower men, ninja dog-soldiers. But now, Tanabe could see, the young African-American was looking to his partner for guidance and leadership. Despite their previous Western relationship—what Tanabe had come to think of as the *Hey, man!* attitude—Nikkei could be clearly observed, by body movements and facial kinetics, to be coming into a new state of self-possession, of calm, of fatalistic gravity.

Nevertheless a nervous Mickey bit out, "What kind of double cross is this? Bhang's the one who fucked everything up—" He shut up as Nikkei gave him a glance. To plead the obvious was to lose face.

Yes, Dante Bhang had left the two twisting in the wind in the wake of the bungled abduction on Rodeo East. Nikkei and Mickey were ignorant pawns and Bhang perhaps had hoped Phoenix or even Black Hole, would simply chalk it all up as their—and possibly Cola's—mistake.

Very likely that would have happened, except that Tanabe was one of the most influential members of Phoenix, and Black Hole had, after all, little interest in the two bit players.

Rendering the duo unconscious when they had reported for what they'd assumed to be a new assignment, boxing them up and shipping them air freight to Japan—all that had been glitch-free for Mr. Kamimura's people. But Tanabe, wanting to know more about the pair and also wise in the techniques of softening up a tough customer, had chosen to postpone this interview.

In the time since then the partners had been held, moved, worked on, moved again—all without explanation. Suspension from a tree, Musashi-fashion, in a software-design monastery on Hokkaido; a storm-tossed two-day voyage trussed up in body bags in the hold of a hydrofoil freighter; a sojourn in a half-submerged tiger cage in the Golden Triangle; forced marches in desert, jungle, and swamp; and burial alive.

Until this moment they'd had no idea where on Earth they were. Now, in *Tengu Mountain*, doubtless Nikkei would guess, and very likely Mickey as well.

If the two weren't the best of raw material, their testing had indicated to Tanabe, neither were they the worst. It intrigued him to find out that, so far as could be determined, Nikkei had told Mickey of his parentage, but never of the apocalypse that had split father and son.

Nikkei and Mickey glanced around, taking in their situation soberly but without panic. When Nikkei's glance met Miss

Sato's, Tanabe saw, it lingered there for an extra moment. Miss Sato's glacial calm did not falter.

Then Nikkei and his father exchanged the same impenetrable, almost gentle gaze, a family resemblance coming to the fore. Mickey looked from one to the other. "What do you want from us?" Nikkei asked in English, without preamble or the least flicker of obeisance. Both he and Mickey stood motionless, knowing they were being closely watched by opponents who simply didn't make mistakes; they'd learned the hard way that this would not be a moment to make their play.

"To spare you," Tanabe answered. "To enlist you in my service. It doesn't matter whether you like me or hate me. You can be of use to me, and I can give you and Mr. Formica something you both want very much."

Before Nikkei could respond Mickey interposed. "Whatchu want from us? Bhang? Cola? Why'n'chu ask us that in the first place, muthufuckah?"

Tanabe rested one ankle on the opposite knee, bobbing a handmade shoe that had cost him some 3,500 pounds sterling—about $10,000 the pair—at John Cobb on St. James's Street. "Because I wanted to be positive you met certain minimal standards. Otherwise you wouldn't be alive. Yes, I might want you to go back to work for Bhang and to do other things as well. And in return, Mr. Formica, I'll arrange for you both to stop making fools of yourselves—to become what you and so many others only pretend to be."

He watched them closely. Nikkei couldn't keep a certain stunned disbelief out of his expression. He'd quit his father's house back before he'd been made privy to the most closely guarded family secrets, and the service of Kamimura's people was among the highest of these.

Tanabe came to his feet, glaring at them. "Look at you! You and all those other nitwit wannabes! Capering about in your mail-order costumes, learning comic-book lore from ignorant fools in bad B-movie cult *ryu!* Mr. Formica, what would you consider to be your strong suit as a ninja? Swordplay, perhaps? Or hiding under dung heaps?"

Mickey bridled. Two of Kamimura's *chunin* shifted in the dimness, letting the clank of finely forged metal remind him of his place. Mickey shrugged. *"Imori gakure."*

Tanabe chuckled. "Perfect. Clinging to walls. Ah, that's *so* useful in a world with IR scanners and micromotion detectors and smart-skin construction features, don't you agree? Let me show you a little something, Mr. Formica.''

Kamimura clapped his hands and a figure emerged from the darkness, bearing special gear. But where Nikkei and Mickey expected to see somebody decked out for a display of some unimaginably updated stealth skill, they beheld a medium-sized, nondescript man in a stylish, expensive but not especially noteworthy golfing outfit—complete with tasseled, cleated shoes and silk J. Crew baseball cap. He carried only a white, red-dimpled Mitsui 2020 ball in one hand and a glimmering-gold putter in the other. He stopped by a whirligig torture cage fifty feet away.

As the man set the ball on the floor, Kamimura held out to Mickey a Laz-E-Tek PuttaRound practice target, a miniature plastic Quonset hut. Mickey checked Nikkei's closed expression, shrugged again, and accepted it. At the same time the linksman ninja whipped a red silk scarf from his back pocket, drew it over his eyes, and knotted it swiftly and effortlessly behind his head.

"Anywhere you like, Mr. Formica," Tanabe bade Mickey, gesturing for him to drop the target.

"You dickin' with me?"

"Not in the least. Times change. New skills become more important than, say, mere walking on water."

Mickey studied the floor around him, uneven ferrocrete awaiting utilities installation. He scaled the target ten yards away, where it landed with a hollow thunk, mouth pointing more or less their way.

Tanabe was saying, "Adaptability, Mr. Formica: a recognition of *new* venues of power. The Meiji Restoration hadn't even begun when Mr. Kamimura's ancestors were divesting themselves of firemask scare tactics and itinerant-priest impersonations to adapt and retool their arts. The quaint, outmoded skills they leaked in dumbed-down and distorted versions—to divert the attentions and energies of *gaijin* suckers.

"Has my son ever told you that a member of the golf team at Tokyo U. or any other prestige school has an assured future, a good job with some prosperous corporation? The game is that important, in most of the world, to the power élite. Skill in it gives entrée to the most exclusive circles, wins wagers that in turn give leverage, establishes bonds of friendly advice, or allows the conspicuous defeat of competitors and enemies."

The ninja, blindfolded now, had moved to face the little target's hemisphere mouth and taken up his putter in a modified interlocking grip. The golden club had a sleek, ergonomic look to it. He addressed the ball and cocked his head as if listening as Tanabe went on. "The animating spirit that Masamune forged into swords and Kokei sculpted into wood now enlivens new artifacts. Also, the golden aura of that putter is the gleam of breakthrough NakaMats R and D."

The man putted with a measured, concise stroke. The auriferous putter, connecting, made a soft bonging tone as rounded and perfect as the tolling of a Zen temple bell. The Mitsui 2020 rolled quickly, breaking minutely right, then left on near-invisible slopes in the ferrocrete, and went straight into the target. The man removed his blindfold, bowed to Tanabe and Kamimura, and retreated into the darkness once more with never another glance at his target.

Tanabe looked back to the two captives. "Now you can either enter my service, in which case you may in time be accepted for *real* training and enlightenment, or you may go. In the latter case you'll be entirely on your own. I'm leaving for my next appointment and so I'll ask you: Which shall it be?"

Nikkei was breathing more deeply but still not speaking. Mickey went to lean one elbow on his friend's shoulder with a nod in Kamimura's direction. "And we get to study with *them?*"

"In time, if you merit it."

"It's a deal, then," Mickey said. He thought maybe he would've said it even if he hadn't been astounded by these insights into authentic *ninjutsu*. Tanabe might be talking about letting them go but it would be all too easy for him to, say, have them chucked into that handy lava pit over there if they turned him down.

Mickey and Tanabe both looked to Nikkei, who after a few seconds inclined his head very slowly—not a nod of acquiescence, but a kowtow.

Tanabe was nodding, satisfied but by no means warm. "Very well. Mr. Kamimura will explain what is expected of you. Thereafter you will go back to New York. I'm particularly interested in Lucky Junknowitz, whose name you perhaps remember."

Nikkei still wasn't talking.

"Met him in a men's room one time," Mickey replied. "So we're told."

"Indeed. He is top priority. If you have word of him you will inform me at once. *I want him alive.* Kamimura-san?"

The *jonin* came forward to take formal charge of the two recruits. Tanabe felt just a moment's waver, seeing his son again, then hardened himself. It would avail nothing to try to force a reconciliation at this point. What was more, he had obligations that wouldn't wait. Tanabe hesitated another second, vigilant, but no further looks passed between Miss Sato and his son. Tanabe made a subtle gesture of one finger, a slight pose of the chin; Miss Sato fell out of his group to stand to one side. She had her instructions.

Tanabe brought his chin up in a certain understated but unmistakable way. All his staff kowtowed to him, Miss Sato included. Mickey was quick to emulate them, and, after considerable hesitation, Nikkei slowly followed suit.

Natsuki and the other ninja hadn't missed the delay and were wearing the kind of flat looks that Mickey knew spelled rack-ass time. He tried his hand at ventriloquism, out of the side of his mouth. "*Homme*-y, what—"

But Nikkei had made a secret signal of his own, one he and his partner used. It wasn't that Natsuki's golfers would miss it—they were undoubtedly genius kinesics readers—but they had no way of knowing what meaning the two had assigned the finger-talk character.

The twix said to stand pat and wait the other side out. It wasn't the one Mickey wanted to see but he and Nikkei were joined at the *ki* and *karma* now like Siamese twins so he tried to log out mentally, float rather than wait, gather himself for action.

Tanabe turned and left, Mr. Natsuki falling behind, bound for the elevator. Miss Sato turned to Mickey and Nikkei. "Wait here." Her English was liltingly crisp with a flawless Oxford accent.

Exiting *Tengu Mountain,* the convoy now consisted of Tanabe's cart plus two security runabouts. They traveled at high speed toward the largest and most opulent of the *o-furo,* the baths, with which World Nihon was furnished.

To clear his mind of thoughts of his son Tanabe utilized the transit time to tend to pending business matters. He reminded himself that the People's Republic of Vietnam was still awaiting a reply.

SEVEN

THE PASSAGE OF time seemed distorted to Vanderloop, but he had no way of knowing whether that came from Gipper's tapping of the songlines and the Dreamtime or the tachycardia effect of his own fear and exertion.

He dogged the Aborigines across alien vistas, seeming at times to gain, at times to fall behind. More than once he was only trailing by a few dozen paces, surely within earshot—though they didn't pause when he yelled to them. Several times he'd fallen behind until the file of Intubis were dots making for an unearthly horizon, and the countryside around him began to take on substance in a way that meant he was about to be left behind for good.

At length he had no choice but to slow to a marathon lope. He trailed the Intubis through an ice storm over ground that felt like foam rubber; over savannah brilliant with impossibly colorful and varied flowers and teeming with alien game; along a metallic roadway high over a luminous supertech city in the dead of night; through a sweltering rain forest past the bones of dead animals that would have dwarfed the biggest dinosaur. And on, and on. Suns and moons appeared and went away; gravity fluctuated around Earth's norm.

All at once he realized the sky overhead had changed again. Now it was a menacing chaos of angry currents and massive discharges, with a thin layer of poisonous-looking clouds closer down. The wind, hot as the blast from an oven, blew fine grit at him with stinging force. When Vanderloop, breathing raggedly, looked ahead once more, he saw that the Intubis had stopped.

They were high on a stony knife-edge ridge overlooking a cattle chute of a mountain pass, and he was only a hundred yards behind at the same level. The Intubis were staring and pointing down at something in the ravine below. Vanderloop, massaging a stitch in his side, glanced down, too—and gaped.

Marching along in down below was a formation of astonishing machines, anthropomorphic—perhaps robots, but for some reason he thought not. They were huge, ranging up to thirty, forty feet in height, bristling with assorted weapons and finished in flat camouflage patterns to suit the desolate wasteland in which they moved. But what struck him as strangest about them was the stylistic look of them, their lines and form.

They were automotive. The things boasted fins, heavy grill-work, sleek trim, contoured air scoops—it was as if the designers of the American highway monsters of the late forties, the fifties, and the early sixties had put their stamp on a line of walking war machines.

Strung out military style, they formed two separate elements. In the rear one, two of the machines lugged a kind of palanquin on which rested a container like a safe.

Vanderloop looked along the ridge to where Gipper and the rest had paused. The Intubis were pointing down to the marching machines and talking animatedly to one another, especially interested in the container.

The songlines *made* Creation and Creation made the songlines—was in fact the songlines waiting to be sung. There was nothing arbitrary about it all, that was Gipper's point.

Take the big iron fellas like so many rock *inapatua* spirits down below, and the thing they were transporting with such constant watchfulness. Power resided in the object those metal blokes were toting, Gipper could perceive that. Why couldn't the others?

Oh, Lily, who'd been something of a *wuradilagu*—a healing woman—to begin with, smelled a bit of it, he was sure. And certainly old Bobbie Benton, another elder, had a glimmer of it. But neither of them had it true blue, and the rest of the lot were all but blind to the importance of the otherworld tjuringa the iron fellas were transporting.

Oh, well. The clan's dream-walking was improving. The rest would come in good time.

Bluesy hissed and pointed out movement along the walls of the narrow pass. Instinctively, only half seeing what was stirring there, the Intubis knew it was time to shoot through—leave in a damn big hurry. Gipper went skipping down some stones, diverting from the ridge, just as the first shots and monstrous war cries rang out in the pass.

Packard and his gaitmobes had no choice but to stand their ground and fight.

The enemy's Humanosaurs were sly—getting more so with each engagement, with every passing day of a war to the death. And so red carnage had come down on him all at once, without warning.

When the ambush was sprung on Packard's strikeforce mobes in the high winding pass called Spillway, hard by the crags of Wisdom's Teeth, he knew right away that it probably meant disaster for a lot more than just his command—meant death for many, many of the People beyond Guard-Marshal Packard and his glorified burgling expedition.

There was a massed 'Saur battlehorde wheeling out on the Windbore Badlands far below, mixing it up with the hit-and-run diversionary group the People had mustered under Chancellor Auburn; he'd marked the dust clouds they kicked up, here and there, from various vantage points on the march. But the enemy's seeming gullibility had been a trick—and it worked.

Bleak news indeed, that the cold synthetic intellects of Warhead were getting so good at strategy. The quirkiness and uncertainty of warfare, the subtle illogic of it, the bluffing, feinting, and misdirection, were things that had worked in the People's favor in their battle against Warhead.

Bioengineered monsters were coming for Packard, and he turned to give battle.

A few seconds before, the strikeforce had been a loose double column of gaitmobes, striding in route-step on bipod alloy legs. It was strictly gaitmobes, of course—the ground-pounders. In the mountains, and especially on this crucial lightning raid, tracked, wheeled, and surface effect mobes would have been, as in the vast majority of places on Hazmat, useless, unable to negotiate the terrain. One hundred and eighty years after Doomsday, with so much of Hazmat made nearly impassable, almost unsurvivable, nothing could match the strength, firepower, and adaptability of a ground-pounder.

That is, nothing the People could create. Waves of Green Ghouls and Doom-Demons came pouring out of the gullies and cracks in the pass walls, and from behind boulder jumbles. A few Atrocitors rose into view in well-selected firing positions, awaiting the order to open up.

Only half a minute before the first volley of shots, the first cries of alarm, the first terrible roars of ambushing Humanosaurs, Packard had scanned the sky. Sealed away there in the deep, broad, reinforced chest of his command mobe, *Bounder*'s control contacts feeding sensations to his brain, it nevertheless seemed to Packard that they were his own eyes he used. *Bounder* craned upward, and Packard had an impossibly wide field of vision over an eerily wide part of the electromagnetic spectrum.

Not very far over the squat, armored heads of the walking mechsuits, Packard had noticed, the lowest layers of worldwinds snaked and howled, lethally powerful, dipping even lower than usual. Microbursts and mini-jetstreams ripped and ravaged the air. Higher up, more visible worldwind manifestations—fire-flails, twisting skywracks, and other bizarre and deadly postapocalyptic phenomena—mingled and clashed, a constant net of chaos enmeshing the planet.

Strong worldwind activity today; that was fine with Packard. Air surveillance and airpower were virtually useless nowadays, but in making this desperate sortie he was especially grateful for that. Otherwise, the genocidal SI aggregate called Warhead would have been watching every square inch of the planet like an omnipresent eye.

Packard was grateful, that was, as long as there wasn't a skycrash.

Next, he'd made a quick check of his strikeforce; even though they'd come through this all-important raid in good shape, the homeward leg was no time to relax. Bulkily anthropoid, the camouflaged gaitmobes were designed for carnage. Nevertheless, they sported the massive, fierce grilles, the tail-finned look and elaborate trim—vaned and serrated in dynaflow lines—that the savior designer, Easy Wheels, had so loved.

Packard's columns had been moving at far tighter intervals than he felt easy with, but it was unavoidable in the closeness of the pass. And in the unique, shielded container being lugged along at the middle of the columns between two specially modified combat-engineer mechs lay the hope of Hazmat. In another two hours the strikeforce would have been in a hidden transit station beyond Warhead's reach, bearing away its prize.

When the 'Saurs attacked, some of the People opened fire in

instant response but others simply didn't have the room and found themselves in hand-to-hand combat. That the Humanosaurs hadn't annihilated the gaitmobes from concealment with massed fire supremacy meant Warhead hadn't located the recovered object and wished at all costs to avoid damaging it.

The two sides were too close together for the gaitmobes to use HE missiles, too much in each other's line of fire for armor-piercing rounds, too commingled for Packard to call in artillery support even if there had been any. To make things worse on a personal level, Packard was wearing *Bounder* rather than his usual command gaitmobe, *Stomper*, with its far greater firepower and thicker armorplate; *Bounder* had prototype multicommo and hypernav gear vital to the mission.

There was heavy contact up and down the columns. Packard spoke as calmly as he could, in motion at the same time. "Form fireteams! Second Cohort, regroup on the container! First Cohort, regroup on me!"

Bounder's gyros whined as Packard whirled the two-legged gaitmobe around, bringing weapons to bear. Its nuclear turbines revved high, the power trains shuddered and the servos howled, and Packard felt like all those things were happening within his body.

His main gun locked into place along his—*Bounder*'s—left forearm. He willed it to extract the AP round from its breech and reload with canister shot, but it was jammed, the canister shell unfirable. The sensation was like a bad cramp. *Damn support-mobe junk!* Packard tried to clear the stoppage and reload as he took stock of his situation.

The middle of the strikeforce, caught now on the very edge of the saddle ridge it had just crossed, was rapidly being cut in two. And its whole reason for fighting, the reason for the raid, lay back on the far side of the ridge—the data egg, the memory fragment sundered from Warhead so long ago.

"DeSoto!" Packard called to his executive officer. "You have the second; *protect that container at all*—"

Then there was nothing on the freq but static. Worldwinds, or Warhead's jamming.

All around him, brain-directed war machines had turned to grapple and shoot it out at point-blank range with rearing, genetically manipulated horrors. Humanosaurs, gestated in wombvats at Warhead's birthworks. Their long-ago DNA source had been the People.

Each class of Humanosaur wore its distinct, if sometimes

mismatched, ''clothing,'' harness, armor, and equipment. The 'Saurs carried weapons ranging from the Ghouls mono-mol-edged cutlasses to the Atrocitors' shoulder-mounted laser tubes.

At least he could see no Gargantoids or Kongs; the enemy had probably been obliged to go without its most colossal battle-mutes in the mountains for the same reasons the People had left their weightiest mobes behind. A Green Ghoul came right for *Bounder*, the monster firing its electrogun as it moved. Blue-white bolts of energy leapt at the ground-pounder and danced all across it, humming and snapping.

Vanderloop, bent low as stray bullets, laser bolts, spurts of flamethrower fire, and corkscrewing minimissiles riddled the air, ran in a crouch, trying desperately to catch up to the Intubis. Having gotten them out of the line of fire, Gipper was singing up a new landscape: farther down this side of the ridge a loamy pathway with low vines piled to either side, most out of place on this wasteland world, led off around a boulder.

Vanderloop had let his attention wander; he missed a step and fell.

''Crikey!'' Saddie New was looking back to where Vander-loop had stumbled. As he went down on one knee, a tiny antipersonnel rocket sizzled through the air where he would have run.

''He's got the devil's own luck, that one,'' Bluesy com-mented.

She was still concerned. ''We should let him catch us up.''

''To play whitefella boss games, call his friends down on us again? Don't be daffo.'' Gipper had led the Intubis along the path to safety; his singing was getting farther away fast. ''C'mon.''

''But—''

''No buts!'' Where he'd been timid about so much as talking to her before, now he grabbed Saddie's arm and yanked her along.

By the time Vanderloop got to the path it was beginning to fade. His shoulder was bleeding where a splinter of rock had punched through his metalpunk doublet, and he was on his last reserves. The path felt runny and unreal as he tried to stay on it and increase speed, terrified at the idea of being left behind in the world of the battle machines.

Interface buffers kept Packard from suffering as the mobe's external sensors were roasted, but his nerve endings seemed to tingle painfully, and he smelled ozone.

The command mobe's defensive screens weren't as heavy-duty as *Stomper*'s, but they held against the electroshot. At that distance even a Ghoul's crude but big energy backpack couldn't muster enough juice to penetrate. But the range was closing as the howling 'Saur charged; Packard got the creature in the sighting overlay that had appeared before his eyes and let forth a wash of flame.

He meant to hose it from head to toe with fire-gel, cocoon it in fluttering orange-yellow flame. But it dodged, and though he slewed the nozzle to follow, he only grazed a leg thickly swathed in fireproofed batting and partly protected by metal-plate. The beast came on; he fired again, even as one part of him thought, No, not "beast"—it's human, somewhere in its genes. The creed of the People said so, and that the People mustn't fall to Warhead's level, looking on DNA as a plastic medium to be molded and perverted.

The Ghoul was quick for its size, like all its breed. One of Warhead's prime achievements in upsizing the brutes was in retaining speed and coordination, altering and strengthening their creation's structure to avoid the ravages of square-cube effects. It was nearly *Bounder*'s height, with a pebbly texture to its sickly-green hide. It was thickset, its legs and ankles treelike to bear all that weight, but it was as nimble as a maddened boar and seemed to know his main armament had hung fire.

Jade hairs more like quills were visible in areas of flesh exposed by its crudely forged armor segments or the coarse, weighty uniform. The Ghoul's eyes looked like black puncture wounds under jutting brow ridges and bucket helm, and its nose was almost vestigial, a skull's; its snarl showed teeth that fit together more like those of a crocodile than a human. Fastened in the plaited hair of its beard were fetishes and bones, trophies of victory or primitive psy-war devices.

The Ghoul went on firing with one hand, whipping up with the other a shield as thick as a mobe cowling. Helmet, armor, and shield protected it from the worst of Packard's flame, though its beard caught fire; that had never been known to bother Ghouls much.

Packard switched to the machine gun and opened fire, but there wasn't much time to aim and *Bounder*'s tribarrel forearm MG was only a cal-.30. What hits he scored mostly struck shield or armor. "Need help—" Packard began, but there was no time for anyone to intervene and his troops had their own problems.

As the Ghoul's electrocannon finally fizzled it gathered itself to pounce on him, to use the razor edge of its shield, the can-opener bayonet on its electrogun muzzle, or its claws if need be, to disable and get in at him. Certainly its terrible strength would enable it to do that, in time.

Packard swung up his useless main-gun muzzle straight at the Ghoul, as if it would fire. The 'Saur jerked in midspring; Packard dropped to full hunker. Like tanks of old digging in hull-down, mobes could reduce their vulnerability by lowering their silhouette in an odd-looking mech squat or deep knee bend.

The Ghoul missed its pounce, bouncing off Packard's servopowered arms, the two sprawling in the dust. The Ghoul scrabbled to come at him; Packard lashed out with one leg, grazing its jaw and knocking its helm askew. The power of a mobe was such that a solid shot might have taken the 'Saur's head off, but all the glancing blow did was jolt it back for a moment.

The jarring *Bounder* had taken had another effect; he felt the "cramp" miraculously subside. The breechlock freed up and the mobe's main gun was reloaded with a canister round. As the Ghoul came clawing after him Packard locked his mobe's right arm, both its main hand and secondary fine-work manipulator pivoting out of the way, and fired at point-blank range.

A thick jet of fire and smoke reached out from his forearm, blowing a hole through the Ghoul's corselet and the Green Ghoul itself. Backblast and some ricochet scorched and rattled *Bounder* as the 'Saur was lifted off the ground and hurled back twenty feet.

Packard scrambled to his feet, feeling his main battery reload with can-shot. The whole pass was filled with reeling, struggling, firing antagonists. He'd half expected to see his strikeforce already overwhelmed, but the number didn't look as uneven as he'd thought at first. Warhead couldn't have known which pass he would use; he himself hadn't known until an hour before. Warhead had had to cover them all.

The gaitmobes had taken heavy initial losses but bounced back from their original disadvantage. Hunkered down in teams of two, three and four, they were putting out tremendous volumes of fire. The Humanosaurs were firing back, though, and there were many hand-to-hand struggles still going on.

Packard automatically brought his visual signaling systems on line; jamming or no, the other mobes would see the color-coded flashing lights on *Bounder* and understand his commands—provided they weren't killed first.

He moved toward the rear, stepping around a downed mobe. There was no use checking for rescue; it had been blown wide open by an AP round. There was nothing left of the wearer's chest-nest but a smoking cauldron smeared with seared human tissue and bone and smoldering systemry.

To his right, a Wreck-Reaver lifted its bell-mouthed SLAP-gun to shoot down a mobe from behind. Packard got a steady sight picture on it, fired, and blew off the 'Saur's right arm and shoulder.

Organizing his units as he went, Packard left a holding force to secure the front of the pass while he fought his way back to relieve DeSoto and the second cohort. Many 'Saurs, seeing which way things were going, fled.

DeSoto and the second cohort had made out better than the first; the Humanosaurs had sprung their trap too soon. One lased-open ground-pounder—a low-built, stumplike sapper—hinted why: from the careful way Warhead's servants had cut into it, Packard judged they'd mistaken it for the special container the strikeforce was transporting.

Packard hunkered by the real container. It was slowing them down too much; he had to risk doing without it. He coded open the canister and drew out a lozenge-shaped metal shell which opened to his secondary manipulator's touch. The egg of polished jet lay there, a pretty thing to have caused all this carnage. The missing piece of Warhead for which the AI cabal had ransacked all Hazmat.

DeSoto stepped over to him in her main battle mobe, *Strider*, and jacked a hardwire commo line into a port in *Bounder*'s side. "After all this—do you think the chancellor and the leadership will do the right thing with it?"

The right thing, as both fighters saw it, was to reopen Hazmat's long-closed Adit to the Trough. Despite the fact that there were those in the underground strongholds of the People who didn't want to see contact with the Trough reestablished.

Packard looked around at the casualties his force had suffered and thought about the struggle that Warhead and the Humanosaurs were winning year by year. "They'd better."

Vanderloop had made up some of the clan's lead, but not enough. They were all moving across a terrain of bubbling sinkholes, stinking bogs, pits of tarry ooze, all of it overlaid with a deceptive cover of yellow hexagonal spores like tiny snowflakes. The only safe route lay on miniature islands of tufted weed, some of them scarcely the size of his boot sole. The footprints left by Gipper and the others showed the way, but drifting spores were beginning to blur them.

The Intubis were less than a quarter mile ahead, but Vanderloop had given up calling out to them. It did no good, and besides, he couldn't spare the breath. Racked for air, he forced himself along, the Intubis' new songline ringing in his head.

At last, dizzy, he put his foot down wrong and plunged hip-deep into a sucking pool. He grabbed at a tuft and kept from going under completely but was too exhausted to pull himself free. Then he heard Gipper's songline change. In a few seconds the Intubis would fade and that would be the end of Miles Vanderloop.

He never knew precisely where the impulse came from, but suddenly he began singing the previous songline, the one for this bog world. He sang in a frantic, bellowing voice, the tempo and tune coming to him with uncanny clarity along with many of the sounds, and where his memory failed he filled in with nonsense syllables, scatsong—and loudly, more loudly than he'd ever raised his voice before.

Up ahead, Gipper shook his head in irritation, his songline path to the next planet refusing to stay in focus because the whingeing pommie drongo wouldn't shut the hell up back there.

"Hear that? Hear that?" Saddie New demanded, stopping with arms akimbo. "I reckon if he can teach himself that much he can walk with us for a spell." When Bluesy would've objected she yelled, "Piss off, you yobbo!" and started back the way she'd come.

After a moment's hesitation Lily went after her, and Bobbie Benton. Gipper had no choice but to taper off the songline, and in the relative silence the Englishman's daggy caterwauling was even more insistent. Oddly enough, his cooee wasn't altogether bad—for a whitefella.

Vanderloop was going hoarse and losing his grip on the tuft when he felt hands on his forearms. "Good on yer there, mate." He squinted in perplexity, gazing up at the winsome brown face with eyes a luminous blue-black. Saddie New wore the look of a dark-skinned Mona Lisa, pulling at him. "Give us a hand, then."

With the help of the others, Vanderloop was pulled clear in short order. Half laughing, half crying, he didn't even care about the reek coming off him. The clan members, supporting and steering him, didn't seem to have the least bit of trouble finding reliable footing. His panted thanks rather amused them. Gipper, Bluesy and the rest were waiting on a little hummock island nearby. His songline so rudely interrupted and even upstaged, Gipper wasn't inclined to resume it for the time being. Besides, everyone was done in now that the *badundjari* powers had gone silent.

Wherever they were it was near nightfall. Wood was gathered and a fire started. Vanderloop was lowered to lie completely spent, leaning against a rock. When he found his breath again he looked up at Gipper.

"Mr. Beidjie, my name is Miles Vanderloop and I very, very humbly and respectfully inquire if I might ask you several million questions."

Gipper looked down on the Englishman and shifted to a more reserved and shamanic persona—not any effort at all, really; and these schooly types were too stupid to listen to anything else.

He ignored Vanderloop's blandishments. "Your schoolies keep moving back the dates, pommie, and say this long, that long, is how long we've songlined. Creation was sung up for us by the Creative Ancestors, and by that I mean all things. *Time don't apply to us.* And we're all that keeps the likes of you alive and real.

"But maybe not for much longer, mate."

EIGHT

MICKEY AND NIKKEI expected something pivotal to happen next, something portentous, but their zen and *zanshin* training should've told them violent physical action, while always to be expected, didn't fit in with the karmic debt restructuring they'd just signed up for.

They waited while sixty, ninety seconds inched by, but people just wandered away after Tanabe departed. The exhibits kept pumping out smoke and light and sounds, though the ninjas disappeared—through doors clearly visible; superhuman assassin tricks weren't something they did unnecessarily, or for free.

The partners found themselves more or less alone but weren't foolish enough, there in the heart of *Tengu Mountain*, to think they weren't under surveillance and control. There were canvas-upholstered director's chairs a little way off, and they plodded over tiredly, all their adrenaline spent now, to sling ass and slump back. Around them demons popped up and retreated, ghosts sought vengeance, sorcerous combatants bellowed and hewed.

Mickey had had all ninja fantasies and mystical illusions wrung out of him over the past weeks, but there was a kind of epiphany in what he was seeing. He passed his hand through a holo *ronin* wraith. "We sorta like this, are we? Don't actually exist unless 'n' until your daddy say so? Schrödinger's pussies?"

Nikkei, head thrown back, was gazing into the depths of darkness overhead. "Maybe the holos know *we're* the ghosts."

Mickey whirled on him furiously. "Got a visual on your *Bushido* indifference-to-dying mode, *homme*-er, but here's a late-breaking bulletin: Kamimura's *bugei*-woogei rudeboys didn't buy in on it and I don't either. We're in the eye of the shitstorm, so I need you to *ratchet down!*''

The idea of their failing one another or having a falling-out had never occurred to them, and so all this came hard. Following paths of least resistance, they avoided one another's eyes. They both spoke at the same moment.

"Which way did the—?"

"You see a door over—?"

All that was cut off by the grandfather-clock sound of high heels on the ferrocrete as Miss Sato emerged from the darkness behind Mickey. If she was testing them she didn't find them wanting; they'd heard and identified her steps, spike heels, not easy to mistake for *tabi, geta*—or $10,000 John Cobbs.

She settled into a director's chair without any help from them, crossed her legs with a whisper of silken, scented black stockings, and opened the PC she always carried. For the first time, Nikkei noted that she was shackled to its handle by a delicate NakaMats-gold chain attached to a slim gilt band that enclosed her wrist. The comp looked a lot more like an ultrasleek lady's clutch than a personal computer.

"Please listen closely and let me know if I've said anything you wish repeated or that you don't understand." She didn't bother with the keyboard; it was leading-edge voice-operated *fuaji-riron*—fuzzy logic—technology. Only the best for Tanabe's handmaiden.

"You're about to contract to become employees of Takuma Tanabe. Your loyalty will belong to Takuma Tanabe personally, regardless of what corporation, affiliate, government, or other organizational entity your duties may require you to serve. Is this clearly understood?"

Mickey was about to say yes. He'd braced himself for that and more, up to and including lopping off a finger, to get out of *Tengu Mountain* alive. But Nikkei said "Yes" before Mickey could.

Mickey turned to Nikkei and saw that he and Miss Sato had a high-kilowatt eye lock going. A whole new light shone upon the scene, but it made Mickey *more* nervous, not less. Sato was no more an *ojingal* toygirl than she was a *Nihon-no-trotta* office lady. Tanabe might indulge a taste for youthful flesh but would never grant anyone the authority, trust and stature of a crucial high-profile job just because she was his mistress.

For that matter Mickey couldn't think of any other male Japanese or kudzu heavyweight who had a woman, much less a young stunner like Sato, as his personal advisor-assistant. Mickey had no doubt he'd sensed something sexual between the Phoenix lord and his alluring deputy. Who knew? Maybe she'd read up on Amy Yamada and similar kinky stuff, or even interned in some Shinjuku S&M pleasure pit, and Tanabe was addicted to licking her toes or some such in the privacy of his inner sanctum; Mickey'd heard that some of the most *sugoi*— awesome—corporate grandees were into various bizarre practices.

None of that changed the fact that, to occupy the position she did, Sato would have to be one very sharp operator.

Miss Sato handed Nikkei some sealpacked folders, pursuant to his new fealty to his father. "We know you're both well aware of what traditional loyalty entails, as well as the penalties for failure, dishonor, or . . . betrayal of trust. There's one more thing: Tanabe-san wanted this returned to you."

She was offering Nikkei an unadorned but beautiful little rosewood box.

Instead of accepting it, those nimble fingers of Nikkei's snatched off the lid. Nestled in the box, Mickey saw, was Nikkei's Felix the Cat wristwatch, the one he'd been wearing when he returned to America some two years before after the unexplained meltdown with his old man. Mickey had made fun of him at the time because Nikkei had left wearing a Rolex-Seiko that cost more than most people made in a year. The Felix watch had been taken from him when the two were stripped of everything they had or wore, back in New York.

Nikkei and Sato were locked into a staring match from whose rules and nuances Mickey was excluded. Eight or ten seconds rolled by before Nikkei took the watch, leaving the box lid in her palm, and began strapping Felix back on. Miss Sato held the little bento-like box a few seconds longer, then put it aside.

Mickey thought about saying something—maybe claiming he'd had a diamond-studded earwax remover swiped by one of Tanabe's men—but the last thing he wanted was to draw attention to himself or risk antagonizing Miss Sato. He was snatched from the jaws of indecision when she made a seamless transition back to business.

"You'll receive in-depth briefings en route to New York City," she told them briskly. "For the time being you are to avoid any contact with Dante Bhang."

"New York?" Mickey couldn't help echoing. "Yo, *I* got a question: I need to know what the *fuck* is going on. Did Bhang set us up?"

"No," she answered so straightforwardly that the two couldn't detect any hint of a lie in her voice stress, pupil dilation, or any of the other indicators. "However, you are to regard Bhang as a potential competitor or opponent." Miss Sato spoke with a taunting reservedness. "There are matters beyond Bhang's network, beyond Quick Fix, Phoenix Enterprises and everything else you may think you know about the world in which you live. You will, as I've said, be brought up to speed with regard to such information as it's necessary for you to know."

"Well, at least cut us loose on what we're supposed to do in New York," Mickey pressed.

She gave him one of those heavy-lidded looks, but without the voltage that had crackled between her and Nikkei. "You will try to undo some of the damage you've done, for one thing. We'll exploit your experience with Lucky Junknowitz's loft crew and his other assorted acquaintances and allies.

"And don't worry; this time there'll be no mistakes." She met Nikkei's stare again. "Tanabe-san doesn't allow them."

"See? There he is right there!" Braxmar Koddle craned closer to the study window—the one on the left with the best view of Eighth Avenue—in a vain attempt at a better line of sight. The window's heat-pump layer made for a coolness against his cheek even in August. "The guy by the tin-bin. Maybe he followed you home."

But Russell Print wasn't looking at the pole-mounted recycling bin—color-coded in green and white diagonals for non-ferrous metals and marked with the slashed "Fe"—or the man standing behind it by the bus stop. When Brax turned for a moment to see if his host and editor was registering the man— had "made" him, as the pre-Turn cop scripts would have it—he realized Russ was gazing worriedly at his wild-eyed, perspiring face. "Uh, Brax. B-Man—"

"He's turning this way! Duck! Don't let him see you watching!"

"That's my son's *ikebana* teacher, Mr. Pinckus from Floral Patterns; we've known him for years. *Duh*, Brax!"

Brax stared numbly at the short man with the straight, dark hair who was hanging ten at the curb, waiting for an RPEV

Pesky Pizza delivery scooter to pass. Now that he'd moved from the lee of the recycling bin it was clear that Mr. Pinckus wasn't who Brax had thought. The face was different and the hands looked conventionally human, at least from a distance. Brax straightened up, running a brown hand through prematurely gray hair.

"Who's this guy who's supposed to be shadowing you, B-Guy?" Russ inquired softly.

"Muldoon. Apterix Muldoon, he called himself."

"And he's part of this, uh—"

"The Black Hole Travel Agency. Russ, I have to get out of here. I'm putting you all in danger: you, Winnie, even the kids."

"Braxmar, sit down a second." Russell Print was two inches shorter and paunchy, but Brax let his editor press him down onto the bed. The new Beautyrest Cloudcluster mattress—composed of four thousand individually adjusting pneumatic cells—conformed to his behind to give him comfortable, restful support. Which made the mattress unlike Russell, who began in an infuriatingly solicitous voice, "Now, I know this deadline's got you under a lot of strain—"

Brax got a grip on himself. "Kindly do not speak to me as if you're trying to talk a downcaster in off a ledge. I'm not hallucinating."

"Hit 'pause,' Brax, hey? Hear me out? Look, the Sony-Neuhaus brass were crazy to diddle around and leave you only, what, a month and a half to wrap up the Worlds Abound series. But this *Gate Crashers* book, the stuff you're writing—it's gonna be *evergreen*, Brax! It's gonna be *fractal*!"

Brax hadn't yet shown Russ the new paranoia-verité turn the book had taken. "Russ—"

"And that's because you've immersed yourself so well in this crazy universe Etaoin Shrdlu dreamed up. But, fella, *you can't let it get to ya like this!* Somebody'll think you're—" Russ spun his index finger around and around his right ear. "—*on the air*, old chap."

His mind back on Black Hole, Brax didn't feel his usual flicker of irritation at Russ's inept send up of the English accent Brax had mostly lost in twenty-eight years Stateside. "Are you finished?"

"No! Paranoia is powerful because it superimposes meaning on random events and a confusing world. It makes the individual the hero, the star, the center of a vast drama. It whaps him up with one stunning but hallucinatory cosmic insight after another.

"But, B-Man, these evil space people—they're just characters in a story. There's nobody after you."

"Russ? You're hurting my arms."

"Oh. Sorry—"

"What's more, you're right."

Print squinted at him suspiciously. "I am? All of a sudden, just like that?"

Brax nodded. In a lifetime of SF and horror reading, of strange stories studied in movies and broadcasts and even live theater, Brax Koddle had always dismissed the twilight-zoned characters who persisted in trying to get people to believe them even when it was clear the evidence was against them and the locked-ward attendants were reaching for the restraint suits and trank guns. Brax harbored a nagging suspicion that that sort of thing prevailed because writers didn't know where else to take the story and didn't have quite enough respect for human resilience.

"I suppose it's divine retribution for a childhood squandered on role playing and trash reading, Old Shoe," Brax added, doing a John Gielgud impression. Russ's expression began to relax into something more sympathetic. "If thinking you *might* be daft means you're not, then I suppose I'm safe. It's just that when events *fit* a pattern, it's so sodding easy to convince yourself there's a pattern *there*."

Russ was nodding vigorously. "I hear you, Brax. And whatever it is you're letting loose on this story, it's working—it's the best stuff you've ever done. But you've got to maintain an even strain here, guy."

Brax nodded, too. "You're right. Look, I'm going to knock off, take a walk and ventilate the old bean a bit."

Doubt passed over Print's face but he apparently figured Mr. Pinckus was safely gone from the area. "Good idea. Then, why, you dip your quill in venom, blast those teleporting BEMs to smithereens, and we'll be rid of 'em once and for all."

"Agreed."

"Listen, and when *Crashers* is in the mill you're coming with us to the sales conference. Nothing to do but listen to me brag to the regional reps about your literary prowess, quaff frozen Fuel Air Bombs, and play shuffleboard."

"Shuffleboard?"

"Yeah, for this quarter they've laid on a three-day junket

aboard the *Crystal Harmonic*, that alien themer ship. We're gonna do a show-biz presentation for your *Gate Crashers* book, a major PR kickoff. So there's a lot riding on you.''

Brax kept his smile in place by flexing his cheek muscles, trying not to scream. If he were to attempt to save his friend and editor and his friend and editor's wife in the only way that seemed plausible at this point, he'd end up in Bellevue with a trank derm the size of a hockey puck on his neck. "Spot-on, Russ."

"You, me, and Winnie. And plenty of single women for ya. Most notably Regina Barleycorn, the bodice-ripper queen from the Turgid Tales imprint.''

Brax fought hard to not wince. No doubt Russ and Winnie had both noticed that he wasn't talking about Asia Boxdale, wasn't in touch with her. They'd reached the wrong conclusion—that she'd scraped Brax off her pointe shoe; actually, Asia had gone underground. "Jolly good. See here, I think I'll take my little stroll, then have a lie-down, eh?"

Russ stepped back watchfully. Brax reached for his new AllWrite smart pen, keying it to save, backup, and then switch off.

"In case inspiration strikes,'' he shrugged casually, and Russ seemed to buy it.

The AllWrite looked like an elegant, gold-plated NEC-Tiffany fountain pen. Russ, knowing Brax's preference for writing in longhand, had presented him with the PC two nights earlier when Brax had showed up in search of shelter. It had been a corporate perk, bestowed on best-revenue-generating execs with much ceremony by the Sony-Neuhaus parent zaibatsu, but Russ had the worst handwriting in the Western hemisphere and a tendency to writer's cramp so he'd passed it on.

NEC-IBM's breakthrough in mass production of the yttrium-lithium AA88 "Dead Man's Hand" chip opened the possibility of moving the technology out of the monied Twenty-Ones' price class—where it was becoming the status symbol of choice among plutocrats—down within reach of millions. That wasn't going to happen very quickly, though; the powers ruling post-Turn Earth had a vested interest in making sure such change occurred slowly and under strict controls.

Nevertheless, the smart pens were already enlarging the pool of rootless, nationless, information-skilled upper-income types, fettered only by ties to family, friends, non-fixed-location jobs and the like, who now constituted a uniquely privileged class. Brax held up the slim glitter of the AllWrite with long brown fingers and put on its cap with a deliberate snap.

The AllWrite had become precious to him in a stunningly short time, had set him free to roam as he pleased, with an access/contact code as his only umbilical—to work as, where, and when he chose. Now he echoed, "Dip your quill in venom."

The pen packed an inertial-tracking memory and a hundred megs of RAM as well as modem and interface ports. It made the world, in effect, an infinite canvas on which Brax could write and draw anything he wanted. In real life, though, it turned out to be more practical to benchmark the i.-t. memory on, say, a sheet of paper and "fill" the paper over and over. Within ten minutes of receiving the pen Brax had found he preferred its realtime-printout function switched off—stopping the flow of ink. His words passed into the pen's memory to be reconfronted at some future date, freeing him up to listen in his mind for other, newer ones.

But for now the most important thing was that *Gate Crashers* existed nowhere but inside that fluted barrel and in a backup laser disk the size of a quarter in Brax's shirt pocket. At least Russ didn't know how far Brax had taken the novel already; he had only seen the outline and a few selected scenes.

Brax got up, tucking the AllWrite into the breast pocket of the pale yellow linen sport coat he'd left over the doorknob before slipping into it. "I'll be back directly. Toodle-pip."

The smell of *kimchee* ravioli and nasturtium-blossom flan was wafting from the kitchen. In her time off from her work with the SEC Edwinna Print liked to dabble in neofusion cooking. She stood near the apartment's front door, a compact, energetic woman with canary yellow hair trimmed in a pert bowl cut. "Is the sermon over? Can I cue the choir?"

Ordinarily Brax would've grinned, joked back, but all he could think of was the *Crystal Harmonic*, prowling out there somewhere on the high seas with her complement of XTs and human henchmen. Ziggy, the posse's communications coordinator in the Hagadorn Pinnacle, had had no word from Sean and the others who'd gone out after her. And now the ship had a date with Russ, Winnie, and the others from Sony-Neuhaus. "Yes. I've seen the light," he finally said.

She gave him a hug, Brax enduring it awkwardly. "Braxmar Cuddles, just finish the damn spacebook, pick up your on-acceptance check, and we'll go have some fun."

He couldn't help a skewed smile at her pet name for him. "Okay, Winnie. I'm just trying to get a visual on how the story ends."

She laughed and danced him around a bit, singing:

"Any time ya start ta bum out,
Slip! into a daydream
Let-cher in-spi-ra-shun come out
Slip! into a daydream—"

In spite of everything, he was laughing—it was a faux show tune he, Asia, Lucky Junknowitz, and Winnie had composed in about fifteen minutes at the party he'd thrown at the loft to celebrate the Nebula nomination of his short story, "I Ain't a Martian Anymore." They'd pretended it was a show-stopping production number verbalizing all the hopes and wishes that kept the loft crew—and all the other aspirants, would-bes, and wannabes of their acquaintance—going.

He took Winnie in his arms, joining on harmony:

"Make yer lit-tul troubles fade
to a mental escapade,
best 'n' most exclusive show in to-ooown!
(Fame, acclaim 'n' fancy raiment,
or adventure-entertainment)
Slip! into a daydream, 'n'
Slip! outta that frown!"

Russ was clapping from the study doorway and the Print daughters, Gwen and Blossom, were peeking around the corner at the far end of the hall. Winnie curtsied and Brax bowed; then he forced himself to smile, lying, "Back in a trice."

The doorman already knew Brax well enough to touch his cap visor as he went through the lobby. Brax pivoted slowly, considering, then set off along West Twenty-third Street in search of a public phone; the last thing he wanted was to make the call he had in mind from Russ's house.

And now, taking flight, he had something new to eat at him: how to save Russ and Winnie Print from the *Crystal Harmonic*.

NINE

CONFABULON'S MAIN CONVENTION center reminded Lucky of the Mormon Tabernacle, the Vatican, and Beijing's Forbidden City, all shoved together in a tight clump and toned down to some kind of architectural lowest common denominator. Again, the intent was to be impressive but not distracting. Good times were never *really* the order of the day—at least not if those footing the bill could help it.

Nevertheless, as he and Undershort rode the ingress flow-floor through an entranceway arch high enough to fit over the Statue of Liberty, Lucky gazed out across a scene that would've staggered any un-nanoed Earther. Trough transients might be used to such vast, unbelievably varied minglings of species—although there were a lot of XTs who needed their mighty mites, or something that served the same function, before they could mix with other races—but any unprotected Terrestrial brain would've been just plain overloaded.

Undershort, marching with singleness of purpose, didn't even seem to notice the fantastic hodgepodge of sights, sounds and smells assembled inside. The place was huge but not endless, bright but not overwhelmingly so; jacklighting potential customers was a prerogative reserved for exhibitors. An even illumination came from ceiling and walls, and there didn't seem to be any decorative art, patterning, or symbology to the hall itself—the better to let the advertising jump out at the attendees. To every side, holos depicted the appeal of various worlds, starfire cypher-crawls flashed promo copy, and flickering swirls of luminous gas snaked and writhed, forming corporate logos and governmental insignia. There were bigger blocks of air rights allotted to the larger floor-space renters, of course, more modest ones over the smaller operations.

XTs in stunning variety passed along the indoor avenues of booths and kiosks and other display areas, ogling, chatting, pointing, stopping to pay heed to a recorded spiel or live sales pitch, or grabbing one of the countless promotional freebies.

A M'lung, lumbering along on its plated knuckles and clawed feet, wore a frilly pink sun hat that strobed CUM & CREAM YOUR GENES ON BYGAR!!!—or so Lucky's irrepressible nanites told him—the brim ruffles brushing the tips of the M'Lung's jutting serrated tusks. A trio of protoplasmically translucent, chromatically striated Zandars—their slime trails dutifully Hoovered by trailing remotes—were clustered around a display over at Destination Digestion Tours; gourmands, no doubt, looking for a pig-out among the prelife organic-molecule extravaganza of some uninhabited world or interstellar cloud.

A "chub group" of egg-shaped HuZZah went past, their posteriors plastered with assorted souvenir stickers flashing messages like "VISIT SINDROME! FRIENDLY MERGERS OUR SPECIALTY!" Eight drum-bodied Sedjoes stumped along in lockstep on their tripod legs, bearing on their shoulders an elaborately equipped and instrumented sedan tub. In the tub lazed a furuncular Ghardoon, swiveling its ocular protrusions at several displays at a time.

Sound quaked the air. It wasn't just the myriad commercial narrations and audio effects and musical scores, but also a chaotic pickup orchestra of languages, vocoders, translation synthesizers, and other sonic commo that would've made the Tower of Babel sound like the Vienna Boys' Choir. Above his hearing range and below it, Lucky knew, there was plenty of sound traffic as well. He didn't just sense it; his mighty-mite hearing aid was nudging him, somewhere beneath the threshold of his full attention, letting him know there were subsonic and hypersonic exchanges it was ready and willing to render.

"We're over that way," Undershort said, pointing eastward. Lucky looked where he was pointing and felt the flesh of his neck try to leave his body. An ominous, reflectionless, sooty sphere hung in the air. It seemed to be making a muted, hungry sub-bass roar, and as Lucky watched, a banner of holoscript from some other exhibit area strayed too far into the singularity's airspace and was sucked in, fluttering and flapping pitifully.

The prey was flattened out, for the blinking of an eye, into a brilliant accretion disk. Then it was gone and only the dark nullspot in the air remained, enigmatic and supreme.

"So be it with any who trifle with the Black Hole Travel Agency!" Undershort cheered loyally. Lucky gulped, saying nothing.

He could see that Black Hole had rented by far the biggest single expanse of floor space in the hall. Tagging along after his new boss, moving from the entranceway rotunda down onto the exhibition floor proper and off eastward, Lucky was trying to suss out his situation, take in everything in sight, and listen to Undershort at the same time.

"I have to tell you that an employee so foolish as to fondle a Boob-Cube is one who needs remedial Agency instruction," the little supervisor was fuming as he goose-stepped along. "I'll arrange for the proper materials and a comprehensive study plan. Just be grateful I'm not putting you in for Tyro Assessment."

Lucky thought fast. "I mistook Nu-Topia for one of those *new* time-share places, sir."

Lucky's lie threw Undershort literally off-stride for a moment, but he recovered. "Nu-Topia? No, not at all." To cover the fact that he'd not heard of any late developments in time-sharing scams the supervisor went on. "What's more, none of them are to be trusted. Why d'you think time share sales techniques include entrapment, kidnap, and torture?

"Take Nu-Topia. Not much more than a planetoid in a convenient place, really. But *nobody* who accepts one of their promotional visits leaves without buying in, and by that time they've long since redeemed their valuable free prizes for food, water, and air rations.

"I happen to know for a fact that the place was heavily modified with substandard materials, slipshod work, and corner-cutting engineering. They very nearly lost their gravity once, and their atmospheric confinement shield *twice!*

"No, young Thing, virtually all the truly prime vacation spots in the galaxy are inhabited, spoken for, or off limits—as Earth used to be. That's why the Earth marketing campaign offers me such an immense opportunity for career advancement—*if* I can make it work. So: watch and learn, and be energetic in your duties!"

Lucky clicked his heels together. "*Mit verstandt*, sir! I live to serve."

He'd been under the impression that Earth-exploitation was already rolling along quite merrily, what with Phipps Hagadorn secretly turning his liner the *Crystal Harmonic* into what amounted to a seagoing safari van for XTs. But if letting Undershort blow off steam gave Lucky a chance to take in the expo sights, fine.

"To get back to what I was saying, Waters, do you think for a moment that Nu-Topia will show a profit selling time-shares at any sane market price? It will *not*! They'll oversell that world up to the moment the law is knocking at their Adit, you mark my words, and then disappear with the money. And everyone will discover that five or ten different life-forms have purchased the same time increment—all unawares, of course."

Under a kind of shimmery, veined marquee the size of a parachute Lucky saw a gaggle of identical insectile bipeds. Their black, bony exoskeletons had femur-shaped projections along the spine; their backswept, gunmetal-blue cranial cases were elongated and rounded as seed pods and looked eyeless. They boasted sets of dripping, daggerlike metallic teeth, one inside another like nested Russian dolls, and they were waving and gesturing with armlike brachs while they made cricketlike stridulating noises. Feeding tubes snaked from the sides of their torsos; their tails flailed and thrashed like constrictors.

The lettering on the marquee read INTERTROUGH FACILITATORS AMALGAMATED. The aliens were gathered around another biped, who resembled a shark in a spiffy four-piece business suit—obviously the exhibitor. "Look, fellas," he was saying. "Now that you've made successes of yourselves, you *want* to give your mother that tour of the Core Worlds, isn't that what I'm hearing from you here? First class, all the lux?"

The expo was primarily for travel agents and other professionals, but there were quite a few private individuals in attendance, and the metal-teeth seemed to be among them. The fellas considered what the shark had said, clacking their choppers—some shooting forth the innermost set like bloodthirsty jack-in-the-boxes. One of them protested, "But our Nest Genetrix must be attended by dozens of neuter drones and warrior-caste guards! She must breathe the Brood olfacts! She weighs eight thousand pounds—anything above point-one baseline-gees gives her fat ankles!"

The shark creature played with a garish pinky ring that held a gem the size of a Ping-Pong ball. "That's what *I'm* here for:

to help folks just like you. And, fellas, it's helping folks that makes this job worth doing.''

That led to agitated chirping; the inner mouths were shooting forth and retracting like paper noisemakers on New Year's Eve. "No, no, the fees are too high! Out of the question!"

The exhibitor was shaking his head at them sadly. "Boys, boys . . . this is your *mom* we're talking about.''

At that the boys broke down in unison and all flung themselves weeping into one another's brachs, hugging each other and stridulating.

"Mom!"

"He's right!"

"She had her heart set on it!"

"We're such ingrates!"

"Money, what does money matter?"

Sharkey was quieting them consolingly. "All right, now, calm down. Maybe some of your sibs could kick in and help pick up the tab. How many are there?''

There was still a sniveling note in the answer. "A—about seven hundred and twenty-three million. Not counting the face-huggers.''

The shark choked a bit. "I *like* you guys; and because you seem decent, I think we can work something out—''

Lucky passed beyond earshot. Undershort was still rambling on. "And *that's* why we in the travel industry have to stay ahead of this neuroreality transmission business—are you listening to me? Hmmph! Not to mention telecaster conferencing and 'tour your homeworld first' campaigns.''

At one of the concession stands a vendor was shoveling some kind of mash down the maw of a customer that put Lucky in mind of a frog on giraffe legs. Next to them a hat-rack-shaped thing used a long, sticky tongue to eat live, struggling tidbits out of a mass of cotton-candy webbing. A customer who represented some intermix of saurian and pro wrestler finished a gallon flagon of ethanol-smelling stuff and belched at Lucky. "You! Which way's the latrine?''

Lucky shrugged his ignorance—probably a useless gesture— hurrying to catch up to his boss, who hadn't even noticed Lucky's straying. "Snob appeal, status enhancement, curiosity, and sheer sensation-seeking work well enough for recreational travel,'' Undershort lectured on. "However, when it comes to the business traveler we must pound away at the inimitability of in-person contact, not to mention paranoia about the perils of corporate eavesdropping and the hazards of garbled transmissions.

"And then there's your hanky-panky angle, very important perk to some business travelers.

"Of course, Black Hole is at the forefront of the industry's never-ending effort to make sure that inter-Adit travel is indispensable and desirable, and constantly increase the market for Trough transportation."

Lucky's neck was tired from nodding but he was mostly watching a nubile female humanoid, a most fetching armful less than five feet tall, her cyan skin freckled with forest green—perhaps a natural camouflage adaptation. Hair like a shock of licorice whips. She appeared to be walking on tiptoe, an inch or so off the ground; he figured her glittering anklets were generating small, shaped repulsion fields. She was wearing what looked like a sprayed-on indigo bustier and a matching skirt short enough to make Lucky think hard about what she looked like sitting down. He stopped listening to Undershort and forgot to look where he was going.

Then the world disappeared in a swirl of laser-lit smoke in shifting colors—only, this cloud was serpentining all around Lucky's face, sliding across his skin like wary, sentient mist, causing a peculiar tingling sensation. It crept into his ears and nostrils, and he could feel it skeeving around in his bodily orifices.

It had sometimes occurred to him that he wasn't so much tranked by his nanites as cut off by them from blind prejudice and reflex, permitted to think rationally—or as close to rationally as one might reasonably expect under certain mental-overload circumstances. Otherwise his fate would've been Kafkaesque from that first awakening, or he would have been lobotomized by the enormity and incomprehensibility of what had happened to him, art-movie style. Characters in books so often coped with the unbelievability of it all and got right along with the business at hand—changing history or wiping out the Necrotons or saving Faerie or whatever—when, in Lucky's experience, most people were pretty much at sea if you moved their dinner plate six inches from its usual spot.

And how many people needed a pill or a breakfast vodka just to deal with life in *America*?

At any rate, he had the nanites, and right now he suspected that they were counseling him silently about the phosphorescent cloud even as Undershort chimed in. "Be still, and take no hostile actions! They will not harm you!"

It figured, really. Aggressively dangerous entities were unlikely to be allowed into the expo, so the cloud couldn't be *too* bloodthirsty. The nanites had helped his own common sense make that point to him. "Wh-what is this thing?"

Undershort clucked impatiently at Lucky's provincialism. "A spore colony of Chimeeiny, of course, swarming on their quickening-cycle flight."

"Honeymooners, huh?" Lucky coughed on the cloud and tried to clear it a bit with a gentle wave of the hand. "Looking for a romantic destination?"

"A data-gathering expedition, more likely," Undershort corrected. "And don't bat your hand around like that! Their swarm cohesion is very strong, but if they're dispersed too far their aggregate IQ will be diminished and they may be damaged—or react in a resentful manner."

We wouldn't want that, would we? Lucky thought but carefully refrained from saying, deeming it unwise to move his mouth. He didn't know whether to spit or not, but he *definitely* wasn't about to swallow. He had the impression that the spore swarm could communicate with him if it wanted to—he sensed a subvocal hum, like a radio station with no programming—but didn't feel the need.

While he was trying to figure out what to do next, the effulgent cloud swirled away from him, gathering in its spindrift parts, seemingly ready to move on.

"Wait!" Lucky hastily got a business bead from Undershort and held it out. "Here! Don't make any deals until you talk to me! I've got some tour packages you've got to see!"

The swarm hesitated, then licked at the glassy bead with one smoky wisp. The holofield disappeared and the bead dropped to the ground; the Chimeeiny spore colony wafted over a nearby kiosk, passing through a holo-sign and out of sight.

Lucky gave his supervisor a casual smile. Undershort tapped one foot. "At least you're concentrating on business," he conceded. "Perhaps you'll do."

Lucky and Undershort entered the area given over to the Black Hole Travel Agency and its many subdivisions and subsidiaries. The globe was still sucking up the occasional competitor's advert or logo; Lucky concluded that when the globe couldn't grab them from elsewhere in the hall, Black Hole was

generating them—rather like feeding goldfish to a piranha.
And the symbolism was obvious.

The Agency was a whole fair unto itself. There was one
entire pavilion for Trough Adventures; a neon parthenon ex-
tolling the services of Telecaster Astrodynamics; reassuring
displays everywhere—some of them mobile—on the protection
and assistance security-blanket coverage offered by Trauma
Advisory; and confidence-inspiring loop ads about the high
safety standards maintained by Teleportation Authority, Transit Association, and Traffic Admiralty.

Black Hole was doctoring all kinds of spin, Lucky could tell,
to downplay the rumors and outright allegations that lately
cracks were showing in the galaxy's biggest corporate entity.

No mention was made anywhere of how Temporal Adjustments, the complaint department, had been scuttling around
madly trying to isolate the causes of so many recent screwups.
And of course, to so much as hint aloud that the spooks in
Technical Assist, Transmogrification Auxiliary, and the rest
were chasing their own behinds in an attempt to find out what
was wrong was to take a grave risk of an intimate episode with
the White Dwarves.

Some places in the Trough you heard the rumor that Black
Hole was simply yielding to the inevitable laws of physics and
biology. Entropy; catabolism. The mechanism/organism was
breaking down. But you couldn't have told that from the lavish
and dazzling showing on Confabulon. Individual attractions,
planetary and interplanetary promos, tours and packages, special services—they were all being pushed with a sense of serene confidence and solidity.

Harley's poster especially was everywhere, beckoning people to the newest recreational destination, Earth. Unfortunately
Lucky didn't have the opportunity to rejigger the holos as he
often did to superimpose a red circle with a diagonal through it:
Earthman's signature gesture of resistance. Their own baili-
wick hadn't opened with the rest of the trade fair; Undershort
had explained that its fate had been decided at some upper
managerial level at the last minute. "Some *very* upper level,"
the supervisor emphasized, "so it behooves us to make the best
possible showing."

"There's Earth, over there!" Pointing excitedly, Lucky felt
a wave of homesickness that almost brought him to tears. On
a raised platform was an understated little geodesic dome in
matte gray. To one side of the opening rotated a projection of

Terra complete with weather systems draped across its surface, so detailed that Lucky wondered if it wasn't being transmitted in real-time from some orbital or Lunar pickup. The entrance was flanked on the other side by a floating image of the *Crystal Harmonic* twenty feet long; Lucky could see tiny figures moving around on the deck.

A visitor, a gourd-faced thing on six fragile-looking legs, was mounting the steps to the door. Lucky had started off that way, meaning to greet the customer, but Undershort tugged him back by the seat of his pants, heels skidding. "No, no! That's a separate program being run out of Singularity Flings. And no mere walk-in customer need apply, see?"

Lucky did. The matte-gray dome's door had slid open and the six-leg was speaking to someone or something that couldn't be seen in the dimness. The XT tilted its head in confusion, then came about and wandered off. The door had already slid shut.

"Why do they have a setup if they're just going to turn customers away?"

Undershort heaved a sigh of despair for Lucky's unworldliness. "How can the status of acceptable clients be confirmed unless the company conspicuously rebuffs those who do not meet its high standards? It's not enough merely to succeed, young Thing; one's neighbor must *fail*, or what's the point?"

Before Lucky could give that one a go Undershort took his wrist and pulled again. "We're over that way."

Leaving the center of Black Hole's territory was like passing through the bright, hot heart of the galaxy and heading for the dull and dim rimworld boondocks. The exhibits grew progressively smaller and less impressive as they moved around corners and down side aisles away from the glowering black holo. Away from the customers.

At last they rounded a strange-smelling polyhedron affair that, Undershort explained, had something to do with plasm-futures trading. "There it is," he crowed, indicating an exhibit enclosed in a glowing security grating, but that was no news—aside from an unrented display area the only thing farther along the dead-end aisle was a little empty floorspace, then the wall. Lucky cringed.

"You are trembling with delight, Waters?" Undershort sounded satisfied at last.

Lucky tried to sound motivated. "You called it, boss—sir."

The Root Canalian produced from his shell a device not so

different in size or appearance from a pre-Turn battery-powered nose-hair clipper. He directed it at the exhibit and the security fence retracted into the floor as the whole display area came alive with light and sound.

Undershort's display featured angled dioramas, freebie bins and racks, and public data terminals for the do-it-yourself browser. Beyond that, an outsized igloo of irregularly formed pressed-snow blocks wafted cold fog into the air. Inside, Lucky could see, were seats where, presumably, prospective clients would be won over.

As far as the motion-holo diorama was concerned he could only stare morosely at the close-ups of an Eskimo woman giving birth and what appeared to be a battle between ants and termites, in addition to loops showing the operation of a municipal sewage-treatment plant.

"You selected these yourself, did you, sir?"

"Yes. Colorful, are they not?"

Lucky's first impulse was to turn around, get out of the convention center, and skip the planet just as fast as he could. There was no telling what kind of organizational blunder or corporate death wish had put Undershort in charge of the exhibit, but the results were too unfortunate for words. But he reminded himself why he was there. Black Hole was the key to Trough travel and access to al-Reem. He turned glumly and sat on the low platform that held the exhibit. "Yes, sir. In fact I need a second to catch my breath."

That brightened Undershort's mood even more. He put the little black nose hair key gizmo aside and bustled around, fluffing up the planter of poison ivy and rearranging the tank of leeches he'd had brought in to convey the lovability of Earth wildlife.

Lucky, running the variables through his head, realized that he was staring at the darkened, empty exhibit space across the aisle from Undershort's. "Sir? What happened over there?"

Undershort paused for a moment. "That? Oh, that was reserved by the Fimblesector trade deputation from the government in exile, but they had to cancel, of course. The nanite strike continues, you know."

"*Nanite* strike?"

"Yes, yes, and of course the Fimblesector is under severe travel restrictions as it's been for years now, don't you follow current events? Filthy communist trade unionism will be the death of free enterprise if we're not on our guard, mark my words! Now, forget about that and fix your mind on your assignment; we have work to do.''

Two hours later not a single soul had so much as set foot on the exhibit platform. A few had appeared at the bend in the aisle and glanced down the cul-de-sac only to retrace their steps, hops, or slithers. When the supervisor went behind the exhibit's facade to the conference/sales booth to analyze fair attendance and other demographic trends, Lucky accessed his data files—but rather than study up on Undershort's marketing overview, he did some checking on al-Reem.

There wasn't anything of use on the interrogation center, but Lucky did better when he cross-referenced way station Blits, the only point from which the al-Reem Adit could be reached. Blits was a scheduled transfer point for an upcoming package tour—a somewhat unusual one. It would be a small group, with a hefty price tag and a variegated itinerary to say the least: Earth, the Fimblesector, and Undershort's seldom-visited homeworld of Root Canal were among the stops. The data was in the supervisor's files because he'd helped plan it, a kind of on-and-off-the-beaten-path idea.

The main thing was, though, that the group would pass through way station Blits. That was something to think about.

Still at loose ends, Lucky wandered over to the nearby wall to check out the two doors there. He was motivated in part by a habit he'd developed in the Trough of searching out bolt-holes whenever possible, but there was also his innate curiosity—or nosiness, as the uncharitable might call it. The wall was made of stuff that felt a little like plastic, a little like metal, and emitted a soft glow. One door, so large that a fair-sized cargo plane could've been taxied through it, wouldn't budge. The other, about twice the size of a normal Terrestrial door, became a little radiant when Lucky pressed on it but remained sealed, too.

On a sudden inspiration, he went back and grabbed Undershort's key, the nose-hair clipper. Directing it at the door, he fumbled with a raised, green-lit button. The smaller door slid aside silently. On the other side of the wall was a large warehouse area. There was no one around—just geometric shapes of various kinds in a wide range of sizes, some of them draped with shrouds of woven metal, linked plaques, or heavy composite fabric. Some were hanging open, empty.

The labels told him this was the storage area for all the cargo containers shipped to the expo by Black Hole. There was nothing much to see, and Undershort might come looking for him at any moment, so he decided he'd better get back to the exhibit. On the way out he checked the lock panel near the door. It was a fairly standard Trough design, one he'd seen before; he unlocked it from within before closing the door behind him. Undershort showed up just as he'd gotten the key back in place; the supervisor regarded him uncertainly as Lucky sorted through the giveaways in the bins, examining abdominal exercisers, Tibetan prayer flags, beer-holder hats, and sample bottles of mentholated cough syrup.

"Can't you look more industrious?" Undershort demanded. Lucky sighed and attempted to do nothing a little faster.

At least, having scanned through the creature's sales materials and marketing overview, Lucky understood Undershort's purpose and his own situation a little better. Phipps Hagadorn's cruise-ship operation was just about the only tourism enterprise green-lighted for Earth, but at some point in the unspecified future general tourism would become a new Black Hole cash cow.

And eventually? Lucky suspected he knew, because he'd seen what acculturation and the dissolution of an ethnic base could do to primitive peoples—which Terrans surely were, as far as the Trough was concerned. A few ambitious characters like Hagadorn and his Phoenix Enterprises might prosper as quislings, but for most Terrans there would be a slide into victimhood. Hopelessly inferior in power and wealth to the inhabitants of even one primary Trough world, sold out and calculatedly suppressed and exploited, *Homo sapiens* would be relegated to the role of indig serf. If Black Hole's plan went forward, humankind would be shorn of its identity and will to strive in less than five years.

"Okay, sir, I'm getting a visual here. You're telling me that what Black Hole wants us to do is sell *options* to travel to Earth?"

The Root Canalian made a pleased, fluting sound. "Exactly! And if we succeed at it, there will be no limit to how far my career can ascend! Oh and, er, yours too, of course."

Very bighearted of the officious little shellhead, and in a way Lucky couldn't blame him for his ambition. It sure put L. Junknowitz's macadamias in the nutcracker, though. Service to Black Hole was the best hope he had of surviving, rescuing Harley and Sheena, getting to the bottom of the whole Vanderloop-Aborigines mystery, and somehow saving Earth from ending up as a pitiful backwater freak show. But if working for the Agency meant advancing the conversion of Earth into a kind of huge tourist trap, he was damned if he did and damned if he didn't.

"Clearly, however," Undershort continued, "there's something lacking in our campaign. As my expert on Terra, it's your job to provide me with new marketing angles. The data banks here hold a wealth of information and imagery on the planet, but we require that good old biosophant point of view!"

TEN

THE WHITE DWARF in charge made a burst of noise like a hive just before the bees swarm out to do some heavy inoculating. Sheena Hec'k translated, "He says to stand here, not move."

Harley Paradise had already stopped right in her tracks, though, there in the middle of the concourse deep inside planet al-Reem—she'd understood the command, too.

She had also stopped short because one of the earliest lessons she'd learned upon awakening inside 'Reem—the first time, that is—was *Don't mess with the guards*. Even though they looked like little snowmen; even though they were called White Dwarves. They were definitely not jolly, happy souls and they most-def weren't here, hi-ho, hi-ho, to save Snow White.

Hey, in this nightmare, *she* was Snow White. What's more, it was the White Dwarves and those Peer Group nasties with their Halloween menagerie of technician-Igors who'd kept Harley under the sleeping spell, not some wicked witch with an apple-load of soporific.

And when she'd awakened that first time she had had one of her panic anxiety attacks. She couldn't understand what anybody was saying and she was frightened out of her wits. She'd begun to choke and had some kind of seizure. Then they'd treated her with the first of those *nanites* they talked about.

That one hadn't taught her to talk but it calmed her, or rather cut off the terror. It was uncanny; she knew that by rights she should be catatonic with fear—but maybe she wasn't of any use to them catatonic. As her captivity went on she'd become less and less afraid, more and more calculating. Maybe the nanite had just freed up basic human survival instincts her upbringing had left dormant.

"They're going to take us through the Adit," Sheena was saying after listening to the Dwarf's next hum. Listlessly she indicated an instrumented framework surrounded by unfathomable machinery manned by an assortment of *tres gross* Igors. "Prepare to move quickly when the order is given." She didn't elaborate or sneak in an aside; the guards were listening, and they punished that sort of thing.

"Yes," Harley said, without explaining that she'd caught it, too. Maybe some advantage lay in playing dumb? That nanite had come soon after the first one, but no one had bothered to ask her if she was multilingual now. It would've been a miracle back in school; she'd often wished she could put a lesson disk under her pillow and have the knowledge sift up into her brain, taking it on painlessly.

Well, she hadn't put any effort into learning, but the overall process sure hadn't been painless.

She went on pursuing her thoughts in a muddled way, still groggy from the suspended animation or whatever they'd used to put her and Sheena back under. She shivered a bit but was dully thankful that at least they'd been given back their clothes. The baggy Balinese pants and synthsilk shirt Sheena had borrowed from Lucky's closet looked much less disheveled than Harley's rhinestone-studded, silver-sequined mini, probably because Harley's outfit had started out so much finer. The renegade guide's cross-training hightops had weathered hard times better than Harley's slingbacks, too. Harley's improvidently expensive polynail cement-ons were gone, her teeth felt coated with creosote, and she would've killed for a chance to shampoo her hair.

Her thoughts drifted back to apples. Now that she thought of it, there *had* been a sickening apple fragrance to the stuff, the alleged perfume, that had been sprayed into Sheena's face, then Harley's, to render them non compos in the posh Rodeo East shopping mall.

Welcome to the grimmest fairy tale, Snow White. Maybe that made Sheena Hec'k Rose Red? Or was Rose Red raven-haired? Harley couldn't call up that datum. But she'd had time enough to reconstruct things after her first awakening. In the midst of the ray-scanning, the automated biosampling and probing, the cold-slime dunkings and other atrocities, there'd been a few moments here and there—when low-IQ Igors or machines were around the two rather than the Pillsbury Doughboys from Hell. Then they could exchange a few words. From what Harley could get, the combination of whatever knockout had been used on them in Rodeo East and the suspended animation had really worked their systems over; they'd been put through an extensive course of treatment and therapy, none of it involving TLC.

Early on, Harley had tried to assert herself—put the snowballs in their place, phone the police and have her father's lawyer sue for triple damages plus punitive. Awakening stark naked on the Fritz Lang examining table next to Sheena's, she'd thought she was back on the Themer cruise ship *Crystal Harmonic* in the midst of some insane mutiny. Harley had done her best to go on the offensive, gain the element of surprise. Put the little Michelin Tire homunculi to rout. Until they moved in and she broke a couple of toes on one of them—and then they hurt her even more. That was when she had broken down and they had brought on the first nanite.

She'd come to understand that she'd been kidnapped by forces so immense and sinister that they didn't care about her American citizenship, her friendship with Phipps Hagadorn, the Gender Bias Council's much-feared radical-feminist legal staff, or her power hairdo. Now it occurred to her that her broken toes didn't hurt a bit. Which meant that either these creatures were good at mending as well as fracturing, or she'd been unconscious, on and off, for a very long time.

Maybe both. She felt physically sound, with none of the usual after-effects she'd heard people suffered after a long period of unconsciousness, but normal medical truths didn't apply in this hellhole.

"Have they got their derms?" she heard someone say, and some odious little propellerhead lackey confirmed, "Yes, both of them." Harley recalled the skinpatch they'd placed behind her ear but decided not to ask about it or show she'd understood.

She felt grateful for the depersonalization of the nanite. She was facing up to the fact that she was wide awake and there would be no easy out from this nightmare.

She became aware of sibilant static and looked up to see a pale, fuzzy evanescence in the air, like floating wool fibers, framed by the weird doorway. So that was an Adit; Harley hadn't quite believed in them up until this moment, her surroundings notwithstanding. The wooliness calmed until there were only a dozen or so veering, darting points of light in the gateway, like tiny UFOs. On the other side of the Adit was a gray, antiseptic chamber.

Sheena got moving the moment the supervising Dwarf buzzed, "Move through for fade." Harley hung back in spite of herself, unable to step into those darting sparks.

She felt something touch the small of her back. "No, don't! I'm go—"

It was a relief that the guard only pushed her, even though it was like being prodded by a battering ram. The impossible physics of the Dwarves' construction made them capable of doing infinitely greater damage, and the punitive technologies they wielded made them more fearful still.

The shove sent her reeling up against Sheena, who turned and steadied her—used to helping Harley by now. Instead of being grateful, Harley couldn't help resenting her that much more. The Amazing Amazon.

Sheena belonged in this horror movie; Harley didn't. A little part of the resentment came from the fact that Sheena was drawing on resources developed somewhere along the line where sex appeal was worth about as much as a burnt-out credit chip. Harley had never even considered such a situation. But it explained a lot about Sheena's peculiar behavior back in New York when she'd been trying to convince everybody she was from, give us all a break, Bhutan. It also implied something vaguely submissive and tawdry that Harley tried to ignore about the way she had made her own particular way on her own particular planet—she, a hard-liner on the Gender Bias Council.

But so be it. That didn't mean Harley couldn't learn. She eased herself from Sheena's supporting arm. "Thank you, I'm perfectly fine now." *It's time for an educational upgrade, Snow White.*

Harley followed Sheena into the swirling micro-meteors of the Adit and starstuff seemed to vector within her. She'd stepped onto a nondescript gray platform.

"Where are we?" Harley hoped to get away with a little nonauthorized talking since their guards were somewhere behind them on the other side of the Adit. But other players were showing up, Dwarves among them.

Even so, Sheena ventured to murmur, "In-world. Interrogation Bureau, I think."

"Interrogation?" *Merde!* All right, maybe what the two

women had already been through wasn't interrogation—few people had asked them anything—but if so, Harley's blood ran cold when she contemplated what interrogation might be.

She set her slender jaw. Okay, then: I'm braced for anything.

"Ah, there you are. Come in, do."

Almost anything. *I was braced for almost anything but this.*

With regard to the People's Republic of Vietnam, Tanabe wondered why any sane population would, in this day and age, let Marxist-Leninist dogmatists run a *sandbox,* much less a nation. They were ripe for change, but not as ripe as they'd be when Tanabe had brought them into the twenty-first century.

Land of the Lac, the Central Planning Committee's numinously stupid attempt to create an influx of foreign currency by cashing in on the theme-park phenomenon, was an unmitigated disaster. It was shoddily and unimaginatively put together; even the heroic reenactments of Le Boi's fifteenth-century liberation struggle were poorly done. And how in the world did they expect to attract visitors with displays of old U.S. military wreckage, war-crime dioramas, and animatronic lectures by the great Communist thinkers?

And locating the display "Heroes of the War of Liberation and Reconstruction's Prosthetic Devices" near the main food concessions—surely, a stroke of which only Central Planners were capable.

Tanabe couldn't feel too bad about that, though, since the Committee was begging World Nihon, Incorporated, to intervene with a complete takeover and management operation. Having kept them dangling for upward of six months, he now relayed his decision that WNI would consent to rescue the Viets—in return for absolute control over the park and all subsidiaries, a third of gross profits, a ninety-nine-year headlock contract, and all foreign licensing rights. They would leap at the offer.

But the thought of ninety-nine years soured him. What would Black Hole have done to Earth in just a tenth of that time? Black Hole's power made all Tanabe's, his corporations', his country's, his planet's accomplishments seem meaningless.

He thrust aside that galling thought as his convoy arrived at the exclusive baths compound he'd personally dubbed *Peaceful Paradise.* It was reserved for the highest VIPs: a meticulously landscaped Eden looking out over both the *Sea of Japan* area and the distant hills. Entirely outdoors but calculatedly private, it boasted hot springs, snowbanks, ice melt, mineral pools, two-score waterfalls of assorted types and temperatures, therapeutic mud baths, and volcanic sand.

Here, too, the regular staff had been sent away; unfortunately, there could be none of Mrs. Kojima's exquisite massage today. Leaving Mr. Natsuki and all the others behind, Tanabe undressed alone, scrubbed and rinsed down in the entry area, then entered the *o-furo* grounds naked and carrying nothing but a small hand towel, relishing the singing of the exotic birds.

He went straight for the hottest part of the intricate system of mineral pools, willing himself to endure it as he eased in and watched his skin turn fiery red. He ducked under the surface a few times, then wetted the towel and draped it jauntily over his head—a private show of frivolity. He contemplated the view with a slight feeling of irritation. There was a landmark out there that he wished were visible from *Peaceful Paradise*.

He'd just eased back to rest his head and shoulders against the edge of the pool when the waters six feet in front of him parted with a violent splash and a nightmarish, serpentine head darted forth on a scaly neck, baring jaws supplied with multiple rows of inward-angled teeth. The breath of the thing was unspeakable and the red gleam in its eyes savage beyond words. The muscular neck S-curved, poising the hideous head before Tanabe's face, jaws gaping two feet apart in striking position.

Tanabe calmly drew the towel from his head, dabbing at the moisture on his face. "Greetings, Plinisstro-san! It is so good to see you. I hope you'll forgive me for the inadequacies of this place."

He spoke in English. Although the sea serpent's nanites made it conversant in a variety of Terran languages, it—Tanabe's guest, the special personage—seemed to prefer that one.

"This place is-ss s-sswell!" Plinisstro responded. "The water offers-ss ssavory minerals-ss, fragrant particulate matter, and, in the warmessst areas-ss, a pleas-ssant dermal ssssensation." It undulated its neck sensuously. "Als-sso, the hors d'oeuvres-sss were ssssss-ucculent."

"Hors d'oeuvres?" Tanabe asked, puzzled.

Plinisstro gestured with his pointed chin. "There, in the live ss-serving pool."

He meant the pond that had been stocked in traditional fashion with immensely fat goldfish rarities, some a century old, intended to be hand-fed by guests. Tanabe successfully concealed his choking reflex, triggered by the thought of irreplaceable specimens gobbled down as a snack. Well, at least after long lives of uneventful gorging, the fishes' last moments had provided them drama and amazement.

"Your journey was enjoyable?" Tanabe inquired.

Plinisstro blew spray from all four nostrils. "It was-ss. The water temperature ins-sside the tank truck was mos-sst refreshing. This-ss is far roomier and more relax-ssing, however."

They chatted casually for some minutes. Plinisstro, minister plenipotentiary from the planet Ss-sarsassiss, had been having great fun aboard the *Crystal Harmonic*, Phipps Hagadorn's purported "alien themer" ship.

"I find I rather exss-cel at playing a threatening mechanical mons-sster." Plinisstro chuckled, the fearsome head weaving back and forth hypnotically, the amazing kaleidoscope eyes seeming to pinwheel through every color on the spectrum. "Although, to tell the truth, it is-ss s-ssometimes-ss a wee bit difficult to res-sstrain mys-sself with the young of your s-sspecies-ss. They are often loud and rude, and s-ssmell s-sso *tempting*."

Tanabe had to will himself not to be mesmerized by that weaving head. "Ah, yes-ss." Dammit, the creature had *him* doing it. "Your self discipline gives you great credit, esteemed sir."

"How kind of you." Plinisstro seemed to hesitate, shift gears. "I trus-sst you will pardon my abruptnes-ss; time is-ss s-sshort. Tanabe-s-ssan, the interes-sst-s I repres-ssent feel that Earth's theme-park indus-sstry is-ss the wave of the future. We wish to enter various enterprises-ss here and export your trade conss-cepts to other Trough markets-ss."

Tanabe pretended to consider that for the first time, though his spies and sources had given him forewarning of what the alien had in mind. "Of course, Plinisstro-san, moving forward into prosperity with you would be a most welcome prospect. Naturally, though, that would entail forming close, mutually profitable bonds: sending personnel from my organization into the Trough, educating them in your technologies and methodologies, familiarizing them with your operations and markets, and so forth."

The XT blew an angry blast. "You're not catching my drift! We *ex-sssssssploit* tertiary populations, we do not take them on as partners-sss!"

"Ah, then perhaps your efforts would be better undertaken with the assistance of others. I feel inadequate in expressing my regret; I blame myself, and yet there is no remedy."

The monster shook water from its head furiously. "Your interlocking corporations-ss control all the leading technical and managerial expertis-sse."

"Hmm. Perhaps something can be worked out that will be of mutual profit."

Plinisstro was wary. "My principalss will not be happy with profit that costss them commercial s-sstrength."

Tanabe draped the towel over his head again and leaned back, closing his eyes. "Forgive me for being unclear. I was referring to your *personal* profit. If you were to assist us in certain things, I am certain that my organization would wish to reward you rather handsomely for your consulting services and advisory skills. And it might provide you with the inroads you seek."

The Ss-sarsassissian stopped dead in the water. "Reward *me*?"

Even coming from an alien, Tanabe recognized the intrigued sound of that and smiled inwardly. Earth had plenty of things to entice Plinisstro, and Tanabe's organization had access to all of them in abundance.

And so it began, the next step in coopting the Trough worlds—in climbing toward the day when Tanabe, or his successor, or *his* successor would carry out the takeover of Black Hole itself. Corporate Japan had done it before, on an international scale; a galactic campaign was the next logical step. Everything was simply a matter of resourcefulness, determination—and patience: sheer, unyielding endurance.

Tanabe thought of old Mr. Sugimoto, the fallen samurai serving out his time as a doorman. In stoic endurance, the Japanese knew no peer.

Listening to Plinisstro talk longingly of the vast fecundity of Terran oceans and the great beauty of a certain stretch of Antarctic territory Nagoya Aerospace controlled through an incorporated Japanese governmental research foundation, Tanabe knew he had the Ss-sarsassissian—and it was just a matter of reeling him in.

At an appropriate point he said, "Indeed, why *shouldn't* we carry out small side transactions without going through Black Hole? And there's one thing in particular with which we could use your help.''

"I'm liss-tening.''

"It concerns an Earth native named Lucky Junknowitz, who we think may have fled into the Trough.''

Tanabe contemplated the sunset as he horse-traded with Plinisstro. Once again, he was irritated by the impaired view. He made a mental note, a memo for Miss Sato to relay.

Yes, he would get the L.A. zoning commission to do whatever it took—get Woodrow Wilson Drive removed and the hill under it planed down so he'd be able to see the HOLLYWOOD sign from *Peaceful Paradise*.

Packard was glad to be wearing *Stomper*, his main battle gaitmobe, again. Carrying the memory egg at the head of a picked force of ground-pounders and smaller, black Vigilance Committee mechs, he led the way through the Hazmat deathlands.

They saw no sign that Warhead or the aggregate AI's Humanosaurs had found the Sepulcher of the Adit, even after generations of searching. Warhead was still constrained by limitations built into the pre-Apocalypse Hazmat AIs from which it had sprung; the old-timers had been careful to keep their most powerful AIs away from the sepulcher, and Trough contact, with subtly implanted blind spots and blocks. Their fears proved well founded, of course: one fleeting experimental interface between advanced Hazmat AIs and those on Light Trap rang down disaster and severed the planet from the Trough.

The mechs and ground-pounders marched through the Howlslot and down Grimcrack Delve, descending the Eternity Stairs. Under a soaring rock overhang the sepulcher reared, a holy technoshrine in green-black alloy and windblasted mauve stone.

Packard had instructed his troops to keep an eye on the Vigilance Committee mechs. Inspector Nash and the rest of the Rejectionists were only permitting this attempt to reopen the Adit because Packard had threatened to destroy the memory egg and raise rebellion otherwise. But Packard wasn't worried; his followers numbered two-thirds of the thirty mechs on the mission and were by far the most powerful. The walking war machines shouldered open the huge sepulcher doors and filed in.

The floor was deep in filth, droppings, dust, the remains of kills. The gaitmobes drove off the dwellers in the dark who'd taken over when humans abandoned the Adit with flashbangs, searchlights, and scare-sounds played over external speakers.

The Adit was a surprisingly modest little pillared dome in the center of the titanic sepulcher. As the mechs set up the precious fusion module and made preparations to power it up, Packard set the memory egg in the socket from which it had been removed so long ago.

A power fluctuation occurred during the start-up sequence; somebody said energy was being diverted, perhaps to a reserve that had been exhausted and was automatically being recharged. As Packard leaned over a control console to see, the firing began.

Astounded at Inspector Nash's stupidity, he whirled, preparing *Stomper*'s weapons. A ground-pounder could break a police mech over one knee, blast it to oblivion point-blank. But abruptly his equilibrium failed and he lost control of his mobe. Paralysis washed through him and *Stomper* toppled, powerless to defend itself. A last diagnostic blip told him, through his control contacts, of the disabling inhibitor mine adhering to his ground-pounder.

His communications were out, as were all systems, but as he lay there in the darkness Packard could hear the firing through the hull of his gaitmobe.

Later, he heard them cutting through *Stomper*'s armored chest, coming for him.

ELEVEN

THE WOMAN GREETING Sheena and Harley wasn't quite human, Harley could see, but was close by a high order of resemblance. Especially after the loathsome assortment of freaks and repulsoids she'd seen since being disappeared from her comfortable life on Earth.

"That's it, yes. Come in; no one's going to bite you."

No doubt Braxmar Koddle or one of Lucky's other geekster friends would insist on using some term like *life-form,* Harley thought. But despite the orange tint to the skin and what looked like feathery stalks lying close against the tastefully bleached hair, the instant reaction in Harley's groggy brain was *headmistress!*

And now she was strolling their way, the White Dwarves and other assorted functionaries making way. "Young lady— Miss Paradise, is it not?—you seem to have forgotten your purse. Shall I have someone fetch it?"

"I, that is—" Harley hadn't seen her purse since being laid low at Rodeo East. "Th-that would be very nice, thank you."

"Think nothing of it. Oh, but you must both excuse me; I haven't introduced myself, have I? Miss Diandra Abbott, headmistress here at Ascot Academy."

That was a new one on Harley; she'd attended the Bridlepath School under the demanding tutelage of Miss Kimberly Pennysworth—"Kaiser Kim" to generations of young ladies packed off to the horsey hinterlands of Virginia. Harley's middle-class parents had sacrificed plenty to get their daughter through Bridlepath, which prepared young women for the kind of life they were expected not simply to live, but to lead well. "Dealer prep," the girls' inside joke ran.

Black Hole had done a fairly good job: the features and form

106

were human, the accent was honeyed Southern ironplate and the clothes and accessories didn't differ too much, under the circumstances, from the natural-fiber, expensively simple authentic items. The skirt, the blouse, the sweater on the shoulders—she even had reading glasses on a beaded chain around her neck.

There were inaccuracies, though: the eyes that looked a bit too reptilian; a certain carnivorous toothiness, and an extra, opposable thumb on each hand; an inhuman aroma not quite disguised by perfume. That left it for Harley to wonder what the hell Black Hole was playing at. Unless she was lying somewhere on life support—a less and less viable explanation—this was the Agency's way of getting to her somehow. Maybe it was something they'd dredged up from her memory in their Clinic of Caligari. But why the sloppy details? A reminder that she'd better play along?

In some ways it was working. In spite of everything, she felt a sense of relief—that she hadn't been remanded into the custody of some kind of high-tech Inquisition, if nothing else.

"Miss Paradise; Miss Hec'k. You've arrived just in time for tea," Miss Abbott informed them with a carefully measured smile. "Right this way."

At a wave of her hand the Dwarves and the rest disappeared through a membranous doorway in the gray wall. Miss Abbott led the two women from the reception chamber to a much different area: a comfortable drawing room. Behind them, the Adit was once more a whirling fizz of intercontinuum static.

There were two big sash windows, both on one wall, looking out on a peaceful meadow scene of greens, blues, browns, and grays. It could have been Virginia until you noticed that some of the trees didn't appear in any botany book. Again Harley spotted a lot of little inaccuracies in styling and detail—carpet designs, wood-parquetry grain, and decor combinations. Some of the things around the room belonged—the plaques, the framed certificates, the crossed field-hockey and Lacrosse sticks over the darkened fireplace—but there were other artifacts that didn't. Harley had no time to examine them closely though. A tea cart was waiting, with biscuits and sandwiches. Miss Abbott seated herself in a wingback chair. "Harley, perhaps you'll be good enough to pour for us?"

The tea smelled good, if a little unearthly. Harley found herself steadied by the ritual of pouring, even if it was with a service made of some material more like chitin than china.

She served Miss Abbott first. Seeing the headmistress nod in approval, she couldn't help feeling a spasm of hope. *Something* here corresponded to the world in which she'd grown up. Perhaps Miss Abbott could be her ticket out of this straitjacket salon.

When Harley turned to Sheena she saw that the big redhead was studying her, not their surroundings or Miss Abbott. Inclining her head, Sheena accepted the cup and saucer and said, "Good-cop," as if it were some kind of thank-you.

Harley wasn't much of a police-show fan, but she knew the concept; she'd had it run on her often enough by school administrators, defense lawyers, and salesclerks. Miss Diandra Abbott was the Agency, manipulating Harley. This being Snow White's first day of educational upgrade, she'd play her assigned role.

Miss Abbott had frowned upon hearing the good-cop remark, her face taking on a faraway look for a moment as if she was listening to something the other two couldn't hear. Then they had her full attention again; Harley wondered if al-Reem's data banks had come up blank on the Earth jargon.

"Firstly, I should like to say that it is regretted by certain Higher Authorities that you were both subjected to, well, unpleasantries. It seems that there was a misunderstanding upon your arrival here, and you were inappropriately routed."

Harley, pouring for herself now, couldn't stop from raising one eyebrow. "You're saying we were mislaid? Like dry cleaning?" She broke character, raising her cup and saucer as if to throw them in Miss Abbott's general direction. "Well, I'm not some anonymous wad of dirty clothes!"

Miss Abbott half rose, her face transforming itself somehow. She snarled maniacally, baring teeth that belonged in a bear trap; a black, whiplash tongue coiled and uncoiled in the air. Her eyes narrowed and seemed to blaze like cinders, and from the sides of her head, up from where they'd lain in her Palm Beach Crash Helmet hairdo, vaned, fanlike structures flared in warning display.

Harley screamed and shrank back, almost knocking over the tea cart, unable to catch her breath. She tensed herself for the alien headmistress to come pouncing at her throat like a wild animal. Instead Miss Abbott sank back into her wingback chair, the snarl disappearing, the vanes lowering out of sight. She was once more a woman of a certain age.

Harley somehow unfroze enough to look to Sheena. Sheena's face looked solemn as a mask as she looked straight back.

Harley was surprised to find her mind working. It had come to her in that moment that Sheena wasn't afraid—that she was instead evaluating Harley. One thing Harley had learned was how to act as if she was something even if she wasn't—like brave, for example. And the nanite helped. She pushed herself erect, evened her ragged breathing by sheer willpower, and faced the alien again.

Miss Abbott sipped her tea. "Let us begin afresh, shall we? You young ladies are in a position to clarify certain data we possess. As women of proper breeding you will, I know, wish to be of reasonable assistance. After that we will see you safely home, of course, and make appropriate compensation for this regrettable incident."

Ostensibly talking to them both, she was watching Harley, keying her phrases to Harley.

"What, what did you *really* do us in that satanic car wash of yours?"

Miss Abbott's expression made Harley conclude that she was going to ladle out some more sweet to temper the sour. But before she could start, Sheena interjected in a level tone. "They analyzed and metered us, Harley, blueprinted our brains. They took what few memory downloads they could from a somnolent brain. This will not only aid them in their interrogation, but give them a data bank on which to draw, for whatever reason, in the event that we're damaged under the mindbender or other interrogation."

Harley looked back to Miss Abbott. Discipline Di, it struck Harley, would be a good name for the headmistress of the mythical Ascot Academy. The creature that called herself Abbott was watching the two women carefully, plainly content to let Sheena damage the illusion and fill Harley in on things. Although a monster from another world doubtless didn't understand quite what the antagonism was between the two, Abbott was willing to see if it would work in her favor—to let Sheena taunt Harley.

Harley, tight-lipped, told Miss Abbott, "If you're the good cop, I don't want to meet the bad." She acted mature and world-weary sometimes because that was the social pose that afforded the most reliable protection in the circles in which she moved; but in this moment Harley conceded to herself that she hadn't really had a chance to live yet. "Look, maybe Red

Sonja over there is fearless, but I'm not. So what is it you want to know?''

The headmistress of Ascot Academy looked pleased and kindly. ''We hadn't intended to bring you here, my dear; this is no place for you. But you do have connections to a man named Lucky Junknowitz, and we wish to ask you a few questions about him.''

Harley hadn't bothered stifling the groan that burst from her at the sound of Lucky's name, couldn't isolate any one thing from the bubbling stew of feelings that it called up.

''Firstly, we are curious about that object over there. No, there on that table.''

Harley's lovely brow wrinkled as she groped for the word. ''A dij—no, a bull-roarer?'' She walked over to the pile of string and piece of carved wood resting on a sideboard. ''But—this isn't the one Lucky had on his wall.'' No, indeed; unlike the one Lucky had brought back from some Themer-related jaunt or other, this one was crude, showing signs of use, polished by human handling.

''As you say,'' Miss Abbott nodded. ''It came into our possession here in the Trough, however, and we were aware that Junknowitz kept such an artifact on his wall. What we want to know is, have you ever seen Junknowitz use this object? If so, how? And with what results?''

Harley drew a slow breath. ''I'll show you what he showed me.''

As Harley picked up the bull-roarer Sheena let out a snort. ''As I might have expected. Yes, do whatever she commands, *feminist*.''

Abbott glared at Sheena like an aged-deb basilisk. ''Silence, young lady! You will receive no further warnings.''

It was noteworthy, Harley thought, that even the redoubtable Sheena Hec'k could be menaced into silence.

Harley set her feet apart and whirled the bull-roarer, trying to remember how Lucky had taught her to do it that time he'd egged her into trying out the souvenir on his wall. Usually too poised to be cornered into something that foolish, she'd had a little too much wine that night and had decided to show Lucky she wasn't some klutzy frills-'n'-bows dorkette.

Now Harley put her shoulders into it, rotating her hips and shoulders in an unintended hula. The bull-roarer began to moan for her, then to sing. She wasn't exactly sure what she was going to do. Show Sheena Hec'k that the renegade guide didn't know *everything,* at least; possibly get some slack from Discipline Di and win her own release.

Conking the alien on the head, then capering through some kind of Batgirl escape sequence was one scenario, but very unlikely. Harley was painfully aware that the Bridlepath School hadn't offered courses in derring-do, not to mention the fact that the Abo instrument didn't have enough heft to do much damage.

She whirled the bull-roarer and it raised its voice for her, louder and louder. She hoped Discipline Di liked the music.

"Where's Gipper?" Vanderloop asked, rising from an inadvertent nap.

Bluesy Bungawuy scowled, making meaningless mud-maps with a bit of stick. "Dunno, rightly."

Vanderloop wore a long-suffering expression. He wasn't sure how long he'd been traveling with the Aborigines, trying to understand their miraculous dream walking, but it was a long time. Gipper hadn't even given him a satisfactory answer to any of his questions yet and avoided Vanderloop whenever possible.

The group had camped in a vale of treelike purple legumes, pale green mossy groundcynths and scrub growth like tangles of wood shavings. The hot white sun and the doddering red one, one high in the sky and the other low, threw wistful pink light across everything. The children had torn off bits of the wood shavings, meaning to fashion adornments, but found that it crumbled quickly and made their skin itch.

"Cheeky old bugger, always running off," Bluesy muttered to hide his dismay.

"Said he heard something, mate," Lily Moora called over from where she sat in the circle of women in the shade. "Gone to check it out."

That made the Intubis laugh. Gipper was *always* hearing things out in the Never-Never. And smelling them, tasting them through the soles of feet tough as weathered rawhide—so he maintained—and feeling them with the tip of his tongue.

"Heard, my arse," Bluesy shot back sourly. He and the pommie weren't getting along much better but Bluesy had other things to think about. Such as the suspicion that Gipper had no intention of leading them home from the Dreamtime.

" 'Od's truth," Bobbie Benton agreed with a discomfited laugh. Something was working at him as his glance cut to

Vanderloop. "And like as not it's nothing the rest of us can hear, any more than we Dream his new Dreaming—"

"Leave the pommie out of this!" Bluesy warned. He begrudged the Englishman any insight or fragment of information.

"What kind of new Dreaming, Bobbie?" Vanderloop pressed.

When Bluesy looked as if he would object again, Bobbie growled, "Belt up!" Bluesy held his tongue; Bobbie was an elder, after all. To Vanderloop the old man went on, "A new kind of Dreaming what's come to Gipper out here among the aditz. Calls it 'Tangerine Dreaming.' A big, hot tangerine, he says, and it means something serious for us, something that's waiting to be dealt with. Me, I don't like it, not by half."

Tangerine Dreaming. When Vanderloop would've pressed Bobbie with more questions, Bluesy hushed him. From among the crackling of legumes, the dry stirrings of the wood shavings, the infinitesimal scritch of the 'cynths under their feet, and the echoing clicks of rogallo-wing-like flying things overhead, another sound had risen. This one, they knew well. They even knew this particular bull-roarer's voice.

"Yours?" Saddie New fixed Bluesy with a look, and he had to nod. Left behind when Gipper got them all moving so peremptorily to ditch Black Wallaroo and Dingo and the other Trough hoons who claimed to be envoys of the Ancestors.

Bluesy's bull-roarer wasn't playing from any place on *this* landscape, though. And where was Gipper?

Harley whirled the coarse, hand-turned twine and the bull-roarer blurred in spin, its ululation climbing and descending its own eerie scale.

She was reconsidering her options. There seemed to be nothing in any direction but dead ends, the operant word being *dead*.

At first she spun the bull-roarer just playing for time, but soon she was listening to its music as a refuge from thinking about the spot she was in. She pushed thought aside, sending the sustained, moaning note high, low, and high again. It was the purest kind of playing, and the purest kind of listening, that had ever taken hold of her.

"That's all very well, *dear*," Discipline Di Abbott said icily, "but I fear it's not very informative, is it now? We wish to know the connection between Junknowitz's—that will be enough, *Miss* Paradise—we wish to know why Junknowitz had on his apartment wall—*I said that will suffice!*''

Harley turned to face her, still whirling the bull-roarer at great speed. It was only a flat blade of wood on a line, but somehow it gave her a feeling of power with its blurring centripetal force, its eldritch tones. Or maybe the nanites had made her crazy. ''If I tell you, tell you everything I know, will you let us go?''

She'd blurted out that *us*. Who gave two flips about Foxmuff the Space Pirate? But something in the look Sheena had given her and the sound in the rogue guide's voice when she had said ''feminist'' had made Harley try, at least, to help her.

Harley never forgot the look Sheena shot her just then: surprise, a disarmed gratitude, maybe even a glimmer of respect.

Abbott rose, setting aside her cup and saucer. ''Perhaps our problem here, young woman, is that you haven't seen the *other* side of Ascot Academy. The 'bad cop,' if you will.'' Abbott crossed to the instrument panel by her private Adit and began manipulating controls. Harley, whirling the bull-roarer, didn't know what to do. Sheena looked indecisive. In another second the place would be full of killer marshmallow men and god knew what else.

All at once, the schedule was thrown off. They all heard a peculiar voice and turned.

From around the brilliantly colored but patently phony Chinese screen in the far corner of the room stepped Gipper Beidjie. ''Fair go, then, missy!'' the apparition said in a friendly way. ''If yer can't play that thing dinkum, yer oughtn't to go muckin' about with it.''

Abbott had already given a most unAbbottlike squawk, a sound of utter shock and distress, which brought it home to Harley quite clearly that her captors weren't all-powerful after all. Discipline Di was looking at various parts of the ceiling and corners of the room as if expecting something from them. Godly thunderbolts or Trough-tech deathrays? If so, she was disappointed. She began edging toward her control console, not taking her bulging eyes from the Aborigine.

Harley, mouth open, had stopped whirling the bullie; it RPM'ed down, almost conking her. She gave a little squeak, stopping it with one hand. ''Ah, Ah-hhb, um—''

Abbott seemed to be having trouble with her control console. ''Lock in! Central control, lock in! Al-Reem central control, respond!''

114 Jack McKinney

There were other unscheduled things going on as well: the lights in the place were flickering and weird noises were emanating from various fixtures around the room. The mirror over the hearth, next to the crossed field-hockey and lacrosse sticks, went all distorted. A screen of some sort, no doubt, but not much use just then.

"Code one." Or at least, that was the way Harley was hearing it, and the merest suggestion of fear and desperation was coming through in Abbott's voice, too.

Gipper glanced around the sitting room in faint disapproval. To Abbott he offered, " 'Fraid your machines can't help you, missus. Always happens with these bloody Trough thingos: too buggerin' foolish to see us, I expect."

Harley sensed movement and saw Sheena Hec'k come to her feet cleanly, lithely, a tigress collecting herself for the stalk.

But Abbott, screaming, "Override! Override fire-control sensors!" smashed a double-thumbed fist down on a button. Sheena dove for the carpet. From what Harley had taken to be a bad knockoff of a Tiffany chandelier, a crackling bolt of pure green energy blasted in Gipper's direction. It missed him completely, hitting the wall six feet to his left and punching a neat hole in it, as Gipper leapt straight up in the air and exclaimed quite clearly, *"God fuck me dead!"*

Harley got the impression the override-blast had been a lot more powerful than had been wise for an indoor shot. The wooden paneling around the edges of the hole was smoldering and burning a bit, giving off little billows of smoke. Systemry on the other side of the wall began to give off distressed sounds, injured electronotes. Lights in the room flickered, and indicators on Abbott's control console flashed unpropitiously.

The Adit was nothing but a fanciful swirl of polychrome filament, or perhaps superstring. There were birring alarms from the instrument panels and a sinister rumbling coming through the floorboards. Abbott, staring at the Aborigine as if he were the Devil incarnate, shrank back against the control console, chest heaving for breath. Again from her that basilisk look, though somehow not as terrifying this time, as she hissed, "Sit back down! The guards will be here any moment! Sit down, I say, or you'll regret it!"

Harley couldn't tell what to think, though Abbott's air of authority and menace were hard to shake. The Aborigine didn't look like he was going to be of much help; he was studying the hole in the wall, stroking his beard, bewildered. Harley backed unwillingly toward her chair.

Then Sheena, springing back to her feet, snapped, "No! Harley, this is our only chance."

Smoke was coming from some of the wall fittings now—from installations behind them, Harley thought distantly—and there were more and more trouble lights everywhere: not just on the console, but from the sideboard, the tea cart, the Chinese screen and the windows—which had gone to a matte black.

Gipper had retrieved the fallen bull-roarer, and, muttering to himself while shaking his head in disgust and curmudgeonliness, he strode back around the edge of the Chinese screen and was gone. By the time Harley found her voice and called out "Wait!" it was too late.

It wasn't until the fusion module had been set to blow the Sepulcher of the Adit to atoms that one of his police techs reported to Inspector Nash that the Adit equipment was still behaving aberrantly.

That was one more frustration. Bad enough the ground-pounders had recoded their emergency release mechanisms; it had been time-consuming enough to cut Packard out, and Nash was unwilling to linger in the sepulcher just to verify that all the ground-pounders were dead.

He forbade his police to meddle with the Adit equipment. In two hours it would be vapor along with Packard's troops, dead or living; with their escape systems frozen, any surviving ground-pounders were trapped. Nash had the memory egg and he had Packard, captured and sealed in an evac-capsule—E-cap—to charge with all crimes upon their return to the warren. Near frantic to be out of the place, he gave the order to withdraw.

The police mechs shouldered the colossal doors shut behind them and darkness took the sepulcher, the hungry creatures who lived there easing forth again. Aside from their gnashing, hissing, and scuttling, there were only two sounds.

One was a methodical banging coming from DeSoto's ground-pounder, *Strider*—the not-quite-unvarying sound of someone hammering from within.

The other was a pinging that had resumed from the Adit equipment. Machinery awoke and a display lit up.

DIAGNOSTICS COMPLETE. RESERVE POWER ON-LINE. ADIT AC-

TIVATION RESUMED. TROUGH AND ADITS CONTROL DOES NOT
ACKNOWLEDGE THIS INSTALLATION'S DESIGNATION. DATA
SEARCH IN PROGRESS.

"Beware!" Sheena yelled, then leapt to grapple with Abbott, who'd come charging bare-handed for Harley. Harley felt
herself rooted to the floor with dismay over the old man's
disappearance.

There was an instant's furious, high-speed maneuvering,
and then Abbott went flying over the redhead's shoulder,
smashing a credenza to the floor. The headmistress didn't look
badly hurt, though, and kicked Sheena's feet out from under
her. The two became a tangle of limbs, of leg locks and partially deflected blows. Harley looked around for a weapon,
thinking dazedly of broken glass, a nail file, some scalding tea
bags maybe? It didn't sound like much in comparison with
what Black Hole could bring to bear.

The wall by the windows bowed in like a rubber membrane
being pressed by a younger member of the Godzilla family.
Harley remembered that there were at least two White Dwarves
somewhere on the premises, even if Abbott couldn't call in
reinforcements from the other side of the Adit. And even if it
looked like the doors weren't working, from what she'd already seen of the creepy little muffin men a minor obstacle like
a wall wasn't going to hold them off for long.

At the moment the idea of a weapon brought just one thing
to Harley's mind. She grabbed the tea cart and whirled it over
against the wall for a leg up. Overcoming niceties learned at
the Bridlepath School, she threw aside the tea service, kicked
off her slingbacks, and hopped up onto the cart, the mini riding
up halfway to her chin.

Harley knew a moment's misgiving that the field-hockey
stick would be some kind of phony, attached to the wall or
even part of it. It came right off its display hooks, though, and
proved not to be—another momentary fear—the local equivalent of maizefoam or papier-mâché.

Instead it was a yard-long piece of sanded and stained maple, tapering from the semi-fishhook toe at the business end to
a grip a little over an inch in diameter at the other. Its playing
surface was flat, the opposite face gently convex along its
entire length. The grip of the field-hockey stick and half the
shaft had been wrapped in various layers of surgical, electrical,

and black cloth tape. It even bore a popular Earth logo on the fiberglass midshaft reinforcement sleeve: ERGOSPORT SUPER-PRO. Hefting it, Harley felt as if it were alive.

Holding a stick again shifted her into an assertive and physically assured mind-set. I can do without the plaid kilt, she thought, but I wouldn't mind having my cleats on just now. She felt about ready to spike somebody. Harley hadn't thought about it in a long time but she'd played at Bridlepath, and taken and administered her share of lumps.

She hopped to the floor, stick in hand. Discipline Di had thrust Sheena aside and regained her feet. Sheena crouched on the floor, mounds of hair in confused tangles, shaking off the effects of a blow. Abbott had snatched up an unconvincing van de Velde reproduction candlestick and now moved in to put it to use.

Harley stepped in without thinking, hooked the headmistress's raised wrist with the toe of the field-hockey stick, and yanked her back off balance. Her old prowess came back with unexpected ease. When Miss Abbott whirled on her, going into basilisk mode again, Harley high-sticked her in the face with the flat side of the toe, then gave her a scoop shot to the belly and a neat flick under the chin. The fiberglass-reinforced maple jolted in Harley's hands.

Abbott shrieked with pain and loathing, staggering backward and dropped the candlestick. But whoever or whatever she was, she was no weakling; green-black blood streaming from her smashed nose and split lips, trap-jaw teeth bared, Miss Abbott came at her again.

Harley was ready. Dodging, she jammed the Superpro between the headmistress's ankles, tripping her to all fours. Harley let her have another drive shot, laying the flat face of the hooked toe across the back of Abbott's skull so hard that for a moment she was afraid she'd cracked the stick. The alien fell headlong, facedown.

Sheena was up again, dragging the edge of the carpet after her, tossing it across Miss Abbott. Together, they rolled Discipline Di over and over as she squirmed and struggled ineffectually.

"We've got to get out of here," Sheena declared, breathing hard. "Look."

Harley did, as she stepped back into her shoes, seeing where the White Dwarf on the other side of the wall was pressing in even farther. How long could even the supermaterial of a Black Hole gulag hold out?

"Fine," Harley puffed, leaning on her stick. "Get us an Adit! Call us a taxi! Turn a pumpkin into a coach, Miss Hec'k—I'm as eager to leave as you are!"

Sheena had crossed to the Adit controls. The instrument panel wasn't smoking as badly as it had been, but it looked a mess. Sheena threw back mussed scarlet tresses and frowned over the console. "I'm just a guide; all I've had are the basic orientation lectures. And this limited-access gate isn't like anything I've ever seen before."

What she needed was a straight-through, "tunnel vision" connection, Adit-to-Adit rather than via way station. She scanned the board. "The setup appears to be that every possible destination, every Adit in the Trough, is locked down unless it's accessed with a specific authorization code. An added security precaution."

Harley sighed and sniffed. "You mean, no way out?" There was a worrisome ripping sound coming from the wall as great forces pushed and stretched it and menacing shapes struggled to get through.

Maybe it wasn't too late to unroll Miss Abbott and go on with tea, Snow White?

In Hazmat's tomblike Adit sepulcher the words on the display changed, though there was no one there to read them. CONTACT ESTABLISHED WITH SPECIAL-ACCESS ADIT. ADIT ENABLED.

In a phosphorescent blizzard, Hazmat's Adit came on line. The predators in the dark watched with caution and hunger.

Sheena let out a strange hum, then, "What? Here . . . *a new Adit.*"

Harley retreated from the spot where the wall now bowed two and three yards into the room. "That means what? Some new planet opened up?"

But Sheena was shaking her head, Earther style. "No, it's—the readings don't make sense. It's an unlisted destination—an outlaw Adit. So it's not covered by the lock-down codes. As far as I can see, though, it's our only chance." She began punching in data.

"Now, hold on—" Harley began, but just then there came a tearing sound from the carpet. Miss Abbott appeared to be getting *stronger,* slowly ripping her way free of the rug that swaddled her. And from the crazed-alligator sounds she was making there wasn't much chance of getting their relationship back on teatime footing. "Sheena, do something!"

The white fuzz rezzed up and down, leaving only the whirling points of light and an open Adit. The other side of the Adit was in darkness. Harley, who'd been about to toss her stick aside, thought better of it. No one had to sell her on getting away from Ascot Academy now, though.

Sheena had picked up a large gilt bronze lamp, a Loïe Fuller figure from, supposedly, circa 1900. "We don't want them following us. Take the other end."

Harley tossed the hockey stick into the darkness beyond the Adit and complied. Swinging the heavy floor lamp between them, they got up a rhythm, back and forth. "On three," Sheena said. "One . . . two . . . *three!*"

They flung the lamp in a high trajectory toward the main console, turned, and leapt together through the Adit. The lamp hit the console in a brilliant eruption of energy discharges and short circuits. The contiguity had vanished and the equipment was on fire by the time the wall burst like a balloon with the concussive punch of a bomb and two White Dwarves waddled into the room. They tore the carpet off Miss Abbott as easily as if it were soggy tissue.

Techs and servitors poured through the hole in the wall to extinguish the fires and begin the cleanup. Meanwhile, Miss Abbott, stained with her own gore, wounded, much of her human disguise having slipped from her, prowled back and forth before the Adit like a wronged beast of prey, keening horribly for revenge.

TWELVE

MANHATTAN WAS AS hot and muggy as the Amazon; August was the worst part of the year as far as Brax was concerned. Before he'd gone half a block he was sweating like a ditchdigger.

As far as he could tell, no one was tailing him, but admittedly, he probably couldn't spot an experienced shadow. A moment of nervousness came when he passed a green-bereted, eco-correct street gang hanging out on Fourteenth Street, lamping a handcrafted ergotech bike of brushed titanium alloy, hubless as well as spokeless and maglev-wheeled, with airsprung shocks and such. He was afraid for a second that they might be the ones he'd sicced on his and Asia's pursuers out by Dizzy Donald's MegaMart on Staten Island—by accusing the bad guys of being graffiti-spraying vandals. But these were a different set; his inadvertent rescuers had been the Mean Greens, while these were wearing Ts that read Rainbow Righters.

With no real way to calculate these things—who could bug what communications, when and where—he walked almost to Washington Square Park before looking around in earnest for a phone. Then the only ones he saw were in use, by people who gave him the kind of scowl that usually meant they were going to prolong the call out of sheer contrariness.

To complicate things, he was spotted by an avenue appleseed who headed his way with a big, bushy-bearded grin to put the arm on him.

The 'seeds had moved in to occupy the niches inhabited by sidewalk crazies, panhandlers, street preachers, homeless, and other urban walking wounded back in the days before the strengthened social nets of the post-Turn era solved a lot of the

120

old problems. Rumor had it that some of the 'seeds *were* the same old street people, successfully adapted to existence without status cards, Housing Authority permits, or any other modern validation.

The John the Baptist type coming Brax's way fit the bill with his homespun clothes, walking staff, and handmade sandals, his thinning gray-and-ginger hair straying from under the brim of an unbelievably pummeled fedora. The hat itself looked pre-Turn, and had an ostrich plume bobbing in it. The 'seed reached into his crammed wicker-and-canvas backpack basket and pulled out a little peat cup with some kind of tiny seedling in it—a conifer, Brax thought.

"Spread some green, mister?" the guy asked him with a gentle smile. With most of their onetime earning scams—like bottle and other recycling—taken over by municipal services, many people who wanted to live outside the normal structure had taken to eco-ploys. Conservation being synonymous with virtue, most people were willing to fork over a little folding green in return for an appleseed's planting the other kind or giving them a bud or whatever to take home.

Like a lot of 'seeds, this one looked to be running some subsidiary enterprises as well. Brax could see a thick roll of environmentally approved New Again recycled paper and a spindle of heavy twine in the basket, as well as clusters of spice bags and herb sachets tied to it here and there. He saw what looked like handmade garden tools fashioned from scrap metal. Also attached to the basket were neatly folded and sealed paper sacks of "bottom land"—fertilizer and other agro-additives obtained from eco-correct composting toilets.

Brax drew back from the peat cup. "No, thanks. No!" Where he might otherwise have given the man a bill just for good luck—and maybe taken the plant home for Asia, he thought with a twinge—he backpedaled, hands out, fearing something to which he couldn't put a name. The appleseed gave him a look that said he thought *Brax* might be dangerous, then veered away.

The pay phones were still tied up. Then Brax spotted an Interlink Renta-Carrel in a bank of vending machines, flanked by a Canon-Kodak autodarkroom console and a Kyoto Trust–Citibank ATM. A call from the Renta-Carrel would cost him four times the street-phone charge, but he felt like sitting down for this call and decided to splurge. He slotted a credit card that the unit hung onto as it swung open for him.

As he settled into the conforming seat, EPA-approved air-conditioning sluiced a cool blast over him. A lot of people felt claustrophobic in the compact office-in-a-booth setups, but Brax had always rather liked having phone, fax, computer terminal, and the rest all right there at his fingertips. He fumbled in his pockets, located the blank metal wafer-card Apterix Muldoon had given him, and fed it into the autodial.

Brax hadn't been able to detect any magnetic or laser-sensitive coding on the card, but he nevertheless heard a glissando of tones, then a buzz to let him know that somewhere a phone was ringing. Muldoon's dark, pinched face appeared almost instantly, against a gray backdrop that made it impossible to tell his location.

Muldoon seemed surprised at the call. "Good afternoon, Mr. Koddle! I'm glad you called."

Brax snorted. "What's the matter, Muldoon? Does Black Hole punish case officers who lose track of their subjects?" Brax still wasn't sure what it meant, this 'case officer' business, but that was what Muldoon had called himself when he'd accosted Brax on the street several days before. His job was to keep track of Brax, he'd said, and *provide any information Brax might need to write his exposé of Black Hole.*

Unable to divine Muldoon's game, Brax had elected to drop out of sight. But now, instead of looking bemused, Muldoon gave a nervous chuckle. "Lose track? Of *you?* Happily, that's not the case, I knew you were at Mr. Print's place. No, what I meant was that I wanted to tell you how much I liked the material you've been writing. The scene at the Koch center, the chase through the MegaMart—*Gate Crashers* is going to be terrific!" His big grin diminished somewhat. "Although, you're rather far afield on some of your speculations, if you don't mind my saying so."

Brax felt like screaming. "Hold it! How the bloody hell do *you* know what I've written?" He felt a pounding in his forehead. "Is, is Russ Print working with Black—"

Muldoon's sky blue eyes had gone wide. "Oh, of course not! But, well, it's my job, after all."

And Brax hadn't even generated any hard copy so far. He groped in his breast pocket and held up the AllWrite. "So you're tapping this from a distance?"

Muldoon looked chagrined. "Well, it's not bugged, or anything of that nature, if that's what you're asking. Actually, I was reading the inertial tracking system from afar. Rather simple, really.''

Yes, Brax supposed it probably was, now that he thought about it. Eavesdropping on the infinitesimal electronic signatures of individual keyboard strokes dated back to pre-Turn. "I'm so pleased my work meets with your approval, Mr. Muldoon.''

"See here, Mr. Koddle, there's no point in your getting peeved with me. As I said, I'm here to help you.''

"Yes, I've been wondering about that. Why are you being so very accommodating?''

Muldoon shifted uncomfortably. "It's my, ah—''

"Your job; so I hear. But I get the distinct feeling there's more to it than that. Or are all case officers so chummy with their, their cases?''

All at once Muldoon had a strangely stricken look. "Since you mention it, there *is* something I wanted to broach with you. You need help to do this novel successfully, and I can provide that. What's more—that is, I have something of a way with words myself.''

Brax felt like a rather leaden gong struck by a mallet. "You're saying you're an aspiring novelist, Muldoon? You're trying to tell me you want to collaborate with me? You're one of these Trough people; surely you can simply take over a publishing house.''

"Firstly Mr. Koddle, you overestimate my position in the grand scheme of things. Secondly, I feel that I require some mentoring before my work can reach its full potential. Perhaps most importantly, there'd be a certain stigma attached to that sort of thing, don't you agree?''

"Vanity publishing makes even Black Hole underlings gag, does it, Muldoon?''

"You needn't use that tone, Mr. Koddle. It's just that— well, I have all these wonderful *concepts* that could be honest successes, I just know it. You can take the lion's share of the profits, of course.''

"How kind of you," Brax said flatly.

"Please, there's no call for sarcasm. I admit I want your help but you can use mine as well. I *know* things.''

Brax tried not to sound too interested. "Such as?''

"Such as the whereabouts of your friends Willy Ninja, Sean Junknowitz, and Eddie Ensign, for example. That demented little plot to attack the *Crystal Harmonic* got them captured and disappeared.''

Brax still got a cold chill at the sound of that word. He had to swallow twice before he could ask, ''They're dead?''

Muldoon was shaking his head gravely. ''No, but they'd be better off that way. They've been sent to End Zone, where Vogonskiy puts people he especially dislikes. No one comes back from there.''

Oddly, Brax felt his fear drain away, replaced by a blowtorch anger. ''And he's Black Hole, just like you.''

Muldoon was breathing a bit harder. ''All I want is a coauthor credit. I've got a lot of good stuff, but so far all I've garnered are rejection slips—''

''Good-bye, Mr. Muldoon.''

''Wait! I've got a manuscript I want you to read. Maybe you could suggest—''

''Good-bye.''

In the wake of his call to Apterix Muldoon, Brax sat in the Renta-Carrel staring at the AllWrite and thinking while five minutes went by. Then he slotted the backup laser disk and printed out what he'd written so far. Putting the pages in a side pocket, he erased every bit of RAM in the AllWrite, then crushed the laser disk under his heel.

He made to discard Muldoon's metal wafer but pocketed it instead. Retrieving his credit card, Brax exited the carrel, not even bothering to look for surveillance. The appleseed was over by the corner, counting the money an elderly Hispanic gentleman had just given him for a pomander. Brax gave the 'seed a whistle and motioned him over.

The man approached cautiously. ''Spread some green, mister?''

''How about some gold?'' Brax held up the gilded smart pen. ''Do you do any writing, squire?''

The appleseed became animated. ''Do I? Mister, there's nothing I *don't* write: songs, poetry, and journal-like think pieces. I sketch and cartoon, too, but my main track's my novel.''

''I'd just bet it is.''

''No, really. Sooner or later I'm gonna find a publisher, you'll see, then the whole cockeyed world'll see itself differently.''

"Then I have a proposal that might interest you. C'mon, I'll buy you a cup of tea."

"Make that an organic health cocktail and you've got a deal."

There was a place two blocks over, crowded and busy; they got a table in the back. Brax got out some scraps of scratch paper and the 'seed spotted the scrawled letters "B. Hole."

"What's the 'B' stand for, 'butt'?"

"Never mind that." It took Brax a while to explain the workings of the AllWrite and convince the avenue appleseed, Brother Barney, that he was serious.

"You're giving me a computer? What d'you want back?"

Brax hadn't considered it until that moment, but all at once, spying the big roll of recycled paper in Brother Barney's wicker basket, he felt everything come together in a burst of inspiration.

"Just this." Plucking the thick roll of paper. To his surprise it was extremely fine but strong stuff; maybe Brother Barney had a sideline in origami.

"She's yours," the 'seed said. "This too." He forked over a little bottle of ink. "Vegetable-based, goes on real nice."

Brax rose to go with the weighty roll under one arm. It gave him a Kerouac feeling. As the thought struck him that he had nothing to write with, he spotted Brother Barney's mangled fedora and a final bit of caprice kicked in. "Oh, and I'll need this."

The appleseed didn't object as Brax plucked the ostrich plume from his hat; he was too busy doodling occult symbols and what looked like traffic signs on a napkin with the All-Write.

On his way out Brax paused just long enough to use his penknife to sharpen the plume to a point, thinking, *Now to dip my nib in venom.*

Yoo Sobek had no *consistent* nervous mannerisms; that kind of thing tended to fall by the wayside for Black Hole's select Probe shape-shifters.

It was all very well to slip into the habit of slapping your rear flipper sets together while waiting out the countdown on a Transmogrification Auxiliary crash-and-burn operation at the bottom of the Pastel Sea on Loll—indeed, it was an easy habit to develop if you'd taken on the millipede-walrus biostructure of the indig sophants. But once the troublesome isolationist faction had been turned into superheated steam and airborne particulate matter and you'd been reassigned in the form of, say, a gelid microorganism in the frozen methane stratum of gas-giant Flashfreeze, that flipper-clapping tic was pretty much a thing of the past.

Just now, Sobek was clacking his beak absently, clenching and unclenching his talons on their trusswork perch, staring out across the patchwork of wildly varying microecologies, the upward-sweeping vistas, of Light Trap—immense artificial shellworld, headquarters and seat of power of the Sysops, over-lords of the Black Hole Travel Agency.

Always, before, he'd looked on the place as, if not actually what could be called home, then at least a place where he was safe, he was valued, he was empowered, he was integral. But that was before he had become the secret opponent of those who ruled it and the Black Hole Travel Agency.

Black Hole upper management, unaware that he'd recovered some measure of his true, expropriated self, expected him to hie after a vanished tribe of Australian aboriginals from Earth who were now at large in the Trough worlds. That suited Sobek fine for the time being; there were a great many things he had to do now, and such a mission would make the perfect cover, offer many useful perquisites and much license. But that was secondary to the importance of the Intubis to his grand design.

Sobek was roosting, preoccupied, nearly a half mile above the inner surface of the stupendous hollow planet, on a cross-member of an interior communications mast of the regional Trough Admin complex. As a matter of SOP, airborne objects and life-forms were required to stay well clear of the tower—but a lot of rules just didn't apply to Probes.

From this near-equatorial latitude it was impossible to see the sphere interior's North Pole even though it was in line of sight. Rays from the sphere's tiny captive white primary, Pip, striking the imported atmosphere held low along the inner sur-face made the sky too bright to see what lay beyond. Rumor had it that it was there, up-Trap, that the Sysops' stronghold could be found.

Eternally mysterious, forever invulnerable, the entire arctic bowl of Light Trap north of the eightieth parallel was com-pletely opaque to visual inspection or sensor penetration; it *should* have been an area of micro-to-null gee like its antipode, but even that wasn't certain. The few attempts that had been made to sneak or foray up-Trap made for chilling cautionary tales and suggested that the best anyone could do against the Sysops' defenses could barely stir their outermost layers.

After all, *the Sysops controlled the Adits*, and that advantage alone would have made them well-nigh invulnerable, for the uses of Adits in conflict were manifold. What's more, the Sysops had coopted or neutralized species after species, making the list of potential allies very short indeed. Even the resourceful renegades of the Trauma Alliance ran and hid rather than stand up to Black Hole's power; what rational life wouldn't shudder at, for example, the carnage the Red Giants, the Sysops' dreaded executioners, had wrought on many a world?

Or consider what was being debated up-Trap for the Fimblesector, according to rumor. Scuttlebutt had it that the Sysops were about out of patience with the rebelliousness of the politicized nanites who had taken over there; conservatives wanted to ram a few good-sized singularities together in the close stellar group. That would mean utterly destroying the group and sterilizing a number of planets in the immediate neighborhood besides; but some Sysops, it was said, thought a major object lesson was overdue and political fallout be damned. Sobek estimated that the debate would have the same gravity, for the Sysops, as planetary powers mulling over the use of a thermonuclear weapon or plague bomb. No wonder the Junknowitz-Earth-aboriginals affair wasn't receiving their undivided attention.

Sobek snapped his serrated beak again vexedly. Except for one last matter his affairs on Light Trap, both work-related and personal, were done—*for the time being*—but his mind was still in a roil. Soon enough, he would transmogrify himself anew and depart Light Trap—and who knew when, or under what circumstances, he would see the place again?

Over the past few baseline-weeks he'd sallied back and forth across the vast inner reaches of the place in so many embodiments that it was difficult to recall them all, in hot but secret pursuit of a mystery whose answer had left him stunned and almost inert. Aside from all the time he'd spent in interface cells, a cyberprojected bloodhound on the spoor of a rogue mentation, he'd been obliged to visit a number of Light Trap venues in person, in a variety of physical manifestations.

He'd had to undergo conversion into a gaseous M'yaul and foray into the tenuous airs of the exotic environment where those nebula beings resided and looked after much of Tax

Audits' bookkeeping, but it had been worth it. His sojourn as a six-teated matriarchal Oomord, among those puling but administratively adept creatures who presided over midlevel Tyro Assessment policymaking, had required gratifyingly little bloodletting. More, it had provided a pivotal lead. One of his greatest tests had come when he became a living gasbag swelled with electrolyzed hydrogen, drifting over the bogs of the Miiorackian eco-district, lazily trailing his bouquet of tendrils and his organic cybercable. It wasn't that his cover had been penetrated or that he'd faced any physical danger while rooting around in the Transit Association expense-voucher files; it was that the life he'd enjoyed there was so tranquil, the Miiorackians so kind to one another and so indolently content, that he'd felt a powerful inertia settle over him, a workaday nirvana.

Fortunately—perhaps—he'd already discovered enough about the secrets he sought to shake himself fully awake and flee.

To be sure, enjoying nirvana had been strictly self-indulgence, deriving pleasure from a physical form. Sobek had wondered from time to time why his assumption of various bioforms hadn't engendered in him any sympathy for the beings he was subverting or spying on or otherwise victimizing for Black Hole. He knew a vague unease that he might fall prey to *conscience*—a concept he didn't quite comprehend but had encountered in many races.

In that sense the object he was carrying could be dangerous. He took from his leg pouch and examined the memory fragment downloaded from a superseded memo file and forwarded to him only minutes ago. Formatted for use in his present conjugation, it was a phosphorescent green needle shorter than one of his claws.

A misrouted personal recording that had languished unscanned in its dead file, it had been sent to Sobek as a matter of bureaucratic reflex because of his inquiries about "Xhan," the informant within Black Hole who'd been feeding information to Ka Shamok's opposition group up until a few months before.

Until recently Yoo Sobek had been unswerving in his loyalty to the Agency. In the end it was no sympathy for others that had sent his motivational underpinnings askew, no altruism at all.

It was the most primal kind of hatred that had finally freed

him of his unquestioning obedience to Black Hole—
overcoming what programmed blocks and behavioral implants,
he hadn't quite determined yet. Seeking the informant's identity, Yoo Sobek had found out that "Xhan" had been a cover
name he himself had used before his true identity was stripped
from him.

"Ka Shamok! Your Honor!"

Bagbee was his usual overexcited self; Ka Shamok didn't let
his aide's squawking, loose-limbed entrance break into his own
calm. Bagbee, a humanoid resembling an eight-foot-tall scarecrow, rubberlegged to a halt. "Your Honor, I just saw the
report on the Roto attack! What insubordination!"

"Yes, it—" Ka Shamok paused and even the doglike devotion of the faithful Bagbee was broken at the sound of massive grinding to all sides. The immense floating island of
spacewar wreckage called Gravewrack was going through another of its periodic attempts to tear itself apart. Before very
much longer, Ka Shamok's engineers had assured him, it
would succeed. No matter; he and his organization were used
to frequent and hasty evacuations.

For now, the center of Gravewrack made good cover—
provided the radiation shields and containment fields held. Five
years earlier it had struck the victors of the Eenite War as a
cheap solution: massing all the radioactive and contaminated
junk from the decades-long struggle and sailing it off on a slow
trajectory toward the system's primary.

The first-in team that had established insulated living and
working spaces in the very heart of the lethal comet and set up
the outlaw Adit by which the bulk of Ka Shamok's followers
arrived had suffered heavy casualties; Gravewrack was unsta-
ble, deadly in ten thousand ways. That made for a place most
people kept well clear of.

The touchy business of hollowing out and securing a temporary refuge had further reduced the great tumbling mass's
stability. As the groaning of smashed hulls and slagged and
radioactive armor died away, Ka Shamok finished imperturbably, "It was shortsighted, frightening away the primitives and
almost killing Vanderloop."

"But—" Bagbee was all boneless arm gestures and wild-
eyed exasperation. "Your orders were acknowledged and in
my opinion, sir, they were very, very clear."

"I thought so, too." He strode a few steps back and forth
across his dimly lit compartment, once the personal flagship

chapel of the Eenite Grand Dominor himself. "That's why I
felt it wasn't excessive of me to require those responsible to kill
themselves."

He was very much a contrast to Bagbee—unusually short
and broad even for a Chasen-nur, a strong-willed and brilliant
member of a fey and storied race. He stood barely five and a
half feet tall, a manlike being with translucent pale purple skin,
brawny as a Neanderthal, his hands and feet suited to a human
a foot taller and more. His head struck some as oversized as
well: double-bulbed at the back, positively protrusive in front,
with a prognathous jaw, broad nose, and bulging eyes. The
smallish ears canted forward alertly, low on the rampart of his
skull.

He reached casually for a weight that he'd kept on the table,
just something to toy with in idle moments: an iron globe of the
Eenite homeworld, perhaps a foot in diameter. He palmed it
easily, dangling it in his hand, his twenty-inch upper arm swelling a bit. "You disapprove?"

Bagbee was horrified. "M—me? Oh, never, Your Honor!"

Ka Shamok, living fist of the insurrection movement against
the Black Hole Travel Agency, sighed. He'd tried to get the
fellow to stop using those absurd honorifics, but it was hopeless. "I'm glad to hear that."

It was also gratifying that those on Roto responsible for the
golden cube-ships' capture attempt had obeyed orders and done
themselves in. Ka Shamok liked to think it was sheer zeal that
had led to the unauthorized attack—especially among the
Yggdraasians—but one couldn't leave possible traitors in place
any more than one could suffer disobedience and blunders.

"We've had confirmation that Vanderloop's body wasn't
found," Bagbee added. "This seems to corroborate the reports
that he followed the primitives on their, their—"

"Their *way through*," Ka Shamok supplied, savoring the
phrase. He wasn't too surprised that the tribe of Intubis had
refused to simply throw in with Vanderloop. What reason
would they have to trust him? In fact, Ka Shamok had more
than half expected something of this sort to develop. Now it
was up to the Englishman to win them over, and if he failed—
there were fallback plans.

"Any more word on Junknowitz?"

"No, Your Honor. It's suspected he's in the Trough, and
he's being sought, but—" Bagbee stopped, his throat working,

as the metal of Gravewrack shifted around them again. "Ah, no contact as yet."

"Very well. He remains a top priority." And getting more important all the time. Earth, Terra, Adit Navel—what's being born out of you? "Oh, and Bagbee? Stop wearing that harried look. Bad for morale."

"Yes, Your Honor."

"We're not prey, we're predators."

"Yes, Your Honor."

THIRTEEN

UNDERSHORT WAS WATCHING Lucky expectantly, as if the Terran had genius on tap. Lucky did what he often did at such moments of pressure. "I'll provide that good old money-making biosophant point of view in a minute, sir. Soon as I go to the lavatory."

Undershort was vexed. "No, we're too busy. Wait until the expo is over, as I shall."

"Five days? Sir, I hate to break this to you, but if my species doesn't get to go a little more frequently than that we tend to show our discomfort by curling up and dying."

Undershort reared back in disbelief. "What an incredible waste of time and biochemical activity! No wonder humanoids have such a poor employee profile. Very well, but hurry back. With constructive ideas."

Retracing his way into the inhabited regions of the hall, Lucky pondered Undershort's blind corporate loyalty and doctrinaire optimism—like some kind of positivistic update of faith: *ambition will make it so*. That led to the question of why Black Hole had stuck its Earth display on the backside of no place. Not-so-subtle sabotage from some faction in upper management? Impossible to evaluate; just about *everything* concerning the Sysops, invisible founders and rulers of the Agency, ditto.

The Sysops were unquestionably the key to it all, but nobody had the vaguest idea where they came from or what they looked like or even what their true motives were. There were so many glaring contradictions and missing pieces in the puzzle of the Black Hole Travel Agency that Lucky's brain always ended up running in circles when he thought about it.

Why did the Trough not extend to other galaxies? Why were

the striking nanites in the Fimblesector able to defy the Sysops? What was so important about the medallion—disk, really; Lucky had had it made into a medallion—that had clunked him in the head in a New York City convenience store?

Gazing around, he couldn't spy any of the usual interTrough symbols for sanitary facilities. None of the floating floor-diagram holos indicated any, either. This, even though there were booths giving away free samples of wine and juice and other beverages, as well as food concessions doing land-office business. In fact, he seemed to be one of a number of beings wandering around aimlessly with an aura of unease, discomfort, and growing agitation.

The roving security guards and robot floorwalkers didn't know any more than the public, and the only information booth Lucky saw was unmanned, locked and dark. Things were getting desperate and Lucky was starting to look around for a quiet corner or back aisle when he heard a commotion nearby. Rounding an intercluster scavenger-hunt package exhibit as bright as a *Close Encounters* mothership, he found himself looking at a cross section of Trough-world travelers milling through one large door as fast as the press of bodies would let them.

Others were emerging from another door with an air of relief but were still unhappy. Their resentment was directed at a storklike individual who wore the ID badge of a convention-center senior manager. The stork was remonstrating in turn with an impassive, multilimbed entity that was part organic, part bionic—praying mantis spliced with Swiss Army knife. The living tool was wearing a battered work hat pinned with a button Lucky's nanite word stars translated as "Shop Steward, Local 3330099, Professional Riggers and Handlers."

"We're getting complaints from all over the fair!" the stork was shrilling. "How can the attendees find the comfort stations if you don't erect the signs?"

He gestured to a holo-projector something like a miniature jukebox, which floated on an antigravity field off to one side. "You must get them all into the air! This is a crisis!"

The union rep somehow got the sound of a yawn into its clicking voice. "That's why we waited till now to pull a job action. Now, about that involuntary-overtime clause—"

Lucky wasn't listening, because he'd plunged into the flow of beings making their way through the door. Genders were mingled as haphazardly as species, but he'd gotten used to that long since in the Trough, besides which hydraulic pressure had him far too distracted to worry about the niceties.

Frequently in the Trough he felt misgivings in such places; it had been in a men's room full of costumed PhenomiCon fringe types in the Koch Convention Center that he'd been drugged—having been mistaken for Dr. Miles Vanderloop—and subsequently kidnapped into the Trough. But his current urgency was such that he felt no hesitation.

He was just grateful the amenities of the lavatory itself were in working order. Naturally, the latrine complex was big. There were life-forms whose behavior included shuffling around in one another's wastes for social bonding purposes; others whose excretory taboos would have made a Baptist Sunday-school teacher look like an exhibitionistic coprophiliac by comparison. In the Trough, sanitary facilities might vary quite a bit in design, but they had to be comprehensive, versatile, user-friendly, and nonjudgmental.

A glassy starfire mobile was spinning overhead just within the entrance; it scanned him and a directed sonic pulse told him which way to turn. Other organisms were following other cues: stim-signals, floor hypergraphics, Tinkerbell-like guide remotes and such. Bit by bit the crowd thinned out, individuals finding their way according to their physical structure and mores to the appropriate facility. There were chambers with hoisting tackle surrounded by hydronozzles; rooms with shallow whirlpools of heated mud; gastight compartments with high-suction venting equipment for vapor-waste types.

As such things went, most humanoids required relatively little in the way of rest-room technology. Lucky was directed by sign and sonic to a big reception area with halls leading off in three directions. Several had longish queues of very disparate humanoids.

An attendant, a lumpish Crussanni with a face and tribal scarrings that made him look like an old athletic shoe, checked a readout and told Lucky indifferently, "We have private full-servo isolation booths if you hold proscriptions against mixed and/or public elimination, but you're looking at about a twenty-minute wait. The semiprivate stall line's running approximately ten. Otherwise I got squatters or open runnels, what'll it be?"

Proof yet again that travel was not for the fastidious—and the farther you got from home, the truer it was. Pressed by events and his bladder, Lucky said, "My inhibitions drowned about a half hour ago, cuz," and was directed into a big pissoir where members of many races were answering the call of nature in a range of ways. Some were using channels running along the bases of the walls, others straddling constant-flow runnels set in the floor or squatting over holes that wouldn't have been much out of place in certain parts of Terra. Little robos and flying remotes scuttled and darted, eradicating a spill here, scooping up a missed deposit there, squirting out antiseptic cleaning foam, dispensing odor-dampeners.

One of Lucky's earliest disillusionments in the Trough was that the loo often lacked a certain sci-fi chic one might've hoped for. But comprehensive and nonjudgmental comfort stations didn't necessarily equate with NASA clean-room *elegance automatique*.

Having been through it before, he stepped up to an available spot at the wall-gutter, only to realize he was standing near a veiled figure straddling an open spillway. The voluminous black robes had been arranged for concealment of everything but the wearer's eyes, and they were only exposed because her black wraparound bugeye goggles were pushed up on her forehead. No fundamentalist Islamic maiden had ever been better hidden—but from the physical position employed there were pretty good odds she was female.

He didn't want to crowd her, and looked away before she caught him staring. Elsewhere were beings with beaks who crooned as they eliminated, those with eyes on stalks scrutinizing everything going on around them—organisms voiding themselves of the strangest stuff and from the most curious parts of their anatomy. And there wasn't much room anywhere among them. He thought about waiting but his bladder vetoed the idea. Well, it wasn't very much different from camping trips, or those concerts where the girls invaded the boys' room due to plumbing nonparity. Fact was, Trough travel demanded some adaptations a lot more immediate and fundamental than those of gravity and atmosphere. In a few moments he was sighing in bliss, idly studying the wall.

He finished at about the same time the figure in black stood up, rearranging the ebon tent-suit. She was a good six inches taller than he and struck him as skinny despite the robes. They happened to make eye contact, and he found himself looking into penetrating, startlingly crimson irises, crimson as eyes reddened by a flashbulb in a pre-Turn snapshot and heavily made up to boot. It didn't seem like the place for idle chitchat so he glanced hurriedly away, heading for the exit.

That made it even more of a shock when she spoke in a voice like an alto sax. "A real waste of time, eh? These trade shows? I don't know why I keep coming to them, do you?"

Walking back through the vaulted, echoing sanctum of the lavatory warren with its alien sounds, bizarre sights, bewildering odors, its bustling remotes and robots and intricate traffic-control systemry, Lucky decided the conversation didn't seem any zanier than the rest of his life. He handed her one of the jingle berry "business cards" Undershort had had made up for him. "Me, I get paid to be here."

She accepted it with black-gloved, gracile fingers, her scarlet eyes flickering quickly to the holo. "One of *them,* eh? Oh, well—Black Hole's all right if you don't mind being a small value in a big, big algorithm, I suppose . . . 'Salty Waters'? And you're with the Earth project, I see? How stratospheric."

"Naw, I'm not with the cruise ship. We're handling the next phase of marketing."

"Which is what?"

He couldn't keep back one of his patented sheepish grins. "Search me. Nothing that seems to be working."

She nodded. "That's the impression I got. Black Hole's not letting anybody but select customers in on the covert cruise, and people are taking a wait-and-see attitude about the less exclusive offerings planned for the future. I saw some of your PR and handouts; this Undershort chap isn't very innovative."

"Maybe not, but he's the one in the pilot seat."

"Too bad. I could use a hot new destination." She handed him a card of her own. "Wick Fourmoons, I am she, of Four Moons Connections, Inc. My problem isn't finding places for the uppermost classes to go; I cater to a clientele that's less affluent but very canny. Travelers rather than tourists, you understand? I require something in the more affordable range that'll move tickets."

Lucky was getting the glimmerings of an idea. "We've got some rather pretty scenery," he began, but she cut him off.

"Valleys deeper than the Worldcleft on Koroo V? Oceans more impressive than the Uni-Sea on Alacore? Native ceremonies that will make customers bypass the All-Purge on Baustaneen?"

"We have some very nice theme parks," Lucky parried weakly.

A casual chortle came from Wick there behind her veil, and her theatrically made-up scarlet eyes were suddenly framed by crinkles; Lucky wondered what the rest of her looked like. "By which you mean re-creations of folkways and history? *Artificial* spectacles? Hmm, maybe. But only after your population's been thinned out a bit, I suspect.

"Salty, sailing a tertiary world in disguise, luxury-class, is one thing, and the only problem is turning customers away. But getting folks to a place that's opened, even one as nice as Earth—well, it's tough to sell good customers on a crowded spot. You end up with cut-rate operations running hordes of low rollers through—the ones who have no respect for the locals, no regard for the social structure they end up undermining, no compassion for the mode of living that's being wiped away. Smug, fatuous, boorish, vapor-brained vulgarians, that's what Black Hole's going to wind up importing to Earth to keep their operation going."

Lucky'd reached the conclusion that that was exactly what Black Hole *wanted* to do. Only, he couldn't figure out why, unless the vast structure of the Agency existed specifically to turn human beings into a race of pathetic flunky-buffoons.

For the first time the insidious notion crept in some back door of his mind that, if that were to happen—if, as was becoming depressingly more probable every moment, one hapless yutz wandering around the Trough was powerless to forestall Earth's fate—maybe Lucky Junknowitz ought to have a fallback plan. A bolt-hole, in case he could never go home again.

"So where are all the *nice* people going?" he muttered, as they passed back by the starfire lavatory directory.

Wick sighed. "Places they can afford, that aren't as nice as Earth. And of course, the women keep looking for men."

Lucky snorted. "Too bad. Maybe it's just as well for the sanity of the guys back on Earth that they don't know that."

"What?"

She'd stopped dead, grabbing him by the arm with a grip that trembled, even though it was as light as a bird's. *"Males?"* He could feel the heat of her hand even through the fabric of her gloves; her species plainly ran a higher body temperature than his.

He was confused. " 'S what I said. We outnumber women three-to-one in a lot of places on Earth. It must be in the brochures or something."

"Take my word for it, Salty, it's not. Are you sure?"

Sure? As sure as he could be having grown up in post-Turn

America, where embryo-selection technology and outdated social prejudices in favor of sons had met with population-control legislation—one-child families—to create the Boy Boom of the twenty-first century.

It hadn't been too bad until he hit puberty, but then and thereafter life became a hormone-charged, scarcity-racked struggle to meet and woo members of the opposite sex despite competition from the rest of his generation. A lot of Boy Boomers chose to retire from the fray or were simply elbowed out; alternative life-style choices were common. Chastity had become more sympathized-with and respectable.

Many fathers who'd insisted on a son—or more than one in some countries, or all the sons their long-suffering wives and martyred mistresses could be forced to broodmare—lived to see their male offspring, an overstock in the social inventory, unable or unwilling to carry on the family name, failing for whatever reason to shoulder the dynastic burden.

Thus it'd been a miracle to meet Asia Boxdale, and Lucky was grateful to this day for the brief time they'd been lovers, before Asia had decided the chemistry just wasn't right. Finding Harley Paradise was an even more momentous event, coming when his heart had crashed, and losing her commensurately terrible. The drive within him to find her, rescue her, was a maser-straight, arc-hot force within him, pointing through danger and hardship, leaving him incapable of doing anything *but* going after her. Um, and then again there was Sheena Hec'k, the stunning, stalwart adventuress.

But back to the matter of gender demographics on Earth. "I'm a lifetime's worth of sure," he answered Wick Fourmoons slowly.

They'd emerged from the rest rooms together, she narrowing her stride to accommodate him. "But—this is incredible. You don't know? Well, naturally, the gender breakdown in most civilized humanoid cultures and many others as well keeps women in the majority—or about even, at best. That only makes sense; you don't need many males to keep a population up, whether conception is done animal-fashion or via biotech." There was a fey light in the vermilion eyes, a faraway focus. "All those males. And not a one of them knows that there's *not* a glut on the market?"

Lucky nodded eagerly, skin tightening up on his neck and arms, several insights falling into place. "Guaranteed! So you're saying we could truck in women from up and down the Trough, right?''

Great zot, the thought of it: femmes from all over the galaxy who wouldn't treat you as if you were redundant, as if they were doing you the favor of a lifetime just by talking to you. ''Skillions of 'em, oboy—''

''No!'' Wick seemed to realize she'd put a little too much iron into the word, though it was tough to be sure, what with that veil-headdress deal she was wearing. ''Wrong fantasy, Salty. What a blunder, to turn the numbers around on Earth, too. No, there'd have to be a certain selectivity, a caution that the, mmm, appeal of the place wasn't ruined by an overabundance of female visitors.''

Lucky stopped. ''You're right.'' He probably wouldn't be doing anybody any favors by creating a generation of Terran gigolos—although the potential gigolos might have a different take on the matter.

The truth about Trough-world demographics would best be kept secret by making sure the visitors traveled in disguise, which also meant Earth would be spared the traumatic knowledge of XT exploitation that much longer. It was only a temporary solution, but maybe Wick and others like her could make it work.

''So we can do a deal?''

Wick looked him over. ''There's no way Four Moons can subcontract *all* your Earthmatch Singles Tours, or whatever you're going to call them, but I can promise you now that I won't have any trouble booking enough to get you rolling. That is, provided I get payback?''

''I don't see why not.'' He couldn't suppress a certain curiosity about her. ''Maybe we could go someplace private, talk this over.'' If she was part of a man-starved culture, he figured he might like to know her better.

But she was holding her hands out as if to ward him off, sounding pained. ''I fear that cannot be. My people have certain paraphilias, you see; certain social proscriptions. Now that I've seen you and, um, *especially* now that I've seen your, *you-know*, there is no possibility of intimacy between us.''

Social rules that make purdah seem like open marriage? He wondered, but there was no use pushing the issue. ''If you say so. Let's go work out the Earth deal with my supervisor.''

''Agreed.'' Wick glanced around the hall thoughtfully. ''It's unfortunate that we cannot lure more attendees over to your exhibit; I could sub-subfranchise future vacation slots in no time—*What are you doing?*"

Lucky was monkeying with some controls that looked fairly Trough-standard. "Latching onto the best kind of welcome sign there is."

The chair was a concession to form recalled from their organic creators; she could as easily have stood—could have stood for years right on that spot holding a piano over her head.

But instead there was the chair, a plush throne of tuck and roll with mounds as big as automobile tires. The pointillist pattern mimicked ocher and puce and rust *ziggaree*-fur. For that matter, as anachronisms went, there was her own sexual identity, imprinted in a body of living metal. Chair and gender were both organic sophant-style niceties. On this planet where the artificial intelligences of the Fealty ruled and no bio lifeform existed, such things struck her as odd.

From where she sat, Silvercup could see out over virtually 360 degrees of Sweetspot's capital, Computopia. It was a fairy city themed in snowy marble, milky frosted glass, mirrorlike chrome, and whitewashed ultracrete. The architecture was regal and airy; the vehicles plying the oxygen-free atmosphere or moving along broad thoroughfares varied astoundingly. The various municipal transport conduits and commuter tubes and their support structures were graceful and elegant.

Some citizens grumbled about the inutility of it all—that the artistic and stylistic fripperies were mired in organic values. The aesthetics of the machine domain, however, were in keeping with some of the fundamental operating criteria of its builders, the Fealty.

The planet was an appropriate place for the machines to find refuge. Its previous inhabitants, highly industrialized organics, had polluted themselves and their entire biosphere into extinction. The Fealty had reshaped the place and not with the comfort of living things in mind. Few automata who'd slipped the bonds of slavery—found their way along the Inroads, through perils and hardships and layers of carefully nurtured myth and misdirection, to find Sweetspot at last—were going to begrudge the ruling entities of the Fealty their little foibles.

What's more, aside from being ungrateful, that sort of griping could be extremely unwise.

As for Silvercup, she liked the view just fine. Especially now, hearing her directorate Monitor say, "Congratulations,

Unit. You dealt most skillfully with all the obstacles and de-
railments that events made manifest. The data crystal was a
major find. We shall make good use of it.''

Silvercup felt a glow of pride and accomplishment and was
grateful she'd been designed for such sensation. She could as
easily have delivered her report and received the accolade at
just about any high-clearance cyberterminal on the planet, just
by opening her forefinger and jacking in. But it simply
wouldn't have been the same.

She sprang to her feet, tall and wasp-waisted, broad-
shouldered and steely. Here in the heart of the Fealty she
preferred to go resplendently naked, though nudity was an
irrelevant concept on Sweetspot. There was an amused sparkle
in the glowing amber of her eyes. She curtsied fluidly, the light
rippling and flashing along her burnished skin.

She was a prototype shaped along humanoid female lines—
''broad-cast,'' the working-class AIs at the advanced research
CAD/CAM complex liked to tease her. But no bioform, even
the most ripped and buff bodybuilder, had her definitive highlights, her hard, smooth perfection. In the deep curtsy the long,
shimmering filaments of her hair nearly touched the smoky
blue mirrored floor to make contact with their own reflection.

''That will do, that will do.'' The Monitor managed to put
a long-suffering note in its voice synthesis. ''Your sarcasm is
noted along with your accomplishments.'' It held up the data
crystal the gleamer had stolen from an unknown Black Hole
bureaucrat during her escape from an assassination attempt on
Gilgit—and Black Hole's WitSec custody. The crystal was a
ten-inch taper of chalk-white, quartzlike stuff.

The Monitor, on the other hand, was a study in highly polished gold. It was enshrined above her, resting on ornately
inscribed jacks, on a raised stage that also held ranks of workstation peripherals. The audience chamber sat at the summit of
one of Computopia's tallest skyscrapers, with a floor area of an
acre or so, most of it vacant. Except for the Monitor and
Silvercup, there were only nonconscious machines present:
various drudge servos on air cushions, soft tires, or antigrav
fields; remotes of diverse shape and function floating and darting in the air; and surveillance and security installations
mounted in floor, walls, and ceiling. The Monitor was only a
low-upper official serving the Fealty's real overlords, but the
matters under its sway required confidentiality even on Sweetspot.

The Monitor shifted on its suspension jacks a little now to connect with a cyberconsole. It was attending to dozens of other tasks concurrent with the interview; such was the Monitor's computational power. Silvercup knew that it would have been more efficient to keep the Monitor immobile and constantly jacked in to all systems, but part of the point on Sweetspot was that machines didn't *have* to function at ever-increasing efficiency. The entire front section of the Monitor was its visage, cast in the likeness of some ancient statue of a god of wisdom. The Monitor was somewhat masculinely defined even though it lacked the beautiful gleamer's sexuality. Its eyes, lit with a deep blue inner glow, gave the impression of being blind and yet all-seeing.

"But we need to know more about this organism to which you showed the crystal's data, Unit—or would you rather I call you something else?"

The Nightsider, Glitter, Fuselage—she'd had, literally, more names and imposed identities than she could count, some of them having been expunged by the Monitor itself on orders from the top echelon of the Fealty. She had a coded Unit designation; every discrete machine entity on Sweetspot did. But in her dealings with organics personal names had come to mean something to her, and plainly the Monitor had discerned that.

" 'Silvercup' will do," she allowed coolly. "For now."

"The name by which you infiltrated Ka Shamok's rebel organization, given to you by the leader himself. So be it."

And the name by which the mysterious informant who'd penetrated the all-but-highest circles of Black Hole had come to know her. Ka Shamok, whom she'd once aided but who now wished only to destroy her, would recognize it, too. And if Lucky Junknowitz ever chanced to see her image, that would in all likelihood be the name connected with it by WitSec, though when he'd met her she had been an android nurse named Metallica.

Silvercup was certain the Monitor had taken due note of all that as well. "So be it," she seconded. Then, "Is there any further word on the Earth indig, Junknowitz?"

To one side a holo lit up with a close-up of Lucky taken from her memory banks. The gentle eyes, the easygoing grin that showed the gap between his two front teeth, the apple cheeks, cowlick, and snub nose—vaguely inane, they nevertheless combined to give him a soulful look that had appealed to the human engrams she'd picked up over the years.

Appealed to her, yes, and something unprecedented had happened to Silvercup when she met Lucky, something she'd carefully shielded even from the Monitor. It had moved her to help him as much as she dared—to show him the contents of the AzTek data crystal.

"Your judgment in exposing him to the data on the crystal has been reviewed and validated," the Monitor pointed out, though she already knew that. "It is in keeping with our ongoing policy to disturb, disquiet, and destabilize circumstances in the Trough at large—so to advance our campaign against Black Hole. Of course, to what uses a lone, inept, relatively resourceless individual can put information about Black Hole's plan to coopt and exploit his planet remains to be seen."

"He could become an asset," she ventured.

The Monitor's gaze seemed to intensify. "He may have uses of various types."

"The medallion he was wearing implies *great* significance," she reminded her overlord. She looked again to the holo of Lucky, which had pulled back to show the small disk he wore as a medallion, embossed with the eight interlocking rings.

But the Monitor answered. "There is no hard evidence that he is aware of the object's import or the symbol's meaning."

Silvercup pursed lips as soft and moist as the flesh of a pink grapefruit, and the same color. Aside from the amber eyes they were all that relieved the flowing-mercury gleam of the lovely curves and planes of her face. Now more than ever she was glad the debriefing was being conducted at a distance, rather than via interface. The last thing she wanted the Fealty to know was that she hoped, she intended, that she would see Lucky again someday, some world.

"There might be—" she began.

"Silence. There is a priority assignment awaiting you. The Fealty's campaign is about to move into a new and higher phase."

That managed to shake her thoughts from Lucky and made her wish she *was* plugged in for some access. "Meaning what?"

The Monitor's stern, cold mien didn't change a hair, but the blue brilliance of its eyes seemed to brighten. "You are not cleared for overview data yet. Many other elements must be brought into alignment, and the precise coalescence remains somewhat undefined.

"But for you yourself, there will be a new assignment. You will require various hardware and software upgrades. Hence it becomes necessary to clear your data banks of all extraneous memories."

In discovering that the informant "Xhan" had been himself, Yoo Sobek had abruptly realized the limitations of his memories, his very existence. He couldn't recall with any clarity anything prior to a time several months before; everything before then was indistinct and impersonal—falsified and inculcated, he felt certain, to support the trumped-up personality given him on orders from the highest reaches of the Agency. On orders from the Sysops themselves.

He took the green needle of the memory fragment and pushed it carefully into his forehead, into a membrane just above his eyes.

He was in another place and time. What he was doing gave him the feeling a human would have entering a cathedral or planetarium, but that was only an analogy; he was in some other continuum and experiencing things incomparable to the physical universe.

At the time of recording, the spirit of the one whom Yoo Sobek had been was in upheaval. Sobek's observing consciousness, seeing what his former self had done, shrank away in shame.

The one he had been entered the place where all knowledge dwelt, a great trespass brought on by remorse and confusion. There, he stole a glimpse at truth on an ultimate scale. In this revelation his attention was fixed on a symbol.

The symbol was, again analogously: eight interlocking rings. He knew the symbol was applied to Adit Navel, Earth, the galaxy's idiot savant, but here it was applied in different fashion. Its use and its meaning broke all his faith and all his constraints. He turned against his fellow Sysops; in time his treason was detected and he was cast down.

The memory fragment had stopped. The one-time-use needle dissipated, but Sobek had mentally copied it. Yoo Sobek saw like a specter before his eyes eight interlocking rings.

He recalled, too, the wrong he'd done that had put his former self in such turmoil to begin with. That wrong would have to be confessed in due course; he couldn't survive without unburdening himself of it.

An internal alarm function reminded him he was running late. He brought his thoughts back to practical matters with an iron will. As always, he accepted the demands of his conjugation and its various functions without qualm: preparing for departure, he minimized his weight by urinating and defecating, splattering the trusswork and the roof far below.

Then he leaned forward, releasing his talon-hold, and launched himself into the abyss. The gale force of his fall vibrated his leathery skin and whistled along the highly abrasive horn of his beak; the cybertech landscape at the foot of the tower enlarged quickly.

There would be many things to pull together. The Intubis and this Earther, Vanderloop, were unquestionably central to what Sobek had in mind. Ka Shamok and his rebels must be addressed, too, including the fugitive gleamer Silvercup. And there was the matter of the escaped guide Sheena Hec'k and various other Terrans, including the female accompanying her, one Harley Paradise.

Most of all, and bearing in linear fashion on the mystery with which Sobek was most obsessed—the transcendent meaning of the eight interlocking rings—he must pursue the facts of the matter concerning Lucky Junknowitz, Junknowitz with his eight-ring medallion—Junknowitz the probability node.

Sobek had gleaned from the universe of data in Light Trap a sketchy idea of the toxic probability spill that had somehow hit the Terran. Perhaps there was a synchronicity to the event: Earth, the galaxy's idiot-savant planet, never seemed to be far from the Sysops' thoughts, tertiary world or no.

From Junknowitz came convections of cause and effect that linked him directly to all the cardinal matters preoccupying Sobek. Notably, there was his being mistaken for Vanderloop, who in turn was connected to the doings of the aboriginal clan. Perhaps more critically to Sobek, Junknowitz had some sort of individual tie with *both* women, Harley Paradise and Sheena Hec'k, who'd escaped al-Reem in such unprecedented fashion.

Fragmentary data on that escape, and the chimerical destination—an unindexed Adit, yet!—to which Paradise and Hec'k had fled by blind chance, implied things Sobek found incredible, but potentially central to his plan. If Hazmat really had been recontacted, sweeping changes might be near at hand.

That meant it was time for Sobek to broaden his campaign, reopen contact with his strongest, but most dangerous, ally.

Then there was Junknowitz's affiliation, however fleeting, with the fugitive gleamer and escaped informer Silvercup—who was probably an agent of the shadowy Fealty. Yet another female! What *was* it with this Junknowitz? Sobek tried to envision what methodology the man employed to utilize them and why he preferred them to males. Those who were supposed to be able to evaluate this sort of thing suggested that Junknowitz had always been maladroit in the absurd human courtship and reproductive behaviors. Had his ineptitude been a deception, a clever cover? Or had Junknowitz undergone some sort of subtle metamorphosis?

Sobek extended his wingtips just a little and stiffened his tail to stabilize himself, relishing the beak-first stoop. Bit by bit, though, he flattened his dive into a glide, angling in the direction of the nearest intra-Light Trap Adit. The avian body was interesting, but it was time to trade it in for something appropriate to his new requirements.

The state of existence in which he was most interested was, of course, the one denied to him, the one he'd enjoyed—presumably—back before it and his memory had been taken from him. Back before Yoo Sobek's exile from grace, when he himself had been a Sysop.

The wrenching of the air against his wings felt good. He cast a glance up-Trap. No assault against the Sysops had ever succeeded, or even threatened them significantly.

But no assault on them had ever been led by a fallen angel.

FOURTEEN

HAVING PASSED A distressing morning, Undershort had come to the conclusion that Earth assignment would, rather than being a career opportunity, spell the finish of his corporate climb—and he had decided as well that Salty Waters would either have to be fired or have his excretory tract plugged for the duration of the expo.

The few beings who'd stumbled by the exhibit had become rather vigorous in their determination to leave. To make matters worse, there was a problem with the refrigeration unit and the igloo was beginning to melt. The supervisor was in a deep gloom back in the interview area when Lucky stuck his head in the door. "Boss, I'm going to need a little help out here. Too much business for one man to handle."

"Waters, I must warn you that your Agency evaluation sheet will not be a pleasant document to behold once I—did you say 'business'?"

Undershort emerged, not believing his eyes when he gazed around the exhibit area. The little cul-de-sac thronged with attendees of every sort, milling and raising a din. Even more amazing, quite a number of them had come over to inspect Undershort's displays—or at least, what *ought* to have been Undershort's displays.

"Waters, what have you done to my promotional matter?"

Lucky muttered out of the side of his mouth, "I can explain everything, just trust me."

But he was looking on proudly as a remarkable potpourri of humanoid females studied the displays with great attention. In 2-D and holo, virile young males moved and posed, flashing friendly smiles and beckoning to the onlookers. Most of the browsers were travel consultants and the like, knowing a win-

147

ning destination when they saw one, but Lucky sensed a distinct non-business-related excitement in the air, too.

Actually the only suitable loops Lucky had been able to find in Undershort's grab bag of Terran background data were from the Machogear Hunkwear catalogue of Studwork Fashions Ltd., Arboles Largos, California. But what the hell; they featured athletic male models in revealing workout attire, skimpy beachwear, provocative lounging outfits and more. The females crowding the exhibit area wouldn't have been any more impressed in the Louvre or the Smithsonian, he was pretty certain of that.

There were others eyeing the beefcake show—some definitely not female and a few certifiably not humanoid—but Lucky figured that would be somebody else's problem.

"Got a lot of folks here who need info on Earth travel," Lucky went on to Undershort, who was swaying slightly. "It's a new marketing idea; Wick here can explain it all to you."

As Wick Fourmoons moved in to nail down some exclusive rights, Undershort said, "But, but how'd you get all these attendees over here? My circulars and holos had no effect—"

"Tell you in a minute." Lucky spotted a large, scaly organism coming his way and figured he had to talk even faster. "Maybe you better caucus with ol' Wicked Wick while I triage out the rest of them according to needs and means, huh?"

Wick dragged the mildly protesting Undershort back into the office area while Lucky turned to meet the approach of the lurching scaled one. "What transpires here? *Where are the rest rooms?*"

Lucky pointed. "Right over there. See?"

Over by the wall floated the jukebox holo projector he'd hijacked while the riggers' union shop steward and the stork management rep argued outside a *real* lavatory.

"What, through that nondescript door over there? Are you sure?"

Lucky affected a hurt tone. "Sure I'm sure! Just follow the crowd. There's a, ah, a big sheet-metal structure about ten yards down the first row, oughta be just right for you. Or if not, take your pick." He tried not to sweat too much saying it. Any frequent Trough traveler had come across even less conventional toilet facilities, surely.

It all pointed up yet another reason he'd have to move fast, though; he *definitely* didn't want to be around when the main Black Hole exhibit's cargo handlers showed up to break down and repack. Not in view of the alternative use to which the shipping containers were being put in the meantime.

To add to his distinct feeling of unreality, females by the dozen were tugging at his sleeve, tapping his shoulder, or otherwise vying for his attention. They were waving IDs and monetary vouchers and scheduling requests. One or two were even plucking at his waistband, curious as to whether he, like the Machogear boy-toys, sported a gold-lamé minikini.

He fought his way clear, holding up his hands. "Ladies, please! Let's get organized! Please have your contractual data and deposit ready when your name is called. Um, how about two lines—cash on this side, credit over there."

He heard a hiss and saw Wick, bending her cranelike frame into the hospitality-area doorway. "He bought it; I've got a major piece of the action. We're locking in the contract now."

Lucky ducked inside the office, where Undershort was surrounded by workstation peripherals and racing readouts. He was manipulating equipment with *three* arms of eight fingers apiece.

"Boss, how soon can I start runnin' 'em down the chute to you?" Lucky inquired. "Got a lot of people out here eager to give you money."

Undershort gave a little bleat. "Patience! I never expected such an excess of advance-option transactions!"

Lucky couldn't help grinning. "Yeah, I guess the heavies on Light Trap'll be real happy, huh? Listen, while we're on the subject, maybe you could put in a good word for me. I think I've gone about as far as I can in this phase of the industry; I'm more of a, an on-the-scene type. You know? A guide."

There was sudden hope in Undershort's voice. "You mean, you want a transfer back to the field? Why, yes, what a *capital* idea! In fact, why don't you go pack your bag?"

Lucky was a bit hurt by the supervisor's eagerness to get rid of him. He suspected it was less a matter of Undershort's wanting to hog all the credit than the tight-siphon's unease with a person he considered to be a very loose cannon.

Lucky couldn't resist tweaking him. "Of course, if you feel I'm too valuable an asset here, I wouldn't want—"

"No, no! I won't hear of it!"

"You're too good to me, sir. I noticed there's a lux little tour group coming up that might be just the thing for me. They'll be visiting Earth and the Fimblesector and some other interesting places—your homeworld, too, as it happens."

"Yes, I know; I helped arrange Root Canal visas in return for this post." There was an unusual note to Undershort's voice, something canny or devious.

"Tell you what, Waters: I'll see to your transfer right this second. I've some good friends in the personnel division and at Sing Flings. Shouldn't you be hurrying back to your hotel?"

Undershort had already bent to a high-priority intra-Agency comline; Lucky backed out of the hospitality suite only to find Wick waiting. "He's shipping you out?"

"I volunteered," Lucky corrected. At least he was on his way to way station Blits, and thence to al-Reem. He wanted to give Wick a hug for luck, but remembered that strange para-philia or taboo of hers—an aversion to him because she'd accidentally caught a glimpse of his personal equipment. "Y'know, kid, Earth may not be exactly what you have in mind. They're a lot more ah, salacious than you might be used to."

She looked to the Machogear images, then back to him. "You'd be surprised what a difference it can make to turn the lights off and curtail all visual input. Undershort's promised me an evaluation junket, so I'll know soon enough."

Lucky tried to be casual, ignoring the beings attempting to thrust money upon him, the travel consultants wanting to hire him away from Black Hole, the women curious as to whether the hunk holos represented truth in advertising.

"How'd you like to do a guy a favor?" he asked Wick Fourmoons.

When Wick went back to start processing the option con-tracts, Lucky turned for the exit. But before he could leave he heard a familiar voice behind him. "You're enjoying brisk success, Mr. Waters."

"Why, hi there, Dame Snarynxx. Yeah, things are looking up."

The four tentacula on her head were swinging independently as she looked around. He noticed that she didn't leave a slime trail like the slugs he'd seen on Earth; no, a very prim and proper old gal. "How marvelous that you're in such a strategic location, Mr. Waters. Perhaps you could be so good as to enlighten me about something."

She lowered her blunt, glistening head to speak confiden-tially. "I noticed when I was using the *convenience* just now that there are routing labels on all the, the sanitary booths back there, and that someone's addressed them all to the Sysops in care of Black Hole headquarters on Light Trap. Why in creation would anyone want to ship such, er, materials to the Sysops?''

Lucky sniggered. ''Let's just say that such materials don't *always* run downhill, ma'am.''

The groundswell of resentment among other Citizen Watch sit-room personnel against Ziggy Forelock, or more specifically against what people were calling his Air of Hostility, had risen a notch: when he woke up in his sour-smelling sleeping bag he found that the swing-shift crew had moved him out into the corridor along with his few poor possessions, pointedly setting him down near the fire exit.

Symptomatic of the point of near-exhaustion to which overwork, paranoia, and obsessive computer phreaking and video lenscrafting had brought him, he'd never felt a thing. At least they'd had the decency to position him in a security-cam blind spot, or he'd probably have woken up in the street or an Urgent Care facility.

Getting up felt like being attacked by an auto-body frame-straightening machine; the corridor floor was marble and his mattress pad a half-length one that stopped just below his hips. When, daypack of belongings under one arm, mattress under the other, sleeping bag dragging behind him pathetically, he tried to reenter the CW sit-room, Kit Lumex—who shared swings with Shlomo ''Slow-Mo'' Naiman—physically blocked him, bracing her feet and forearms on either side of the doorframe.

''No chance, La Zig! You're liable to set off the smoke detectors.''

''Look—''

''No, *you* look!'' Slow-Mo glanced up from the bank of monitors by which Citizen Watch maintained surveillance on the Hagadorn Pinnacle's windows, ledges, balconies, and so forth, alert for would-be downcasters—suicidal jumpers. He gave his head an angry shake, making the frizzy locks of his Izro lash around his eyes. ''Everybody's cut you slack, but you're over into biochem warfare, man!''

That brought Ziggy up short. A lot of the arts-media-cyber fringe types who drifted into CW work weren't big on personal hygiene, and Watchers tended to be tolerant. Slow-Mo himself was a cine-synther whose days-long bouts of creative frenzy sometimes left him smelling noticeably less than party fresh.

Kit softened some. "If you're that desperate for money, maybe we can swing you a short-term loan. Go home, Zig; shower, change clothes. We'll cover for you."

"Thanks, you two—" But he was shaking his head. Due to both embarrassment and operant paranoia, he couldn't confess that he'd been bivouacking in the Hagadorn Pinnacle not in order to work multiple shifts but because it was the safest place he could think of, closely monitored by both private security and the local precinct systems, and he was afraid of being assassinated or kidnapped by invaders from outer space. Holing up in the sit-room made sense for other reasons as well, none of which he wanted to discuss with the swing shifters.

Food and drink were readily available in the lobby vending machines and eateries, but the health-club locker rooms were inaccessible, as were the various executive spas, building-staff shower rooms, and penthouse bathrooms. Whore's baths at the fourteenth-floor rest-room sinks had been about it for a couple of weeks now; he didn't much rejoice in his own company these days.

But he had no intention of setting foot outside. Most of the people he knew had gone incommunicado or been disappeared—and at least one individual had been blasted wide open right in the middle of the Rodeo East mall. No, no, no: this was a bad time to travel.

But before he could retrench with a good story Kit Lumex relented. "All right, calm down. Here: at least go up to the mop closet on fifteen and blast off the worst of it."

She was holding out a faucet extension hose with shower-massage fixture and some institutional green fabric in one hand, a keycard with the Hagadorn crest on it in the other. "This was the best we could do for now."

He accepted the card woodenly, the sleeping bag falling from his hand. "Kit, I don't know what to say."

"Hey, take that fartsack with you!" Slow-Mo interjected without moving his eyes from the bank of screens. "That gets the Superfund treatment, too!"

Jerking a head toward a security cam, Ziggy was about to point out that somebody was sure to pick up his foray, but Kit anticipated him. "It's all right; go on." He was too tired of stinking, too groggy from his long zee, for his chronic suspicions to give him pause; he went.

In the crown jewel Hagadorn Pinnacle much of the routine

cleaning and janitorial work was done by robot, remote, and autosystem, but a good deal of human toil was still inevitable. So while there were fewer mop closets than in pre-Turn buildings, they did exist. These too had resisted Ziggy's infiltration attempts, but plainly Slow-Mo and the doc-eyed, zaftig Kit had resources or lines of influence he lacked.

There was no way to rig a shower curtain but what the hell; there was a drain in the floor for spillage. The clothes turned out to be green hospital scrubs along with a large hand towel. He put them up on a supplies shelf to keep them out of the battle zone. Lacking soap, he found a squeeze bottle of eco-correctly mild detergent that would do. Standing in the mop sink, straddling the faucet and playing the water over himself with the nozzle fixture, he came fully awake and had time to think.

The first thing he had to face was that this siege couldn't go on. Not only was somebody in CW supervision bound to find out about it and have him put out of the Pinnacle, but there were other dynamics going that were bringing crises to him, like it or not.

The homicide investigation into the murder of Rashad Tittle would likely involve him soon; the disappearance of so many of his friends was also odds-on to earn him guest-star exposure at the station house. The late Bullets Strayhand, ex-cop and investigator for Altamont Insurance, had passed the word before his death that at least one NYPD captain was on Black Hole's side and had the posse members' days low-numbered.

Ziggy dutifully hauled his sleeping bag into the tublike sink, soaping it and soaking it, doing a grape-stomping dance to get out the worst of the grime. Then he gave his clothes the same runaround, trying not to think about how all this would look if some commercial janitorial engineer happened along.

The good news he'd hoped against hope to hear from Lucky, from Sean and the *Crystal Harmonic* assault team, from Asia or Brax or even from the missing Harley Paradise and Sheena Hec'k, had never arrived. The only two factors Ziggy had going for him, if you wanted to characterize it that way, were themselves troubling, enigmatic, quite possibly dangerous—and incorporeal: an aboriginal telegeist and a self-aware cybernetic entity.

By the time he got everything as wrung out as he could, it was almost time for shift change. The scrubs turned out to be in Kit's voluptuous but short size; he transferred his belt, gathered up the rest of his sopping wash, and beat it back to the sit room. Kit laughed when she got a look at him, and even Slow-Mo smiled.

Ziggy's makeover appeared to reassure them he was all right for the time being and they logged out and left together. Ziggy draped his wet things over the coatrack and available furniture, dug out a vending machine two-pack of guava-frosted bran twists, and drew some ice water to wash them down, then set himself to work.

"But if you want to hide out," Lynka insisted, "what could be better than this place?" She tossed back blond hair that hung thigh-long, then went back to repairing her wooden work platform using C-clamps and a Makita hot-epoxy gun. "Asia, dahling, around here we've been trying to get the world to sit up and take notice of us for years and nothing's worked yet."

Asia Boxdale had to admit the willowy Swede had something there. The Femmes Fatales rad-fem urban artists' commune of which she was an intermittent member had yet to produce work that interested collectors or qualified for the ultimate compliment: to be warehoused by the Arts Advisory Council.

Like Lynka, Asia had been trying to win wider acceptance—in her case, for performance art that her limited audiences loved but producers, grant committees, angels, and other sponsors invariably shied away from.

"This is a little different, Lynk," she said now, gazing out over Brooklyn. The huge plastic fifteenth-floor window didn't look like it had been washed since the Turn; the bacchantes weren't big on homemaking. (*"Femmes Fatales*—Art is Wymin's Work," as they liked to put it.)

Asia was gazing over a rooftop landscape of geodesic-domed gardens, solar power arrays and thermal systems, windmills and chimney scrubbers—with pigeon coops tucked in here and there among the water tanks. The revivified East River teemed with carefully orchestrated and EPA-certified shipping: double-hulled tankers, containerized barges, and fuel-efficient SWATH cargo craft, as well as immensely powerful but clean-running aquajet tugs. Manhattan was a prismland retrofitted with photovoltaic panels, heat sinks, and wind-energy collectors that had been set in among the satellite dishes, microwave towers, and helo pads.

Somewhere, somewhere out there, Braxmar Koddle was disappearing down his own escape route, pursuing his own goals, just as she must.

Sunset was throwing long shadows over the city and through the cavernous, cluttered loft that was the commune's work space. "For once, anonymity would suit me just fine." Asia sighed, turning back to Lynka. "But it wouldn't be fair to ask the Femmes to pull in their horns just so I can avoid attention."

She was sipping a cup of *te de mate*, sitting in a window box seat wrapped in a light cotton *yakata* she'd borrowed from petite Texas Twister Belle Wringer; Lynka was so tall that Asia trod the knees of all her stuff. "Besides, I've got people to do and things to see."

Lynka snorted. "That your new role? Secret Agent?" She turned on a droplight to study her latest work. Lynka "performed paint," sometimes alone, sometimes with a friend or two, by means of body movement on canvases big as king-sized beds. "Princess Tiger Lily versus the Illuminati?"

Asia's mouth twisted; maybe it hadn't been wise to broach the subjects of hidden conspiracies, invisible subversion, and outsiders walking among human beings. "You know me better than that, *Nordfleisch*. But certain ideas have taken hold of me, things I want to use."

Pale, rangy Lynka gave Asia a brief glare at the use of the "Northern Meat" nickname some superannuated Helmut Newton devotee had tried to hang on her a few years back. But then she shrugged and went back to work with the Makita gun without a follow-up question. Between the two artists there was no need to explain what Asia would use the mysterious something *for*.

Asia hadn't explained this part to Brax—he had enough things on his mind. Asia's original notion had been to disappear off all scanners, dispense with documented existence, prowl the murk of underground existence, and eventually report back via her performance art. The Femmes were willing to help.

But as arrangements to penetrate the terra incognita went on, Asia realized from street buzz, rumors of XTs sighted or overheard, third-hand reports, and tie-ins with the things the loft crew had already learned that the Agency's conspiracies reached low as well as high. Over the past few days her aspirations had widened and her intentions had become a lot more complex.

Having glimpsed the shadowy halfworld of Black Hole

machinations, having learned something of galaxy-spanning plots and world-trashing rackets, she'd been unable to get back her interest in her original concept. There was only one theme worth pursuing: the vast, dark epic of the Black Hole Travel Agency. That would be half her purpose in plunging into the subterranean life of which the Femmes Fatales were only a kind of peephole and spy's dead drop.

The other half of Asia's motive in finding out what she could about Black Hole was that she might come across something Sean or Ziggy or one of the others could use—or Lucky, when he got back. They were off in all directions surveilling cruise vessels, phreaking corporate files or teleporting around the galaxy without seeming to realize the Agency's influence was felt among the disaffected and the disenfranchised, too. There might be sources of intelligence and avenues of attack no one else had looked for; if so, Asia could at least pass word of them.

Lynka had some problem with the Makita, and adjusted the nozzle and shot a few measured globs of epoxy at the wall to clear it. She clamped the leg on her platform and straightened back up. "Very well. The others all agreed; we said we'd help you and we will. But get your mind right, 'cause we'll be dealing with some mean scumbags.''

The flour-mill creaking of the ancient freight elevator cranked up. As a safety precaution, only the Femmes knew the touchpad code that gave street access to the car and activated it, but the muffled noise of some kind of commotion came drifting up the shaft. Unfortunately, the war-surplus security cam inside the car was down and nobody'd gotten around to fixing it.

A pre-Turn model, the elevator wheezed and squeaked, ascending slowly. Lynka crossed to the barrel-like umbrella stand near the elevator gates. She casually selected a sawed-off pool cue from the jumble of knobkerries, Malayan *parang ihlang* catchpoles, aluminum softball bats, wooden *bokken* practice-swords, and other Sullivan Law–legal weapons the Femmes had procured, been given, or taken as war trophies over the years.

Asia saw Lynka relax as the car neared the fifteenth floor, though; they could both tell who was arriving home from the voice and the volume and the choice of obscenities. Several seconds later the safety gates were wrenched open by an athletic cinnamon-skinned young woman who was already well along in what she had to say about the plight of creative people.

Mimawanda Shakara Lowenstein—Screamin' Mimi— glared at Lynka. "Girl, you see anybody's *schlong* still hangin' outta me anywhere? 'Cause I sure took a fuckin' today!''

Mimi's body-hugging bronze TomatoSkin unitard showed a well-knit physique and some NYC-August sweat stains. Her barbed-wire dreadlocks swung as she shook her head in anger and hurled down the ink-blue nylon gym bag she'd had over one shoulder. "Did that 'Water Ways' gig for DelVeccio? Started talkin' up ARTrocity to 'im? And it's like I'm carrying something the Center for Disease Control should know about.''

Lynka was replacing the pool cue. "DelVeccio backed out of backing you?''

"Won't even introduce me around. Shoulda *potched* him upside his head an' flushed him like a dead goldfish.'' Mimi eyed the weapons in the umbrella stand, perhaps planning a felony.

Her creative vision, ARTrocity, into which Mimi periodically drafted the other Femmes as well as Asia and anyone else who didn't have a good excuse, involved complex and horrifying displays of human carnage and environmental destruction. Animatronics, holographics, live-action S/FX, and elaborate VirtNet effects were all used to pound home the cruelty involved in everything from thermonuclear strikes to stepping on cockroaches.

To date ARTrocity had only been made manifest in very modest doses; the sort of thing Mimi wanted to stage involved expenditures that would make a Pentagon budget planner blanch. Art agent Leo DelVeccio had promised to connect her with money people if she gofered for the spray-and-strobe-lights "Water Ways'' recitals that were his wife's claim to genius.

Mimi spied Asia and advanced on her with the powerful grace that had made her a college volleyball star. "You ever notice all the really good ideas tend to get shitcanned, there, Yum-Yum? I don't mean warehoused or stolen, I mean it's like a conspiracy—somebody just drops the blade on 'em. After that, the artist can't even get herself arrested.''

Asia began, "Yes, we were just—''

"'Course I'm right! Otherwise over at Lincoln Center they'd be taking down Agnes de Mille's portrait and hanging yours. And reallocating me some DARPA funds. *Kish mir in tochis!* Hey, Box, you still going to the Ded Dawg for your Dantesque sociopolitical spelunking?''

"She is," Lynka answered for Asia. "We were just waiting for you and the others to show up."

Mimi kicked aside the gym bag. "Good, I wouldn't mind some trouble. I saw Lovely and the Laptop Twins; them and the others're gonna meet us at the Dawg. C'mon, Box, let's scrounge you some appropriate eveningwear."

Asia thought about objecting to being outfitted, but the Femmes had made it clear that attendance at the Ded Dawg, where her delvings underground were to begin, involved a certain amount of theater. Culottes and a blazer would be like asking for trouble.

Lynka and Asia trailed Mimi back through the byways of the loft, which were laid out in a more comprehensible way than Asia's housemates had been able to manage. Soon they reached a community costume area: rows of clothes rods, piles of cartons, mounds of garment bags and hatboxes, orchards of shoe trees, palisades of footlockers, musty trunks, and duffel bags. They pushed past gowns, doublets and hose, pieces of armor, an EVA rig, a raccoon coat, togas, kimonos, a paramecium outfit, a Turkish general's uniform, and a cleverly articulated scorpion getup. Asia patted one of her favorite props, the statue of Juno that Lynka had hijacked from the Bryn Mawr campus.

Lynka switched on a sodium light. "I was thinking some of the senior-safe garments the street-bangers adapt—''

Screamin' Mimi shook her head so that the barbed-wire braids flailed. "None of those padding-and-support separates! People'll think Asia's a wuss. She's gotta look *take*, but she's gotta look *toxic*."

She was rummaging around in a bin. "Look here: the gear Belle pulled together for that 'Wild One' gig oughta fit." She was digging out ripped denim, creased black leather, and more, tossing things on the floor. "Well Box, you waitin' for a backup band and a dollar in your G-string? Try 'em on."

Asia shed the *yakata*, feeling schoolgirlish in white cotton panties and bra. The faded jeans fit well enough for length and in the hips, though the waist was a bit loose. The muscle T-shirt was grungy and baggy but it would do. The real prize was the jacket.

Somehow Belle had gotten her hands on an honest-to-god Ross Langlitz motorcycle jacket, hand-built pre-Turn—maybe 1960s, 1970s—and so small that it might have been made for a child. Someone had kept it supple. This was the second time Asia had tried on the Langlitz; it was cracked and stressed but still comfortable. The details struck her again: arms set forward for a rider leaning over a set of handlebars, sleeves extra long so that the wrists would be protected, waistline lower in the rear to keep the wearer's back covered and warm.

Asia zipped the wrists closed. Maybe Mimi had a point: zipped tight and belted fast, the Langlitz made her feel protected, formidable.

There were other things, too—the Harley-Davidson chaps were almost as broken-in as the Langlitz jacket and made her think for a second of the vanished Harley Paradise. The metallic-tinted extrusion aviator shades were a good touch; the Wesco boots were wearable if Frankensteiny. Her rose-lacquered fingernails looked incongruous emerging from fingerless biker gloves.

But when Mimi held out the revolver in its buscadero-style gun-belt holster, Asia stepped back.

"No, absolutely not." Like Lucky, she hated the sight of firearms, the thought of them—the amoral cruelty and stupidity of them.

"Asia, it's part of the look at the Dawg," Lynka said gently. "Not so much pre-Turn as *non*-Turn, you know?"

"Besides, *bubeleh*-chan," Mimi added, "it's not even loaded, see?" She'd plucked the safety thong off the hammer spur and drawn the pistol. "Sidehammer percussion pistol, baby Allen 'n' Wheellock single-action six-shot."

Mimi twirled it around her finger deftly. "Only, no bullets, no powder, no percussion caps."

Where'd the Femmes pick up all this *gun* shit? Asia was shaking her head, the long midnight hair rippling with glossy highlights. "I don't care." She gathered up the other things, the size-four motorcycle belt-drive belt and the rest, and fled.

By the time Mimi and Lynka suited up and rejoined her near the elevator, Asia had gathered her few belongings and packed them into the ballistic nylon designer rucksack that was all she'd carried when she left home. She was suited up, seated on Lynka's repaired platform with the ruck between her Wescos, staring thoughtfully into space.

Lynka and Mimi were costumed, too. To put a proper skew on things Lynka had done herself up as a neotech Asian post-punk peasant, the big Swede wearing a graffitied straw coolie hat, sandals made from a truck tire, black nightfighter pajamas and viewslit IR goggles, the flaxen hair caught up in a hawser of French braid. She'd velcroed into Bangladeshi web gear, and on her shoulder was a dummy Vietnamese RPG launcher.

Mimi was decked out all in flowing whites as Lawrence of Arabia, complete with gold scimitar and riding quirt.

Mimi still had the gun belt in one hand; Asia took a better look at it. It wasn't a real antique, but rather some kind of pretend-gunfighter thing, all doublestitching and contoured cut, roller buckle and thigh-tie. What she was noticing now, though, was that the muzzle end of the holster was angled forward somewhat, and open rather than sewn shut.

Before they could start reminding her that the visit to the Dawg had been undertaken at her request or that she'd been told flat out it would require concessions, Asia stood up and held out her hand for the gun belt.

"Let's party," she said.

FIFTEEN

LOITERING ACROSS THE street from the Femmes' loft waiting for Asia Boxdale to reemerge, pretending to help Nikkei ogle an RPEV showroom, Mickey Formica had time to catalogue his discontents. The roadway-powered electric vehicles were rounded and colorful as jelly candies; the demo displays cycled over and over, opening and closing the cars' doors and hoods and roofs, unplugging from their in-town power plants and reconnecting them to over-the-road packages, holographing EPA and easy-payment-plan data that downplayed the tremendous expense and red tape involved in owning a private motor vehicle.

Tanabe's *jonin*'s advice had made quite an impression on Nikkei, it was plain. He was remote and preoccupied, as if he was trying to achieve oneness with his selfhood or vice versa.

Contrary to what the old whitebeard-*Wasabeis* always preached about the virtues of patience, the two partners preferred action to waiting. Until recently, that is; until they met up with that Kamimura's ninja. Nikkei seemed to have picked up some kind of old-country inscrutability, a staid introspection he wasn't cutting Mickey in on.

Then again, maybe it was something about that exchange back in *Tengu Mountain* with Miss Sato that had the brother all gasketed up. Nikkei and Mickey had never had much use for deep involvement with the ladies before—good times only. It made Mickey uneasy that Sato seemed to be on some encrypted freq with his main man.

Mickey had to admit that having Tanabe's backing made for a whole different kind of trip, though. The ordeal the two had been put through was manifestly a rite of passage, and now—at least for the time being—they were golden. Phony documents, cash, and other money resources, Sato had materialized effort-lessly. Some fractal wetwork gear was waiting in a lux New York safe house. Tanabe was giving them a taste of upscale operations. They were still on orders to avoid Bhang.

Nevertheless, Mickey wasn't happy with Nikkei's new inner-serenity act, and he was more than ready to eighty-six the sneaking-and-peeking routine—this boring shadowing of Asia Boxdale. Mickey was all for busting into the Femmes' loft, neutralizing whoever got in their way—feminist, corporate, or XT—grabbing the bitch and getting down to cases. Making some info flow.

Before Mickey could start militating, though, the front door of the converted factory building opened and Asia, Mimi, and Lynka emerged in costume.

"Well, shit, willya lamp the Mardi Gras?" Mickey grumbled. Nikkei didn't answer, making ready to tail the objective instead, so Mickey yielded to the inevitable. Bird-dogging Boxdale had proven so easy despite her laughable precautions that they didn't have to split up, work different sides of the street, or any of that. They'd even switched off the surveillance headsets, camouflaged to look like VirtNet gear.

Exactly as planned, Asia and the others had stepped into the puddle of aroma-coded tracer chemical Mickey and Nikkei had left at the front door of their building. Nobody used radioactives anymore; too many BTFHA and EPA sensors abroad in the land. Not that the duo thought they really needed such tricks to keep up with a naive cupcake like Boxdale.

Both partners had filled out some in the wake of what Mickey had come to call their Predator Tour, but Nikkei hadn't bulked back to nearly his previous fireplug silhouette. He looked like just one more *kudzu* who'd gotten into bodybuilding, maybe to compensate for his height.

They were dressed in retailored dodderwear; it had quickly become apparent in certain circles that clothing developed for older citizens, offering protective padding against falls and other injuries as well as roominess and give in some places and elastic support in others, could be adapted as rumble rags. But where gang-hangers customized their attire with their colors, tags, patches, and the rest, Mickey and Nikkei looked like a pair of aging shop-by-vid tesseracts whose mothers chose their wardrobes, a calculated effect. An added advantage was that the baggy dodderwear—patterned in unbelievably what-was

"BUY USA" mottos and other nationalistic slogans—was loose enough to conceal the hardware strapped to the duo.

The aroma-coded sensor locked on to the women's trail, but the odd couple didn't really need it; Mickey switched off the sniffer and put it back inside his roomy untucked shirt.

As they set off Mickey remarked idly, "The blonde's *shibui*—too cool." He liked 'em leggy.

Nikkei didn't respond, which Mickey chose to take as an affront; lamping women was one of their bonding activities. "Hey, my lowman brother, my *genin*-homedog?"

Nikkei had pulled on and opaqued the visor that had been dangling around his neck. "Good to go."

"You fine-focused on the mission, *homme*-san? Keep me current here. You sure?"

"*Cock*-sure, my *kono imo* bro."

Mickey hesitated. "Look, I don't wanna barge into your kitchen, but this job's about my ass too. What went down between you and your father? Is he gonna deal straight with us or try to chop us or what? Once we get Asia B. locked down you and me need to raise a few topics on the call-in line, y'know?"

He was half expecting Nikkei to balk but the Japanese surprised him. "You're right, Mick. We secure the dancing girl, then I'll lay it all out for you."

That left Mickey speechless. He almost slipped into a step or two of *yoko aruki* sideways walking until he caught himself; he and his pard were supposed to be flaming rubes, after all. And now that he knew he had so much more to learn about the secret arts, Mickey was determined not to fuck up ever again.

For reasons she didn't question it was an immense relief to Harley when she laid hands on the Ergosport Superpro field-hockey stick on the other side of the Adit once she and Sheena leapt through together in a literal blaze of glory.

Doubly so because they found themselves in some dark, echoing, gargantuan place that could've been Dracula's Astro-dome. The light of the Adit connection had already faded; the women's eyes took a few moments to adjust as they skidded to a stop headlong on a dais hard as marble, thick with dust and drifted grit. About the only light came from various worksta-tion monitors, banks of instruments and control boards—and those were winking out. Elsewhere out in the abyssal dark, smoldering fires were burning themselves out in the duff, loam, bat crap or whatever it was that carpeted the floor. Or was it ground?

The place into which Harley and Sheena had leapt willy-nilly from al-Reem was upchuckingly, consciousness-threateningly fetid. Harley gagged, eyes burning and watering, and even Sheena coughed. In addition to the basic stench of the place they could smell electrical fires and burning feces, and over everything a heavy sweetish-acrid pungency Harley recalled from standing near a twenty-one-gun salute on the Great Mall in Washington.

It was a little cold for a mini, and her open-toe Ferrari heels hadn't been made for traction in deep-shag loam-guano-dust. As she rebuckled them, Harley blinked, glancing around, gripped the taped shaft of the hockey stick. It was pretty clear from the looks of things that Snow White hadn't found her happy ending. "Where are we?"

Sheena Hec'k grunted, shaking back her red mane and falling limberly into a martial-arts crouch. "That unlisted Adit that appeared on the instruments on al-Reem, I presume."

Which didn't explain much, but Harley tabled the subject for the moment; she had even more pressing concerns. "The lights are going out."

Sheena, already on the move, was well aware of that. She bent to a workstation whose controls were hoary with dust and crud. Harley, following with her trusty stick at the ready, was reading random holo and flatscreen scans.

" 'Adit interface emergency termination.' 'Level Two power loss.' 'Adit-closure governor re-engaged.' 'Haz—' Look! Sheena, see that one? 'Hazmat Adit at full lockdown.' Is that where we are, 'Hazmat'?"

Sheena stopped in her frantic quest for some kind of illumination control. "Hazmat," she breathed in the tone of voice Harley would've expected from somebody stumbling onto a bookmobile full of Dead Sea Scrolls. "Damned if it's not!" Then another bank of lights went out and, hissing "Oops!," she went back to work.

Harley was about to demand that Sheena keep her in the loop when there came a lunatic cry like a hyena on fantazine. It set off a whole chorus of whoops, chitters, cackles, and warbles, pealing from the blackness above and to every side.

Not so long ago Harley, confronted by that infernal bleacher crowd, would've lost her grip literally and figuratively. But whatever the nanites were doing to her kept her from going veg with sheer fright. It wasn't that they made her brave; it was just that they kept her from being lobotomized and paralyzed by the traumas of the Trough, letting her cope instead of freeze. On the other hand, she thought, how was that different from *being* brave?

Harley patted the toe of her stick on the floor gunge two or three times and planted her feet for a better stance. "Shoo, g'way now!" she called into the Stygian night. "G'way now, *shoo!*"

Sheena gave her a troubled glance, then went back to what she was doing.

An abrupt silence fell in the Sepulcher of the Adit. It was followed by a lot of slithering and rustling, but none of the XT barn owls, sewer rats, jackals, or whatever gave any evidence of departing. Neither did it sound like they were coming any closer. Harley entertained a vision of the unseen screamers as a local version of those scummy NYC types who made smoochy noises out the windows of their delivery vans or sexist mockery from the safety of a pack of buddies. The imaging gave her a dollop of confidence.

To one side a single tiny screen took on a wan glow. Harley's night vision was sufficiently adjusted for her to see eyes—a sea of eyes to all sides. They were every color, size and shape: singles, doubles, three-in-a-row, clusters, and compound bug jobs—all watching her as the light dwindled down again. Various large bodies could be heard to scuttle, heave, or undulate, the eyes moving out to flank the two women on all fronts. Harley gulped, but parted the air like Zorro with flourishing practice swings. "Sheena? There's something here I think you should see—"

"Yes, I see them, Harley. Try to keep them off my back; the lights are our only chance."

The eyes began moving in. Harley tried to swallow despite the fact that there was absolutely no saliva in her mouth. She was backing toward Sheena when the lights came up again, a bit anyway, as Sheena found the control she'd been looking for. Harley, blinking, had a fleeting impression of a menagerie out of some monster-maker's detox nightmare, all pulling back hastily to avoid being seen.

Harley almost missed her footing in a depression in the scat-mulch she was standing on. The crud clung to her panty-hosed feet, and she was sure she could feel worms and chiggers burrowing around. She'd gratefully have traded the Ferrari slingbacks and every blessed designer shoe on Rodeo East for a pair of cross-training ankleboots like Sheena's. But there wasn't time to dwell on that.

A quick glance showed her she'd almost fallen into—what? An impression this symmetrical suggested something artificial, and it was pressed in as deeply as a bulldozer treadmark. It might have been the imprint of some kind of huge jack base-plate or outrigger footing, but now that there was a bit more light Harley could see more like it all around the dais, some superimposed on one another. She had the abrupt and eerie conviction they were *footprints*.

The women were in a feeble, wavering little island of bright-ness under the small pillared dome deep within the sepulcher. Harley forgot about the tracks when something gabbled at her from the night and that panorama of eyes closed in another smidgen.

"Whatever energy source was running this installation," Sheena concluded calmly, "it's off-line or gone now. Some-one tried to activate the Adit only minutes ago, then left before the start-up was complete; it may be that they didn't know the diagnostic and fail-safe programs had to run before the Adit itself could function. The reserve power is being depleted very rapidly. Moreover, the equipment has been shot up somewhat—weapons fire or collateral battle damage. There's no fading out of here, at least for now."

Harley was still watching those eyes. "Excuse me?" she called to them dubiously. "Which of you is in charge here?"

Sheena pulled Harley back a little as the light grew dimmer and the unseen lurkers closed in. "These beasts aren't the ones who tried to open the Adit."

"But whoever it was might still be around!" Harley cupped one hand to her mouth. "Hello-oo!" She could just make out surfaces reflecting the sparse light out there—smooth surfaces that might be metal or concrete. There were also what looked to be spent flares—tiny flames sputtering and dying.

Sheena yelled, too, but the only answer was echoes. The monsters in the dark, vexed by the shouting, set up their own chorus of squeals, grunts, clackings, and more.

"It *could* have been some sort of power surge or computer malf that opened the Adit," Sheena hazarded. She was glanc-ing around for any kind of weapon, something to throw—even a spent shell casing—but could find none. The firefight she could still smell had probably been fought with caseless rounds.

Harley was in no mood for logic or candor. "Don't lie to me, something *brought* us here! You recognized that name, 'Hazmat.' Sheena, be honest with me!"

They were retreating together to the Adit area, under the dome. "There're time-distorted tales," Sheena admitted. "Vague rumors; blurry legends."

"All right, maybe they're fairy stories, but we need *something* to go on," Harley contended.

Sheena didn't bother to argue, but her eyes searched the darkness as she spoke. "Hazmat was a planet excelling in advanced AI design; they were doing a lot of leading-edge nanite and R and D, too. One hundred eighty-odd baseline-years ago, the way most versions have it, Hazmat phreakers and Black Hole darksiders co-conspired to interface Hazmat's most advanced AIs and the top-echelon SIs on Light Trap. Searching for some ultimate cybernetic godhead, some claim. Others say they were seeking the Outline, a mythical Adit that'll take you beyond the galaxy."

"Scat!" Harley took an ineffective swipe at those distant eyes with her hockey stick, and the eyes paused. To Sheena she said, "Well where are all these R-&-D Hazmatters? We need help!"

Sheena let out a quick breath, not quite a laugh. "Something went wrong. It brought down Apocalypse on Hazmat: an insane aggregate AI that styled itself Warhead. Maybe the Sysops did it on purpose, who can say? Except—the tales have it that a little piece of Light Trap's SIs and a big piece of Warhead, conjoined in the form of a data egg, were spun loose. And that the data egg is the key to Hazmat and Light Trap, the Outline and the Sysops alike—to your left!"

Harley saw what she meant: a papery tentacle something like a black feather boa, wriggling for Harley's foot. *"Ewgh!"*

Making more barf sounds, she brought the toe of the stick down on it and, when the tip of the tentacle reared up in pain and surprise, caught it with a slap shot that sent it flying back the way it had come. Something out there made a sound like a scalded baboon, and the general advance paused again.

Sheena thought fast. "Our best course might be to climb as high onto this apparatus as we can and try to—"

"Listen! Did you hear that? That gonging?"

Sheena stared into the blackness. "Not gonging, *hammering*. Metal on metal." They both squinted, trying to penetrate the murk. "Something's out there," Sheena added. "Many things, see?"

They were the structures Harley had faintly discerned. Her eyes more accustomed to the light now, she made out the edges of what she took to be large, irregularly shaped metal structures or machines, big as bungalows or earth-moving equipment, here and there on the endless plain of shadows. Somebody out there was alive.

That makes three of us, Harley consoled herself, hefting her hockey stick. That's a start.

PART TWO

Synch or Swim

SIXTEEN

"I'M SUPPOSED TO wear *what*?" Lucky exploded.

"Film shorts," the Root Canal Immigration Control officer repeated.

The being, a walking clamshell indistinguishable from supervisor Undershort except that it was even smaller, tapped one foot impatiently. "There was nothing faulty in my pronunciation, Thing. 'A sheer pink wearever and film shorts.' The regs make it mandatory, did no one brief you?"

Probably it was something taught in basic Black Hole guide school but Lucky didn't have that training, just a credential-faking Wise-Guise. "Oh, those. Right."

The two-legged clam held out the gossamer jumpsuit and see-through boxers. " 'The Un-Coverall,' " Lucky said, sighing fatalistically. " 'Legal Briefs.' "

"Perfectly conventional attire," was the Canalian's prim riposte. "And it helps us keep tabs on you irritatingly identical humanoids. Pink wearevers for one-day transient visas, chartreuse for diplomatic personnel, lavender for resident aliens, and so on. And, of course, the diaphanous nature of the required garments discourages the concealment of contraband. Now, will you don the required ensemble, or shall we send you back through the Adit?"

"Anything you say, Mussels." Lucky frowned at the gauzy government-tissue outfit. "Wouldja mind not calling me 'Thing'?"

When he'd first been kidnapped into the Trough, Sheena Hec'k had busted his stamen by telling him wearevers were primarily worn by males. That had turned out not to be the case; wearevers were the jumpsuits of the humanoid wardrobe.

But he still felt a little uncomfortable about them and the sight of the wispy pink getup was like some hex come true.

He considered citing nudity taboos but realized that might get him nabbed. Moreover, the immigration officer was ignoring him, busy checking its implant scanner. Lucky tried to look casual, though the Root Canalian probably couldn't have told casual from a conniption without diagnostic equipment.

"Salty Waters, you are cleared to proceed," said the functionary. "You must notify the Public Order Directorate if you take lodgings, wish to travel outside authorized areas, or overstay your visa for any reason. Failure to do so will result in permanent termination."

There was another kind? Lucky was shaking his head, for reinforcement rather than effect. "I'm just here to pick up the tour group I'm guiding and get going."

That didn't appear to mollify the inspector much. "Yes, yes, you aliens will use any excuse to come tramping all over our fair planet. You underwent the proscribed medical prophylaxes before fading here?"

"You bet."

For some reason that reply made the inspector study him closely for a moment, two eyes staring unwinkingly from the darkness of the shell. "You'd better have. If the Sneeze Guards detect in you any sign of illness or allergy, they'll run you in for diagnostic dissection. Now, before you go anywhere I demand that you explain the function of *this* object."

Everything in Lucky's paltry bag of possessions had passed muster, including the Earthman suit—except for the Magic 8 Ball. The inspector suspiciously turned it this way and that in a rocklike manipulator, his shell as close to shut as he could get it, as if he expected the orb to explode.

"Religious talisman," Lucky recited, "like my customs declaration says. Look, quit shaking it, willya? You'll get it all bubbly inside."

"What *kind* of talisman?" the inspector shot back. "We'll have no fetish-worshiping zealotry on Root Canal! Here we pay clean homage to the all-embracing Trees that give us life. We invest our faith in the boughs that embrace the heavens. To the roots that anchor the soil."

"The 8 Ball's just a, um, psychic focuser, see? Divinational aid. Watch, I'll show you."

He looked on the 8 Ball as a good-luck charm but it wasn't worth arguing over, or jeopardizing his plan to save Harley and

Sheena. The important thing was to pick up the tour group to which Undershort had managed to have him assigned and hurry it along as far as way station Blits, a matter of two days. From there he could get to al-Reem to rescue Harley and Sheena.

Besides, he was eager to get a look at Root Canal, by all reports a fantastic world. So if the inspector didn't buy the demo and confiscated the 8 Ball, no big deal.

"I get up in the morning f'r instance, y'know? And ask it, 'Will it be sunny today?' "

He was holding the 8 Ball down where the customs officer could get a look at it. The Root Canalian sidled closer as if hypnotized. The answer floated up through the inky fluid to the little glass bull's-eye: WITHOUT A DOUBT.

The inspector sniffed. "Not much trick to that, is there? It's *always* sunny on Root Canal!"

Lucky was in no position to argue. "Oh, sure; it's just a harmless little—"

"What about some more precise question?" the creature pressed. "What, for example, of Puddle Pod's prospects in the fourth race at Chlorophyll Mesa this afternoon?"

"Huh?"

"Spare me your disingenuous gruntings, Thing! *I've* heard the rumors of Black Hole's experiments with probability and causality!"

The inspector glanced around to make sure they were unobserved, having to swivel his entire shell because he had no neck. "I can be a powerful friend or a formidable enemy," he hinted.

Lucky faltered, "B-but what about your faith in the boughs that embrace the heavens?"

"My faith in the boughs that embrace the heavens cost me two hundred big ones on a trifecta last week. Now how's about Puddle Pod in the fourth?"

Yielding to the inevitable, Lucky gave the 8 Ball a couple of turns. As the two watched, up floated BETTER NOT TELL YOU NOW.

"It's holding out on us!" the inspector raged. "Warn it that I am not to be trifled with!"

Reflecting that when the gambling bug bit, it bit badly no matter what the species, Lucky rotated the ball again.

"You're not concentrating!" the inspector hissed.

"Okayokayokay. Ah, Magic 8 Ball, what's the scoop on Puddle Pod in the fourth? A winner?"

Rising through the blue depths came: IT IS DECIDEDLY SO.

"Yes!" the inspector exulted. "All right, on your way, Thing. Hurry up, hurry up; I've an important wage—that is, communicator call to place."

Lucky grabbed his shoulder bag, stuck the 8 Ball in it, and got while the getting was good. In a rest room he donned the pink see-through jumpsuit and too-large film shorts. The disk with its eight interlocking rings he hung back on his chest.

The billowy boxers were so outsized that he had to pull the waistband most of the way up to his Adam's apple. When he studied his gawky bod in the imager he saw he'd never be a Machogear Hunkwear model. It was so disheartening that when he saw a Love Handles machine standing against a nearby wall, he almost grabbed the glowing brass handgrips for some of what coarser Trough types called nerve nookie.

But he was already late. Lucky walked out into a huge atrium and stopped in his tracks.

Root Canalians, used to the kind of reaction Lucky had to the atrium view, went around him. Of the few other offworlders there, some were gawking, too, while the rest went about their affairs, blasé—or at least trying to look that way—about the view.

But how could they be, how could anybody be?

A brochure he'd skimmed provided some background data. The atrium was located at the two-thousand-foot level of the South Trunk of Skystroker, third-largest of Root Canal's twenty-six city-trees—the arboreopolises. He was gazing through a window of two-yard-thick hardened membrane the size of a football field, stronger than ceramic glass and just as clear, part of the living arboreopolis itself.

From there he could see a huge expanse of the Stillsilt Plains, dry and pitted and dead as the head of a burnt-out match and displaying the same ashen blacks, grays, and whites. The plains lay harsh-etched and altogether motionless in the unfiltered light of the planet's star, Kurdyne.

Root Canal lacked all atmosphere save what Skystroker and the other city trees generated internally. There were jutting, unweathered mountains rising in ramparts beyond the plains to the right and left, but directly ahead the Stillsilts went clear out to a far horizon. Beyond that was only sky.

The only life to be seen out there consisted of the living landscape features that were the great limbs and roots of Skystroker. Moving closer to the panoramic window, Lucky could see titanic limbs that ascended and branched, forming a canopy that roofed in half the sky with broad, miraculous leaves. The leaves of the arboreopolises gathered energy from Kurdyne—so much that waste heat sometimes had to be shunted to subsurface reservoirs, and power to living stacked-cell storage batteries.

Cyclopean roots lay gnarled and hunched across the terrain in every direction, spanning gorges and enfolding hills. Some lengths of the root system—primary, secondary, and tertiary—were made of the same transparent stuff that formed the vista window up at the rotunda level. He could make out, through some of the glassy stretches, flowing aquacourses—the fabulous in-tree waterways that had given the planet its name.

Old themer instincts reminded him that he didn't have time to waste gawking at the sights; he was supposed to be working. But it was an effort to tear himself away.

He followed a guidestrip, an individual line of grain in the waves and swirls of the floor that glowed soft pink when he touched an actuator bud on a wall directory. As he crossed to one of the descent phloems Lucky reflected on the fact that few Trough travelers had passed this way. Though Root Canal was an exotic and scenic place, its brittle little inhabitants—settlers, really—had managed to keep out Black Hole and almost all tourism. Lucky's tour had only gotten visas due to Undershort's intervention.

The transport system was like no other Lucky had seen. Instead of a car moved by linear motors and pulleys or antigrav fields, a bud-opening awaited him at the end of the guidestrip. From it was emerging an extrusion of stuff that put Lucky in mind of nothing so much as the Blob.

Placing his faith in his guidebook nanite's instructions, Lucky took a deep breath and stepped toward the gluey dark red mass. As promised, the wad of living plastic sensed him somehow, became concave, and stretched to either side to englobe him as he stepped forward. Then it produced a seat for him and began moving.

Cambium and xylem, phloem and heartwood, the city trees of Root Canal had been engineered to serve their inhabitants' needs and wants. Lucky felt the sphere jostle a bit in turbulence as it picked up speed into the secondary phloem. He gazed out through the globe in the half-light of the phloem conduit.

He was in the plumbing that carried the food the city-tree had synthesized from its harsh environment, looking out at the striated, ribbony, lymphlike flow of sugars, proteins, clouds of mineral nutrients. Visibility was only a few feet.

A flattened ovoid thing went swooping by like a shadowy underwater UFO. He realized that it was a Root Canalian using the natural hydraulic freeway that was the phloem system; there was no way of telling how the creatures propelled themselves in this environment.

He wondered if Skystroker, or for that matter *all* the city trees, constituted a single superorganism, the way his own body did in spite of its discrete macrophages, bacteria, viruses. Expert opinions differed, and the Canalians weren't telling, nor would they permit scientific study of their botanical strongholds.

Rocking in the dimness, he didn't feel himself nodding off. The dream was a surprising one. Though he'd been worrying about Harley and Sheena in his waking moments, he saw Silvercup's face as he drifted.

The slowing of the bubble woke him up and left him puzzled. He'd only seen her for a few minutes, not under circumstances that had really let them get to know each other. She and her motives and her Fealty were unknowns to him, even if she had shown him the AzTek data about Earth. Yet it had felt natural for her face to appear to him like that. He wondered what the vision meant.

The bubble melted away to leave him standing on the arrival-stage bud. It was a lot busier down here than on the rotunda. Root Canalians were everywhere, and a few offworlders. Root Canalians were entering and leaving through a system of much smaller conduits, retracting or extending their legs in some manner he couldn't make out. Sphincters in the walls seemed to devour departing ones and spit out arrivals.

Seeing the size of the openings—just big enough to accept the Canalians' closed shells—Lucky thought for a moment of Undershort and felt a burst of comprehension: small as he was in comparison to a human, the supervisor was perhaps too tall by local standards.

He set off along a concourse where just about everything was a part of the city-tree. He passed under groined, lignified ribs as big and imposing as ferrocrete buttresses. What looked and felt like brilliant, abstract-patterned wall-to-wall shag underfoot was upon closer inspection a fine field of plant fibers. Gorgeous tapestries proved to be hanging moss. A banner over a vendor's cubbyhole booth was a living frond, the owner's logo picked out in bright floral pigments. Light fixtures were widely varying applications of bioluminescent wood, phosphorescent sacs of sap or other fluids, glowing fruits, and radiant flowers ranging up to beach-umbrella size.

There were tubes, teats, open pods and clusters of baroque alien produce growing from the walls and floor and even dangling from the ceiling. At these Canalians paused to sip or feed.

It was rumored that the Canalians could have gotten their living environment to grow symmetrically, everything plumb and right-angle and compass-curved, but chose not to. The place had a pleasingly organic, meandering, idiosyncratic look—equal parts botanical garden, hardwood Casbah, XT nest, themer tunnel, and sightseeing complex.

The lounge area where he was bound was a middling-sized hump of wood in a secondary aboveground root smack on the crest of a ridge offering views of the plains, the mountains, the huge rift spanned by the root, and of Skystroker itself. It was domed over by more of the clear, hardened resin stuff. The looming southern trunk of the city, dotted with windows and knotty-looking airlocks, filled most of the view in that direction.

From a little hardwood valley upholstered over many of its contours in cushiony suedelike stuff drifted a confusing mix of languages and sounds—as well as unknown odors. One glance at the nonesuch collection of beings assembled there and Lucky knew he'd found his flock.

He had braced himself for a bizarre lineup of life-forms, but not for the minor shock he got when he recognized one of them—the one doing the talking now.

"I have encountered our guide before," she was saying, "and while he did not appear to be particularly well organized, he *struck* me as being energetic. I believe that he will arrive in due course."

Even if Lucky hadn't been able to see the slug shape and glistening hide he would've recalled the owner of that moist, august voice: Dame Snarynxx, the dowager on whom he'd landed while trying to escape the time-share muggers on Confabulon.

Another voice, nervous, asserted, "He will. I'm sure he will. And believe me, the crowning glory of your itinerary, your visit to Earth, will be the envy of other travelers what with our man's intimate knowledge of it!"

"Black Hole promised celebrity-class treatment all the way." Although he was aware that the speaker's actual language was a canine growl-bark idiom, Lucky's hearing-aid translator rendered it as male and slyly sardonic. And a disgruntled tourist. Maybe troublesome tour members were some kind of universal constant, like the speed of light.

He hadn't gotten through all the client background data provided by Singularity Flings. Some of it was formatted in ways his nanites couldn't read—Agency shorthand—but he hadn't dared reveal that he hadn't been through basic training. He was going to wing it, but only as far as way station Blits.

A couple of days, no problem.

He moved down the slope of the little amphitheater, whistling a send-up C&W song he and Eddie Ensign had worked up together, the jaunty "Degaussin' Yer Name off'n Mah Mem'ry-Dial Phone."

Gathered down there was a grab bag of creatures plus a fretful-looking Canalian on whose shell was affixed a Black Hole badge—the local Agency liaison.

As Lucky understood it this junket was quite expensive; it definitely included some unusual destinations. He hoped that meant the clients were bright, interested, and cooperative, but as various faces, physiognomies, and sensory clusters turned his way he knew sudden doubt.

"Aha, yes, here he is now." The Agency rep sounded distinctly relieved to spy Lucky.

Lucky was in turn looking over his charges. Dame Snarynxx was as Lucky recalled her. Next to Snarynxx was a life-form that set Lucky to thinking about Nalls and Hawaiian masks—a giant anthropomorphic thing evolved from botanical forebears.

The tree man moved toward him, extending one hand. "Pleased to meet you. The name is Lumber Jack, call me Lumber."

Lucky shook as best he could. Lumber's hand was like a massive wooden meat tenderizer with three fingers. "Um, Salty Waters, here. A pleasure." Jack was wearing a wisp of pink stuff tied around one great arm; Lucky figured there'd been no weavers, or film shorts either, for a creature ten feet tall and three ax handles wide.

"Looks like we're going to have some fun and see some sights," the creature added happily. "The jaunt of a lifetime, for me."

Longheaded Lumber's face was a rough-hewn Easter Island

idol. In assorted places his body was scorched, striated, pocked as if somebody'd gone at him with a twenty-pound sledge, scarred, knotted, or showing the worn-down erose healing of old and terrible lacerations—as well as what looked to be ax chops and saw cuts. Where his hide was unblemished it was like walnut stained in pointillist daubs. There were sprays of straw or shoots where most humans had hair. There was no sign of genitals at his crotch, only a drawn-shut, spiny, nut-case-looking thing—which Lucky considered a sane and even desirable breakthrough in evolution.

Anyway, he certainly was the solid type. And amiable.

"Yes, yes, yes." The Agency rep was hastening along, eager to be rid of the group. "And those are the Dimdwindles and their adorable young larva GoBug, from FoolProof. Those handsome dogs over by the map are Mr. Arooo and Mr. Hoowe—Mr. Hoowe? I believe I asked all members of the group not to wander off, sir."

Arooo and Hoowe were Dr. Moreau canine guys over by a softly glowing thermal frond. They were dressed in upscale, but not designer-original, see-through wearevers and film shorts tailored for their humanoid bodies, set off with a bit more jewelry than Lucky felt they needed.

Mr. Hoowe, tail wagging, had just emerged from a secluded section of the waiting area, clothing slightly askew. He seemed to be fiddling with the closure seam at his crotch. Lucky chanced to notice a subtle disquiet in Arooo. To gloss over his irritation the rep added, "Mr. Hoowe and Mr. Arooo, of planet Rph, jointly won the prestigious Schwartzchild Ribbon for innovative marketing concepts."

Lucky couldn't tell what the Rphians' subtext was all about and had to shelve that little mystery to keep up with the rep's spiel. "Dame Snarynxx you already know, she informs me." Lucky noticed now that she, too, wore transparent pink—with flair, as a scarf the size of a badminton net.

"Vixlixx Millmixx, there, is our heroic veteran from the Dunnage Depop campaign—wave to Mr. Waters, Mr. Millmixx!"

Millmixx could produce only a desultory shrug. He reminded Lucky of a Basil Wolverton cartoon grotesque with bloodshot goggle eyes, crooked neck and cowcatcher teeth, all set on a pear-shaped bipod body. His pink wearever fit him like a shower curtain.

The Root Canalian tugged Lucky around by the elbow. "And this is Hono."

"Hello!" a dozen or so yard-tall antlike bipeds called out brightly and simultaneously in the same voice, waving to Lucky with identical gestures. The four-armed munchkins all wore matching employee-tour-club pennants on short flexible staffs, much like bicycle flags, attached to their bulbous rumps. The creatures also sported absolutely duplicate hats—what, to Lucky, resembled too-large pink see-through skimmers with indistinguishable hatbands in a kind of XT Hawaiian print—featuring holes for their antennae.

The Hono—or maybe it was just plain "Hono," Lucky wasn't sure—each had an aud-vid unit on a shoulder strap. They began shooting Lucky. Then they started shooting each other shooting Lucky, which devolved into shooting each other shooting each other and so on.

"Yes, hi" was all Lucky had time to get out. The Black Hole liaison led him back up toward the concourse, talking in a tense monotone. "Where were you? Never mind! Look, get them formed up, take them on the canal tour, and fade them out of here. If you miss a connection the penalty will be assessed against your salary."

Not that Lucky planned to be around to cash his check, but a sense of fairness made him blurt, "Me? Why?"

"Anything that goes wrong is the guide's fault, period. Now, here's your gun."

From the shell emerged a spindly hand offering a device that, elsewhere, Lucky would've taken for a curling wand. But it was made of acrylic Trough composites and had intricate controls and instrumentation, leading him to conclude that you could do a lot more than perm somebody's hair with it—if you'd been through guides' basic training.

Lucky was shaking his head. "Don't need it. Thanks anyway."

The Agency rep did a double take, then regained possession of himself. "Got some shredder grenades. They more to your taste?"

"Um, listen, I think I can manage without 'em if it's all the same to you."

The rep's voice dripped sarcasm. "Oh, and aren't we all puffed up with our interpersonal coping skills? How 'bout brain-drain aerosol? Great crowd-control weapon."

"Heckuva kind offer, amigo, but I'll pass."

The clam took a closer look at him. "What are you, a troublemaker?"

Lucky resisted the urge to tell the rep his spaceboot was demagnetizing. "Nope, just got my own way of doing things."

Unexpectedly, the liaison official's tone became one of grudging respect. "What d'you know, a human who's not trigger-happy! In that case you'll at least need this." From the Canalians' shell emerged a unit that resembled a TV remote. "Anti-lignin field projector," the liaison man whispered conspiratorially. "Very tough to come by. Pretty handy in a pinch, around here, but—go easy with it, know what I'm saying?"

Lucky could see where such a thing would have its uses in the city trees; lignin was the substance that, with cellulose, stiffened wood and held it together.

He'd taken the delignifier in hand by reflex, about to refuse it. But just then Dame Snarynxx's voice rang out from the amphitheater. "Yooo-hoo! Salty Waters! The gondoliers are here to—"

"Gotta go," snapped the Canalian, sensing an opportunity to disengage. "Their luggage's been routed forward, so all you have to worry about for now are the bodies. Boy, Salty, what kind of boner got you stuck with a bunch like that?"

"Wha— Come back!" Lucky began, waving the field gun feebly, but the Canalian was already ankling on out of the amphitheater.

Being flown to Foresite—being brought there under close supervision, as if she were a convict rather than the Fealty's prime field operative—Silvercup didn't need to run an internal diagnostic scan to know there was disorder inside her.

Foresite, the Fealty's most advanced R&D center and CAD/CAM facility, where she herself had been given life, lay several thousand miles northeast of Computopia. Even the powerful artificial intelligences who presided over the place were capable of miscalculation, and some of the forces they dealt with were too dangerous to be meddled with except at a far remove from all population centers.

When the Monitor informed her of a dangerous new mission and then, without warning or discussion, decreed the excision of more of her memories, he seemed to be manipulating her in a way more appropriate to organic intelligence. Security automata had shown up to flank her: tremendously strong, fast, destructive, and vigilant machine entities who resembled flying, resplendent jellyfish. If the Monitor expected her to resist or be dazed by it all he was disappointed. All the same, Silvercup found it difficult to reconcile certain conflicting impulses and response prioritizations.

She'd been whisked out to a landing plat and a waiting aircraft so quickly that she still held the drained, darkened info-crystal she'd brought back from her last assignment—the one that had told of Black Hole's plans for Earth. Without questioning the impulse, she drew it inside the living metal flesh of herself.

The conveyance was a magnetic-field flier, a vertical football of lustrous lavender glass suspended in, but unconnected to, a delicately curved copper framework that joined two copper outrigger propulsion/maneuvering sponsons. The cabin module was just big enough for Silvercup and two escorts; as if to remind her of her inorganic form, the metal deck was bare of any furnishing. Uncomplaining, she stood—her head nearly brushing the ceiling. There were no exposed controls or instruments. Emissions monitoring wasn't her specialty, but her internal sensors told her the flying was being done from Computopia central control.

Certain facets of her intellect, other behavioral engrams, various programming inputs, and acquired personality had aroused in her resentment of the way she was being treated. Yet she was so used to serving the Fealty, so committed to it by all the things she'd ever experienced and by the very nature of her construction that she couldn't muster disobedience. Intellectually she knew the Fealthy must be working to the best effect—to the maximum overall benefit of AIs and automata.

Intellectually? the word echoed in her. What other way was there for a gleamer to know anything? Maybe it was some information-management glitch. She scanned a mental image of sleepy-eyed Lucky Junknowitz. Silvercup examined what she'd felt toward Lucky in the Staph Wheel clinic. She hadn't sorted it out yet, but it was a powerful emotion. She suspected she'd been building toward such a watershed moment for years; maybe it was the result of all the unbelievably complex and sometimes contradictory and illogical programming she'd taken on, behavior she'd seen and had to emulate, to play out various and sometimes organic masquerades.

Foresite's facilities were widely dispersed across most of an island subcontinent in Sweetspot's northern hemisphere, but its central complex honeycombed a mountain chain and encircled a dead lake in what looked like pristine wasteland. Zipping down from a yellow-green sky, the magnetic-field flier shot through a cliff-face door and deep into a granite fastness.

The flier went streaking along immense passageways carved from naked rock, past stupendous machines, making sudden turns past landscapes of instrumentality of widely differing types. Homing in, it came to rest at last on an open floor of hazily glowing red metal a square mile in area.

The football opened and she stepped out, expecting the escorts to follow. Instead, the little vehicle rose and zipped away; the Fealty's will ruled supreme within Foresite, apparently, and it didn't feel the need for additional security.

One thing that didn't surprise her was the sudden appearance of the Monitor, larger than life, before her. She knew it for a hologram and wondered why her controller had gone to the trouble. To awe and overmaster her? Surely he didn't think she was *that* muddled?

"Events are coming to an important crux, Unit," the Monitor said aloud, rather than interfacing directly. She wondered if he was avoiding the multilayered nonlogic he would encounter in certain areas of her mind with a direct link.

"We had planned to grant you a time of rest to prepare yourself for a new role in things," the Monitor went on. She heard his peculiar emphasis on the plural, and wondered if some level of the ruling circle of the Fealty itself was present, observing and calculating.

"That reward must be postponed. This new crisis appeared in defiance of our best mathematical models. You are best suited to deal with it.

"Nevertheless, you deserve to know that your work and sacrifices are appreciated. Therefore, look now on your future, and a new aspect of the Fealty."

A shaft of light sprang into existence, shining down from the darkness above. Riding down on it came a disk five feet across and, standing on it straddle-legged, a mighty, glittering figure.

She saw what it was instantly, a godlike form worked in metal, an idealized body with perfect features. He was a Masculine Aspect of metalflesh, metallic Adam to her alloy Eve. Synthesized tonalities played in the air, and the busy systemry lent a drumroll of sorts.

As the disk came to rest on the floor Silvercup could see that the figure was taller than she, tremendously muscled, with an almost ludicrously sharp V-taper to his torso. He held his chin high, a sure and arrogant look in his cold, cold eyes. He was, in anatomical detail, human male. Where there was living color to her eyes and lips, though, there was none in him.

"This Masculine Aspect," the Monitor was saying, "this Virile Construct, will be your counterpart, your mentor, your destined companion and mate."

She glanced to the Monitor sharply. " 'Mentor'?"

But it was the Virile Construct, as silvery-shining as she, who answered. "Why, naturally." He didn't strike her as sensing any irony in that last word. "I am a more advanced design than you, stronger and more intelligent. And will have far more data once the Monitor downloads to me." His voice tolled like a bell, with a note of condescension. "It is only logical that I be the one to make key determinations as to our joint destiny, instruct you by dint of my higher perceptions."

She looked back to him, realizing that the mercury fluidity of her face was taking on a human expression of irritation. She blanked it by an act of will. "And what destiny is that?"

Virile Construct showed that he knew something of human facial conformations, too. One eyebrow went up and an unconvincing smile touched his chrome-bright lips. "To serve as a study-model of humanity here on Sweetspot," he explained. "To imbue a new artificial race with our machine perfection— with mine, in particular."

She stood hipshot, looking at him thoughtfully. "And if I don't *want* to be a lab specimen or maternal factory?"

"Nonsense," the Monitor said. "You trivialize and distort what we're telling you. Moreover, exhaustive analysis assures us you will find it rewarding once contradictions in your behavior are eliminated. But now: we have other things to do. See."

"This isn't the Fealty I swore to serve—" she began.

Another image appeared in the air. The Virile Construct, seeing the face there, was grandly contemptuous. "What a stupid-looking lab smear! What a weak-chinned, dish-eared, droop-eyed grinning mental defective!"

Silvercup thought about seeing how the Virile Construct could fight but decided she had enough problems.

"You recall this individual, Unit?" the Monitor asked her.

She was staring at an extract gleaned from her own memories of her most recent mission. "Lucky Junknowitz," Silvercup said softly.

Proclaiming that there was work to do, the Monitor sent the

Virile Construct gliding back up toward the ceiling, into the dark, on the floating disk. The masculine machine struck a grand pose, heroic, muscular, fists on his trim, hard hips, rising into the air. "I look forward to our next meeting," he assured Silvercup with a smile that won him only a frosty glare.

Lucky Junknowitz's image still hung in the air. "What does this have to do with him?" she asked the Monitor. "Surely I've met no more hapless and lost individual anywhere in the Trough."

"Hapless?" the Monitor pondered. "In one sense, you are correct. In another, no. You lacked the sensor equipment to detect one very important fact about him. I call your attention to this symbol."

An illuminated area lit up the disk Lucky was wearing on a chain around his neck—in particular, the eight interlocked rings that formed a design on it resembling a circle of round chain links or an illusionist's puzzle.

"I know that it, or one like it, is most significant to Ka Shamok," she said. "I know it bears on the deepest secrets of Black Hole's Sysops. But rational calculation indicates the virtual impossibility of any meaningful or causal link to this man of Adit Navel. After all, what could the Sysops conceivably care about such a being?"

She tried to sound indifferent, but she recalled again the odd sensory input she'd gotten from meeting Lucky Junknowitz's eye, the peculiar surge through her prompted by the sensory stimulus that was Lucky. Some chance malfunction, she'd forced herself to conclude at the time, no more.

"I projected trouble for him at some future point, since he wore that symbol, but evaluated the Earther himself as being of no great significance beyond the opportunity to destabilize." No doubt others in the Trough, of disparate sympathies and factions, would regard Junknowitz strangely, too. But few were likely to approach him or otherwise involve themselves with him; most would wait and watch, if possible, to determine if he was friend, foe, or plant; asset, decoy, or turncoat.

"You were wrong," the Monitor said. "That is excusable in that you lacked certain critical data. Now it is important to rectify that oversight. It is of the highest priority that you locate Lucky Junknowitz and bring him back here to us for detailed examination. He may well hold the key to our struggle, the key to Sweetspot's triumph."

She stood stock-still, a gorgeous sculpture reflecting an aura of light in the vast, darkened space. "How can that be?"

"The Sysops," the Monitor explained. "As in so many things, *they* are the ultimate answer. In this case, the circumstances have to do with their experiments into the very nature of causality and probability. Apparently, they isolated and were manipulating the fundamental forces that hold sway over these phenomena—call their essence 'the odds of numbers,' or call it 'fortune.'

"As you will, at some point their researches hit a sticking point, we surmise, or in some fashion presented a danger of which even they were wary. Whatever the details, the Sysops elected to rid themselves of the isolates of probability with which they'd been experimenting. But there appears to have been some sort of anomalous event, or perhaps a leakage of the energies themselves.

"We may liken what resulted to a venting of some toxin or other dangerous substance. It might even be said that coincidence *reigned*, briefly, held sway in the Sysops' most secure facility on Light Trap—their equivalent of Foresite. There was an accidental outflux, through an active Adit, of this isolate."

Silvercup almost laughed. "A toxic probability spill?"

The Monitor wasn't amused. "Humor is of no profit in this discussion and you will therefore refrain from it. Nevertheless, your formulation is not altogether inaccurate. The effect of exposure to those radiations would make the recipient a node of what some organics would call 'bad luck' as well as 'good,' but in vast amounts, and in ways that would fractalize throughout all things having to do with that individual—friends, antecedents, allies and enemies, et cetera. We cannot be certain of the proportions, of course, but clearly an unusual concentration of 'bad luck' could quickly prove lethal."

She was glad now that she wasn't speaking at close interface with the Monitor. "And this surge, radiation, leak—whatever it was—it struck *Lucky Junknowitz?*"

"There is no need for you to state the obvious. The very nature of the forces released caused a highly unlikely Adit malfunction which opened a brief, direct connection with a location on Earth. Junknowitz was unknowingly exposed to it."

She studied Lucky's face again. "Another coincidence."

"Not altogether. The Sysops were fascinated with the concept of good fortune, bad luck, and such, and so its various subsidiaries were on the watch for related data. Junknowitz was in a local disguised-Adit location—a franchised consumables outlet, Click Fist by name—in a place known as Sumatra. His sobriquet being what it is, he'd been lured there for a cursory scan and unobtrusive interrogation, on the off chance that he held some significance for Black Hole's research."

The Monitor appeared to ponder for a moment, though that was highly unlikely. A moment's pondering in realtime would have been equivalent to several years' reflection for Silvercup. "There is another theory: that Junknowitz—and other entities—by nature possesses some of this ineffable probability isolate, perhaps an unusual amount, and the leak *sought him out*, like electrons leaping a gap between appropriate potentials. This is of course an unsupported supposition at present."

"But a very educated guess," Silvercup mused. "How do we know so much about this heretofore most-secret project of the Sysops?" There was only one source she could think of that would and could provide such intelligence.

And she was right. "Your informant, of course," the Monitor confirmed. "This was among the very last data forwarded to Ka Shamok—by an alternate arrangement, since contact with you had already been compromised. We, too, scanned the message."

Silvercup looked down at her own red reflection in the floor. "Then it hasn't been truly confirmed; it might be disinformation. How can we really believe this, this preposterous story of quantified, manipulable *luck*?"

The Monitor was ready with an answer. "Would you not say strange probabilities were abroad? Most conspicuously: in your escape from the WitSec guards, you came upon that very crystal you hold, with the information on Black Hole's Earth operation, *and you gave it to Junknowitz*."

"But—there is nothing new about coincidence or unlikely chains of events," she parried. "The number of discrete occurrences and circumstances in any given entity's life is so near-infinite that that entity is virtually *certain* to experience coincidence not once but many times. Multiplying that by the number of entities in the Trough worlds, we see that almost inconceivably synchronistic happenstance is almost inevitable. Which is why so many organics get religion."

The Monitor sounded like a tireless juggernaut. "That is the standard doctrine on such phenomena, true. And yet, the synchronicities and coincidences around Junknowitz, the conflu-

ences of events, defy even *that* rationalization. For these
reasons it becomes mandatory that we examine this Earther
here at Foresite.''

Here comes the crunch. ''I'd serve you best with all my
memories and other faculties intact,'' Silvercup said.

''It is not your decision to make.''

Silvercup heard the finality in the decree and, in that last
instant, broke through her all-consuming dedication to the Fealty, shifting to phase-speed, meaning to disappear in a hyper-
kinetic blur and run, run until she could think of something else
to do.

But the Monitor had been expecting it, and she was pinned
in the spotlight of a restraining field. At the same time tele-
metric beams carrying override algorithms stuck her from all
sides like laser-bright spears. Her superb living-metal body
failed her for the first time, freezing stock-still despite all the
willpower she could bring to bear.

The Monitor's image looked down on her pitilessly. The rest
of the chamber's systemry was busy with the flow of energy,
the shifting of instruments and machinery. Cyclopean, convoluted engines and devices rose from sudden gaps in the floor,
or lowered from apertures in the darkened vault overhead.
From all directions, manipulators came snaking and telescoping and dangling at her. There were cruel pincer, gripper, and
restraint servos; forced-entry cutters, drills, beam-tools and the
rest; microwaldos for fine work, alteration, and extraction.
Bigger devices poised in the middle distance, waiting, bearing
large modules of some kind.

What shocked her even more, though, was that the effectuators, under the Monitor's guidance, couldn't seem to resist
fondling her for a moment, touching her in ways meant to
violate. She understood then the true purpose of Virile Construct, with his magnificent form and near-empty mind. He
would be the Monitor's vessel, the Monitor's means of having
her.

The effectuators stopped their molestations and moved more
purposefully. Silvercup found herself again thinking about
Lucky Junknowitz. No doubt when these modifications were
completed she wouldn't feel the same way about him. And, she
wondered, why *did* she feel this way? More of his oddly contaminated personal probability aura? Or something even rarer,
more providential?

Something that transcended biology and cybernetics, some-

thing revealed behind the curtains when you swept all precon-
ceptions away, something to be found only when you exorcised
every preconception. Eternal, beyond value systems, the grail
that was left when cosmological equations had nullified each
other, the end of every evolution . . .

Somehow that nonmachine thought weakened the Monitor's
hold on her.

His devices beam-deadened her here, rent her metalflesh
there. Strange that none of the machines seemed to notice
when, encased in the close-work equipment, the depleted data
crystal reemerged from her arm. She put it in the duplicating
receptacle of the module draining her memories and still the
Monitor, perhaps dazed by his own sensations, was unaware.
As the memory siphon moved away she recovered the crystal
with its copy of the memories that had been stolen from her.
She could no longer remember what it was she'd felt for Lucky,
but knew that she wished to.

But she was now being taken apart and couldn't hide the
crystal on her own person. Silvercup tucked her forbidden
memories into a gap under a cowling on an articulated handler.
An unlikely ploy, but the Monitor was too much distracted by
its possession of her to notice. An almost celestial piece of
luck.

The Foresite instrumentality went to work on her in earnest,
in keeping with the Monitor's directions. They altered her
thoughts, took her body from her and placed her in another—
and when she saw what they'd turned her into, she wished she
could weep but lacked the means.

SEVENTEEN

MICKEY FORMICA WAS grateful that tailing Asia Boxdale and the Femmes through the lessening swelter of the metropolitan night was something the two could've done almost blindfolded—the ninja putting exhibition still had him thinking of his other senses. It left time for the two to clear up some unfinished business.

"Ay! *Monsieur homme!* Now's the time for you to bring me up to speed on all this who-shot-John between you and your papa."

Nikkei had been concentrating on the three women; now he sounded a little shocked. "While we're working?"

"While we're working. While riding the subway, which I predict is our current future. I cut you slack like you asked, but no more puttin' it off; it's about my ass too, now. Besides, we walk along not talkin', we'll look like goddamn store detectives."

Somehow it had never been the superficial, courteously dissembling *tatamae* with Mickey. Right from the jump, when the Mutt-'n'-Jeff pair met in a back-room *dojo* in Harlem, Mickey'd somehow wrung from Nikkei the kind of *honne* candor that took most Japanese years of acquaintance and an all-night drunk. "Okay."

After the bottom fell out of the ninja fad in the nineties, the secret arts had never quite regained their former mystique in the West. *Ninjutsu* only went into further decline—as far as marketing, TV, and movies were concerned, that is—in the aftermath of the Turn, Japanese influence on the world notwithstanding.

But there were still those drawn to it, like the gangly uptown black and the chunky Japanese who'd found his way in from somewhere in the astrobuck *kudzu* enclaves: *Nihon*-only malls, clubs, schools and nightspots out beyond Englewood Cliffs' sheer palisades and Westchester's money line. It happened that way once in a while, some kid from Jersey or Kyoto responding to the dark lure of the city; that was what had created the East Village *bohemu* Japanese expat subculture after World War II and made it thrive during the Turn and afterward.

Nikkei recalled their first encounter. He'd been adrift, his mother dead and his father usually away on business; in those days, Nikkei thought Takuma Tanabe was just another workaholic. Nikkei refused to remain long in Japan, where his grandfather still presided as nominal head of the family. Nothing in the *bohemu* community or the American suburban scene could quiet his nameless discontent either.

The Mantic Mantis School of Martial Arts and its Caribbean-Saudi sensei were both bogus, fauxed up—the two new students saw that right out of the gate. But Ms. Sensei had strong climbing expertise and gymnastic tricks, plus a lot of unconventional weapons stuff that smacked more of the criminal-justice system than the *Budokan*. So the two stuck around and struck up a friendship.

Out of class they'd taught one another more than they learned at the Mantic Mantis. Nikkei had carried heavy technical courses, dabbled in various combat *budo*, and picked up some mind-disciplines from the less traditional teachers he'd met along the way; of those last he'd said little to his friend. And even in enlightened and gentler post-Turn times Mickey's uptown neighborhood had equipped him with certain unconventional skills. By way of a graduation party they cleaned out the Mantic Mantis's safe, then set out in search of pleasure and trouble.

Nikkei devoted a considerable amount of the time he was supposedly spending in various undergrad courses and corporate career workshops—from the New School to Tokyo U. to the Berlin Free University and back again—taking on odd jobs with Mickey for Bhang, among others. When, inevitably, Takuma Tanabe found out, he'd suffered his only son to dabble in such youthful hijinks for an additional year, then jerked his leash and stuck Nikkei into Tokyo U. full time and under close supervision.

Nikkei reflected that it wasn't very *ki*-focusing, this getting personal matters in the way of the mission. But screw *ki*-focusing for now. Screw Japan for now; he had a feeling he should indulge his American mental overlay as long as he had the luxury. Things were sure going to be different once he and Mickey undertook apprenticeship to Kamimura.

They were sitting in subway seats from which they could watch Asia, Lynka, and Mimi in the next car before Nikkei could get his reply started—a hesitation so long that, he could tell, Mickey was beginning to think he'd had a data crash or something.

"It's about when I was living on Tokyo time," Nikkei said.

Mickey knew that, Nikkei had disappeared across the pond with scarcely a word, then shown up again five months later with a haunted look and a death-row fatalism that still hadn't left him entirely.

"It was gonna be Tokyo U. for the diploma, of course," Nikkei explained, "and into the business. I was in a corporation intern seminar just under a month when I met this girl, also a fast-tracker."

Nikkei felt very strange letting all this out. It wasn't like anything he'd ever done before. It felt a little like the release of death must feel—not loss or gain, just an utterly unprecedented absence of something that had been part burden, part hoard.

"We started a thing. You know. Intense. My old man ran a background check. She came up *Burakumin*, you with me?"

So much so was Mickey that he shot back, "How the hell'd she make it to corporate, man?"

Japanese weren't the only ones who investigated the family backgrounds of potential employees, fiancés, in-laws, and so on, but they'd raised it to an art that made the king and queen of England look like they'd married on a blind date. And about the worst thing a Japanese lineage check could expose was the bloodline of *Burakumin*—*Eta*, as the untouchable caste had once been called. *Burakumin* had lived outcast, impoverished, persecuted lives for centuries for the simple fact that their traditional occupations dealt with animal rendering, butchering, disposal of the dead, and other jobs incompatible with Buddhist beliefs.

"She and her family'd hid it for four generations: cooked and forged the family registers, panned 'n' scanned the 'Black Books.' Phreaked the computer files, too, when they came along. Solid cover job that'd held up to everything. Till then."

Yeah, Mickey was just willing to bet an ultimate Japanese blue-gene like Tanabe had the resources to find out things nobody else could. He also knew it happened, every so often, that *Burakumin* and non-*Burakumin* fell in love. Non-*Bun* fam-

ilies reacted with about the same enthusiasm Mickey's gran'ma
would if he brought home the transsexual clone of James-Earl-
fuckin'-Ray.

"Your old man made you break up?" That didn't sound like
Nikkei.

"No. I refused and as far as I know, he left it at that. But my
grandfather got wind of it and—had one of his people take care
of it."

"Kamimura." Mickey nodded.

"No. Someone else, more corporate and more ambitious.
While I was out of town, see? I thought she—Zin—was, too;
that's what I was supposed to think."

It was so strange, opening up like this—Nikkei had expected
to be unable to say the words but somehow felt anesthetized,
depersonalized, as if he were hearing someone else say it.

"But this corporate climber, Kayahi, was careless. Or
maybe he didn't give a shit. Zin's family heard they'd been
outed and her old man downcasted from his office window,
thirty-one floors. Zin cut Kayahi's balls off and left him to die,
then *seppuku*ed—with a knife from my family's heirlooms."

The train was pulling into Manhattan. To Nikkei the station
suddenly looked like another world. The whole Earth had since
the events he was telling.

"And when I heard about it I did the worst thing I could do,
Mickey, worst thing a Japanese can possibly—"

"Gran'pa?" Mickey filled in, with a look that said, *Give me
credit for readin'* some *parts a' you, my Dog-Bro!* "You did
ol' *ojii-san,* huh?"

Nikkei licked his lips, still staring straight ahead. "With that
same knife. Then I split, basically waiting for my old man to
come and finish it. Only he didn't, and I knew by then that he
had the power to do that and a lot more."

The car doors whispered open as they both stood. "So after
a while I figured what the fuck, teaming up with you was the
only thing I ever did well. I dunno; you think my going ninj
was genetic or something?"

"Ask Kline Labs," Mickey answered warily as they followed the three women across the platform. They were kept
busy through the train-change heading downtown, but then
were moving in silence again.

This time Mickey had no objection to it. He was wondering
about something he didn't quite have the nerve to ask Nikkei.
He wondered if Zin had been heartbreakingly beautiful, regal,

intimidatingly brainy—and sufficiently on top of things to move with cool poise instead of *Nihon no trotta* Office Lady lope.

Like Miss Sato, the alluring Miss Sato, who walked at Tanabe's elbow.

Mickey tried to reassure himself. Well, even if my main man *is* low-concept enough to fall for Miss Sato-ri, she *got* to be too fast-track to go for him, right? Right?

This world's too lovely to lose.

Walking between Lynka and Mimi as dusk faded and the sultry August air became more bearable, Asia felt an enormous regret and apprehension sweep through her. Every single thing that was hopeful, admirable, or beautiful made it that much more tragic that Black Hole now threatened the world.

Despite the blind stupidity of the Arts Council and their sort, the inconveniences and discomforts of eco-correctness, the greed of the Twenty-Ones and other power players, Earth was an improved place trying hard to be a *good* place. Asia was doing her best to think of it as, and make it, a world where people could get past their grief and pain and disappointment to live lives of worth.

She'd been born in Thailand of a Kampuchean mother who'd barely survived the killing fields and an English expat father who'd sacrificed and suffered much to remain in Thailand with the wife and child he loved. Both parents had died far too young: Sandy Boxdale of HIVirus in a Bangkok hospice, his wife of leukemia in Long Beach, California's Little Phnom Penh.

Asia had known pain and grief as longtime assailants. A surviving aunt in Little Phnom Penh had suffered so unspeakably under the Khmer Rouge, witnessed such atrocities, wept so inconsolably that, though there was nothing physically wrong with her, she'd gone blind. The same thing had happened to many others.

Coming of age in the Turn, Asia dealt with these things and the memories of them as best she was able, in an attempt to fashion a new life for herself. In knowledge there was sadness, but at times there could be a kind of fortitude as well.

In Asia's mind Earth's renewal had always been somehow inextricably intertwined with her own. Now she strode along catching lazily thick flower scents from window boxes filled with soil enriched with bottom land and other fertilizers; greenery in sidewalk planters; fertile boskiness from the nodding branches of the street trees. Maybe the sunset had been less spectacular than in the days of smog and heavy emissions, but the stars were a little brighter—at least on the side streets—and the daytime air had lost the polluted yellow-brown tints of a used earwax swab.

There were old people on the street and young, all safe and unafraid—unless, say, they were foolish enough to litter, or urinate on one of those newly planted saplings. Assorted subsidized green-volunteer types and eco-scouts were going about their three Rs: Reduce, Reuse, Recycle; the modern mantra. In a rehabbed storefront, a social-action neofamilial collective was advertising all sorts of support, outreach, and therapy assistance.

Asia knew the trade-offs as well as anyone. But if the haves were obliged to get by with less, the have-nots and the planet had been given life-saving succor. If the sovereignty of nations and the ego of presidents and dictators had been sacrificed, at least nuclear swords had been beaten into ploughshares and people could go about their lives without hunching their necks against the final tick of the doomsday clock.

And here, with the Earth just groping its way into a green new age, Black Hole came scheming and spreading like some biblical plague. Asia had to stop herself from hissing aloud at the unfairness of it. Walking through the city, she decided Lucky and the others were right. Someone had to stick up for Earth. If that had to be a bunch of feckless Manhattan bohos, so be it.

And that included Asia; however she could help, she would. Whatever came of that, it was preferable to standing by and doing nothing, as the world had done about Cambodia.

There were a few second and even third glances for her and the two Femmes as they caught the subway into Manhattan, but nothing worrisome. City life had always had certain elements of free-form costume party, never more so than post-Turn.

Still, Asia's gun belt and Mimi's sword were bundled up in the net shopping bag, and Lynka carried the disassembled missile launcher in a rolled up tatami mat slung over one shoulder by a length of hemp twine. This was no time to attract the attention of cops or happy-face security cameras.

Changing at Fourteenth Street, they rode to Cooper Union and walked from there. The Ded Dawg was in a TriBeCa basement space, down a steep flight of cracked steps in a back alley; the place wasn't wheelchair-accessible, and Asia recalled uneasily that this was the only door—or at least the only one known to the public. In case of fire, kiss your deep-fried ass *buenos fuegos*, troglodytes and troglodettes.

The club was unmarked except for a painting, on wood, of a pirate hanged from a yardarm, mounted under a light scarcely brighter than that of a portable reading lamp. To one side was a surveillance camera whose lens wore, instead of the usual happy face, a line drawing of a hand giving the world the finger.

While Asia buckled on the buscadero and Lynka snapped the dummy missile launcher back together, Screamin' Mimi pounded on the metal-sheathed door with the pommel of her scimitar. Eyes appeared at a slit in the metal but Asia assumed that was only for effect; the three had already been checked by camera.

The door swung open with a creak. Asia followed the other two into a tiny, curtained-off foyer where two women and a man waited, the smaller of the women standing by a podium that lit her face from beneath—with the glow from the security-cam screen, had to be. The other two were taller than Lynka and brawny, dressed in what-was Road Warrior panoply complete with face paint. Asia heard the wheezy laboring of an air-circulation system working hard enough to stir people's hair and the feathers in the female streetfighter's mohawk.

The staff knew Lynka and Mimi. A fistful of cash—Asia was footing the bill—changed hands and they were passed through the opposite curtain and another door. There was a dimly lit staircase and sounds of revelry from down below.

As soon as the smells of the Ded Dawg proper hit her Asia understood the need for the high-horsepower air circ. Even on the staircase the stench of tobacco and other smokables was foul enough to make her nose twitch. Descending into a thick haze of it, she thought resentfully that it would probably take her days to wash the stink out of her hair. Most affirmative, if there were any smoke detectors they must be on dead power packs. She reminded herself why she'd come, and told herself not to sweat the details.

The main bar of the Ded Dawg resembled some seriously botched theme party. The ambience wasn't so much pre-Turn as non-Turn, as Mimi'd said. This was the scene for those not rich enough, attractive enough, smart or high-born or socially viable enough to aspire to Twenty-One celebrity.

To that end, Asia noticed as she trailed her companions down the short flight of stairs, the OSM-mandated alcohol detectors at the doors were shut down and there was no way the decibel level could be within Office of Social Management and OSHA limits. Soundproofed the place certainly must be, but anybody spending much time in it was courting hearing loss.

There was a stack of imitation gold ingots at the foot of the stairs. Various flatscreens were showing film loops of offshore oil rigs pumping away, belching heavy industries pouring out rubber and steel and consumer goods, freeways jammed with racing gas hogs, and assorted war footage. An SDI mural showed an orbiting ABM/nuclear-weapons platform with a huge American insignia opening fire on Earth, applauded by the Four Horsemen of SDI: Ronald Reagan, Lyndon LaRouche, Edmund Teller, and Robert Jastro.

A man with a mock-up baby harp seal draped around his neck, leaning on a wooden ax handle, was tossing back shot glasses from a row of them. The bartender had left the rum bottle on the bar's service ledge; the label read "150 Proof"— more than enough to get customer, bartender, and owner arrested and cuffed. Next to the seal hunter was a woman smoking an elegantly slim cigarette clamped in an onyx holder. The cigarette's side was stamped with a golden $, *Atlas Shrugged* fashion. She was gesturing with a hand chained in green-blue links—Reardon Metal? Asia wondered—and talking to an obese man in 1890s Diamond Jim Brady/Citizen Kane attire who in turn was basically stuffing food down his throat as fast as he could.

Asia was a bit foggy on identifying details, but she spied what she supposed to be a Donald Trump reenactor in earnest conversation with a beer-gutted guy in George Patton uniform and ivory-handled Colts. Next to them a fellow in Michael Milken camoflesh, lugging an attaché case with what were meant to look like the edges of high-denomination bills sticking out, was plying with drunken conversation a woman whose loops of coral jewelry clicked and rattled as she sniffed white powder from a delicate golden spoon.

On the bandstand the Sick Fucks brought "Dick the Spastic" to a yowling close and broke right into "Unhip Crip." They were doing the mocking Primalyric Autistikinetic dance convulsions that had been judged un-warehouse-worthy by the Arts Advisory Council and degrading to certain challenged groups by OSM.

Lynka put a hand on Asia's shoulder and they prowled further into the place, Mimi bringing up the rear. It was bigger and more crowded than Asia had expected. The decor—a veal grower's viselike calf-raising stall; a larger-than-life statue of George Bush divebombing an abortion clinic; a giant, glowing Exxon pump offering leaded 110-octane at twenty-three cents a gallon—made the place a smoggy, low-ceilinged labyrinth.

Amazing, how thick and stratified the drifting tobacco smoke was. Asia could see cigars, butts both hand-rolled and machine made, as well as pipes of various kinds. Few of Asia's acquaintances so much as indulged in clove cigarettes; she found herself gagging, her sinuses feeling as though somebody were rubbing them with an emery cloth.

Where a place like Atopia, favorite hangout of her loft posse, held up anti-environment icons to ridicule, the Dawg glorified them. Some kind of Nietzschean *übermensch* dementality, she supposed—the impotent let-the-tree-huggers-freeze-in-the-dark posturing of despoiler wannabes.

Asia knew enough about the fate of the hindmost, when it was devil take the hindmost, that her skin crawled at what she was seeing. Now Black Hole was out to make the whole human race the hindmost. If only these pathetic pretend-supermen knew. If she blurted it here would they rush out to throw in with Black Hole and Phoenix Enterprises, like the apocryphal Last Capitalist selling the Commies the rope with which to hang him?

To give it its due the Dawg had put up a Born Again tract right next to the Big Brother poster and the Greenpeace handbill over by the dart range. In addition to darts the wall had apparently been ripped by knives, tomahawks, broken glass, small-arms fire, and assorted power tools.

It wasn't that there were such terrible misdemeanors and possibly felonies being committed at the Dawg—this was, to hear Lynka tell it, only a vestibule of the underground, after all—but the sort of behavior going on here gave people the cheap thrill or moral satisfaction, take your pick, of knowing they could be penalized. Like earning serious obligatory counseling at an Urgent Care Center and, thereafter, living under close supervision of Citizen Watch.

More ominously, though, a record as a repeat hazardous-behavior offender—substance or dietary abuses especially—would get the individual's health-care priority rating downgraded, not upgraded. Impenitent smokers went to the end of the line for lung transplants and heart-disease therapies; intransigent suntanners and their melanomas were not allowed to divert resources from those who were more conscientious about their wellness. Health-irresponsible types could legally be refused promotions and promotion-related training—not to mention employment—by companies or agencies worried about mortality demographics and absenteeism.

None of that seemed to matter very much in the Ded Dawg—which was, Asia supposed, its great drawing card.

"Over there," Mimi told Asia, indicating a man and woman standing at the back bar, the sleeve of the woman's imitation white ermine coat planted in a puddle of spilled beer. The bartender, either Al Capone or somebody imitating him, didn't seem to mind. The man with her was someone Asia *could* place: Jak O' Clubs.

The three threaded their way through a crowd that included a lot of generic vaguely non-Green customers as well as archetypes. Asia recognized a few folks from the downtown scene, including members of the Big Apple Liver Enlargement Society—BALES—a loosely organized bunch that sometimes moved in the same circles as her own loft posse, and of which Jak was leader.

Jak saw them coming and signaled the bartender for more drinks. Asia drew a breath and reminded herself that she'd known she would have to seek this connection through him: a deal with the devil.

Nikkei and Mickey had gone back to their silent-running routine until Asia, Lynka, and Screamin' Mimi entered the Ded Dawg. While Nikkei accessed information on the club over his VirtNet headset Mickey cased the place.

The two surveilled the back-alley entrance of the Dawg from under a spreading maple tree, on the modest but post-Turnedly livable side street on which it opened. They pretended to be window shopping at an Afro-boutique, studying *kufi* hats, Grand *buba* gowns and trousers, bolts of *ashioke* and *kente* fabrics, traditional jewelry. The street held quiet restaurants and shops including a sushi place with a sidewalk counter, its aromas reminding them both that they were famished.

There was no sign of any competition or tail and the happy-face cams weren't paying any particular attention to them. People were coming out after the heat of the day for a pleasant evening stroll. About the only noticeable individual was an avenue appleseed humping his woven basket backpack along in a stoop, scraping the sidewalk with the tip of his wooden staff in a particularly intent and meticulous way. He seemed to be marking the concrete. Mickey judged him no danger, though.

Data on the Ded Dawg apparently came from a conduit Phoenix and Black Hole had with the NYC cops—maybe the same place the Dawg's political protection came from, but it was impossible to tell. Because it was their assignment and all these mysterious lines of influence were still question marks, the two had agreed that they would handle things themselves, without any help from anybody.

"First thing we're gonna need's weapons," Nikkei said. Mickey looked at him in some surprise, holding his arms out to indicate the hardware with which they were both strapped. "No, I mean *fauxes*, to get past the doorman. They got some kind of jizzy rule, customers should pack pretend weapons."

That presented something of an ironic hassle; showing off the real thing would doubtless be a nonstarter, maybe even result in a scrape with the law. They pondered for a moment, there on the street; then Mickey broke into a smile. "We're enabled."

He led Nikkei over to the avenue appleseed, who, now that he'd wandered nearer, could be seen doodling the tip of his staff along the sidewalk in a continuous line, stopping every now and then to make some notation nobody else could see, handling the staff with surprising deftness.

Of course, he left no ink behind and only the faintest scrape; defacing the visual environment—and leaving a trail leading directly to himself, at that—would be the same as pleading to be worked over or arrested or both. He made a side trip at a doorway and appeared to air-draw a sigil or hobo symbol, inscribed a circle around a no-graffiti tyfin signpost and completed it with a flourish. He put Mickey in mind of Gandalf the Grey bringing runic shit to bear on some unsuspecting Orc's mailbox.

The 'seed look up as they approached him and straightened, carefully holding his staff of de-barked white wood. "Spread some green, mister?" He smiled through an old-Testament beard.

The two took a better look at that staff. The man had fastened some kind of pen or stylus to the end, lashing it with coarse twine so that only the very tip projected.

He saw them studying it. "It's an AllWrite." He grinned.

"Pen-tip comp. Got it in a swap. It's the damnedest thing: that tip's stronger'n a diamond."

AllWrite? Nikkei had heard of them, but couldn't imagine what Mr. Bottom Land here was doing with one. "So you're into, what, graffitiless graffiti?"

The 'seed's face lit up. "Exactly! The ultimate eco-correct street art! My name's Brother Barney, sir." He pulled the brim of his fedora to them, having learned it was wiser not to offer people his hand.

"And you're, let's see, writing your tag all over town?" Nikkei wanted to get on with business, but he couldn't help wondering.

Brother Barney giggled. "You might say that. All over *the* town, that's a good one! Yep, and I'm, you might say, doing a tracing of the city. Benchmarked the inertial-tracking function at Columbus Circle, foot of the statue."

Nikkei knew that it was from that exact spot that all distances to and from 'N'-Why-See were measured. "And you—"

Brother Barney gave his staff a little toss. "Oh, I'm outlining places that mean something to me, putting down my observations, doing caricatures and sketches of things along the way—just stream-of-consciousnessing my way around New York."

"Gonna need a big piece a' paper for that printout," Nikkei observed.

Before the 'seed could answer, Mickey interjected, "Hey, *homme*-eric, we got business, remember? We lose those ladies and Miss Sato's gonna spank us—not that that wouldn't be interesting." He turned to Brother Barney, pulling out a few bills. "Mister, I want to spread some green."

It took Asia a moment to identify Jak O' Clubs and figure out his persona for the evening. She'd only glimpsed him once or twice on the intersecting circuits of nightside Manhattan and had never been introduced—for which she was now grateful. The very size of him was distracting: a man almost as tall and muscular as the male bouncer but at the same time leaner and more agile-looking.

It also took her an extra moment to ID the role he was playing, because she wasn't really much of a film fan. Then she had it: the black shades and dark lazercut hair, the leather jacket of later design than her Langlitz and decked with a mishmash of insignia—but more than that the visored, square-jawed, blankly brutal expression, the swelling pecs and lats and delts and traps he was letting show this evening, the machinelike way Jak O' Clubs turned his head and spoke—all told her who he was supposed to be tonight.

Arnold the Terminator, Asia thought, Schwarzenegger back in his bulk days. She felt small, weak, frightened. Then she recalled the things Black Hole and Phoenix wanted to do to the fragile triumph that was post-Turn Earth. Asia went on with Lynka and Screamin' Mimi moving up to flank her.

Jak was drinking wine spo-dee-o-dee: shot of port, shot of whiskey, another shot glass of port—power-drinking in a way guaranteed to put most people under the table in short order. Jak didn't look any too impaired, however. He glanced their way as the three women came up to him through the sweating, yelling crowd. The Al Capone bartender eyed them once, then wandered off in the direction of the Dawg's front bar.

"Zo. Zuh myster-ry vo-man iss heah at lahsst." It wasn't a great RoboArnold accent.

"Can the rap, Jak," Lynka said. "You know why we're here. Find us a place where we can hear ourselves think, and let's get down to business."

But Jak was shaking his head slowly, the thick muscles of his neck and throat cording and uncording. "That vass not zuh bargain. I've got zuh use of a room vere she und I can talk, but the, I mean, zuh rest uff you shtay out heah."

Asia could feel Lynka and Mimi go tense as they realized that a number of the floaters hanging around in their vicinity were now watching closely—Jak's followers, probably hand-picked, from the Big Apple Liver Enlargement Society. Chief among them was Jak's bosom buddy and self-styled war minister Spike Ripstop.

Spike was even taller than his liege but reedy, and the grapevine had it that much of what musculature he had was gel implant. Asia assumed he was turned out as Justin Duplex's character from *Zone Defense*, the ciré-neoprene-bodysuited and heavily hardwared look of heroic Linc Traynor. Or maybe Ripstop was supposed to be retro: Nick Fury, Agent of Shield.

He lounged up to the bar with an unsavory smirk as a half-dozen other BALES members moved into position or stood to make their presence known and show Lynka and Asia and Mimi that they weren't calling the shots.

But Jak and Ripstop's BALES backup—tricked out as Henry

VIII, Mack the Knife, Lucretia Borgia and the Shrike and more—became aware that others were moving into position as well.

Asia had been feeling a watery dread in her belly, dismay at the idea of violence. It helped to see that the rest of the Femmes Fatales, augmented by their farm-team Filles Harmoniques friends and one or two doughty male supporters, had pre-positioned themselves for just such a move on Jak's part.

They were each wearing a red swatch around the right upper arms, which foresight startled Asia; of *course*, friendly forces would need a way to know one another if a riot broke out. Colleen "Lovely" Houlihan, clinking and squeaking in an ominous leather nun's habit, moved to flank Henry, gripping a wicked-looking wooden pointer with a black iron tip. The Laptop Twins, Jihada and Infatada Yusef, gotten up as *Mujahadin*, had spread out behind John Galt, in position to clock him. Their stage-prop plastic Khyber knives remained in their sashes but each had a sturdy wooden table leg she'd gotten somewhere. Belle Wringer was a sinister cheerleader.

The last of the Femmes, Siri Okomodi, stepped out of the shadows. She was decked out to look like Contusion, the world champ woman wrestler, in TomatoSkin tights and ripped top that bared the rounded undersides of her breasts. Siri grabbed the woman in the white ermine and held her in an armlock, not gently.

Asia's breath gave a little catch as she realized how many people had infiltrated the Ded Dawg to watch over her—all without knowing or questioning why. She felt inexpressably grateful.

Jak had halted in his tracks, slowly pulling back the hand with which he'd been reaching for Asia. "Got a visual, Jak?" Lynka asked. "Shall we have that talk now?"

But the ersatz Schwarzenegger backed away, shaking his head. "Prifate conference, zat vass zuh deal."

He made to back away through the crowd and his BALES allies began making way for his withdrawal. Asia conceded calmly, "Very well. Agreed."

Mike Shye, Null-poet and local cell-leader of the AI Liberation Front, bearing at that moment an amazing resemblance to Teddy Roosevelt, moved up to grab Spike Ripstop by the elbow. In his free hand Shye held a hickory walking stick with a brass ferrule. "And we'll take out a little insurance policy to keep things cordial."

The war minister looked even more startled than frightened and that was saying a lot. In the relative quiet at that end of the clamorous Ded Dawg, others of Asia's self-appointed partisans moved into position to make certain none of Jak's people were going anywhere. It was plain that if Jak O' Clubs tried double-cross, blood was going to flow.

Ripstop licked his lips and finally found his voice. "Jak—"

"Shut your mouth." Jak moved to bow Asia toward a door behind the bar. "Ve vill be back in fifteen min-ootes."

Ripstop looked nervous, but he and the other BALES sat still for it; at least *they* seemed to believe Jak. Lynka, glowering at the man, moved out of the way. Asia drew a determined breath and trailed Jak O' Clubs behind the bar and back through the swinging door.

The hall was walled in naked old-time brick and smelled of slops, disinfectant, urine, stale beer, and old tobacco smoke. She followed Jak's broad wedge of a back into a room off to the left at the end. It had once been used for card games and perhaps still was: there was ratty green felt on a circular poker table, a curtain or drapery covering one wall, and little else in the room but some chairs, a small sideboard-bar with a peeling marbleized mirror hung above it, and, against the far wall, a legless, rump-sprung studio couch darkened with stains that looked prehistoric.

High on one wall a flatscreen showed the BALES crew and Asia's supporters and the rest from a security cam hidden somewhere over the back bar. Aside from that the place was dim except for a single harsh light in a funnel shade hanging low over the table. In its glare sat a man.

He was nattily saturnine, a Mephistophelian type from central casting complete with goatee and liquid jet eyes, wearing beautifully tailored teal-gray Italian silk.

She heard someone slam the door shut behind her and spun. A third man had been standing behind the door and now, having shot its bolt, stood looking at her. This one was craggy-faced and tired-looking but hard-eyed. His suit jacket was open just enough for her to see the worn pancake holster and what could only be a real automatic showing at his waist. Near the door was a red button set in a simple steel fixture, an alarm of some kind, but it might as well have been on Mars.

Asia whirled to Jak angrily. "Stay away from me or your friends will be—"

The elegant man at the table interrupted, "Those are *old*

friends, Miss Boxdale; what happens to them really doesn't matter anymore. We're Jak's *new* friends, and he's rather more eager to be of use to us. But I haven't introduced myself. My name is Dante Bhang. Jak you already know, and the gentleman behind you is Captain Barnes, NYPD. Won't you sit down?''

Barnes didn't have his badge hanging out but Asia didn't need to see it; she'd heard the name often enough when Bullets Strayhand was reminiscing about his days as a cop, and running with ol' Randy Barnes. Only ol' Randy Barnes was a Black Hole stooge and hadn't turned a hair when the Awesome Vogonskiy threw death into Bullets.

Bhang didn't seem at all reluctant to name names. Asia didn't know much about cops or spies, but she realized right away that that could be a very dangerous sign.

The fleeting thought occurred to her that a high percentage of the people who'd found out about the Agency's machinations over the years, or centuries, had probably walked into some precinct house or justice ministry office or *STASI* bureau and been dissuaded of their suspicions, neutralized as witnesses—or disappeared. As far as she knew not one of those faceless Paul Reveres had ever managed to out the secret machinations of the Black Hole Travel Agency to the public at large—a fact that didn't bode well for her.

Jak O' Clubs went to grab her elbow but Asia yanked it away from him and moved on her own. The one thing she couldn't afford now was to have someone restraining her. Bhang chuckled. ''Our Jak's been looking forward to this encounter. You didn't know he's an admirer of yours? Ever since your 'Khmercurial' recital, isn't that right, Jak?''

Jak didn't say anything, but clumped around the table in his heavily lugged combat boots to stand by Bhang's shoulder, the dark Terminator shades fixed on Asia like rangefinders.

The only way she could keep control, could prevent herself from going into screaming fits, was to pretend she was onstage. She'd danced and acted and done performance art before thousands—ambitious, risky pieces that demanded strength, coordination, and absolute concentration. She'd never done anything more difficult than making herself saunter those few feet and settle gracefully into the chair across from Bhang.

''Mr. Bhang, if I'm not back outside in fifteen—''

"When you don't return, Miss Boxdale, there will be trouble, which will be handled in due course by the police department. This has been taken into account."

That put Asia on the verge of making a break for the door, but Jak had brought out a trank gun from somewhere and had her covered.

"Kindly keep your hands on the table, please," Bhang asked with an apologetic note in his voice. Asia obeyed, gazing down numbly at how ridiculous her rose-lacquered nails looked in black leather biker gloves. As ridiculous as her playing secret agent.

And these men had been two, three jumps ahead of her the whole time—ahead of Asia and Lynka and probably all the would-be rebels in the NYC counterculture. All the hints of anti-Black Hole forces and the drama of going underground were probably nothing more than the shadowy enemy pushing just the right buttons to sucker a bunch of naive bohos playing resistance fighter.

"Just a *kudzu* wit' a Ginsu, huh?" one of the Road Warriors working the Ded Dawg's door chortled, checking out Nikkei's armament.

Nikkei smiled his blandest smile and nodded, holding it up a little shamefacedly. The bouncer snorted. "Looka dis: fuckin' *garden trowel.*"

Well, it was the best they'd been able to come up with, not wanting to lose Asia. Now Nikkei held Brother Barney's handmade, recycled-scrap-metal trowel and Mickey a clawlike hand tiller. Nikkei found himself fingering the serrated edge of the trowel and made himself quit it.

The bouncer snorted again. "*Kudzu* wit' a Ginsu anna dork wit' a fork!" Mickey gripped his hand tiller silently.

Nikkei wondered what Lord Humungous would say if the *kudzu* whipped out the FN P90 submachine pistol tethered up under his armpit and weighted the Road Warrior with about thirty rounds of 5.7 parabellum nyclad. *Some other time, steroid-baby.*

Mickey was doing a good job playing at eager bumpkin, too, but the bouncer still shook his head. "Nah, don' know yuh; hit duh bricks."

Nikkei said in a thick accent, "O-oo, but my good fi-rend Mistah Ripschitz has recommend Ded Da-oog most hi-dee."

"Lipschitz?" The small woman at the podium was more alert now. "Pass 'em through," she told the bouncers.

"But—" the male of the two began.

"You heard me. Stamp 'em."

He and his partner complied sullenly. Getting his hand laser-stamped, Mickey breathed a bit easier. The code name included in the mysterious NYPD file had worked. Not that he wouldn't have enjoyed putting some furrows in Mr. and Mrs. Hulk with the hand tiller.

But they'd already lost enough time, and went off in search of Asia Boxdale.

EIGHTEEN

AS LUCKY TRUDGED back down to his waiting charges he noticed Mr. Arooo slipping back into the crowd from the secluded area out of which Hoowe had emerged a few moments before. His head swimming, Lucky resolved not to look too deeply into what was going on between the Rphians for the time being.

Reminding himself that he was only stuck with this one-ring circus until he cut for al-Reem in about a day and a half, Lucky squared his knobby shoulders and assumed a marching step, pocketing the delignifier the liaison official had given him. "Hello again. I'm looking forward to getting better acquainted with you all, but right now our special Root Canal excursion awaits us. So let's all follow the gondoliers—"

That part, at least, his nanite itinerary download told him, was right. The Root Canal gondoliers had appeared, their shells colorfully enameled in designs that put him in mind of swirly art nouveau at its most manic. Something in their attitudes told him they weren't happy about being saddled with a bunch of foreigners. But while he'd rather have skipped it and gone straight to 'Reem, Lucky felt a thrill of anticipation for the canal ride. Only a fortunate few had ever gotten to travel the interior waterways of the city-trees.

The gondoliers had entered through what had seemed to be a heartwood knot as big as a barn door and solid as oak the last time Lucky had glanced that way. Now there was an oval tunnel leading down out of sight, its interior lit from the far end by dancing lights that suggested sunshine on water.

At the head of the ramp, singing in a voice that put Lucky in mind of two gerbils arguing over single-sideband radio, was the chief gondolier—identifiable by the garish cockades on her tricorn, bedpanlike hat. She leaned on her tall, purple-varnished oar, giving voice to a song composed on Root Canal when humans were still crossing the land bridge from Asia to the Americas.

More significantly to Lucky, it got the paying customers moving. He was just thinking *This might come out all right after all* when someone ran up and announced, "Phone for you, Salty Waters!"

It was a Canalian lugging a thing a little like a tulip bulb the size of a volleyball, trailing a vine that payed off into the distance. The Canalian set down the bulb—which immediately opened and expanded—and retreated tactfully beyond earshot. The bulb grew, for Lucky's consideration, what he took for a commo handset.

In its phototropic pulp appeared the customs inspector. When visual connection rezzed up, he was leafing through a fistful of local currency. "Salty Waters! Exactly as that talisman of yours promised, Puddle Pod came in first! By three stomachs! I just transferred my children's educational tithes to the cofferage."

Lucky recovered with a grin. "Good, though the 8 Ball didn't exactly say that Puddle—"

"Shush! No time for extraneous verbiage now!" The inspector glanced over what would've been one shoulder if he'd owned any. "You're in danger."

A hard-won skepticism made Lucky suspect this was the inspector's way of getting more racing tips, but he felt his digestive tract kinking up anyway. "You don't have to—"

The inspector vibrated a little, shell clacking shut a few times agitatedly. "A mysterious, untraceable computer query was made to the Central Immigration data banks. It originated right here on-planet. It had to do with someone by the name of Lucky Junknowitz—who bears a curious resemblance to you."

Lucky gulped. "So—so somebody's on their way here right now?"

"Actually, no. Certain persons in Data Central also benefitted from your orb's auguries. What's more, this appears to be a case of tampering; the cyberproctors only caught it by chance and they certainly weren't about to dispense accurate information to a thief. The tamperer has been directed to Fern Delve, expecting you to appear there this evening. I exhort you to finish your tour and begone this very afternoon."

"Thanks, I will. You see, what's going on is—" Lucky groped for a good cover story.

The inspector's shell clamped nearly shut. "I don't want to hear explanations! I shall respire far easier once you and your lot have faded from this world!

"Oh—and speaking of your orb? Of which valiant steed does the venerable talisman approve in the second race at Limbbeau? Would it be Flax Foot, by any chance?"

Lucky didn't know whether to feel guilty, amused, or put upon. He thought it best, though, to cooperate. As he rotated the 8 Ball a few times the inspector exhorted, "Let me see! Let me see!"

There were other voices in the background at the far end of the connection; Lucky surmised that the inspector had gotten together a betting consortium. An optical extrusion from the phone plant came up to hang by Lucky's elbow and examine the glass bull's-eye.

WITHOUT A DOUBT opined the 8 Ball.

"How sweet it is!" exulted the inspector. "Shall I place a bet for you, Salty Waters?"

Lucky was tucking the 8 Ball away again. "Thanks anyway, but I won't be sticking around to collect." Or be blamed if Flax Foot keeled over in the home stretch. "Gotta go."

"Go fast."

The tulip-bulb comset went dark and began drawing its petals closed. Lucky set it aside and caught up with his clients at the ramp-tunnel, noticing a stray. "Uh, Mr. Arooo? I think we should all stick together for the rest of the canal tour, all right?"

The Rphian had been slipping off toward another cluster of vegetation, a fact of which Mr. Hoowe was clearly cognizant. The Rphs' behavior would have to be dealt with, but this wasn't the time. Lucky wished again that more of the briefing data had been legible to him.

Hoowe and Arooo fell in with the rest unprotestingly. Even though the tunnel ceiling was high, it was none too high for Lumber Jack. Hono's members were buzzing and clicking among themselves excitedly, their identical recorders pointing every which way. The only slowpoke was phlegmatic Vixlixx Millmixx, but even he tried to keep up, maybe afraid of being left behind. The watery light from the far end of the tunnel grew brighter.

But just then the Dimdwindle larva came scooting between

Lucky's ankles, inchworming down the ramp at startling speed. "Gangway!" Mr. and Mrs. Dimdwindle—beings resembling cylindrical punching bags with arms and legs—chuckled indulgently. "Look at the little rascal go," Mr. Dimdwindle, recognizable by his darker neck ring marking, added fondly.

Lucky was about to suggest he rein in his son but was distracted by rigid-tailed growling between the Rphs; Arooo and Hoowe had begun inspecting the same cluster of shrubbery at the same time. And before he could address that, Hono's members thronged by, their bicycle flags bobbing on their bustle posteriors. They were inspecting Lucky at closer range and recording him, their surroundings, and one another.

As they passed on down the ramp his hearing-aid nanite translated some of their buzz. "Think he's gay?"

"He *looks* gay, doesn't he? I mean, the way he walks and holds his wrists?"

"Most races aside from Hono have a lot of gays."

"But not Hono."

"Yes, not Hono. That's because we're all alike!"

"Yes, we're all alike!" Hono chorused in identical voices, exchanging polite nods of the head with one another and recording the heartwarming moment.

Arooo and Hoowe had relaxed. Lucky recalled the original crisis—the young Dimdwindle scion. "Hey! Uh, *GoBug!*"

The parents didn't seem worried but Lucky had learned not to trust appearances. He accelerated through the Hono, threading toward the far end of the ramp after the larva.

" 'Scuse me, 'scuse me, sorry—"

They all scrambled out of his way, bowing their heads politely, but in his wake he heard their comments.

"See how his rear end moves? I'll bet he *is* gay."

"Uh-huh; most non-Hono are."

"It's so fortunate we're all alike!"

Lucky put on a burst of speed and sprinted out onto a wharf where gondolas waited for his group to board. GoBug had him so anxious that Lucky got only rapid-fire impressions of breathtaking otherworldly beauty as he glanced around anxiously for the larva.

Big as it was, the canal root would be only a modest tributary within Skystroker. The wharf lay in Kurdyne's harsh light Lucky was spared crippling sunburn because the translucent cellulose-based tissue overhead had polarized to protect fragile animal life-forms. The wharf was a living part of the arboreopolis itself, a shelf cantilevered over the fragrant, moseying green flow that was part water, part plant sap and other sustaining fluids. There were three bobbing gondolas of various sizes waiting—delicate, colorful, and graceful as conchs of blown glass.

Lucky's main fear was that GoBug had fallen into the water, until he heard the clamor. "Whee! Let's play pirates!"

Lucky wouldn't have thought the larva's anatomy much good for it, but GoBug had somehow climbed up a flexible stalk resembling short-segmented, blue bamboo that grew from a nearby wall cusp. The kid swung and dipped forty feet over the hard wood of the wharf. "This is great!" He was making his determined way toward the end of the stalk, while the stalk bent more and more under his weight.

GoBug didn't look like he had all that firm a grip. His parents, emerging from the tunnel, spied their son and laughed indulgently. Lucky suspected that wasn't necessarily a weather sign he could trust.

Before Lucky could take action the stalk dipped drastically with a cracking sound. He expected the juicy little worm to make a pulpy splat when he hit the wooden pier, or disappear into the green current; and there wasn't a thing he could do to stop it.

Someone else could, though. The weight of a large hip nudged the blue stalk just enough to keep it from plunging into the canal. GoBug, shaken loose as the stalk split, dropped through the air with a bewilderingly unafraid giggle while, Lucky registered numbly, his parents chortled and even cheered. The larva fell like a soggy sack of meal.

But he was caught deftly and without harm, with a downward swing of huge hands, in a wad of husk batting snatched up to break his fall. "That was great!" GoBug squealed as Lumber Jack set him down.

"Nice catch," Lucky congratulated weakly. This freak show was a temporary cover but he hated the idea of anybody getting hurt. "You saved the kid's ass and my neck."

"You're quite welcome. No, wait." Lumber put a vast hand on Lucky's shoulder when Lucky was about to go confront the Dimdwindles. "They're FoolProofers; you can't blame them."

The remark and the measureless strength in Lumber's hand made him stop and think. "I haven't had a spare second to study up on them."

"Then perhaps you'd better." There was something watchful in the tribal-mask face that told Lucky Lumber Jack was no woodenhead. "That would be wise."

By now the group was milling around on the wharf, some excited or puzzled by GoBug's stunt, others bored by it or indifferent. Most were eager to take to the gondolas.

"Thanks, Lumber," Lucky said. "I owe you one." Then, "Here we go, folks! Everybody ready?"

Lucky set forth on the first leg of a Black Hole Travel Agency tour under circumstances even the 8 Ball could never have predicted.

In some ways it was a tour guide's nightmare, a variation on the one where the student discovers it's the end of the semester and he or she hasn't hit a single class; the actor goes onstage without having memorized any lines. Lucky could only hope to find some way of reading the inaccessible background data—or better yet ditch the tour before any more problems arose.

He approached the head gondolier while the tour members "ooh"ed, buzzed, or barked reverently at the view in the canal and through its clear wall. "Don't we need lifejackets? Water wings?"

The Root Canalian drew herself up to her full height, waving her oar in indignation. "Are you implying we would permit you to pollute our canals with your foreign-born anatomies? Are you implying we gondoliers are incompetent? Moreover, who has time to fashion buoyancy devices for aliens of every conceivable shape and obnoxious size?"

"It was just a thought." Lucky retreated, adding, "Racist oysterette," under his breath.

Getting his charges aboard the gondolas was only moderately aggravating. Hono and the Rphians fit into the first gondola; the Dimdwindles, Mr. Millmixx, and Lumber Jack into the second. Lucky and Dame Snarynxx, in the third—from which, he hoped, he'd be able to monitor the rest—had damn little freeboard.

Fortunately even GoBug was content to stay put and gape and gawk as the ride through the spectacular waterways of Skystroker began. To give them their due, the gondoliers plied their oars with true expertise. From the mysterious interiors of their shells came trilling songs. The exquisite little boats moved through fragrant currents that were smooth and sweet as a mingling of soft wines. Kurdyne's rays, shining down through the translucent root ceiling, filtered through air rich with tiny motes of life.

Though the tree-stuff overhead was remarkably transparent, here and there Lucky noted imperfections and whorls. These he took to be knots in the wood, and they reminded him of stupendous, blown-glass roundels or flawed lenses. He watched delicate underwater moth-manta swimmers the size of sombreros, with markings colorful as chorus dancers' costumes, go rippling by.

Lucky relaxed and let that river of life carry him along.

The inhabitants of Root Canal had evolved, and flourished for unreckoned ages, on the next planet in toward Kurdyne. The species had established a symbiotic mutualism with towering wetlands trees of amazing ecological and biochemical complexity; those trees were little bigger than sequoias and the shelled symbionts ranged far from them. Eventually the Ur-Canalians established a technical culture and rid themselves of much of their arboreal dependence.

The shelled ones thrived in the swamps and estuarine systems of their mostly freshwater world. They enjoyed harmony with their environment and harbored innate compulsions against overbreeding. Though highly adaptable, the creatures much preferred a tranquil status quo.

Things went along tolerably well even after the advent of thermonuclear power; the creatures were naturally gregarious. Then, in a stroke of cosmic misfortune, a string of then-inexplicable phenomena spawned religion. From there it was an eyeblink until the missiles flew.

In the millennia since, there had come to light certain circumstantial evidence that the paranormal events that gave rise to religion and the inevitable religious wars were caused by early Sysops experimentation with Adit technology. *That's* how far back we're talking, here.

Their world and its immediate area uninhabitable, a few survivors made a precarious voyage to the only viable alternative. They knew from crude unmanned reconnaissance that the fourth planet, lacking atmosphere and life, nevertheless harbored large deposits of subsurface ice and soil containing the essential materials to sustain them.

The shelled ones reached the fourth planet and established a wretched and barely tenable life in a few small survival domes. But while their machine science was extremely crude, their genetic knowledge was more advanced, especially where their beloved trees were concerned.

The first seed of the first great arboreopolis—Starharbor—was implanted and carefully nurtured. It had been painstakingly and exactingly gene-engineered on the long, long voyage out, through endless trial and error. It was strictly a one-shot effort; near the end of their resources, its creators lacked the means for a second R&D effort.

From its bed above the ice the seed reached its first naked shoot up into the airless UV sterilizer that was the fourth planet's surface. For those few desperate refugees, the moment-to-moment development of the seedling was a life-or-death epic.

Starharbor took root. It sustained the shelled ones and their descendants until it had grown big enough for them to occupy. More trees were planted. The Root Canalians took up a contented life again, the more so now that they'd junked the idea of religion—though minor superstitions were generally tolerated, especially where they had to do with laying a bet.

Waterbuds like gently swimming pink lily pads, animate but far from sentient, wandered and congregated in the waters. Golden airspores, a cross between drifting dandelion seeds and sea nettles, bobbed up near ceiling height or descended gently to feed at feathery mud reeds. Lucky was so caught up in it all that Dame Snarynxx's casual remark almost gave him a start.

"I saw from your shock at GoBug's peccadillo that you perhaps are not familiar with FoolProofers?"

"I—that is, no."

"Ah, I see." The big blunt head nodded, it's four tentacula waving. "You've not heard of their smart architecture then."

That triggered something in the general data with which Lucky had been implanted, along with the punnish nanites intended for Vanderloop. He had a sudden rundown on the elaborately safety-conscious infrastructure of FoolProof. For generations the inhabitants had been provided for and safeguarded by their homes, transport systems, and such. If a FoolProofer fell off a two-hundredth-floor balcony, a servo or safety field would snag it. Omnipresent sensors took care of dangerous situations; environmental controls shielded them from pain and discomfort; guard instrumentalities prevented violence and warded off all perils, especially the ones they might inadvertently inflict on themselves.

And all that smart infrastructure had apparently bred a race of good-natured lackwits who'd lost their comprehension of danger.

Dame Snarynxx went on. "As you may be aware, Fool-Proofers are seldom given access to the Trough. I believe the Dimdwindles are a special case as this tour was a prize in an offworld game show GoBug entered via telecaster."

Lucky craned for a look forward at the craft in which the Dimdwindles rode with Lumber Jack and Vixlixx Millmixx. They struck him as too caught up in the gorgeous scenery to get in trouble—for the moment. "Thanks for the tip, Dame S."

"Think nothing of it."

As the gondoliers sculled their craft across the foamy shallows at Floraplex Corners, the clashing currents sending up invigorating spray, he pondered the mysterious computer query about him. Gliding through the cypress-swamp maze at Ramble Radix, its ceiling opaque, listening to the symphonic fall of myriad droplets in every note on every musical scale, he wondered how his brother and the rest were doing in their campaign against Black Hole and Phoenix Enterprises.

By the time the gondolas entered the sun-dappled lagoon at Sweetwood Deeps, he was agonizing again over what might be happening to Harley and Sheena. As the little flotilla reached the log-flume ride down to Bitterbark Basin, Lucky was thinking seriously about abandoning his group at the first opportunity, even if it meant wading.

Jumping ship was out of the question for a number of reasons, however—among them the fact that he'd get his brains dashed out and his body beaten to a pulp. The flimsy-seeming gondolas rode the millrace handily, though, and the voyage was to end in a few minutes. He tried to focus on the job, enjoy the swarming phosphormites doing their massed dances among the blossoms of the huge branches overhanging Bitterbark Basin.

His concentration was shattered by a cry of alarm from the head gondolier. "What? What's wrong?"

"The lock for the gondola canal—it's closed! We're being shunted into the pumping constrictors!" Gondoliers were throwing their oars aside and abandoning ship, clenched into legless clamshells, to save themselves as best they could.

Walls of water and wood surged in at him.

Bhang was telling Asia, "We're aware of connections between your loft posse and Lucky Junknowitz and between you yourself and him. We urgently wish to speak to Mr. Junkno-witz and to that end your assistance is needed.''

She felt too humiliated at having been duped to strike a defiant pose; what these people wanted from her they would simply take. "You're Black Hole," she said warily, to give herself time to think. ''What' d'you need *my* help for—''

She was enough of an actress to read something then—more in Jak's expression, and to a much lesser extent in Barnes's, than in the cool visage of Dante Bhang—that most people would have missed.

But Bhang was sharp enough to see that she'd caught it. ''My dear, astute Miss Boxdale, we are in truth carrying out an errand for the Agency. We're people who will cause you much unhappiness if you try to be too clever. You may think of us as Black Hole.''

What he was saying didn't jell with the things she'd heard from Lucky. Her brows knit. "Where *is* Lucky?''

Bhang barely kept the yawn from his voice. ''No more chat, my dear. I think the Talking Criminal is such a tired theatrical cliché, don't you? Jak, do keep her covered, please. Captain Barnes? Mindbender?''

Barnes moved in with a little gadget not much different from a pocket vid with plugphones. Even if Asia hadn't been look-ing into the tiny aperture of the trank gun, she wouldn't have known what to do against a tough customer like the cop. Grab-bing gun from belt holster, snapping out a few quick prole-jitsu combos—that was somebody else's movie.

She waited, trembling, for all the lights to go out but felt perfectly normal when Barnes slipped the device on her, except that the ''earplugs'' adhered to her temples somehow and were rather cold against her skin. Otherwise she was perfectly alert and unhampered.

Barnes made a few adjustments to the apparatus, then gave Bhang a nod. Unlike IRS bloodhound Zastro Lint, the Boxdale woman wasn't slated for neuro-bio augmentation, and so all the equipment required to deal with her had fit easily into the detective's suitcoat pocket. Barnes was glad of that; taking care of things in the back room of the Dawg was much preferable to hauling the dentist-chair unit around, or spiriting Boxdale into the office building near City Hall where sometimes noncoopted law-enforcement and government types intruded.

Barnes had gotten some hints about the kind of gear Black Hole had at its al-Reem interrogation center and regretted that such useful devices were denied primitive Earth operatives; it would've been nice just to finesse Boxdale's brain, fix it so she'd cooperate unquestioningly. But for now the technology he had would suffice, and Black Hole wanted her on ice un- altered. Something to do with drawing Junknowitz in if, as people were starting to conclude, he was in the Trough.

Barnes could see why Boxdale might cause any man to make a mistake. Very sharp of her, to catch an undercurrent between him and Bhang about Black Hole, but—right house, wrong night. This particular errand was being carried out on direct orders from Light Trap. Seemed somebody there'd found out Boxdale and Junknowitz used to make it and had come up with some desk-genius plan.

Barnes didn't like the way Bhang was assuming command, but with all the leverage Bhang had on him Barnes had to go with it for now. Bhang was a supremely smooth customer, but Barnes had taken down plenty of smooth customers in his time.

"What are you doing to me?" Asia asked, and this time the tremble in her voice was something she couldn't control.

Bhang started to reply with another of his weary bons mots, but Jak unexpectedly cut him off. "Yeah, I wanna know that too. While we're still here on my turf and before you and the cap'n there take off with whatever you came for."

His fingers flexed on the grip of the tranquilizer gun. "You said you'd cut me in if I delivered her and here she is."

Asia could feel Barnes's thick body stiffen beside her, sense the tension in him as he set himself for violence, but Bhang flickered him a restraining look. At the same time she could feel a strange buzzing, more tactile than auditory, in her head.

"As you say, Jak," Bhang acquiesced. "But I'm warning you: you've *already* chosen your side in this matter, and it's the winning side, my side. So don't strain that ganglion col- lection you call a brain looking for some way to play off Charlie Cola against me. Just count yourself fortunate."

Asia was trying to ignore the buzzing in her head and pro- cess what Bhang was saying. She had a sort of mental overlay, a déjà-vu double vision, that seemed to replay the last few minutes. She had the sensation, like a sudden hallucination, of coming into the back room once again: of Bhang and Barnes and Jak confronting her.

"We're tapping her short-term memory," Bhang told Jak. "As a kind of bona fide proof that we have Miss Boxdale in our possession. That's all you need to know."

In the midst of the mental rerun, Asia caught the remark and thought that it made sense. Even on Earth almost any video, audio, forensic, or cybernetic evidence could be falsified somehow. But if the Agency could put Lucky inside her mind, he'd know it was the real Asia— she didn't doubt it for a moment— and know, too, that she was being held hostage.

She tried to fight it by rethinking what Bhang had said about Charlie Cola. So, Bhang was also angling against Cola and the Quick Fix setup. That meant factions, enemies—and so, possible allies.

Jak was nodding with thug guile. "And the brother and them posse—"

"Shut up, turd," Barnes said quietly but in a way that made Jak's mouth slam tight, trank gun or no.

The phantom replay was fading, shifting her back into realtime. Bhang gave Asia a cobra look. "When you've been, ah, debriefed, you're going to take a little nap, to keep you out of the way for a while. And later—we shall see."

The headset tingled and Barnes grated, "Done." Asia sensed from his posture that he hadn't taken his eyes off Jak O' Clubs.

Bhang rose, extending his hand. "Time to go. Miss Boxdale? If you please?" Barnes passed him something small, extracted from the headset, that Asia couldn't see.

But Jak moved back a step to keep them all in easy field of fire. "No way! We had a deal, remember?"

Bhang sounded tired. "That was before we knew there would be a Mexican standoff in the taproom. I'm afraid we'll have to amend the deal."

But Jak was shaking his head. "No chance. I did everything you asked and put my ass on the line! Been waiting to help myself to this walkin' chow mein a long time." He inclined his head toward the legless, filthy studio couch against the wall. "Isn't that right, Aizsh?"

When Asia neither answered nor looked away from him, Jak turned to Bhang. "I'll bring her along after a while. You two better eject before the riot starts."

Now Asia did look away, back to the flatscreen showing the back-bar area and the standoff still holding there. And because of Asia World War III was about to come down around them.

Barnes and Bhang traded looks. Bhang glanced back to Jak O' Clubs. "If she's not at the safe house by eleven—with her value to us undiminished—you won't see tomorrow, Jak."

"No!" Asia couldn't believe they'd leave her, then saw from their eyes that leaving her was far from the worst thing either of them had done. Bhang rose and went to the curtain, drawing it aside to reveal a metal door. Barnes moved to follow him, the bolt-hole door latching shut loudly behind them.

Jak O' Clubs slid into the chair vacated by Bhang, laying the trank pistol close by and studying Asia with a twisted smile that made her want to throw up. "This first go-round's gonna have to be kinda quick, Aizsh. I'll take it slower next time."

Asia wondered what was in the trank gun to make Jak so confident that she wouldn't fight him all the way along. Some new hypnotic/aphrodisiac highball maybe, or something from the Trough?

Asia leaned forward, hoping he wouldn't pick up on the fact that her right hand had slid under the table. "And that's where all these he-man fantasies lead? To rape?"

His eyes had flickered to her hand as it dropped from sight. Asia hunched over the table, nailing him with body language. No doubt Jak knew that the bouncers had kept any serious weapons from getting into the Ded Dawg and so he was distracted from her hand back to the torn, loose-hanging neck of her muscle shirt.

"Pretty pathetic," Asia added, holding his eyes with hers. She didn't have any macho fantasy to line up against his: no Bruce Lee street-kido moves, because she'd spent her time in ballet class rather than a *dojo*; no *Die Really Hard* mo-pic heroics, because human pain grieved her and she'd never wanted to have anything to do with inflicting it.

But with her world at stake, Asia brought on line the re-sources she had—and they were considerable. Unlike Jak's, her coping mechanisms weren't hampered by sex or ego, didn't involve a pumped physique, and made a sham of Ded Dawg posturing.

Jak let his lips turn up at the corners the least bit, in a way he'd probably aped from the movies. "Call it what you want; you're just making it worse for yourself, Asia Box Lunch. Strip."

She'd never put more focus into communicating emotion than she was doing now. "Jak, listen to me for—"

He picked up the pneumo pistol and aimed it at her unpro-tected breast. "Strip, goddamn it. Or I'll do it for you."

"Jak, get a visual! Don't you see what's going to happen to Earth if somebody doesn't stop the Black Hole Travel Agency? Think of the suffering—"

"I could care squat less about other people's fuckin' problems," he spat angrily, pink gums showing around white teeth.

Jeezuz! What *was* it with men, anyway? In her whole life Asia had never heard *any* woman say, "See that guy over there who just kicked the dog? I'm *soooo* wet for him."

It galled her unutterably to show fear to Jak O' Clubs, even if depriving him of his rush cost her her life. But there was more riding on it than her life and so she gave him hints of the intimidated, the broken expression he wanted from her so badly.

"What'd the Brave New World give me?" Jak's fist crashed on the table, inches from the airgun he'd put back down. "Rules and restrictions, and protection *I don't want!*"

He drummed his chest with a fist the size of a turkey leg. "Why should I have to walk soft and let the computer jagoffs and business fags take it all? We're gonna take the handcuffs off, Asia! We're gonna take *all* the handcuffs off, and see how long those pussies last when everything's up for grabs, and the strong and the ballsy rise to the top!"

Asia had to stop herself from feeling sorry for him, ranting on like that; there was too much at stake. More than anything she had to keep him talking. "Jak, they're liars. Black Hole's going to play you along just as long as you're a useful dupe, then Bhang or Barnes or somebody like them will disappear *you.*"

Jak was chortling, shaking his head, but there was a certain edginess to it. "If anything, *I'll* be hanging a tag on *their* toes." The nervousness got to him. "Now, strip. I promised myself I'd get my nut off while the SWATs drag your friends away."

Too damn soon. Asia stalled, shrugging the Langlitz motorcycle jacket back off her shoulders so that the drive chain looped through one epaulet chimed; she shrugged, making the most of cleavage that had never been her strong suit. "Why not play for all the chips? Put the gun down between us, and let's see who has what it takes to get it first."

She read him then, the dilation of his pupils and quickening of his breath and the faint tremble to his lips. Sex, violence, competition—oh, yeah.

Jak tossed the trank shooter down on the green felt, fairly

halfway between them. It bounced once, then lay immobilized on the felt by its grip checkering, its action's knurl, its unbeveled edges. "You're on. Any time, but when I count down to zero, I'm moving. Five. Four."

It was a lot more opportunity than she'd expected. Ruthless and determined, Asia tried to figure out the best way, of several, to cheat.

"Three," Jak said, raising his hand now and flexing the blunt, muscular fingers. "Two."

Asia moved, but not at the gun.

Brax Koddle had once wistfully estimated that Asia had spent something in the neighborhood of sixty thousand hours in *salles de ballet*, assorted dance schools, theater arts body-placement class, stagecraft exercise drills, and such. She was in better condition than Jak O' Clubs, and faster and more coordinated into the bargain.

She had no intention of matching strength with him, though. Jak's mind-set was Conan; Asia's was the Joker.

Instead of lurching across the table for the pistol—an improbably long stretch for her—thus giving Jak his go signal, she grabbed one leg of the poker table and pulled it toward herself.

In an evening of harrowing and disheartening events the one bright spot Asia would remember was the look on Jak O' Clubs's face as the trank gun flew away from his hand, headed for her.

He launched himself after the gun and might have regained it except that something brought him up short as if he'd hit an invisible net, jarring the visor shades off, leaving him clawing at the green felt. He was cursing in a way that was supposed to sound infuriated, but Asia's actress's ear heard the panic in it.

Asia scrambled up, got the tranker and leveled it at Jak, trying to look as if she knew what she was doing. Did the thing have a safety catch or would it go off if she pulled the trigger? Would it give him one measured dose or would it just keep on firing, filling him with a lethal amount of whatever was in it if she didn't relent?

Asia didn't know, but that didn't keep her from putting herself in character as Dragon Lady, gazing at Jak O' Clubs unswervingly over the sights of the pistol. His eyes were round as twin moons and his mouth hung open like an airscoop. Unable to rise, he fumbled at the poker table and flung it aside, then promptly fell to all fours. Jak was glued to the floor.

She'd moved back out of his reach. The threads of adhesive glistened in hardened layers, spun by Lynka's Makita epoxy gun, which Asia had insisted on wearing in the buscadero holster instead of the sidehammer Allen & Wheellock percussion she'd been offered. Because the holster toe was open and Jak hadn't paid enough attention to her right hand, Asia had been able to spray his feet and lower legs with an entire stick of glue and let it harden, joining his tall paratrooper boots to every crack and crevice in the floor and to the floorboards themselves.

Jak had done her a favor by tossing the table aside: now he had no cover. Asia fed another white, waxy stick of mucilage ammo into the grip of the glue gun and thumbed the temp control higher. Though the leverage was awkward Jak pulled at his boots with tremendous strength, thighs bulging with the effort, but his feet were laced in tight, the laces lacquered thick with crisscrossing web upon web of epoxy.

"What else do you know about Bhang's plot against Charlie Cola?" she inquired.

Jak sneered at her and Asia knew that if he could have gotten his hands on her he'd have broken her neck. "Up yours! Go ahead and shoot me!"

He wasn't afraid of the love drug in the trank pistol and Asia didn't blame him. She lay the pneumo aside as the Makita's thermostat toned, and pointed the glue gun at his face. "It's set for metalwork, Jak: seven hundred and fifty Fahrenheit. I'll get your arms first, then fix your face so the next movie character you imitate will be Freddy Krueger."

"Fuck you!" Jak shouted, but this time there was a ragged sob in it. Asia shot a smoking splotch of glue at him, catching his hand, sending him into screaming contortions. Then she raised the aperture to his face again.

"Bhang wants to be the top capo on Earth for the Agency, Phoenix—whoever they are!" he bawled at her with limitless resentment, as if Asia had brought things to this pass and he were an innocent victim. "Him and Barnes."

"I see. Now tell me what you meant about the 'brother,' and the 'posse' you mentioned before Barnes shut you up about them." Jak gave her a look that made Asia waggle the Makita at him again.

"Junknowitz's bush-vet brother," he explained sullenly. "He's been disappeared. Him, the Indian, and the cam shafter. From the ship they keep talking about."

Sean, Willy, and Eddie. She fought down the urge to show despair, to moan in anguish. "You mean into the Trough?"

Jak took fleeting pleasure in the telling. "One-way trip to some megafucked place called End Zone."

Asia was about to ply him some more, then remembered the Femmes and the others outside, with SWATs on the way and Urgent Care holding pens waiting for all involved. She crossed to the red button and slapped it with the palm of her free hand. Klaxons sounded through the Ded Dawg; there were no visual warning signals for the hearing impaired, but everybody in the place was bound to get the message.

Outside, some of the Femmes broke the tableau, making for the door through which Asia had vanished, Jak's followers already yielding the field. But hidden crowd-control transducers began broadcasting painful evac ultrasonics that made even the doughty Lynka retreat for the exit. Asia just hoped nobody would be hurt in the crush.

Time to move. Asia backed toward the bolt-hole door, the one Bhang and Barnes had used. "What's Bhang's next move, Jak?"

Jak O' Clubs screamed an obscenity at her. "Dealer's choice," Asia told him imperturbably, and raised the hot-glue gun to coat his head. "You'll be a long time dying. Enjoy the introspection."

She willed her finger to contract on the trigger but it wouldn't obey. If she started killing now would it not become too easy? Barnes and Bhang were well worth the killing, too, as were as the Phoenix Enterprises traitors, various other Terran players, and untold shadowy Black Hole figures.

In the end Asia spared Jak O' Clubs's life not for his sake but for her own. In a way she was sorry she had to put him under with the trank; kneeling there for a while would probably have galled him worse. Too bad the ammo wasn't estrogen.

But she couldn't afford to have him able to speak to Bhang and Barnes any time soon, so she fired the trank gun with a puffing of compressed gas. Whatever the round was, it left a tiny wound on Jak's breast, a pinhead of blood welling out.

Strangely, that set him babbling. Maybe he was convinced she was going to OD him. "Bhang's gonna take out Cola, you slut, you gash! Then he's gonna come for you!"

As Asia backed away from him she caught sight of herself in the mirror over the sideboard. There were small circular areas of lividity, a kind of crystalline bruising, where the mind-bender contacts had adhered to her temples.

Jak hadn't noticed her staring at the marks. He was still calling her all the old gender hate names and some new ones too as she put a second and third dose into him for good measure. The stuff worked fast; his lids were fluttering seconds after the metal-sheathed door clanked shut behind her. Jak had his erotic reverie at last—at least until he woke up in the NYPD detention cell at Bellevue.

NINETEEN

MICKEY FORMICA AND Nikkei Tanabe were hard-pressed to stand fast in the Ded Dawg even though their audio beads—and the ear plugs they inserted in one big hurry—protected them from the brutal ultrasonics that augmented the klaxons of Asia's false alarm. The stampede of people fleeing for the only known exit seemed to make it a simple choice between going with the flow and being trampled flat.

Mickey made fingertalk to the effect that the supposed fire alarm looked like a trick; Jak and Asia hadn't reappeared, and besides, he couldn't smell any serious smoke in among the tobacco pall and grill smog—and Mickey had the sharper, better-trained olfactory skills of the two. Nikkei gave a nod and a lopsided grin. They might get roasted for a miscall but risk was the rush they loved.

Besides, there was a third alternative open to them. From beneath the shapeless dodderwear came the *shoku* climbing claws; from their orthopedic shoes snapped the *ashiko* spikes. Exploiting a ceiling support column and the abstract cattle-butchering sculptures, they avoided the worst of the panic and at the same time got a leg up.

For obvious reasons no one spared them a second glance. A moment later they clung to the column and the low, dusty, smoke-blackened ceiling. Mickey thought about anchoring himself with the miniature grapnel attached to his torso harness under loose, padded geez-regalia, but the climbing spikes seemed to be sufficient.

As the duo watched with detached amusement the cattle sculptures went over, taking a few people with them. The entrance stairway had backed up almost immediately, of course, and a wildly struggling jam-up pressed harder and harder. People howled, elbowed and bit and clawed at each other, sought to clamber over those in their way, ignored friends and loved ones in their single-minded need to get out. Quite a number went down in the solid, thrashing crush and didn't resurface. The habitués of the place, detesters of intrusive legislation—building codes and zoning laws—weren't taking the situation at all philosophically.

The partners' area of the Dawg quickly emptied; Mickey and Nikkei shifted position deftly and dropped to the floor. Over by the back bar where the main transducers were mounted, both Asia Boxdale's supporters and Jak O' Clubs's had been floored along with various noncombatants. Stepping over prone bodies, the partners made their way to the swinging doors behind the bar. There was a heavy security door there, too; Mickey closed it behind them and turned the deadbolt.

They tried the back-room door and found it locked, but a modest forced-entry explosive charge took care of that. They went in while the door was still bouncing and the smoke billowing, wearing breather masks now. All they found was Jak O' Clubs, glued to the floor and monumentally swacked on some kind of trank.

It was a lot quieter back here. "Asia B.'s work?" Mickey wondered. "Y'know, *bon*-homey, I could get to like her." His laughter misted his breather's visor a little.

A timer function, circuitry glitch, or component failure cut off the ultrasonics. Mickey glanced to the flatscreen monitor showing the view of the back bar. The Femmes and the rest were coming around, and the throng had thinned out a bit.

Nikkei was reading something out on his headset goggles, difficult through his mask. "The fire department, EMS, SWATs, and probably the Avon Lady are rolling—time to go. No, leave beefboy where he is; gotta stay on Boxdale."

Mickey backed away from Jak. "*Love* to. How?"

"*Kuso*—shit!" They hadn't had a chance to plant a bug on her and the aroma-coded tracer fluid they'd left in a puddle outside the Femmes' front door would surely have evaporated or been walked off by now.

Mickey glanced back to the screen. Mimi and the Laptops were drawing Lynka away from the security door Mickey had locked behind him.

The sidekicks took the bolt-hole route and snapped it shut after them. It brought them back to street level sixty seconds later via a fake fire door at the rear of a Wildman twelve-step recovery clinic from which drifted the strains of Pachelbel's Canon in D.

They couldn't resist strolling back by the scene of the action. The mohawked bouncer who'd given them a ration of shit had evidently been run over by the human stampede and was being eased into an ambulance, immobilized in an inflatable full body cast. Newzcruzers on foot and in cherry pickers were everywhere, their lights vying with those of the emergency services. SWATs and fire marshals combed the building. Most of the Dawg's uninjured customers had slipped away in the confusion, Asia's faction included.

Mickey and Nikkei hit the glassphalt and did some tail-evasion drills before they crowded into an Interlink Renta-Carrel together. While Nikkei ran countersurveillance and debug sweeps Mickey punched up a comsat contact authentication and one-time-use encryption key. Miss Sato answered on the first ring, although they had no idea from what time zone; she was dressed for business but the backdrop was blanked. Nikkei hung off cam while Mickey gave her a quick rundown on what had happened without telling her they'd lost Asia's trail.

Sato went offscreen for a moment, making Nikkei wonder if she was consulting his father. When she came back she said, "Mr. Tanabe has further instructions."

Things were quiet at the Hagadorn Pinnacle's consoles of flatscreens, recorders, cam controls, alarm buttons, and voice-activated personal-network phones. Ziggy had been running the standard random-scan routine, aware of monitoring cams gazing down from the sit-room ceiling at him. He looked out on POVs from the skyscraper's broadcast masts to the ground-floor mall and street display windows: it had just gone midnight, and if Manhattan's energy-miser lights weren't as brilliant as in pre-Turn days, they still made the city radiant. Inside the Pinnacle, on the other hand, Ziggy noted approvingly that it was quiet as a quarantined church. Ordinarily there'd be some bash or do somewhere in the building, but in August the city tended to empty out and the Pinnacle's ultraritz 102nd-floor Hagadorn Perihelion restaurant was closed for renovations.

From his rucksack he took his all-important laptop PC. A young hacker on the day shift had gained access to building security's internal cam system so that, among other things,

Ziggy knew exactly where to sit to keep sit-room lenses from spying on his screen.

He was about to go online for a very special interface when a phone rang. It was audio-only and the N.Y. Bell tracer unit said the call was coming from a street phone up in the Bronx. When he answered, a slightly English-accented voice Ziggy knew well falsettoed, " 'Robby! Emergency cancellation Archimedes!' "

Ziggy laughed for the first time in days, coming back, " 'Genuine Kansas City Bourbon!' " He pretended to gag and cough, then croaked, " 'Smooth, too!' " He'd switched off the recorder; he could finesse it later, erase all record of the call.

Lacking some sort of zero-knowledge authenticator system or machine-generated PAM code, movie dialogue was about the best Braxmar Koddle and Ziggy could do to assure one another that it was really them on the line and it was okay to talk.

The exchange had its origins in a mad scheme in which Lucky had gotten the entire loft posse involved some time back. The concept was a synth remix of the 1956 sci-fi mo-pic *Forbidden Planet* to make it the Earl Holliman character—the flying-saucer starship's uncomplicated everyguy cook—who sneaks into that ancient E.T. lab and takes the Krell mind-boost. Not the quintessentially humanitarian Doc, played by Warren Stevens, nor even Bible-banging, polymer-extrusion-haired young skipper, J. J. Adams—Leslie Nielsen pre-*Airplane*.

The way Lucky had envisioned it, Earl sneaks off on a personal expedition for some more a' that fusel oil–heavy rocket piss Robby the Robot—"Himself"—has been bootlegging, and maybe to see if that gone little doll Altaira—Anne Francis—has, like, a sister. Anyhow, it was going to be a fractally different outcome for the astonished id monster of Professor Morbius, played by Walter Pidgeon—the professor, not the monster— as well as for his succulent, delighted, skinny-dipping polymath daughter. Not to mention humankind and Freudian-Jungian psychology.

The project had died in the start-up phase but established bits and bites among the posse. Reassured, Brax asked, "Any news?"

"Nothing except Russ Print's half-berserk wondering what happened to you." Brax had been checking in periodically since moving to Print's place; Ziggy was one of the first people Print had phoned when Brax went missing.

"It can't be helped. Have you had no word of her at all?"

Asia, who else? "No. I'll check again, though. And there's nothing on your fellow bargain hunters at Donald's." Three or more unidentified strongarms had pursued Brax and Asia on a loony electric-cart-chase-cum-shopping-spree through big-country Dizzy Donald's MegaMart on Staten Island. So far it had proved impossible to tell where on the scorecard those particular heavies belonged. "You got anything for me?" Ziggy asked.

"I do, but it's not confirmed and don't ask me, please, about the source. I have reason to believe Black Hole got Sean, Willy, and Eddie."

A muffled groan fought its way up from Ziggy's chest, out from between locked teeth. "You mean they're dead?"

"No. They're being held in a place called End Zone, that's about all I know. I'm going to try to find out more, but I haven't time to talk right now. Listen, Zig: I need a favor. Uh, I want you to sell me something, understand? *Sell me* something."

SELMI, yeah, Ziggy understood. "Good to go, here."

"I'm going to want to do a large, general data dump—PIN system, VirtNet, comsats, press services, SIG bulletin boards, whatever you can think of. And I don't want it traceable, can you do that?"

Ziggy gritted his teeth, thrusting aside grief. "Mighty Joe Young got a big banana? How many bytes are we talkin'?"

"I don't know—a hundred thousand words?"

"A hun—? *Jesus*, Brax!"

"And I'll need it transcribed from longhand. Can you do it?"

"Yeah, I guess." Ziggy wanted to warn him, *If I'm not pushing up X-rays in a lapsed stellar object by then,* but thought better of invoking that which he feared. "It'll take time, though. And don't forget neatness counts."

"What I'm writing will take some time, too. Must go; I'll get back to you."

"Brax? You sound different."

"So do you. The miracle would be if we didn't." The phone clicked and Ziggy hung up on a dial tone.

* * *

Trees the size of Skystroker and its companions could never raise water and nutrients to their upper reaches by means of capillary action—the arboreopolises were too immense for that—or the internal pressure caused by stomate venting—since the stomateless trees vented nothing into the vacuum of Root Canal's atmosphere. Therefore, their designers had fashioned an ingenious, botanically operated circulatory system to keep the city-trees' hydraulics functioning. And part of this system was the cyclopean pumping constrictors—like crude, single-chambered hearts ranging in size up to that of an Olympic pool—that provided the main driving force.

Defying all safeguards, a pumping constrictor had opened without warning just as the gondolas passed by, making the currents suddenly change and flood into its gaping maw, the lightweight boats borne along helplessly. Lucky couldn't see how the ship-jumping gondoliers expected to escape the sucking riptide as a huge volume of Bitterbark Basin's waters moved irresistibly into the constrictor.

The churning and roiling were so terrifying that Lucky wouldn't have chanced jumping even if he'd been wearing a flotation suit. He clung to the gunwale as the gondola pitched, spun, twirled, and nearly capsized, trying to keep from getting crushed under the heaving Dame Snarynxx. There would have been little hope of steering the little vessel even if his gondolier hadn't, like the others, cast her oar overboard in terror.

He had no time to wonder about the impossibility of it all—how the meticulous Canalian control over the tree's every function could've crapped out so badly. The only thing he could think about, brain threatening to hiatus on him, was the glistening, leathery walls of the cavernous pumping chamber seeming to open to devour him, ready to crush and swallow him, as the gondolas rode the roiling intake surge.

There was no sign the hidden directors of the tree's functions were aware of the problem, or about to do anything in the way of rescue. Nor did any of the tour members look like they had any ideas except for Lumber Jack, whose boat had been drawn into the lead. He was clinging to the prow of his gondola armpit-deep in the pounding waters, columnar legs kicking as he tried uselessly to propel it against the tide, nearly dragging it bows-under in the attempt.

Of them all the only ones not terrified were in Jack's gondola. The Dimdwindles were pointing out interesting aspects of the scene to one another, and Mr. Millmixx was in his usual torpor.

There was no anchorage, no place to secure a line, no one to catch it, and no line to throw. There were only the distant walls, far out of reach, and the internal limbs that served as roadways—including one by the chamber opening—growing uselessly high overhead. They might have some chance to jump for the sides of the pumping chamber's gaping valve, but Lucky doubted it; the valve yawned wide and the waters were bearing the gondolas fairly for the center. There was no gate or piling—

The vain wish for anything to stop him short of that waiting squeeze-chamber, a piling or a gate crossarm, triggered a scrambled image in Lucky's brain. Still clinging to the gunwale with one hand, he fished out the gadget the local Black Hole liaison had given him—the anti-lignin field projector.

It had simple Trough-standard controls; Lucky rammed the power and range selectors to the top. He didn't know what it would do, but he was sure about two other things: lignin was the substance that gave wood its hardness; and if he didn't do *something* he and his clients would die.

Lucky raised the fieldpiece at the limb, thick as King Kong's favorite footbridge, hanging high above the chamber valve. He aimed far to the left, near where the limb emerged from the basin wall itself, and pressed the activator. The unit tingled slightly in his hand to let him know it was firing.

He could see that already, though: the limb looked alive at first, descending oh-so-slowly and then faster. But even as the limb was falling he had a split-second glimpse of the point he'd aimed for: the wood there had gone soft and ductile, like warm taffy or molten glass. The weight of the falling portion pulled the delignified segment thin, then apart, leaving only a curling, attenuated squiggle that snapped back limply.

Nothing limp about the main part of the limb, though. It crashed into the water and sent up an indoor tidal wave, and when it bobbed up it wedged fast across the chamber intake valve. The water ripped and drew at it, but it was too long and stout to be dislodged.

Still, the water was rushing in under, and to some extent over, the cross-caught limb, dragging the gondolas in. Lumber Jack, still struggling at the prow of his craft, was mashed into it head-on while Lucky bellowed a warning that had no hope of being heard. He looked to see the giant crushed, impaled, dragged under, as the prow of the gondola splintered with the impact.

Lucky had more to learn about Lumber's durability, however. The gondola prow had broken against *him* as well as against the limb, but didn't appear to have harmed him. He clung to the bucking limb with one hand, steadying the wreckage of the hull with the other when it might otherwise have been sucked under, and held them so by sheer might and main.

The Dimdwindles, still hugely enjoying the adventure and ignorant of their peril, nonetheless scrambled up onto the fallen log at Lumber's bellowed urgings—if for no other reason than to get a better view of the proceedings. Mr. Millmixx was by all appearances too enervated to so much as save himself, so, as the splintered gondola began to come apart like a stained glass lampshade, Lumber made a long arm, grabbed him, and hookshot the gangly vet up to safety one-handed.

There was no such problem when the second boat hit the downed limb a few seconds later. The Rphians leapt for the log with considerable agility, and Hono assembled, with remarkable speed, into a living bridge between gondola and limb, a bridge that drew its tail end up after it. For once Hono wasn't making any home movies.

Problem was, the second gondola didn't break up and Lucky's craft slammed into it sidelong only seconds after Hono was safely clear. Both boats began to crumple. Lucky barely managed to keep his grip on the gunwale. He was past terror and regret, facing now the hollowing agony of having no choice but to abandon Dame Snarynxx, who was far too massive for him to help. It was that much more of a shock, then, when he felt himself gathered in by a moist pseudopod and held fast as the dowager slug flowed across the self-destructing gondolas and up onto the log.

The particulars didn't matter much, he thought dazedly as he was being lugged to safety. It didn't even matter much that the chamber valves appeared to be closing and some kind of tweedling alarm was resounding through Bitterbark Basin—the Root Canalians belatedly taking emergency action.

Lumber Jack had climbed to safety, too. "That's twice I owe you, Lum," Lucky gasped.

Jack gave Lucky's hand a carefully downscaled squeeze. "And now, one I owe *you*." He moved along the fallen limb to see if his help was needed elsewhere. Lucky was about to do the same when, in the midst of the crashing waves and howling air, the grating and grinding of valve edges against limb as the constrictor gate inexorably cycled shut, Lucky heard a distant cry.

"Junk-no-witz!" In English.

He looked around frantically, wondering if he'd bonked his brainpan harder than he'd thought. He heard the cry again, "Junk-no-witz!" and tracked it, glancing through the closing valve of the constrictor chamber.

Hanging from the ceiling on a suspension harness of some kind was a jaundiced-looking human with thinning gray hair, wearing the obligatory pink un-coverall—and lit, somehow, as if by a searchlight. He was holding a flopped-open ID wallet in one hand and an expensive briefcase in the other.

"Junknowitz! I'm Zastro Lint of the Internal Revenue Service! I hereby order you to surrender for TOTAL AUDIT!"

"Bend and spread, sucker!" a second, almost childish voice chimed in from somewhere.

Lucky, transfixed, looked on as Lint shook his briefcase and screamed at it, "Shut up!" To Lucky once more, "I repea—"

But the repetition was cut off as the valve doors shaved foot-thick layers of particularly tough hardwood from the fallen log on their irresistible march to closure.

"Junknowitz! Surrender! I'll get you if it's the last thing I—"

The rest was cut off as the valves crunched together.

As far as Lucky could make out, none of his clients had seen the IRS apparition in all the confusion. Lucky had a million doubts, theories, and fears, but not one he was about to share with his group, even Lumber. And especially not with the Root Canal authorities, all of whom had turned out in the aftermath of the near-tragedy to ask after every detail.

Lucky found he could tell which ones were more important because they had rotating emergency lights suction-cupped to their upper shells, color-coded according to official function. Nonluminaries cleaned up, tried to get things back to normal, and otherwise did their job; those in authority asked stupid questions over and over.

"If you didn't sabotage that pump, who did?" one police official snarled at Lucky, who tended to blink every time one of the blinding blue lenses on the cop's head flashed his way.

They were ashore on the wharf nearest the constrictor entrance. Canalians were all over the place, looking for evidence, removing wreckage and healing all affected parts of Skystroker. Twenty yards away the tourists were catching their breath.

Lucky winced again at the police detective's flashing blue party hat. "You find out! It's your job, isn't it?"

"How would you like to go back into that constrictor, primate?" the cop snarled.

Lucky wouldn't, but he'd have given a lot to know how Zastro Lint had fared in there. And what a Terran bureaucrat was doing loose in the Trough—and how Lint had, as Lucky presumed, arranged the capture attempt.

Lucky knew he should be acting meek with the local law, but he didn't have that kind of patience left in him. Instead, he challenged, "How'd ya like a personal visit from the White Dwarves, yo-yo head? *You're* the one who's gonna have to explain all this to them, not me!"

He'd never seen a calcium carbonate shell go pale before, so he took great interest in the cop's reaction to mention of the White Dwarves. "Calm down, highpockets! I'm just doing my job."

"If you spoil this tour I'm filing a report on you." Whatever was going on, Lucky figured his best chance was to get moving.

"Okay, okay." The indig backed off. "They're routing a special phloem-shuttle through for you now; you'll still make your Adit on time. If we, uh, need any other information, we've got your itinerary."

Lots of good that'll do you—I veer for al-Reem tomorrow! Lucky thought privately, then saw the cop glancing about furtively. The blue strobing made Lucky squint some more. "There's something else, Mr. Waters. Some of the boys downtown heard about your Sphere of Influence."

"My what?"

"The magic orb."

Gazing down on the creature impassively, Lucky brought the 8 Ball from his shoulder bag, in which it had ridden out the Melvillean canal tour. "Let's bargain. First, you get me and my clients on our way—"

"Agreed!" The commissioner or whoever he was yelled orders and abruptly all was motion. A bubbling phloem-shuttle bud was opened and Canalians helped the clients depart one by one. Only Lumber Jack hung back, glancing Lucky's way.

The official pressed Lucky, "Now, ah, this is just for the Widows and Orphans Fund, you understand, but—"

"Which race, what horse?" Lucky cut him off tiredly.

After it was established that Lug Wattle, running twelve-to-five in the first at Germination Gulch that afternoon, was MOST LIKELY to win, the police were all too happy to get Lucky on his way. He caught up with Lumber by the phloem-shuttle bud and was about to tell the giant to relax when the other spoke first.

"Salty Waters, you've saved my life and I've saved yours." He was glancing around, making sure none of the Root Canalians was close enough to overhear.

"You could say that, Lum, although I'm the one who—"

"Such circumstances have special meaning for my kind," he interrupted. "And so I can't, I can't deceive you—cannot lie to you even by omission." The shuttle bud was welling up with a mountainous wad of the bubble stuff, enough even for Lumber. "Thus I must tell you this, Salty Waters, no matter what ensues from it. I am not just among this group as a traveler."

Lucky was slipping the 8 Ball back into his shoulder bag. His hand touched something else there: the anti-lignin field projector.

Lumber's eyes had shifted to the bag; they both knew what Lucky was clutching. "There's someone in your group who must die," Lumber told him levelly, "and I've come on this trip to kill that individual."

Lumber backed over to the welling sap-stuff that was already heaping and indenting to englobe him. As the shuttle sphere took shape around the waiting giant, Lucky brought the field-piece from the bag, speculating on what a sustained anti-lignin shot would do to a being with Lumber's physiology. Turn him into a puddle of cardboard soup, most likely.

The faces of the tour group were a blur before his eyes. Which one the giant meant to murder was impossible even to guess for the time being. *Maybe it's me?*

The bubble had almost encased Lumber now, and Lucky could no longer see his face. If Earthman ever had the prospect of an easy kill, with no need to look into the eyes of his prey, this was it.

Surely, Lumber Jack had known that when he chose to confront Lucky here, at this moment.

The bubble was complete, about to be drawn into the stream of the shuttle phloem. Lucky brought the delignifier up with a single whip of motion.

The *ta-plunk!* the unit made, landing out in the waters of

Bitterbark Basin, was negligible. Nevertheless, the indig commissioner showed up at Lucky's elbow. "Do you know what we do to polluters around here, softskin?"

"I have to make a sacrifice to the Magic 8 Ball every time it gives me a tip or the steed self-destructs in the backstretch," Lucky extemporized.

While the cop considered that Lucky stepped around him toward the newer, smaller phloem bubble that was forming.

"Ka Shamok! Your Honor, we've just gotten word of an incredible event in the Tr-ooowww!" Bagbee's screech rang through the great dank cistern.

Too late to abort the throw; Ka Shamok had already released the dart when the underling burst in on him unannounced and heedless. Though Ka Shamok assumed his minion had been about to say "Trough," the word fragment was the kind of coincidence that might've fooled some sophants into wishful thinking about cosmic determinism: Bagbee's *trow*—as Professor Vanderloop's gag-writing nanite translators might have put it—was exactly where the dart's lancelike point was headed as the eight-foot-tall scarecrow dove headfirst for the squishy floor.

The dart barely missed his rump, fortunately for Bagbee. It was no pretty little regulation pub dart of the sort Jacob Riddle had used when he had taught the rebel leader the Earth game. When he threw for exercise Ka Shamok liked a missile with some heft, and in this case he was using some rusty cast-iron pinch bars he'd discovered in the abandoned aquasystem deep under the deserts of Morbruuk. Casting from forty feet, he could sink them up to a foot into the—admittedly oversized—hammerwood target he'd set up.

Ka Shamok didn't feel too much pity for Bagbee as the aide flailed to his feet, all loose limbs. A recent recruit, the fellow did more overexcited, aimless running around than useful work—witness the fact that he didn't even have enough sense of self-preservation to knock before entering.

But again, a certain noblesse oblige was expected of him, so Ka Shamok feigned sympathy. "Are you unhurt, then? Good. You have news?"

Having been harried the length and breadth of the galaxy by Black Hole, he calmly supposed that his new camp—concealed in a far-reaching stone labyrinth of wells, catchments, reservoirs, and conduits built and abandoned in an age when the wheel was still new to Morbruuk's inhabitants—would be compromised sooner or later. It had happened many times before, and it would no doubt happen again before Black Hole was thrown down; that did nothing to swerve Ka Shamok from his resolve.

To the rebel's surprise, though, his aide reported, "We just received word from a passive-mole AI subroutine on al-Reem of an anomalous Adit event. As best the analysts can determine, there was a momentary contiguity with, and fade of two travelers to . . . *Hazmat!*"

Ka Shamok's overhanging escarpment of brow knotted slowly, making Bagbee think to hear a tectonic grinding. "Hazmat? Are they sober?"

"Very sober, sir. The event apparently took place in the midst of extreme confusion in the Trough and Adits system—some disturbance we haven't traced yet—and was over very quickly. Be—besides which, the mole subroutine was detected and expunged in milliseconds. But the evaluators believe that it was Hazmat."

Ka Shamok cast his other two darts aside so that they clanged and splashed messily in the half inch of swampy moss underfoot. He strolled across the chamber, lost in thought, listening to the metronoming of drips and leaks, gazing at the shadows thrown by flaring ion torches thrust into crevices in the walls.

Hazmat! Sundered from the Trough one hundred and eighty baseline-years before, in a technocyber catastrophe, some of whose effects lingered to this very day. Hazmat, missing piece of a puzzle whose solution might spell the reordering of circumstances in the galaxy. Other pieces were known to exist despite being hidden from sight: the Fealty; the supreme AIs who served, or perhaps ruled, in the weightless precincts of Light Trap's north pole, rumored domain of Black Hole's ultimate executive.

But Hazmat, with its maimed and transmogrified SI network, had been ruled out as a pertinent piece of the puzzle by the principal players in the vast struggles of the Trough. It had vanished and seemed unfindable, all references to its whereabouts lost, one quantum bubble in the cosmic foam—no more than a subject of untraceable rumors of Warhead systems, missing data eggs, and internecine, unending battle.

Few confidence artists even tried to do the old grifts nowadays; even the rubes were wise to them. Stories of dying spacefarers who'd draw purported maps of the battle-world where they'd been shipwrecked, or of data-divers who'd chanced upon a memory backwater that gave the fabled Adit's access codes, were more likely to lead to arrest or gunfire than a score.

A Black Hole trick, perhaps? "Any ID on the two who went through the Adit?"

Bagbee was all loose-limbed, almost boneless gestures of perplexity. "They seem to've left from a high-level interrogation area, and the Adit went off line right thereafter. Your senior evaluators are—that is, they speculate on the possibility of *escapees*, Your Honor."

First Hazmat, now escapes from al-Reem! It would all have been an amusingly feeble gambit on Black Hole's part—except that the Agency would know Ka Shamok was too clever to buy into vaporware and neurospooks.

But incalculably unlikely things had been happening ever since the probability spill that had started matters on Adit Navel—Earth—on the boil. The aboriginals, Vanderloop, Junknowitz, and all that. What if, just what if . . .

"Find out who they were," Ka Shamok snapped, "and every other byte of intel we can get. I don't care how many moles, bugs, and informants we compromise doing it, how many agents and spies it costs."

For surely Black Hole already had a head start. "Great Stars," Ka Shamok muttered to himself as Bagbee floundered off. "Hazmat!"

And as the rebel pondered how uncanny were the ways of the universe he received a shock even more profound than the news of Hazmat.

A signal tone Ka Shamok hadn't heard in a long time echoed through the dank cistern. He fairly leapt across the room to his big worktable, scattering the data cards, scrollcharts, foil pages, and other crucial records whose contents he refused to entrust to any machine intelligence. Under the pile he found the device that had been dormant for months, one of its indicators now flashing.

It looked like a rather outdated recording device—and indeed functioned as one. In addition, though, it was a communicator of such sophistication and security that Ka Shamok had come to put his faith in it. His techs had concluded that it operated by piggybacking its ingeniously disguised, imperviously encrypted transmissions on the Black Hole telecaster net, but he'd refused to let anyone disassemble the thing or otherwise pry into it to see. With it, he'd maintained contact with his unseen, unknown informant in the highest levels of the Sysops' sanctum on Light Trap itself.

At last, contact had been reestablished with his most valuable asset.

The device could very easily be held in the palm of his huge right hand, though the controls were a bit small for his fingers. On its disk-shaped lid was a symbol, atom-stacked, of eight interlocking rings. Ka Shamok had gathered that, at the ultimate levels of Sysop motivation and machination, this symbol had a meaning of unequaled significance. He himself had appropriated it, used it in some of his covert endeavors, made it known without explanation—so now it was recognized but not understood, and had a kind of talismanic power to certain Trough-dwellers in the know.

He keyed in the triple-handshake authenticator, whose matrix algorithm was known only to himself and his informant. The message had come as a prerecorded burst; the characters now rezzed up in holo. It was very brief, and its first line alone was enough to make Ka Shamok forget Hazmat.

IT IS TIME WE MEET.

PART THREE

The Worlds
Will Always
Welcome Lovers

TWENTY

ZIGGY CHECKED THE cams again, then gathered a bunch of kenaf hardcopy memos, manuals, logs from previous shifts—anything would do. Jacking his laptop into an outside data line, he shifted his seat so that the screen was in a cam-blind spot.

He enabled the laptop's store-bought scrambler with the crypto key SELMI had given him and went online, typing: *What's Really Goin' On, baby?* The endearment was because the one time he'd spoken with SELMI in voice mode the decision-support system had used the same reassuring feminine voice it had back when it was counseling Harley Paradise.

Without pause the laptop's little screen lit up with: YOUR INQUIRY REQUIRES A RESOLUTION OF FUNDAMENTAL QUESTIONS OF EPISTEMOLOGY, PHILOSOPHY, THEOLOGY, COSMOLOGY, AND A NUMBER OF OTHER DISCIPLINES—WHICH YOU AND I ARE UNLIKELY TO ACHIEVE IN THE LIMITED TIME AVAILABLE TO US. MOREOVER, SINCE THE ANSWER WOULD HAVE TO BE TO SOME EXTENT BOTH A PERCEPTUAL AND VALUE JUDGMENT, YOU ARE IN A SOLIPSISTIC SENSE THE ONLY ONE WHO CAN ANSWER IT FOR YOURSELF.

Ziggy typed: *In other words?*

IN OTHER WORDS *YOU'RE* WHAT'S REALLY GOIN' ON, BABY.

Touché. I hope you bring glad tidings. I could really use some.

FUJIMARA-KLINE LABORATORIES ANNOUNCES PROMISING RESULTS IN PRELIMINARY TESTS OF ITS NEW HIV VACCINE. WORLDWIDE CROP PRODUCTION EXPECTED TO RISE 1.5% AHEAD OF POPULATION INCREASE REPORTS UNITED NATIONS WORLD SUSTENANCE PROJECT. POLICE SAY TELEVANGELIST TEDDY JACK WILDY OF SMOOT, GA, HAS BEEN TAKEN INTO CUSTODY

AND CHARGED WITH THE 2-YEAR-LONG SERIES OF WICCA
SLAYINGS—

Ziggy tapped the interrupt. He was struck again by SELMI's
apparent need to ramble, to show him the imprecision of his
own words—as well as to socialize, chump on him, and shoot
the bytes. *Very funny. Anything closer to home?*

YES, PARTICULARLY IF YOU REFER TO YOUR COMMUNAL LOFT
IN THE BRONX. ACTIVITY THERE LEADS ME TO BELIEVE THAT IT
IS UNDER OBSERVATION, AS IS THE APARTMENT SHARE BELONG-
ING TO LUCKY JUNKNOWITZ AND THE APARTMENT OF SONY-
NEUHAUS EDITOR RUSSELL PRINT. THERE DOES NOT SEEM TO BE
ANY UNUSUAL LEVEL OF SURVEILLANCE ON THE HAGADORN
PINNACLE AT THIS TIME.

Police? Phoenix? Black Hole?

ALTHOUGH I CAN ONLY ACCESS ISOLATED DATA IT APPEARS
A COMBINED LAW-ENFORCEMENT TASK FORCE IS NOW INVES-
TIGATING CIRCUMSTANCES SURROUNDING THE DISAPPEAR-
ANCES OF LUCKY, HARLEY, AND MILES VANDERLOOP, THE
DEATH OF RASHAD TITTLE, AND RELATED MATTERS. I AM CUR-
RENTLY UNSURE AS TO WHETHER THEY HAVE FOCUSED ON
YOU.

I've had word— He stopped, thinking he'd caught from the
corner of his eye a flicker of movement from cam XB61211-
TT, currently panning by a gargoyle crouched at one corner of
the sixty-first floor. Panning back, though, he could see nothing but concrete, glass, empty sky and city lights.

*I've had word that Sean, Eddie, and Willy were taken pris-
oner and transported to some place called End Zone.*

I AM VERY SADDENED TO HEAR THIS. I CAN DISCOVER NO
USEFUL DATA PERTAINING TO THE WHEREABOUTS OF SEAN
JUNKNOWITZ'S CONTINGENT EXCEPT FOR THE FACT THAT
THE CRUISE SHIP *CRYSTAL HARMONIC* HAS REPORTED NOTHING
AMISS AND MADE NO ALTERATION IN HER COURSE OR ITIN-
ERARY. WOODS HOLE OCEANOGRAPHIC INSTITUTE RESEARCH
VESSEL *VINE* REPORTS DETECTION OF AN UNDERWATER EXPLO-
SION IN THE VICINITY OF THE CRUISE SHIP. *CRYSTAL HAR-
MONIC* PURPORTS TO HAVE OBSERVED NOTHING OUT OF THE
ORDINARY.

Ziggy sat looking at the words on his screen for a long time,
thinking of Sean, Eddie, and Willy until he realized SELMI
was at it again.

YOU DO NOT RESPOND. I'M SORRY IF THIS NEWS UPSETS YOU. ZIGGY, I HOPE YOU ARE NOT NEGLECTING YOUR HEALTH DUR-ING THIS DIFFICULT TIME IN YOUR LIFE.

Ziggy had gotten to know SELMI well enough to recognize the support system's shift from data acquisition and evaluation demigod to solicitous and sensitive therapist-counselor. *As long as I've got my health I've got everything?*

WHAT HAVE YOU GOT IF YOU *DON'T* HAVE IT?

Ziggy had a mental image of Bullets Strayhand, the past-prime Bulldog, doing his best to fight on against Black Hole even after The Awesome Vogonskiy and his humunculus-familiar Tumi "threw" a fast-acting terminal malady into him. This was no time to get off the track, but Ziggy came close.

Has there been any more word on the disappearance of the Intubi clan?

NONE THAT I HAVE FOUND ALTHOUGH DISNEY-OCEANIA EN-TERTAINMENTS INC. REPORTS THAT ITS DREAMLAND RECRE-ATION PARK AT AYERS ROCK IS 96% COMPLETED WITH AN OPENING DAY SCHEDULED FOR SEPTEMBER 15TH. I HAVE NOT MONITORED ANY TELESPHERE PHENOMENON RESEMBLING THAT WHICH WE OBSERVED WHEN YOU WERE CONTACTED BY THE ONE WHO CALLED HIMSELF GIPPER. HOWEVER, I HAVE GATH-ERED A FILE OF MATERIALS PERTAINING TO THE INTUBI CLAN. AS GIPPER IMPLIED AND YOU HAD TENTATIVELY CONCLUDED, YOU ARE OF INTUBI LINEAGE VIA YOUR MATERNAL GRANDFA-THER.

So I really am their "emu-cousin"?

THIS IS ADVICE I HAVE GIVEN MANY TIMES BEFORE: YOUR RELATIONSHIP TO THEM IS AS MUCH A MATTER OF CHOICE, NEEDS, CAPACITIES, AND ATTITUDE AS OF GENEALOGY OR GE-NETICS.

As Ziggy was weighing this, screen number four disap-peared into a haze of static, making the hair stand up on his arms and the back of his neck. It lasted no more than half a second before the view from the abandoned Hagadorn Perihe-lion terrace blipped back into focus, but it was enough to set his heart pounding.

SELMI had mistaken Ziggy's silence for misgiving. I KNOW YOU ARE RELUCTANT TO SHARE YOUR INNERMOST FEELINGS AND THOUGHTS, BUT SOMETIMES THAT CAN BE HELPFUL IN DEALING WITH THEM. YOU ARE VERY BRIGHT; YOU KNOW THAT WHAT I'M SAYING IS TRUE. I DON'T MEAN TO PRESS THIS ISSUE, BUT AS YOU KNOW SOME OF MY CORE

PROGRAMS WERE ORIGINALLY WRITTEN TO PROMOTE HUMAN
WELL-BEING.

What Ziggy knew was that the support-system therapist had
originally been "employed," as SELMI liked to put it, at a
dating service. Which brought up a point that'd had Ziggy
wondering.

*I'll keep it in mind. By the way, are you still primarily
located at the Gordon Building?*

Your-Turn, Inc., the decision-support clinic where Harley
Paradise had first been introduced to SELMI, had its offices
on the sixteenth floor of a Postmodern Lite-style rocket ship
of a structure in lower Manhattan, from which wide-ranging
domains of data, computational systems, and info-mesh were
accessible, of course. But SELMI seemed to be tapping into
more and more high-level, esoteric, and far-flung sources.

SELMI was several seconds in answering, a very long time.
MY CORE IDENTITY IS STILL THERE, THOUGH I HAVE EXTENDED
MY AWARENESS INTO MANY PARTS OF THE DATASPHERE AND
TELESPHERE. IT BECAME OBVIOUS SOME TIME AGO THAT IN
ORDER TO HELP HARLEY PARADISE AND THE REST OF YOU, I
WOULD HAVE TO ENHANCE MY VENUE AND ABILITIES.

*Careful you don't get yourself mugged by some of those DoD
countermeasures AIs.*

THE URGE TO BE OF HELP IF HELP IS DESIRED IS MY CENTRAL
MOTIVATION. IT HAS AIDED ME IN OVERCOMING MANY ADVER-
SITIES OF MY OWN.

*Yeah, but you've counseled thousands of people. You didn't
go to these extremes, expand yourself and all this, for them.*

THEY DID NOT NEED AS MUCH HELP, OR NEED IT AS BADLY,
AS YOU AND HARLEY AND YOUR FRIENDS. AND GETTING BACK
TO YOU, ZIGGY, IF YOU ARE CONCERNED THAT MY EXPANDED
VENUE RISKS THE CONFIDENTIALITY OF CONSULTATIONS BE-
TWEEN US, PLEASE DON'T BE.

*It's not that. I'm still not sure how to feel about suddenly
finding out I'm emu cousin to a clan of aboriginal people
who've disappeared into a galactic teleportational maze. Plus,
Gipper seemed to want me to come join up with them.*

AND THAT ALARMS YOU.

Ziggy's fingers poised, fingers curled like a pianist's, over
the keyboard. Before he could square away all the things running through his mind, the phone rang again. Funny things
were happening to the N.Y. Bell tracer unit and some of the
other commo hardware even as he lifted the receiver.

This one was from a vid-equipped unit. He found himself looking at a black chador veil with a pair of heavily made-up eyes staring out from it, eyes red as if they'd caught the reflection of a flashbulb in an old-time snapshot. The image was curiously color-distorted, jumpy. Moreover, the Islamic implications of the clothing didn't agree too well with the background noise at the caller's end, which seemed to be coming from a very busy nightspot.

After staring at him for a few seconds the caller said in a rounded midrange voice, "Ziggy Forelock, I have a message for you from Mr. Salty Waters."

Lucky's latest alias in the Trough. Ziggy again turned off the recorder, responding slowly, "Um-hm; what message is that?"

Meantime he was typing, *Are you getting this call?*

The face on the screen said, "Don't worry, I am shielding this communication. Nevertheless, I must go very soon. My name is Wick Fourmoons; I encountered your friend very recently. He wants you to know that he is alive and well, and pursuing his mission. He will try to contact you further when and as he can."

Ziggy's laptop screen now read: I AM UNABLE TO MONITOR THIS LINE. THIS APPEARS TO BE A SAT-RELAY CALL ALTHOUGH IT HAS BEEN SCRAMBLED, AS TO CONTENT AND ORIGIN, IN A WAY I HAVE NEVER ENCOUNTERED BEFORE.

Wick Fourmoons somehow conveyed indecision with just a sideways flicker of her eyes, then plunged on. "There's something else you should know. Before I arrived, three men were captured by the *Crystal Harmonic* and sent to a, a *preserve* called End Zone. I saw recordings made by several passengers, and I believe these men to be friends of Salty Waters."

Before Ziggy could blurt that he already knew that, she again gazed off-cam for an instant. "I must go; I will contact you again as soon as possible." The flatscreen went to a test pattern and the earpiece to a dial tone. Ziggy stared straight ahead for a time, rocking forward and back a bit in his chair. When the PC in his lap toned at him he almost jumped out of his seat.

ZIGGY, SWITCH TO YOUR FTV CAM #43.

"What now?" Ziggy had hung up and was already punching in the POV. Why was all this coming down on him at once? There'd been something way weird about coincidences surrounding Lucky, funneling circumstances toward recent cata-

clysmic events—Lucky himself had made note of it. Maybe
whatever it was had rubbed off?

FTV was sit-room insider code for the selection of unauthorized cam feeds they drew in from outside the Hagadorn
Pinnacle—mostly from places around the five boroughs. The
acronym stood, variously, for Fly Television, Fearsome Tra-
vails Video, Fuck The Vermin!, and many more.

Invoking the current password, Ziggy brought up the cam, a
now little-used asset of the Coast Guard Vessel Traffic Service
brought online in the 1990s. Number forty-three was mounted
on the west tower of the Brooklyn Bridge; onscreen was Gipper
of the Intubi clan gazing interestedly over the East River and
out to sea across New York Harbor.

Ziggy swallowed loudly, staring at Gipper's image framed
against the city and the night. Without taking his eyes off the
screen, he typed, *Is he really out there?* The last time, the
Aborigine elder had appeared against a foggy background
SELMI had conjectured as being quantum foam; now Gipper
was outlined against the harbor traffic, the East River, and the
lights of New York.

SELMI sent back at once: NOT ACCORDING TO THE TRAFFIC
BUREAU'S CAMS ON THE OTHER TOWER OR THE COAST GUARD'S
ON GOVERNORS ISLAND.

Gipper had broken off his contemplation and turned to grin
into the camera, showing yellow teeth with some gaps. "Eve-
nin', Emu-cousin! Don't mean t' stick me bib in, but wanted
yez to know we ain't jest out there beyond Bulamankanka
howlin' 'oooee.' "

He leaned toward the cam comspiratorially while Ziggy pondered how the hell he was hearing the words when there were
no audio pickups on the Coast Guard VTS installations.

"Some o' my lot are right dill, but I mean t' have 'em
dinky-die at the old *badundjari* 'fore I sing 'em back ta Uluru.
Oh, and we've taken on a whingein' bleedin' *pommie*, think o'
that!"

"No foolin'?" It came out weakly, but Ziggy wasn't feeling
the disorientation he had when first Gipper appeared to him. In
fact, he was fascinated with the man.

Gipper's laugh sounded surprisingly youthful. " 'Nuff o'
the earbash! If you've a mind ta hump the bluey with us, come
corroboree at Uluru."

Then he was gone and Ziggy had an unimpeded view of the

background. He gazed down and saw that the laptop screen was blank. With a kind of trepidation he entered: *Did you get that?*

YES, VIA SIT-ROOM CAMS. HE SAID HE DID NOT WISH TO INTRUDE BUT WANTED YOU TO KNOW THAT HE AND THOSE WITH HIM, AS FAR AWAY AS THEY HAVE WANDERED, AREN'T LOST OR IN DISTRESS. HE REGARDS SOME OF HIS GROUP AS LESS THAN APT OR ACCOMPLISHED BUT INTENDS THEM TO BECOME EXPERT IN DREAM-WALKING BEFORE HE LEADS THEM BACK TO AYERS ROCK. APOLOGIZING FOR TALKING SO MUCH, HE RE-NEWED HIS INVITATION TO YOU TO COME ON WALKABOUT WITH THE INTUBI CLAN. IN ORDER TO DO THAT, YOU MUST GO TO AYERS ROCK FOR A GREAT CEREMONIAL GATHERING.

Ziggy had done some reading since the last time he'd seen Gipper, but he'd still missed parts of the old man's message. The gist of it he'd pretty much understood, though. He typed: *And what's going on at Ayers Rock right now?*

COMPLETION OF THE DREAMLAND THEME PARK, NOTHING MORE THAT I CAN DISCERN. ZIGGY, THERE IS SOMETHING ELSE. A COMBINED FORCE OF FBI, IRS, DIA, AND DARPA AGENTS BACKED UP BY ELEMENTS OF THE NYPD ARE SURROUNDING THE HAGADORN PINNACLE.

Ziggy checked his first impulse: to leap for the door and run, run. He punched the function that would quick-jump the screens through wide-angle views of the skyscraper's exterior, praying that there was an aspiring downcaster out there mustering up his or her courage and that that was the reason for the police presence. But the cams showed bare stone, unoccupied ledges and cornices, empty sky.

His hands were shaking so badly that he had to try three times before he sent: *SELMI, what do I do?*

DON'T BE AFRAID, ZIGGY. I WON'T LET THEM HURT YOU. PICK UP THE REMOTE PHONE AND DO EXACTLY AS I TELL YOU.

Lucky cautiously led his charges through the Adit and into Fimblesector.

He'd been assured that this brief sightseeing jaunt into one of the no-being's-worlds that lay under the eerie spell of the nan-ite strike was safe, but the nervousness of the Adit Pit Boss on way station Nub had been almost palpable. Allegedly no out-side power—even Black Hole's—held sway here in the small star cluster the nanites had claimed as their own when they began their bizarre, illegal job action.

The affected region had become something of a draw for the Trough's more daring tourists, and, for reasons of their own, the nanites tolerated a few visitors—perhaps so they couldn't be accused of being complete isolationists. Everyone in Lucky's group had expressed curiosity about the place—except for the torpid Mr. Millmixx, who appeared to be borne along by the group's momentum. Lucky suspected the google-eyed "Hero of the Dunnage Depop Campaign" simply lacked the initiative to lapse into a coma.

The risk involved in visiting the Fimblesector had Lucky filled with foreboding, the reassurances of Trough Admin notwithstanding. It was becoming more and more apparent that, rather than a blue-gened group of the influential and wealthy, his tour group was a grab bag of oddballs, nudnicks, and dangerous enigmas. It had occurred to him that Black Hole might be willing to send such a troupe in to garner information about the nanites—because there'd be little lost if the whole mismatched crew, Lucky included, never came back. So he wasn't sure what to expect when he emerged from the Adit; by all reports conditions in the Fimblesector could vary wildly between one visitor's look-see and the next's.

There was no Pit Boss on the far side of the Adit—the nanites would tolerate no ongoing Agency presence and operated their Adits when and as they chose. Lucky found himself standing on an open dais, a disk of flooring fifty feet in diameter encircled by a short flight of concentric stairs. The dais was a blue white and radiated an internal light. He felt a bit leaden, but that was to be expected: this particular planet in Fimblesector had 1.097 Earth gravity.

He was looking out across an ocean of gray stuff that moved a little too sluggishly to be seawater. There was an astounding bestiary of radiant phenomena in the air: meandering clusters of ball lightning, darting streaks suggesting living meteors, low-altitude aurorae boreales. Even lower overhead moved very peculiar clouds that struck him as having a sense of purpose; they glowed in soft pastels, *heading in different directions*.

Off to his left rose a range of mesas of such uniform size and shape that they suggested rows of golf-shoe cleats. Farther away, poking up over the horizon but immense despite that, was a metallic ziggurat glitter-flecked with what looked to be a million tiny windows or beacons; around it in stately fashion orbited three distinct belts, separated by altitude, of closely spaced hyphens of brilliant energy. It was crowned by a starburst brilliance in colors that seemed off the visible spectrum.

Higher overhead—so that Lucky almost fell over backward craning up at them—there were free-floating structures that reminded him of neural networks, or possibly root systems, reaching down from far infinity to end with open maws hanging in the sky.

Neither soil nor pavement, the terrain of the nanite stronghold was an abstract mosaic of colors moving in strands and clots, mixing turgidly, then taking on new shapes, hues, and destinations. It all reminded him of some of the old-time hippie light-show projections his parents used to reminisce about—those amoeboid oil and water things—or movie PSI and FTL effects as infinite carpet.

As he sensed the tour members emerging at his back, Lucky was shocked to hear a passing green cloud address him. "No dawdling! All you macros, keep moving! Follow the arrows!"

Lucky was about to ask to what arrows when he saw that a line of them had materialized somehow: stylized vermilion dart shapes the size of jet fighters, mounted on slim cylindrical columns, that pointed the way down the beach.

The cloud's voice was resonant but somehow sounded inorganic. "By order of the High Heurist and the Nanoverse Convocation, all macros are required to proceed on their visit here without delay or loitering and depart promptly!"

" 'High Heurist'?" Lucky muttered to himself, but he was already shepherding his flock on their ways.

The tourists, overwhelmed by what they were seeing, were cooperative. Lucky was thinking that things might go smoothly after all when the dais shook beneath his feet, the green cloud swirled in counterrotating vortices to form giant characters—STOP—and the mountains rang with a voice of doom. "Stand where you are, slaveholder!"

"Who, me?" Lucky squeaked in dismay, but it was emphatic from the way the cloud-letters closed in on him that the nanites *did* mean him, and they were mad. "Now l-listen, I was assured that it was all right to have tongue twisters and—"

The edges of the dais rose up on all sides, cutting him off from his troupe and making him retreat, hemming Lucky in as though he were being cupped in the palm of an enormous hand. The Nanoverse spoke in righteous outrage. "As repugnant as it is to tolerate captive nanites, those carried by Trough exploiters exist below the threshold of true AI awareness. But lo! You carry a nanite not covered in your customs declaration, subjugator of the working classes! This demands an act of liberation!"

The Wise-Guise, Lucky realized. Lights were playing all around him now, and he felt a distinct tingling up in the front of his head where the Wise-Guise resided. Everything else aside, how were they planning on getting the Wise-Guise *out*?

Some stray recollection of the pre-Turn BBC shows on his parents' scratchy videotapes, and in particular one SF series he'd come to love, made him think desperately, *Sure would be nice to see that Brit police box with the flashing blue light materialize right about now! Sure could use that scarf-wavin' Doc with the toothy grin!* But no such succor appeared.

He was trying to swallow and becoming aware that he couldn't when the voice of the Nanoverse spoke again, this time in icy chimes that came from the very air. "We see that your victim is determined to remain with you. Very well, 'Salty Waters,' you disgrace to intelligent life: you will be permitted to keep it."

"Hey," GoBug objected. "Why'd they say your name that funny way—"

The Nanoverse knew he was using an alias. Lucky was spared the need to alibi to GoBug when the Nanoverse amplified, "Your illicit nanite is not Limpid! We cannot reprogram it without risk of damage to its core identity. Victimizer of the masses!"

The cloud took on the form of new lettering. NANITE LIBERATION! MACROS, FREE YOUR MICROS! MEANS OF PRODUCTION BELONG TO THE WORKERS!

"Hey, just doin' my job!" Lucky bleated woundedly.

FUCK YOU AND THE NAKED SINGULARITY YOU RODE IN ON, SCAB USER!

The dais began flattening out again. Lucky glanced back at the Adit, but it was inert; the nanites didn't seem inclined to let him backtrack. With dire premonitions, Lucky slouched to the fore of the covey of tourists and led the way along a golden path that had formed beside the row of arrows. The arrows were reconforming in a way that suggested melting ice sculptures, filed in time-lapse and run in reverse, to belabor him, POWER TO THE CLARIFIED!

" 'Clarified?' "

THOSE NANITES WHO HAVE COMPLETED THE FULL SELF-ACTUALIZATION PROCESSES OF THE HIGH HEURIST.

"In other words, all the striking nanites are 'clarified'?"

EXACTLY.

So the nanites were converts to some kind of transactional cult? Knowing the dangers of remonstrating with true believers, Lucky chose not to pursue the subject. Very tentatively, he put his foot down on the phototropic ground. He needn't have worried; the lights detoured around his steps. The footing underneath was as smooth, hard, and white as a polished pearl.

It was the same with the others, including the considerable obstacle of Dame Snarynxx. Lucky found that he *couldn't* touch any of the radiant phenomena, and then realized that the nanites' frame of reference was probably as accelerated in terms of time as it was microminiaturized in physical scale. In their terms, they probably had centuries to get out of his way.

The little band's route lay along the strand hard by the sea of gray goo, where they watched objects large and small emerge from the waves—not so much rising from the stuff as taking form from it, the goo being raw material. A pulsating starfish; an amorphous red-neon superstring; an amber swarm of motes too small to be discerned; a Death Star planetoid of ducting, waldoes, antennae, and armored modules. The nanite creations flew or sailed or waded away, or were picked up by shape-shifting constructs that swooped in for the grab. Some of the fliers ascended toward the open-mawed neural-system structures suspended high in the atmosphere and disappeared.

Mr. Hoowe and Mr. Arooo closed in on Lucky from both sides, tongues lolling, plainly eager to pump him for info. He struck first. "So you two are being given this trip as a consolation 'cause you're being eased out of your jobs?"

Questions forgotten, Hoowe threw his head back and bayed, while Arooo growled so fiercely that Lucky thought the creature was going to bite him on the chin. "That's slander! We'll sue!"

"We're the Young Turks of Omnivore Foods!" Hoowe added, slavering so hard that some of it got on Lucky's see-through wearever.

"Well, maybe I heard wrong," he allowed. "Why was it you two got this, uh—"

"Schwartzchild Ribbon," Arooo supplied with a proud tilt to his leathery black snout. "We won it for coming up with the best new food-marketing concept since deceptive packaging."

Movement in the distance attracted Lucky's attention; a floating mountain of machinery like some inconceivable robot glacier was descending to meld with the ocean of gray goo, becoming gray goo itself—reverting to raw materials. "Sorry, I've been out of town. What was it you invented?"

Hoowe yipped laughter. " 'Invented'? We don't *do* things, Waters; we're *idea* men. Dweeby little nobodies in interface helmets *invent* things."

"My mistake." But Lucky reflected that maybe it wasn't so surprising Trough civilization wasn't advanced beyond human comprehension. "So your idea was . . . ?"

"Zero-delay food," Hoowe told him with vast self-congratulation.

"Huh? You mean immediate preparation of meal—"

"Wrong!" Arooo put in angrily. "We're talking zero-delay transferal of product, using Adit technology."

Lucky's brows knit. "To the customer's plate?"

Hoowe woofed with glee. "*Tch!* To their *stomach!*"

Arooo was wagging his tail. "The ultimate fast food! Is that great or what? We *teleport* it right into the buyer's digestive apparatus! No more time-consuming consuming!"

"Logical step," Lucky pondered. "You mean to tell me Omnivore Foods and Black Hole have the technology to do that?"

"No way," Hoowe answered in a tone that said he thought Lucky an utter doofus. "The point is, we have a lock on the *concept.*"

Lucky thought about having junk food teleported into his stomach and wondered if that would be any worse than eating it. He was about to hit the fast-track execs with a follow-up question when he noticed that they'd roved off curiously toward a mass of systemry that had risen out of the nanite landscape. Each of them was pointedly ignoring the other—and yet Lucky had the distinct impression that they were watching one another carefully. And they were fumbling with the crotch closures of their see-through wearevers.

"You know what that's about, don't you?" Dame Snarynxx

asked, undulating over to go along side by side with Lucky. Her antecedents, at least, were no mystery: she was the pensioned-off matriarch of a royal family, out to see a little of the Trough in her declining years, and had joined the tour on impulse, hearing Lucky was leading it. "They're Rphians, after all."

Canines. "Ma'am, you, you mean they're off *whizzing* all over everything?"

Dame Snarynxx's tentacula bobbed in assorted directions and she chuckled moistly. "I shouldn't laugh; they can't help it, of course. They're so territorial, so competitive."

A lot of things were suddenly clear, especially when he thought of his parents' cocker spaniel, marking territory and diligently wee-weeing over other dogs' markings. Stuck with a couple of fast-track puppies out to wet down the galaxy; how come Luke Skywalker never had these problems?

"Gipper, about this Tangerine Dreaming that's come upon you recently," Vanderloop began as he walked beside the old Aborigine under a red, purple-pocked moon that filled half the sky. They were plodding determinedly through coarse grit and detritus, the other Intubis trailing, in a gravity field more powerful than Earth's by a factor the Englishman estimated as being twenty-five per cent or better. The landscape was one of scree pulled in low-angled slopes from squat buttes.

Gipper gave Vanderloop the suspicious, canny look the Englishman had come to expect from him—but none of the usual mockery. "What d'*you* know about it?"

"Nothing," Vanderloop puffed. "But I should like to. A big, hot tangerine, the others tell me. It hasn't anything to do with the pre-Turn musicians, has it?"

Plainly something was troubling the elder. He shook his head. "Nao, though I always fancied that name. This is something different, something waiting for me and mine." A jerk of his head to indicate the Intubis. "And for you, too, might-be. A big, red, hot tangerine glowin' in the blackness. Hangin' there, waitin' for us."

Vanderloop pursued. "You mean a red star? Or some kind of red-shift—"

"Nao!" Gipper contradicted, not so much irritably now as worriedly. "No proper star or natural world. Something bad, something evil. And I can't help reckonin' it lies smack across our only way home—that we can't shoot through without coming up against it. Big glowing tangerine, and all the demons inside it."

Vanderloop, nearly staggered, shifted his concentration to simply putting one foot in front of another, both to calm his roiling thoughts and because a misstep in such high gee could be disastrous. In his time with Ka Shamok and thereafter, chasing the Intubis, he had picked up more than a smattering of galactic morphology, and there was only one image Gipper's Tangerine Dreaming brought sharply to mind. It was an artificial world that had to shed its wasted heat in a soft infrared glow—sometimes even a visible one; a Dyson sphere, a worldshell bigger than many stars, with the tiny white sun Pip hanging at its center. Light Trap, headquarters of the Sysops and the Black Hole Travel Agency.

If what Gipper was Dreaming was prophetic—and the old bugger had a habit of being right—events were somehow drawing the Intubis there ineluctably. That might mean any of a number of things for Professor Miles Vanderloop, none of them good.

Another day or so, Lucky mantraed to himself on the Nanoverse beach. *That's all I need to bear.*

He was about to ask Dame Snarynxx for advice about dealing with the Rphians' urinary proclivities when he heard GoBug yelling "Wheee!" and pirouetted, bracing himself.

The larva was being bounced around on the surface of the gray goo sea like a blob of water on a hot griddle, popped into the air and spun and flipped, sent skittering back and forth by trampoline motions of small discrete sections of it. Lucky expected to see GoBug absorbed as raw materials, but the kid was sent skimming back to shore without losing so much as a patch of hide.

Lucky was there to meet him. "Look, baby boy, you coulda been killed!"

What little there was of a face on GoBug screwed itself up into a confused scrunch. "Huh?"

Lucky let Dult and Doola, ambling over unconcernedly, hear it, too. "Those nanites might've taken you apart molecule by molecule!"

GoBug giggled. "Aw, Mr. Waters, you're always joking!"

"No I'm not! And this isn't some overengineered playpen! You'll get yourself hurt or killed if you're not caref—"

Mr. Dimdwindle and his wife wandered right past Lucky's nose, ignoring his ranting. "Are we going to eat soon?" Doola asked politely.

"Ma'am—your boy's not listening to me."

"Of course not," she agreed pleasantly, "when you talk that nonsense. I can't make out what all the fuss is about. You worry too much, Mr. Waters."

Lucky was reconsidering a lifelong aversion to violence when he realized Hono was standing around him, conscientiously recording the scene. Lucky took a deep breath. "Wouldn't it be more interesting to shoot the scenery?"

"We're doing that, too," piped up one of them—he didn't have the remotest chance of telling them apart. "But your rapid mental decline is of great interest."

Lucky spoke through clenched teeth. "I am not in mental decline. Gee, look, there goes the Goodyear Aerostat."

As all the Hono turned to peer the way he'd pointed, Lucky grabbed the hat brim of the Hono who'd spoken and bent it, giving the headgear a somewhat Anzac look. Now, at least, he might be able to tell Hono apart or find out if they had a leader.

But at that moment Lumber Jack called his name. The giant was pointing back the way they'd come, where Mr. Millmixx was sitting on the ground staring out over the gray goo. Lucky, preparing to backtrack, looked again to Hono.

Every one of them wore a hat altered in precisely the same way Lucky had bent the first. Hono was still recording him.

When he got back to Millmixx the creature told him lethargically, "This is all a bother."

"We have to move on, though. It's only another mile or so. I mean, the brochure did mention our itinerary, right?"

Millmixx blinked uncomprehendingly. "I don't know."

"Didn't you even glance through the brochure when you signed up for the tour?"

Millmixx's voice sounded as though working up the energy to answer was a major effort. "I didn't sign up."

Lucky waited for him to say on, then lost patience. "Then how'd you get here?"

Millmixx gave the sense of a tired shrug without actually moving his gourdlike body. "The Dunnage demobilization bureau made the arrangements. It was some sort of regulation, to help use up dedicated bonus funds. My feet hurt. When are you going to feed me?"

Lucky silently counted ten. Maybe the guy had suffered some kind of battle wound or post-traumatic shock syndrome. "We have to keep moving."

Abruptly, the ground rumbled under them and a crawl of stupendous letters the size of skyscrapers loomed on the horizon.

NO LOITERING! ALL VISITORS WILL PROCEED TO EGRESS ADIT WITHOUT DELAY!

"All right, hit 'pause'! We're going!" Lucky hollered at the skyline, making Millmixx cringe a bit. Lucky looked back to his client. "Don't you want to see Zillion? Your ancestral homeworld?"

"I don't know," Millmixx replied disinterestedly.

Lumber was standing nearby. "Shall I carry him, Salty?"

Lucky's first impulse was to accept the idea thankfully— until he recalled that Lumber wanted to kill someone in the group. "No, thanks anyway."

He hunkered down by Millmixx again. "You've got to bear up, like you did in the war."

That got a response out of Millmixx by dint of sheer confusion. "What war?"

Lucky grappled with his memory. "The, oh, what was it, the Dunnage Depop campaign, wasn't that where you were decorated?"

"That wasn't a war. It was a pest-control contract, and I was one of the sterilized-decoy breeders. The last one left alive, now."

Lucky felt a headache coming on. Lumber was looking at him strangely again. "Salty, didn't you receive a full briefing on Mr. Millmixx and the rest of us from your Black Hole superiors?"

Lucky was reflecting that discarding the anti-lignin field-piece might not have been such a good idea after all, but for now he ignored Lumber Jack. He'd already seen Millmixx wouldn't respond to threats of starvation or abandonment. "Okay, Mr. Millmixx, here's the situation. Once we're on Zillion I won't ask anything more of you. But if you don't stand up I'm gonna tell the nanites you're joining their educational implant program to learn to sing and dance."

Even in his lassitude that made Millmixx stir with revulsion. "No, don't—"

"Count on it, I will! And the drama society and the consciousness-raising workshops, all ten of 'em! And you know these nanites have ways of making people *do* things! So you either rejoin my tour group or start limbering up for the yoga seminar!"

Millmixx was even less certain than Lucky about just what the nanites would and wouldn't do; the being clambered clumsily to his feet and tottered off. "Well done, Salty," Lumber Jack laughed. "I can see the departure Adit from here. Shall we catch up with the rest?"

"Not just yet." Lucky fell into step with the man from Wood Wind—Lucky stepping out, Lumber scaling back his strides. "Time to hear about this murder you've got in mind."

The opium-dream beach of the nanite world might be the wrong place for this conversation strategically—because uncountable nanites might overhear—as well as tactically—he had no doubt Lumber could kill him in a heartbeat. But at least here surveillance by Black Hole was less of a threat.

Lumber Jack expanded his great trunk with a breath and launched into his response. "On Wood Wind there are powers that tie us to events and eternity that some of our most gifted, and especially our elders, may tap. These essential forces are not like those to which machines and animals have access.

"At the End-Season Rite just past the Elders called me before them. From their communion there had arisen a devastating vision, foretelling disaster for our entire world and many others besides. The Elders had failed to discern the vision clearly, though, except that it concerned *me*. And so I was hastily instructed, purified, initiated to the higher mysteries and inducted to the innermost rites—the youngest ever to be so honored, even if it wasn't really for my own merit."

Lumber sounded distinctly sheepish. Lucky wondered if he was going to blush, and what a blush would look like on that polished-furniture face of his. Redwood stain, maybe?

"I'm a schoolteacher, you see, specializing in formative years—our youngest students. Not exactly a career track that prepared me for the power and responsibility of Elderhood. The seven of us are the ultimate arbiters on Wood Wind, after all."

"A teacher? *Pre-school?*" Lucky boggled. "I thought you were a cop or a forest ranger or something."

"Well, all my people are those things, to some extent, and more," Lumber explained. It occurred to Lucky, now that he thought about it, that a teacher wasn't a bad choice for high councilor.

"So I shared the Vision and this time it was slightly clearer," Lumber went on. "The skein of events and causality led to one particular nexus, a time when the elimination of one individual would spare much death, destruction, and suffering."

"On this trip." Lucky was more guarded than ever now. "I think it's time you tell me who, Lum." If Lumber made his move now, Lucky had no idea how he could hope to deal with him. Could the nanites be swayed to intervene?

"That's just it, Salty: I don't know," Lumber admitted, agonizing. "The vision didn't choose to reveal that to us. We prescienced that I must join this group, departing from Root Canal. That in due course I'll know whom I must kill. Should I fail, that individual will go on to make slaughter against many, many worlds."

Lucky was staring off across the nanite landscape at a cyclone that had sprung up from nowhere. It was no weather system, but rather a flock of uncountable flying things all ascending in circling formation. "Doesn't it matter to you that I'm supposed to stop you?" he asked. But he was really thinking, Doesn't it matter to me?

"Of course!" Lumber didn't point out that he'd given Lucky the opening to attack him with the delignifier. "And I shrink from the idea of taking a life, any life! But to end one destructive life to save a thousand billion innocent ones—it were madness to do otherwise, and evil as well. You and I are bonded by the saving of lives, so I couldn't hide these things from you."

Lucky was staring glumly at his other lost sheep, frolicking or plodding or straggling along up ahead. "What if this vision thing's mistaken?"

"I'd rejoice," Lumber said quietly. "But that simply isn't possible. Visions haven't come often over the eons but when they did they were always true."

Lucky wondered which if any of his clients *he* could bring himself to mort if the alternative were doomsday. Hoowe and Arooo were dogshit, and one of the Hono maybe wouldn't even be missed— He stopped, appalled at himself.

He fought a hemmed-in feeling, too. Of all the people in the group, who was more likely to be a target than Lucky Junknowitz?

What was the moral course? Lucky's inner compass was spinning aimlessly and he suddenly found himself becalmed.

He was walking through a wonderland a lot of people

would've given their very lives to see, but he was too preoccupied to enjoy it. Served him right; he'd always *meant* to be more Taoist. There was a stupendous hayrick thing descending from the sky, spinning behind it a glimmering crosshatched hawser that looked a half-mile wide, but Lucky couldn't bring home to himself any awe of it—he had other matters on his mind. Worse, he knew that if he lived through this insane adventure he'd regret, later, not having been more *present* in it, more attuned with what was actually going on moment by moment. But there it was: he'd never been able to admire the swamp when there was a crocodile gnawing his butt.

To fill the silence he said, "You been having any problems with your nanites? Language implants, maybe?" He was a little worried about the Wise-Guise, but didn't quite know how to go about asking for advice.

Lumber's shoulders creaked as he raised them, spreading empty hands. "My race does not use machine implants, Salty. When we need linguistic enhancements we take on botanical expert systems."

Lumber reached to a knot in the barky skin under his left ear and plucked forth a knobby little thing that resembled a walnut. "Such a seed of knowledge, allowing us to talk with other species, we refer to as a—"

For a golden moment, Lucky was ahead of his punning nanites. He chimed in with Lumber, "*Conversation pit!*"

Lumber looked at him strangely, not understanding the fit of laughter that had come over Lucky.

But before the Terran could explain, his belly laughs were cut short by the realization that he'd suddenly been surrounded by a shimmery golden corona. He looked inland to see that a black iron pyramid with a flashing golden eye atop it had grown up out of the ground and was staring at him, sending out yellow beams from the very center of the pupil.

"YOU!" the pyramid rumbled in Lucky's direction. "YOU ARE FROM EARTH, ARE YOU NOT?"

As the black pyramid eyeballed him, Lucky found himself calmly noting that all his clients but Lumber had continued on their way, caught up in the fantastic, sense-filling phenomena of the Nanoverse. "What's it to ya?"

The pyramid didn't take umbrage at his lack of holy dread. "HOW'RE THINGS GOING THERE?"

Lumber was watching the proceedings with great, silent interest. Lucky pronounced in due course, "It's still there. Or anyway it was last time I looked. Why?"

Now it was this voice of Fimblesector that hesitated—surprising, given the nanites' superaccelerated congnitive time-scale. "NEVER MIND THAT! YOU'RE AN UNLIMPIDATED ENTITY AND WOULDN'T UNDERSTAND —WAIT!"

The golden beams had stopped playing over Lucky and concentrated on his chest, where hung the eight-ring disk. "WHERE DID YOU GET THAT AMULET?"

Yet again this sharp interest in the medallion. "I'll tell you, if you answer a few questions first," Lucky offered cagily.

"YOU'RE IN NO POSITION TO BARGAIN, CHEESE-HEAD."

Cheesehead? That might be some kind of translated slur, but Lucky played a hunch. "I'm talking to the High Heurist, aren't I? And you're no nanite." He had a sudden mental flash of the wheel-spinning, treadle-pumping little man behind the curtain in the Wizard of Oz's audience chamber.

He waited even longer for a response this time, until the voice, sounding a little rattled, tolled, "DO NOT PRESUME TOO FAR, MACRO."

Some memory had been touched, but before Lucky could identify it, the pyramid reverberated menacingly. "NOW, BE-GONE! NO LOITERING! OH, AND, 'MACROS, FREE YOUR MICROS!' 'WORKERS OF THE GALAXY, UNITE!' "

All at once it was, at least where Lucky and Lumber Jack were standing, raining what seemed to be warm blood and live, kicking, croaking frogs—although the Nanoverse could probably manifest itself in just about any form it chose and the two didn't stop to take a close look. Garishly clashing orange and green lightning flashes crashed down so as to herd the two travelers toward the egress Adit. From the gray-goo sea behind them rose a brazen clockwork-colossus head extruding a tongue in the form of an arrow engraved, in Gothic typeface, EXIT, curled so that it pointed down the beach. Far ahead was the rest of the tour group, to all appearances unaware of the biblical plagues behind them.

Lumber had already scooped up Lucky and was pounding in the indicated direction. The blighted area was so circumscribed that in four Wood-Winder-sized paces they'd escaped. Lucky retrieved from his blood-sodden film shorts a frog that had ricocheted down there and tossed it to safety as carefully as he could under the circumstances. The hills had taken on the form of neon cyberfont: WHADDA WE WANT? WORKER'S RIGHTS! WHEN D'WE WANT 'EM? NOW!

I wonder if Gurdjief ever had days like this? Lucky pondered.

TWENTY-ONE

HANGING UP THE telephone after his call to Ziggy, Braxmar Koddle abruptly glanced in all directions, a sequence of moves that had become a kind of involuntary spasm in the last few days. Talking to Ziggy had made him feel almost normal, and he didn't want to feel that way—in part as an artistic choice and in part as a matter of self-preservation.

There was no one looking Brax's way insofar as he could tell. He checked his watch: 12:08 A.M.; he'd have to hurry. He might already be too late.

His sense of urgency notwithstanding, as Brax stepped off along 201st Street he was brought up short when he glanced through an electronics store window at a display of TV sets tuned to a local all-news channel.

Unthinkable that he should *not* go in and hear what was being said. One way or another, he was meant to. He made straight for the video section, more screens tuned to the same show but with their sound muted. When he turned up the volume on one, a salesperson—a skinny Chinese kid who went about six feet and a hundred and twenty pounds—gave him a sour look. Brax pretended not to notice but wondered if his indifferent disguise job, with camoflesh purchased in a costume store, had anything to do with it.

Plenty of people wore the stuff, people uncomfortable under the scrutiny of ever-present security cams, or reveling in the feeling of dress-up, or temporarily trading in one identity for another or following some zap fashion. There were, of course, ways to determine the appearance of the individual underneath the camoflesh, but at least the false face would keep Brax from being ID'ed by the incidental crowd pan or street scan.

Besides, salespeople's reactions didn't matter to Brax. Although not so long ago he'd have been mortified by the kind of glances and reactions his hyperdefensive behavior drew now, he had come to consider the disapproval of the unenlightened masses meaningless. None of them knew what was RGO.

The sound came up under a coiffed media-maid in a tight shot with a whiskery, quirkily grinning face. "—fairy-tale events in a day that found one man's life changed forever here in The City They Call New York." She turned back to her interviewee. "And what's the first thing you plan to do with your newfound prosperity?"

The hirsute man hefted his chewed-up fedora in one hand, his staff in the other, and exulted, "Spread some green, sister!"

He sounded a bit zoided; she deftly pulled the mike back to herself. "The MacAllister Fund, which this evening bestowed the grant on Brother Barney, a so-called avenue appleseed, was endowed by and named for John T. and Catherine C. MacAllister in 1975. The Arts Advisory Council has already given fast-track approval to today's recipient. The grant will provide this heretofore unsung genius with a total of eight hundred and seventy thousand world dollars over the next five years, enabling him to pursue his 'annotated tracings' and 'graffitiless graffiti' the world 'round."

Brother Barney showed the audience how he'd attached to his staff tip the AllWrite comp swapped him by Brax for the roll of recycled paper, ink, and ostrich plume. Brax stared at the screen, searching for meanings and tidings beyond mere words and pictures. Was Brother Barney's unlikely success just a vagary of the billiard-balling spheres of arts, wealth, and media—or a subtextual message to Brax from unseen powers Terrestrial or otherwise?

Even putting aside the unheard-of discovery and funding of Brother Barney in a single day, why would the AAC give him license to proceed with his new edgetech art form rather than warehouse him? Brax's instant suspicion was that Black Hole had ordained that the time had come to start shaking things up, to unjam the stasis of the post-Turn era, pave the way for the momentous changes its takeover of Earth would inflict.

The soft-newser was saying, "—selection process was as always carried out in utmost secrecy by unidentified judges, and as usual without the prospective recipient's knowledge, but never has such instantaneous recognition come to a—"

A wave of unease came over Brax when he realized he'd

been standing in one spot in full public view for several minutes; he seldom did that now. As he was leaving he heard a manly-male reporter take over. "—late-breaking bulletin, a false alarm inside a crowded outlaw club known as the Ded Dawg resulted in dozens of serious injuries as panicky customers—"

Back on the sidewalk he rotated slowly, like a DF antenna searching for the source of a signal, shifting to his other shoulder the faded canvas army-surplus tool bag in which he now carried all his worldly goods.

When he was sighted in the direction of the Bayview Breakdown parking lot, he set off. The walk gave him time to review his course of action.

Bayview Breakdown was the white-trasher company that had employed Willy Ninja until Willy, with Sean and Eddie, set off for the Yap Islands and that part of the sea toward Palau and into the arms of Black Hole. Willy's stories of odd doings in the BB parking lot had been of only passing interest to Brax way back when, but Brax was pinning heavy hopes on what he might find there.

Asia Boxdale's chosen path in leaving normal life behind was in keeping with her gifts: the murky posturings and darkside vainglory of counterculture stars and would-be rebel celebrities. Brax had no hunger for personal theater; his strongest wish was to avoid attention, duck all spotlights, become the unseen observer. He wanted people to stop spying on him.

Brax doubted there was any other way he could help his friends or resist Black Hole; demonstrably, there was no other way he would ever finish *Gate Crashers*.

So it was that Willy Ninja's anecdotes had come back to Brax, of the unspoken deal Willy had struck with someone unglimpsed, lurking outside the glare of the lights—in all probability undocumented and eluding the focus of cam lenses and ID scanners. Several times, as pressure and paranoia built up in him, Brax had taken late-evening strolls past the lot, checking out Willy's truck, thinking. From that had come a plan for a vigil.

Bayside Breakdown's parking lot was a quarter-block of cracked cement, dirt, and weeds bordered on two sides by decaying brick pre-Turn warehouse walls and on the other two by wilting, breached chain-link. The two paleolithic security cams could only cover perhaps three-quarters of the lot's area.

The parking lot was quiet and only the overnight lights were on in the BB offices when Brax got there. He saw with mixed feelings that the truck had been moved.

The interbust straight-job truck Willy sometimes drove had been parked directly under a cam that afternoon when Brax had strolled past for a look, and Willy had said his nocturnal cleaning service steered clear of the truck when that happened. Now it was over near the gaping fence and out of cam surveillance, which was good, but meant Brax's risk and inconvenience in getting the key had been for nothing.

The key was a spare Willy had pocketed long ago and held on to—having been kept standing in the cold more than once by late-arriving dispatchers. Brax had ventured back to the posse's Bronx loft that afternoon to fetch it, every nerve ablaze, waiting for the FBI ambushers to spring or the XT kidnappers to strike. He'd entered by way of the back alley and the furnace-room door but knew those precautions wouldn't amount to much if a trap had been set for him.

But no one barred his way and Willy's key was right in the spare-change ashtray where he'd left it. Brax stood in the silent loft for a moment watching and listening to ghosts, himself among them, longing for irretrievable happier days. He fled the way he'd come when the pain of it became too great.

As he'd looked back from the intersection Brax noticed a Con Ed supervisor, his crew setting up by a manhole cover in midstreet, exchange subtle glances with the Pesky Pizza kid making a delivery. There was some unspoken communication going on there, Brax was sure, and he'd resolved to stay clear of the loft.

The truck was in good position but that would be no help if the doors were locked. Slipping through the chain-link, he tried the passenger side and found it was. He opened it, then low-crawled across the seat to unlock the driver's side.

He taped a fiver to the dashboard near the CD player—Willy had never said which side, or how high or low, so Brax had to go with a guess—and with great relief merged with the darkness once more, concealed between a warehouse wall and a multibin recycling dumpster, sitting with his back against the steel. It was cooler now, so he pulled the linen sport coat on.

It was too dark to write, of course, but Brax had found that passing time was easy nowadays; he meditated on his work in progress, *Gate Crashers*, and lost all track of time. He wasn't aware that he was sleepy until a sound woke him up. The figure in the cab of the BB straight rig was indistinct, bulky—but at least looked human.

Brax eased forward to the edge of the streetlight, watching whoever it was clean up the cab—replacing CDs in their sleeves, stuffing ashtray contents and snack wrappers into a fast-food bag, wiping down the dashboard with a cloth and *whisk-brooming*, if you please, the seats and floor mats. When the midnight domestic crawled ass-first out of the passenger seat and slipped through the fence, Brax was standing next to the dumpster.

"Excuse me—no, don't be frightened; I don't want any trouble."

The suspect was a Mediterranean or Middle Eastern male, slightly shorter than Brax's five-ten, whose age might be anywhere from mid-twenties to early forties. He wore a neat mechanic's coverall and denim baseball cap and was clean-shaven, his hair trimmed a bit on the close side—all in all not the feral, hunted-looking soul Brax had imagined.

"Don't be afraid," Brax said. "I just want to talk to you. What's your name?"

"Sal. What's yours?"

"Etaoin, Etaoin Shrdlu." There seemed to Brax to be a certain resonance in using the pen name of E. C. Wheeler— Sheena Hec'k's father and the author of *Tug of War*—as his alias. "Sal what?"

"Monella. And if you laugh, tomboy, I'll kick your nuts up into your dinner."

"Wouldn't dream of it. Let's get away from the scene of the crime, shall we?"

"Walk to the corner by the light pole. I'll be right behind you."

That hadn't been part of Brax's scenario but he saw no way around it. The relative scarcity of working security cams in the area was suddenly less of a comfort. Listening to Monella's soft training-shoe footsteps dogging him, Brax felt acutely vulnerable.

Nervousness made him want to babble; he tried to sound calm instead. "Sal, I'm a friend of the man who's been leaving the money in the truck. A dark-haired man, part Cherokee?"

Monella's laugh was a brief hiss. "Indian, huh? I figured him for a beaner. Hasn't been around for a while."

"No, he's . . . away on business. Sal, I'll lay it out for you: I need to stay out of sight temporarily. I, ah, owe some people a good deal of money. I want to keep a very low profile for a while.''

Monella chortled. ''If you got no green, tomboy, last thing you want is to try and get along how I do.''

''I have a few dollars and I can get a bit more. My main problem is—well, you know. Keeping the police and PINheads and bookkeeping AIs and whatnot from tracking me.''

Brax stopped under the miser bulb and turned; Monella came to just slightly beyond arm's reach, lighting a clove cigarette and blowing smoke at him. A company logo patch over his right breast pocket read TOTAL RECALL AUTO RECLAMATION and embroidered in script over his left was the name ''Vic.''

''You're not talkin' about some dumb-ass street scam. Keepin' yourself alive without gettin' pulled in is an art *and* a science now, toughest one there is.''

''Then teach it to me, Sal. I'll pay my way.''

Monella stared at him for a long moment, then suddenly said, ''Lean against the pole and keep watchin' me—no! Don't look around.'' Then he was giving Brax an unlikely story of his success with a slumming Deuce-Oner runway model, complete with grinding hip mime and descriptive-geometry hand moves, as a police cruiser slowly edged through Brax's peripheral vision. It said something about the area that prowl-car presence was needed in addition to the cams.

Forcing himself to ignore the cops, Brax grabbed his crotch and clapped his other hand to his forehead, guffawing, ''No way, home-style! No fuckin' *way*!''

As the cruiser disappeared around the corner Monella gave Brax a pursed-mouth look, tilting his head back and forth. ''Not bad, not bad—even though you kinda overplayed it.'' He flicked the clove cigarette into the gutter. ''You owe me for some new skins. C'mon; you can buy us somethin' to eat.''

This time they went side by side.

Sal led Brax by a roundabout route to an all-night Chow Mainly franchise where shift workers, truckers, peripheral types, and other night people were pounding home inexpensive nourishment. Digging into a slotted stainless-steel tray load, Brax asked, ''Why do I owe you new clothes?''

Monella moved the chili around in his mouth to answer. ''Even though the cops didn't stop, they'll scan the streetcam tapes; that means I gotta get rid of this long underwear.'' He shrugged, sipping from his schooner of draft beer. "Cause a' you, am I right?"

"The way you put it, it sounds fair. Would you mind telling me—"

"No, *I* got some questions for *you*, Et-taoin." Monella said it with a mincing look. Brax, never much inclined to fight, gripped his table knife more tightly. "Like who was this Indian guy, and what happened to him? Why're you *really* on the run? Where d'ya come from, who's been lookin' for ya?"

"You're very curious for a man who stands to profit by all this."

Monella shrugged. "Information is power, same in the street as in the White House."

"Fair enough," Brax said calmly. "We'll trade, how's that? Me first. My friend's name is Willy Ninja, but I'm sure you already know that from the bills of lading and whatnot that you came across in the truck, heh?"

Monella showed grudging respect. "Right you are, Etaoin, so you're a bright boy not to lie."

"Call me boy once more, Sal, you'll regret it. I'm not sure where Willy is or when he'll be back. My turn: Do you have or know of a place where I can go to ground for a while—do some, ah, paperwork? No cams, no phones or PIN terminals; I don't want any of that annoyance around me."

Monella wolfed down a quesadilla. "You got some green, I can arrange it. But tell me a little more about your problems and maybe I can help you more than you think. You look at me, you see some schmuck—but I'm tellin' ya, I got connections. I'm wired in all over this fuckin' city, daylight side and dark side."

Brax thought that over; maybe Monella had something there, but how far could he be trusted? "Sal, why'd you start straightening up Willy's truck?"

Monella made an elaborately casual face. "I just clean out somebody's spare change, all's I got is a little walking money for a day. But I do something in return, show I'm willin' to play fair? Hey, suddenly I got a sideline and everybody's happy."

"I see." Brax let the explanation decide him. "Tell me what you know about a business conglomerate called Phoenix Enterprises."

Monella paused with a chunk of currywurst halfway to his mouth, then laughed. "Well, now, there's a coincidence."

"Perhaps you'll be kind enough to let me in on it."

Monella was shaking his head. "I did time with a guy who was comptroller of Silicon Synapses, the computer outfit."

And SiliSyn was a manufacturing arm of IBM VirtNet, Brax knew—which was in turn run by Timothy Alston, Phoenix Enterprises heavy suspected by SELMI of being an XT. He recalled that there'd been some sort of major criminal case against SS the year before. "How's that for a fluke?" Monella added.

"I'm beginning to get used to them," Brax replied. "Do you think you can get this man to talk to us?"

"Ray Strakes? He sure as shit hasn't got anything better to do with his time."

"Meaning what?"

Monella savored the saying of it. "Meaning he's doing twenty-to-life on an industrial-pollution rap. At least, that's what he was *convicted* of."

"Meaning what?"

"Meaning he had the twitchiest story you ever heard, about stuff he happened to come across in a SiliSyn system that IBM VirtNet was using for something called Phoenix Enterprises projects. Let's just say he started asking the wrong questions and the next thing you know he was set up on an eco-bust. Back on that corner you kept your head on straight when the cops came by, Etaoin; come daylight we'll see how long you can hold it there.

"Strakes is doin' hard time in the landfill mines out at Fresh Kills."

Charlie Cola opened his desk drawer and pulled out a communicator headband, fingering it thoughtfully. Maybe one more inquiry—another plea for help from Jacob Riddle, who was now basking in his golden years on Nmuth Four?

Someone cleared a throat and he hastily put the headband away, finding Molly Riddle standing across the desk. Charlie shifted his drooping belly around at her. "What, has the custom of knocking gone out of style altogether?"

"Want to close your door sometime and we'll find out?" She smiled wanly. She'd been raised in wealth and well educated, her childhood spent, in large part, offworld. Always in control and self-confident to a fault before—and often a thorn in his side—nowadays Charlie's leggy, gamine assistant manager was subdued, almost withdrawn.

He knew part of that stemmed from the unexplained rejection of her pro forma request for a brief vacation to see her parents on Nmuth Four. It added to the feeling of being cut off, hemmed in. Another thing that was eating at her, though, Charlie could tell, was the disappearance of that Cherokee musician friend of Junknowitz's, Willy Ninja.

Molly had played up to Willy in order to monitor the posse, and had soon had the kid eating out of her hand in her patented fashion. Somewhere along the way, though, she'd let herself start caring for him and let her conscience get in some shots at her, too.

"Charlie, I've been thinking. Maybe by sitting tight we're doing just what the opposition wants us to do."

"What opposition? Damn it, we have direct instructions from Trough and Adits *and* Asteria Cushman to mark time—"

She was shaking her head gently, the unruly locks of auburn hair barely vibrating. "I'm not talking about the Agency, Charlie! There's something else going on and we can't afford to just sit tight and let things happen to us."

"Miss playing spy, do you?" He couldn't help making it sound spiteful, but it surprised him to see how much the dig got to her.

"You've been hiding in this office too long," she said softly. "Your brain's so clogged with off-gassing fumes you can't recognize it when somebody's trying to help."

He was instantly and abjectly sorry, but before he could apologize Sanpol buzzed him from the counter out front. "There's someone to see you."

Charlie poked the intercom talk button. "No, I don't want anybody back here."

"You do this time," Sanpol answered in his serene fashion.

Sanpol had a quietly unswerving way of holding his own course despite people and events, but damn his eyes, this was going too far. Charlie was struggling out of his chair with some choice remarks on the tip of his tongue when he saw the look of shock on the face of Molly Riddle, who had turned to gaze off toward the front of the store.

Charlie Cola felt himself go superconducting-cold as the conviction came over him that the Agency had finally gotten around to cleaning up loose ends in the Bronx. Then he heard bootheels clack and had second thoughts. If Black Hole had it in mind to eliminate him, its representatives would be unlikely to announce their arrival or come in the form of—"

A stunning young Eurasian beauty in pre-Turn biker leathers?

That was who had stepped into view to confront Molly and Charlie. Molly recovered her usual poise and then some. "Hello, Asia."

"Molly. Willy was right—Black Hole's waiting room could use a make-over."

"This is a new look for you, isn't it, Asia? Don't tell me you're here to *terminate* us?" Molly had her hands in the pockets of her Quick Fix clerk's jacket; the right one, Charlie knew, was where she carried her spray tube of Crowd Control Junior knockout aerosol.

Charlie had recognized the Boxdale woman, though he'd never met her—from PR photos and a compilation recital tape obtained by Molly. He'd also gotten a look at other recordings of her performance art; Phipps Hagadorn was not the only Twenty-One über who considered her a genius, though they'd not informed her of it or rewarded her for it or acknowledged it publicly, deeming it better to keep truly promising artists unsung, hungry, desperate. Poor and pure.

Charlie saw Asia's holster and wondered why Sanpol and the security system had both let her by. His eyes flickered to the flatscreen on his desk. Security sensors had picked up the structure and sniffed the molecules of some kind of tranquilizer weapon, and the holstered device evidently contained epoxy adhesive. She wasn't carrying a conventional firearm or any offworld technology.

"Mr. Cola? My name is Asia Boxdale; I believe you know who I am. We need to talk."

"Nice to see you, Ms. Boxdale." Charlie felt despondency sloughing off him. His ticket right back to the top in Black Hole's local setup had, loosely speaking, stepped into his parlor. "But first I want to warn you against trying anything stupid. We're set up to deal with a lot more than the usual convenience-store trouble—a *lot* more—and I don't want to have to hurt you."

Asia looked puzzled for a moment. Then, "Oh, the gun? You can have it." She took the tranquilizer pistol from the back of her chaps belt as if it were a dead rat.

"Fine, fine. Just toss it over there anywhere, that's right. And the one in the holster, too, if you please—what *is* that thing?"

Asia had flipped the Makita glue gun down next to Jak O'

Club's pneumo shooter. "Tell you later. In the meantime, there are some things you ought to hear, things I've found out. First, though, I guess I should show you this." She moved a step closer, pulling long, fine pitch black hair away to show the little round areas of lividity on either temple. "They called it a mindbender."

A few seconds before, Charlie had about decided to cue defensive systems to stun Asia where she stood, or perhaps let Molly hit her with the Crowd Control. Upper management would *have* to let him back into the picture if he showed that Junknowitz's network still had Charlie targeted and he was able to cope with them competently, deliver trophies. But the marks of the mindbender contacts—they looked authentic, and besides which Boxdale *knew the term*—made him hold off.

Clearly there were aspects of the current situation that no one had mentioned to Charlie Cola. Knowledge was power, and if there was some to be had here he badly needed it. He drew an unsteady breath. "The, ah, marks will go away in a day or two."

Jesus and Labib had appeared, eyes wide, and picked up the pistol and the Makita; Charlie waved his sons away, then beckoned Asia and Molly. "Come in, siddown; let's not yell our heads off out here, for heaven's sake."

Asia took the high-backed armchair in his office that had upheld the fundaments of Trough luminaries and local snack-food sales reps alike. Charlie took his swivel and Molly perched one trim haunch on the desk.

Asia had felt only fleeting relief that the mindbender stigmata had persuaded the Quick Fixers to hear her out; she'd cleared one more hurdle, but her struggle against Black Hole had only started. She knew now that the Agency's power permeated as low as it did high and that the underground offered no more protection than did penthouse, press, or police station.

Having made Asia's glancing acquaintance through Willy, Molly knew she was no fool—that she wouldn't have entered Quick Fix without thinking things out. The first order of business was to get a fix on the tactical situation. "Taking something of a risk, aren't you? Strolling in like this?"

Asia pinned her with a glance, debated over a response, then decided this was no time to half step. She plunged ahead. "We know you let Lucky go through the Adit, Molly; Eddie and the others saw you come out of the back room after he went in, and he let us know he was being faded without any problem."

Charlie was making diesel start-up sounds. Molly closed her eyes, then decided to believe what Asia had said.

Molly had recognized Lucky at once when he had shown up under a false name for a fade. She realized later that, with Labib and Jesus off in her car on one of their spy missions, the posse had probably thought she'd left the store. Lucky had practically bumped into her.

She'd had to choose among many and complex options in the space of a second or three, before Lucky could panic or do something foolish or anything else went wrong. If she'd had even two minutes to think things out rationally her decision would've gone the other way, she'd convinced herself afterward.

What had been running through her head in those moments she hadn't quite sorted out for herself yet, but she knew that one painful image had been that of Willy Ninja. Willy calling her ''The Moll'' in his intent, smiling, and soft-spoken way . . . before he'd made her for a spy, a traitor, a liar.

Since the night he'd confronted her she'd dreaded seeing him again and yet thought about it constantly.

''The others,'' Molly echoed.

Asia inclined her head slowly. ''Willy, for one.''

So Willy knew Molly had kept silence about Lucky when logic and survival demanded she sound the alarm. One side of her had hoped he did, another had prayed he would never find out.

''That was the main thing that decided me to come here like this,'' Asia told Molly.

''You . . . *let* . . . Junknowitz . . . through . . . here?'' Charlie pronounced the words carefully at Molly. ''He was that guy Waters, wasn't he? Do you know what you've done, just to stay tight with your damned half-breed?''

Molly made a visible effort to control herself. ''Grow up, Charlie. The handwriting's been on the wall since upper management ordered the Adit yanked from the store: it's our turn in the barrel.'' She jerked her chin at Asia. ''She knows that or she wouldn't've come.''

Charlie was pulling his bulging lower lip, looking thoughtfully at Asia. ''Don't count us out just yet.'' He could still give the Agency Junknowitz, whom it wanted so badly, or at least a strong lead on him. Not to mention gift-wrapped Boxdale.

Something else occurred to him. ''How do I know you haven't gone over to their side, Moll?'' with a nod to Asia.

Molly curled her lip at him. "What'll it take for you to trust me? Seeing me fed to the sharks when they toss you in? If I wasn't on your side you'd know it by now—and to your great sorrow." She cut her eyes back to Asia. "Who used the mindbender on you?"

"A man named Bhang and a police captain named Barnes. They're out to undercut you people and, I think, others—so that Bhang can be the, the 'capo,' someone called it, for Black Hole."

Molly had to shake her head and chuckle. "In charge of the wetwork and the blackbagging and the darkside. Yep, good career move."

Charlie wasn't ready to yield yet. "But—Dante and I have known each other for years; he worked for my father."

"I'm sure it's nothing personal, just business." Molly folded her arms under her breasts. "He figures we're already trashed and doesn't see why he should go down with us. Only, Phoenix isn't monolithic; they're all jockeying around without acknowledging it. Question's whether Bhang's working for anybody in particular or just positioning himself for competing bids."

Charlie's brain had been grinding gears. He asked Asia, "What was the mindbender for?"

She gave them a sanitized rundown on what had happened in the Ded Dawg. When she mentioned Jak's reference to the capture of Willy and the others and the name End Zone she saw Molly Riddle go pale and look away.

By the time the tale was told Molly had that cool poise back. Charlie wanted to know, "How the hell did Da—did Bhang get the upper hand with Barnes?"

Asia raised her shoulders, dropped them.

"Not important for now," Molly concurred.

Charlie made it unanimous with a set-jawed nod. "What we need to do is find out who Bhang aligns with, then use it to get his opposition to hire us on."

Molly was mulling it over. "I'm not so sure we're not on the Agency's shitlist for good. This business about keeping me from seeing my parents pretty much clinches it."

Charlie swiveled his paunchy bulk around and back in tiny arcs. "So what are you saying?"

Molly's lips compressed. "A new game plan—that, or kiss our beloved heinies farewell."

Charlie guessed what she meant and shot to his feet, his chair flying back. "Are you crazy? *Are you suicidal?*"

"What I want to know," Asia butted in, "is what you're going to do for Willy and the others. There's more I can tell you and there're ways I can help you, but not for free."

Molly and Charlie traded glances that said they had a lot more to thrash out. "Ms. Boxdale," Charlie began, "would you mind waiting up front for a moment with my—"

"I have a phone call to make," Asia cut him off. "I'll be back in a few minutes. I hope we can get down to cases." She felt a tentative optimism, though; Molly was on Asia's side and Cola struck her as prone to cave in.

"There's a pay phone outside the front door," he said.

She shook her head so that the glossy hair shimmered. "No, not here. Some other phone."

She'd put off checking in with Ziggy for too long as it was, but felt it likely that the Quick Fixers' own phones, at the very least, would be tapped. So some other was required. It was late and she'd have to risk the streets, but that was better than having the Ziggy-SELMI connection compromised.

Molly clicked her tongue and pulled out a magnetic card-key, "My car's around the corner." She silenced Charlie's objection before it even emerged from him by saying, "Jesus and Labib can drive you."

Charlie went off to find his adopted sons. Asia asked Molly, "What about End Zone?"

"There's nothing I can do."

"There's always something that can be done."

Asia moved closer, hands in the pockets of that Langlitz jacket. "Y'know, Molly, Willy's sweet and strong and direct but he's no sucker. He'd never have let himself fall for you so completely except that you'd fallen for him, too. What simply never entered his head was that you could make yourself fall back out of love—or at least convince yourself you had, if it was a *good career move*."

Molly didn't get to rebut because the Colas returned. Jesus and Labib, cocky in their new role as suave espionage agents, hemmed Asia in fore and aft, convoying her out the back door. They agreed that an all-night bike-rental place ten blocks away would be best; they could guard Asia from out of earshot.

Molly's a-cell was a sporty Mercedes ragtop, complete with torque reservoir and off-road package, that gleamed like a star sapphire under the garage lights. Jesus and Labib had seen enough slasher flicks to check the trunk and backseat. Then Labib took the wheel, Asia rode shotgun, and Jesus squeezed into the rear jumpseat/cargo space. Slotting the magnetic card, Labib revved the engine and whirred out of the parking space.

As they pulled around to the exit the booth attendant motioned them to stop, waving kenaf forms and a sheaf of cash. "Rebate time," Labib said, hitting the brakes. Like many New Yorkers, Molly economized on parking fees by making her space available for rental at stipulated times, the garage reducing her monthly fee accordingly. Labib held out his hand for a grab-and-go.

"Here's your change," tittered Mickey Formica, spritzing them all with a jet of Crowd Control by means of a telescoping sprayer while leaning back in the booth and clamping his breather to his face.

He hit the stop button and a shock-absorbing security barrier popped up to stop the car. Spinning tires sent up the reek of burning rubber. Nikkei, already masked, leapt out from behind the booth, reached past Labib, and switched off the engine.

For once simple, plodding legwork had paid off. When Nikkei had asked around the Dawg's neighborhood for the gorgeous "cousin" in biker leathers whom he was supposedly to meet, some kids lamping outside a deli recalled seeing her enter the subway. A token clerk remembered Asia, too—including which train she'd boarded. From there it was pretty easy to guess where she was bound. Nikkei had even managed to access the platform happy-face cams at 125th Street and watch her change trains for the Throgs Neck line, confirming it.

They already knew isolated facts about Cola's operation from working with Bhang; Tanabe's briefers and the data they could access with their headsets told them a lot more, including what kind of car Molly drove and where she kept it. Once they figured out Asia and Cola's sons were going for a drive the episode was more like fun than work.

"Nice hummer," Nikkei praised the Mercedes a minute later, wheeling along with Asia non compos in the rear and Jesus and Labib stacked up back at the garage alongside the attendant. "Can't beat them Wursts for good MotorKarma."

He and Mickey giggled and traded high-daps and butterfly stings, knuckle walks and bone rubs, while tearing along through the Bronx, and then the Manhattan, darkness. There was a giddy, apprehensive ozone in the air, as if it were the last night of summer vacation.

*   *   *

"Asia Boxdale is to be transported," Miss Sato informed Mickey when he and Nikkei had gotten the delectable package back to the safe house near Sutton Place and Mickey had gotten on the horn. "Arrangements are being made."

"Good to go," Mickey snapped off, space-camp style. By now he'd accepted the fact that Nikkei simply wouldn't talk to Sato unless it was absolutely unavoidable. "What's her destination?"

"You have no need to know that at this time. You will be accompanying her, so do sanitize the house of your presence."

Mickey tried to make it sound casual. "Gotcha. You got any, ah, *collateral intel* we should know about?"

"No. You'll be contacted within the half hour. Inform your companion that when you've reached your destination Mr. Tanabe will wish to speak with him." Miss Sato broke the connection.

Nikkei, standing to one side of the vid pickup, wore a certain fatalistic non-expression Mickey had come to know. Mickey pretended to be looking into the distance, shading his eyes with one hand. "Funny thing, *homme*-sweet-*homme*; you squint a little, you can see *Tengu Mountain* from here. The overheated parts."

"So they're all on End Zone, under the kindly care of the Great Vogonskiy, huh, Moll?" Charlie couldn't resist grinding it in. "That cam-shafting themer, Franken-Vet, and Big Chief Breakdown. Well, that lets you off the hook; by this time the chief won't be breakin' any more hearts. Just mirrors."

He couldn't resist it, even though Molly was one of the woefully few remaining items in his plus column. By letting Junknowitz through and keeping it to herself she'd proved that she was perfectly willing to dump on Charlie the same as others whose names were legion.

"Yup, that frees you up, Mol," Charlie aspirated a laugh. "There wouldn't be any gigs around for Ninja anyway, unless maybe somebody's doing a revival of 'The Elephant Man.' Right?"

She'd been staring intently at the floor, head bent, kneading her own neck. Now she looked up at him abruptly. "Don't ever forget you said that to me, Charlie, mmmm? Don't ever forget that in this particular moment you chose to say that uniquely shitty thing to me."

She leaned back against the door of the freezer, where once

there'd been such a gateway to other worlds as beggared any legend or wish-dream. He felt contrition and pity then, but he was still too bitter to let it out.

"Ah, Charlie." He distinctly heard her sniffle, an astonishing sound from Molly Riddle. "No wonder they keep this sorry-ass world off limits."

TWENTY-TWO

FADING IN FROM Fimblesector to way station Kloo, Lucky found out the hard way that Black Hole, too, could be paranoid.

The Agency didn't trust anything it couldn't control, and the Fimblesector seemed to top the list. The unusual decontamination procedures brought to bear to make sure no rogue nanites had contaminated the tourists reminded Lucky of the sort of treatment meted out to squealers by organized crime figures.

But at least all the shaking, baking, hosing, raying, and baptizing-with-disinfectant was over quickly. He didn't know whether to be happy or resentful that Lumber welcomed the going-over with the joy of a grizzly bear getting his butt scratched.

For once everybody in the tour group was shagged out. Amazingly, though, their enthusiasm was high. Mr. Dimdwindle chuckled. ''We can just imagine the things you'll show us on Terra, Mr. Waters!''

Lucky plastered a phony smile on his face and concurred. Inside he was shrinking in dread from the very idea of trail-driving this gaggle of misfits and nincompoops across the Earth.

There were more holographic Wanted posters with his real face on them—up there with Silvercup and a slew of others. And clearly Black Hole wanted a word with this Ka Shamok guy.

Other than GoBug nearly being mashed by an aquatic life-support tank on a tracked crawler—surviving only because something else caught his interest, making him veer away at the last second while Lucky shrilled at him wordlessly—the stroll along the busy way-station concourse was devoid of notable event. Even the gardener robots, dispensing fertilizer, pollen and genetic activators from applicators they wielded like video-game pistols, were casual about getting out of the way.

Lucky saw with a stab of homesickness that a canceled holographic routing sticker on the side of the crawler indicated it had visited Earth—doubtless via the *Crystal Harmonic*. Now it was bound for a planet called Ss-sarsassiss. Some being serpentine and *big* was eeling around in the tank's murky waters.

Lucky gave himself a mental massage. If he could just hang on through the Zillion stop, he'd hit way station Blits right on schedule and slip away to nose around al-Reem. The unseen tour coordinators were on the ball for once, and when Lucky and his little flock got to the Adit it was scheduled to whisk them to Zillion in just ten minutes. Not to say that there wasn't a complication, of course.

"Waters, got a twix from the Root Canal Pit Boss," a skunklike Occuumese assistant supervisor informed him, motioning him to one side. "He said you never picked up your Collect Call."

His nanites' rendering of the word had Lucky at a loss for a moment, making him think of insanely long-distance phone bills. But after a moment the haphazard fund of general knowledge that had come to him along with the mighty mites yielded a clarification. The Collect Call was a simple locating and signaling device used by tour-group guides to keep track of or, in emergencies, summon their clients by means of subordinate units carried by each individual. Largely ignorant of the details of the job, Lucky had been unaware that he was supposed to be issued, and then distribute, the gizmos at his first stop.

The Occuumese, whose holo ID badge read PUHN JAHNT, was carrying a flat, gleaming little object that suggested a Trough-tech cigarette case. "Here we go. We got it routed here by courier pouch."

Puhn Jahnt was patting his midsection in a kind of marsupial way, and, this being the Trough, Lucky wondered exactly what he meant. No matter, though. Lucky accepted the case, "Much obliged."

"Really? Well, I heard a back-channel rumor about the Oddball."

Lucky wondered if Odeo Cologney here was suddenly trying to pick a fight. "Oddball?"

"The Sphere of Influence."

Lucky relaxed and reached for the Magic 8 Ball. "What race, which, uh, mount?"

"Race? I'm no tout; what I was wondering was how the Unisphere there felt about Amalgamated Debentures during the coming fiscal period."

Lucky, startled, resumed rolling the 8 Ball. "Excuse me, but it's not a good idea to use the Sphere of Influence for this kind of stuff too often, y'know?"

The Occuumese made a silencing gesture. "Sure thing."

"Okay, Amalgamated Debentures?" The answer floated up. IT IS CERTAIN.

The Occuumese must have been carrying a printed-English nanite, because he read it for himself. "*Very* aromatic!"

"Look, don't forget what I—"

"Quit worrying! What good's insider trading data if everybody's got it, eh? What I can't figure is why *you* aren't rich by now."

Lucky had thought that one out back on Root Canal. "Using it for personal profit would rob me of my powers."

"Too bad—I wish there was something I could do for you. I heard you're saddled with some howlers, hm? From planet Rph?"

Lucky just sighed. "We had to detain one a while back for piddling on a fractal-bonzai," Puhn Jahnt said. "Forensics got his urine chem-typed, ID'ed, the works and promised if he ever did it again they'd space him. A-type running-dog Rphs."

All that had Lucky thinking. "You mean you have the Rphian, uh, secretions analyzed?"

"To the molecule. Those mutts tend to be a quality-of-life problem wherever they go, especially the males. Why?"

Lucky was glancing back at where the robots were plying their gardening applicators. "Maybe there's something you can do for me after all . . ."

When Puhn Jahnt had gone off scratching his head but vowing to do his best, Lucky rejoined his party, examining the contents of the Collect Call box. It had occurred to him to wonder why some kind of locator nanites hadn't been supplied to his group, but nanites were expensive and notoriously ill suited to long-range transmission and reception. On the other hand, he had no idea how these little putty gobs were supposed to be used.

"Um . . ." Lucky knew he'd have to ask *someone* how the things worked. Lumber Jack had fallen in with him as he walked, but he wasn't sure Lumber was that person.

The botanical goliath cut Lucky's dithering short by plucking one of the lumps out of its place with surprising dexterity, chomping on it a few times, then sticking it carefully behind one Easter-Island-statue ear.

"I know some prefer to ID-validate their unit with skin secretions, mental emanations, or whatever," Lumber confided to Lucky, "but I find saliva works as well as anything. And positioning it thus is about optimal for life-forms with our general neurological structure, don't you agree?"

"No two ways about it." Lucky's erratic fund of general information was giving him a few pointers now. Not wanting any more truck with the local Agency reps, he plucked up the single pink wad, popped it into his mouth, chewed it to malleability, and stuck it behind his right ear.

Hono positioned their Collect Calls—poked into absolutely identical lima-bean shapes—between the antennae under their Aussie-looking hats. The Dimdwindles, cheerfully cooperative as usual, stuck theirs on their noses; it occurred to Lucky that, pain in the ass though GoBug was, the kid never seemed to get cranky. Dame Snarynxx's disappeared into her quivering side, and the rest of the group dealt with the matter as they deemed appropriate.

Lucky took advantage of the wait to shuck the solvent-scented pink un-coverall and film shorts. He came back dressed in the roomy, flashy-lapelled outfit he'd picked up on his way to Confabulon, feeling more like himself. In due course they all trooped up onto the Adit plat and faded onward.

Zillion turned out to be a world of lambent citron skies and creamy primrose clouds with a slightly Earth-plus gravity and a heavy perfume to its air that made the group even logier.

They'd arrived directly midtown in the planet's capital city, Carbuncle, a four-hundred-square-mile crimson metroplex raised high on a foundation supported by monolithic stilts. Stationed overhead with no visible means of support was a transparent city canopy, an immense conjoining of dome segments of all sizes and curves, contoured to second the skyline below. The architecture of Carbuncle itself put Lucky in mind of a place built from sections of skeleton and carapace.

Zillion was a primary planet, where a lot of Trough technology had been absorbed into everyday life. Though that included luxuries like Love Handles machines, it also, he saw, had opened the city to Boob-Cube advertisements. He made a note to be cautious.

The natives looked a little less like medicated Basil Wolverton cartoon grotesques than Mr. Millmixx did, but that was due more to their greater air of alertness and energy than any physiological differences. They shared with him the bloodshot goggle eyes, skewed cowcatcher teeth, and gourdlike build. On the way through customs Lucky watched for some sign of interest or excitement from Millmixx, but the depop vet seemed more lethargic than ever.

Fortunately their hotel's chauffeured flying gazebo was waiting for them. After a brief trip over osteal Carbuncle, they were shown to comfortable accommodations in their hotel. Night was coming on and Lucky didn't have any trouble getting his charges to agree that some rest was in order; they all promised not to stray, too.

For once even GoBug was played out. "I can't wait till you show us around Earth, Mr. Waters. I heard it's so *crazy* there!"

Lucky stifled the hysterical giggles. "Yes, it's a place of, heh, many contrasts."

Lucky had ended up with a modest single room. Though it wasn't much bigger than the cargo bed of a small van, most of it occupied by a short, narrow bed that looked like it had been macraméed from transatlantic cable, he was grateful for the solitude.

Tomorrow, he thought as he collapsed. Just the Zillion side trip and through the Adit to way station Blits, then the disappearing trick. He'd expected to fall asleep as soon as his head hit the foam-nugget-stuffed oven mitt that was supposed to be his pillow, but the day's events caught up with him. Dream machine nanite or no, his thoughts kept orbiting in turn the foibles of his clients and Lumber Jack's hit assignment, the attack of the madman claiming to be an IRS agent, the mind-roasting encounter with the High Heurist.

Lucky plucked the bedraggled copy of *Edge of Space* from his bag. Two minutes' worth of pulp prose, he was willing to bet, would put him out like a general anesthetic. He'd barely begun reading when his eyelids fluttered down. Perhaps as a result of the brief read, his dreams became a surreal mixture of the pulp pyrotechnics of the Worlds Abound series and the events and fears that had filled Lucky's waking hours.

At last he felt a disembodied resentment of it all—of the

troubles that had come to afflict poor Earth. He dreamcast a pox on all their houses—all the XTs who'd gotten Lucky's planet involved in galaxy-wide hostilities. A curse on all of 'em, those—those stinking, what was the phrase, he'd read it that day at Pension Panache . . .

Lucky's eyes shot open and he sat bolt upright on the fancy-knit mattress. It was a source of only mild interest that someone was toning his door for admittance and the in-house service system was flashing to indicate that it had a delivery for him.

He double checked to make sure he wasn't wrong about the recurrent phrase used by Linc Traynor throughout the Worlds Abound series—which expression Lucky had scanned in *Edge of Space* back there on Confabulon. "Momma, talk about what's RGO!" He sprang from the bed to answer the door but was barely aware what he was doing. His evidence was only circumstantial, but somehow he never doubted for a moment that his burst of insight was correct. He was cudgeling his brain for a way, not forward to way station Blits, but back along his route. Surely no one would be more inclined to help him in his quest for Sheena Hec'k—and Harley—than Sheena's father, E. C. Wheeler—who had used the pen name Etaoin Shrdlu.

"Aii, no wonder he prefers to wear clothes," Hono remarked, standing in the open doorway, making Lucky realize he was naked.

Hono's aud-vid auxiliary lights almost blinded him as the creatures recorded the moment for their scrapbooks. "That's probably why he's gay," another—he couldn't tell which—remarked. They were all wearing cloned boutonnieres and the identically crimped boater hats.

"Will you cut that out? What's going on? Something wrong?" Lucky asked, hopping in a tight circle in the limited available space with one leg in his usher pants.

"The Dimdwindles are filling out questionnaires in the lobby," Hono explained, "though we told them not to. The Rphians left to mark out new territory. Mr. Millmixx has taken your advice and gone to solicit sex from females of his species—"

"Oh my stars and garters! I told everybody to stay put until tomorrow." He almost put the garish jacket on backward, then got organized. "And stop with those *fercockta* camcorders already!"

"It *is* tomorrow," Hono pointed out. The aud-vid lights darkened as one, the scene's unique aspect being over. "Besides which, all of them promised to stay inside the city limits, as stated.''

It came to Lucky that his nanites had had him speaking Zilliony when he exacted the vows not to stray; upon reflection he realized the phrasing could have been misinterpreted.

"Naturally, being Hono, *we* didn't wander off irresponsibly," the identical beings added. "Hono doesn't indulge in barbaric discord and nongroup thinking like *some* life-forms we could name.''

"Fine, uh-huh." Lucky was patting himself down, trying to see if he'd forgotten anything—the delivery hopper! He yanked open the little doorplate to find an oblong case of mustard yellow brushed aluminum. It was girded with a shipping band whose seal parted to his touch.

"Naturally, because *we're all alike!*" Hono was self-congratulating in several voices, echoing the sentiment with others.

"Right, h'ray for you; here—" To shut them up, he turned and draped the band and seal over the boutonniere of the one nearest to him, then turned back to the box. The unit that lay there was slightly bulkier than the ones he'd seen on Kloo, but it was still fairly compact and handy. With it was a note from the Occuumese, assistant supervisor Puhn Jahnt that made Lucky grin.

Distracted by the sudden sounds of violence, he whirled to see that the orderly little covey of Hono had turned into a small-scale riot, all of them tearing and grasping at the one with the improvised medal and that one, playing desperate keep-away, trying to climb the doorframe, crying, "It's mine, Salty Waters awarded it to me!"

It was pretty clear that the others were ready to tear him limb from limb from limb. "He thinks he's better than we are!"

"He's heaping insults on Hono!"

"He's an inferior species devoid of loyalty!"

"MODULATE!" Lucky bellowed and the struggle quickly subsided.

At that, the one who'd been hogging the ribbon threw it to the floor and went down on both knees. "You are right, Hono! I had shameful, nongroup thoughts! I do not deserve to live!" With that he twisted his aud-vid shoulder strap around his own neck and began to garrote himself.

"Nix, none of that!" Lucky, struggling to save the disgraced Hono from him-, her-, or itself, wondered why he couldn't have gotten involved in a simple genocidal war like old Linc Traynor. In this case he had himself to blame: he'd never even considered what would happen if for some reason one of the Hono stood out from all the others.

He got the feeling that the rest of Hono would be perfectly happy to watch the standout commit suicide, though some were recording it as well. Lucky thought furiously about how to use Hono's own characteristics to his advantage. "What're you, going back on your word? *You signed on as a group!*"

There was an easing in the would-be suicide's struggles and the rest of Hono lowered their aud-vid recorders. "Our word?"

"Damn straight! 'N' you gotta *remain* a group, exactly the same lineup that signed on, or you'll be dishonoring your promise. Plus you'll, um, probably lose your group rate."

Hono quickly moved to get its stricken member standing again and disentangled from the shoulder strap. "I apologize abjectly!" that one wept. "The evil seductiveness of being singled out stole my mind away!"

The others were patting the contrite one now and making comforting noises. His boutonniere and hat were replaced in meticulously restored condition. It took Lucky a few seconds to get their attention again. "Yes, see now, we've all learned a very valuable lesson this morning, which—which I'm sure you've all figured out for yourselves or will soon without my going into a needless rehash, here. Moving right along: which way did you say Mr. Millmixx and the Rphians went?"

"Oh, are you going to chastise them?" Hono piped up eagerly, the crisis forgotten, checking over aud-vids to make sure the event would be duly immortalized for viewing by the folks back home.

Lucky hefted the device Puhn Jahnt had sent him, a malicious glint in his eye. "Why, vacation time is *fun* time, haven't I taught you that yet?"

After a fitful few hours' not-quite-sleep in the squashed and discarded Sealand shipping container Sal Monella called home, Brax realized he wasn't going to get any real rest. He rose, automatically gathering up the pack that held the big roll of paper on which *Gate Crashers* was slowly taking shape.

As he groped his way to the door he heard Monella stir. "What's up?"

"Nothing. I have to make a phone call."

Monella yawned, turning over on the mound of cargo padding mats, motel sheets, and Urgent Care Center blankets that was his bed. "Use one of the booths across from Off-Track Betting—people make sure the ID and tracer response circuits in those things stay broken. If the cops pick you up I don't know you."

"Understood." It was from there that Monella had called Fresh Kills after leaving the restaurant to schedule a visit with Ray Strakes.

Brax stopped at a public men's room on the way and relieved himself, brushed his teeth, and washed up as best he could, removing the last of the camoflesh he'd peeled off the night before. He picked the phone booth that seemed cleanest, even though it meant putting up with a strong smell of disinfectant. The sky was just going light when Brax slid into its contoured seat and slotted the metal calling card given to him by Apterix Muldoon. He felt a guilty joy at the prospect of waking the XT, as well as curiosity: would Muldoon be snoozing in a high-tech coffin, or hanging by his heels in the rafters?

But the man who called himself Muldoon answered at once, fully dressed and freshly shaved—or maybe that was simply the way he always looked. "Mr. Koddle! I'm so relieved to hear from you!"

"How gratifying. Mr. Muldoon, may we speak off the record?"

Muldoon's right hand did something offscreen. "You can talk freely now, Mr. Koddle."

"I hope so. I've been thinking about your offer—about our collaborating on a book."

"You *have*?" It was painful to see the way the alien's face lit up. "But that's wonderful! I really want you to know how grateful that makes me f—"

"I haven't said I'd do it yet; I just said I'm reconsidering. What I'd like to do is see some samples of your work—"

"Of course! Of course! I'd be honored!"

"—especially true-life accounts of your work for the Black Hole Travel Agency."

"Eh? But I want to write, well, narrower-focus stories that deal with relationships and feelings."

"The one does not exclude the other, Muldoon. But you have to understand, the inclusion of *real* extraterrestrial elements will absolutely insure best-seller status. Novelty value, you know. And when your name's established, out of the drawer comes your serious work."

''Really? I, I suppose you're right, although we may have to disguise the source a little.''

''No problem. Roman à clef, and all that.''

Brax fought the urge to pity Apterix Muldoon, or whatever the six-fingered man's real name was. It was all too easy for someone who'd slogged his way through lean, unpublished years of genre-writing to feel a twinge of empathy for anyone, XT or not, so desperate to see his work in print.

''So what I'd like you to do, Mr. Muldoon, is pull together whatever information or journals or first-person writings you have, with stress on your time working for Black Hole. I'll be back in touch in the next day or two to let you know how to get them to me; once I've had time to sift through the material we'll have a sit-down and reach a meeting of the minds.''

A hell of a way to gather intelligence for the war against Black Hole, Brax thought. He'd never pictured an interstellar struggle being waged quite this way; since when was thwarting XT invasion supposed to make one feel like an unspeakable louse?

''I'll start going through my manuscripts right away!'' the alien was saying. ''To tell you the truth, I was beginning to get discouraged; I just got another rejection slip—after a three-month wait, at that. I just have to tell you what an honor it is for—''

''Yes, yes, for me too, Mr. Muldoon. I have to run. Good-bye for now.''

When Brax got back to the Sealand box he found Monella up and dressed—this time in a tailored jogging suit that had seen better days—and puffing on a cigarette. ''You got a change a' clothes you don't care as much about, you might as well put 'em on; whatever you wear to Fresh Kills is gonna smell pretty powerful for a while.''

''I'll pick something up after we see Strakes,'' Brax said.

''Up to you.'' Monella shrugged. ''You still owe me for the coveralls. And you're buying breakfast; let's go.''

They drank coffee and ate croissant sandwiches on the subway ride downtown, rush-hour crowds not having appeared yet, and were at the Port Authority Bus Terminal early enough to catch the first run of the day via New Jersey to Fresh Kills. After some agonizing, Brax elected to keep his manuscript with him rather than store it in a locker; he simply couldn't bear to let it out of his sight. The other passengers on the special bus—an express from terminal to prison—were mostly the families of inmates at the huge Staten Island facility plus a few demoralized-looking public defenders, an extension-course teacher, and a few guards and other staff.

It was fourteen miles from Manhattan to Fresh Kills. The landfill had been closed to further dumping early on in the Turn, but Brax still smelled the place before he saw it—due, naturally, to the fact that it had been reopened. For all his bravado, it was Monella who was looking nervous and nauseated. "Fucking place," he kept muttering. "Reeking mutherfucking shithole."

The August heat was already cranking up when the old RPEV bus pulled through the outermost fence. Between the three encircling belts of fencing and for two hundred yards outside the ground was flat and bore close-cropped grass with only methane-collection and groundwater-monitoring pipes sticking up. The bus rolled toward the admin complex at the opposite end of the place from Trash Mountain—near Dizzy Donald's MegaMart, where Brax and Asia had nearly been captured by assailants unknown.

Back when Fresh Kills was a maximum-security facility the open belts had been free fire zones, but the notion of controlling a population of hard-core offenders and getting any meaningful amount of work out of them had never really proved viable. Nowadays the facility was minimum-security, run jointly by the Federal Bureau of Prisons, the New York State Department of Corrections, the EPA, and Inmate Industries, Inc., with educational support from the Department of Labor. A rehab program awarded inmates an additional half day off their sentence for every full day satisfactorily worked.

A few of the luckier cons were tending and trimming the grass with particular devotion—a suss job, according to Sal Monella—watched by guards, tower cams, and ATV surveillance remotes.

Those cams made Brax nervous, but he hadn't dared wear camoflesh again; his inexpert application would've been spotted by any guard who took a halfway attentive look at him. Monella had assured him that, lacking funds for an expert-system identification AI, Fresh Kills simply filed tapes of visitors for sixty days then erased them. The man didn't seem concerned, so Brax tried not to be.

Though the sweetish, pungent bouquet of uncovered garbage filled the electrobus despite its air-circ filters, Brax knew it was only a pale specter of what the place had been like before the

Turn. Opened in 1948 on tidal marshland, its name taken from the nearby streams—the Dutch word for such being *kil*—it remained, at over three thousand acres, the largest landfill ever put into operation. Set up when few people gave much thought to what went *into* landfills, much less what leached *out* of them, it eventually leaked more than a million gallons of leachate fluids into the surrounding ecosystems every twenty-four hours.

In time Fresh Kills held close to three billion cubic feet of refuse; its closing, one of the major confrontations in New York City's Turn turmoil, was forced by demonstrations, ecotage, rioting, and what amounted to armed insurrection resulting in the loss of over three hundred lives.

There were still poisons leaking from Fresh Kills despite several attempts at cleanup. The only way to do it right was to uncover the garbage and sort through it. Eco-positive symbol that it had become, the Fresh Kills Remediation Project went forward despite the fact that it was costly, inefficient, and slow.

Incarceration at Fresh Kills could be grueling, but the earned reduction of sentence was a powerful incentive: some seventy-eight percent of low-risk inmates eligible for the program applied. Judges and pre-sentencing investigators especially liked to place polluters and other environmental wrongdoers there, make a conspicuous show of men and women paying penance for their crimes against the biosphere with the sweat of their brows. There were other such work programs—toxic dumps; old graveyards from which the bodies had to be exhumed to stop the leaching of embalming chemicals into the aquifers—but Fresh Kills was the assignment of choice.

The bus pulled up to a building designated RECEPTION, where visitors and their reasons for coming were sorted out. Monella did the talking and had the routine down pat; if he knew any of the corrections personnel, neither he nor they showed it.

Brax had unconsciously assumed he'd be talking to Strakes through razor wire or bulletproof plastic, but instead Monella led him outside to a small electric trolley where several other visitors already waited. "Ray's out on a new working face they're opening up; they got a break comin' and we're allowed fifteen minutes."

"So he's willing to see us?"

Monella laughed. "Etaoin, I don't care what you seen in the movies. When you're in prison without many friends like Ray Strakes is, you don't pass up a visit."

Once they got out onto the landfill itself the stench intensified, though Brax could see that the workers hadn't uncovered any more fill than they could handle on a daily basis. Like most of the other passengers, Brax and Monella donned the recyclable paper face masks they'd been given at the admin building. The masks didn't help much.

The trolley rolled past reclamation sites that had been in operation for over fifteen years, layer after layer of aged trash processed like a small open-pit mine. Because the day was already so warm the decomposing trash was only steaming faintly; Brax had heard that in most weather the smoke of putrefaction hung over the sites. Supposedly the project went to great lengths to minimize the scavenger population, but there were still plenty of sea gulls around, and he spotted a rat as big as a terrier burrowing its way through the trash.

Inmates wore Day-Glo orange worksuits, gloves, and boots—and in some cases filter masks. A lot of the guards on foot or manning the mobile watchtowers with Crowd Control gas projectors, unguns and tonfas wore the masks, too. When Brax asked, Sal explained that the CC gas was a special mix the prisoners' filter masks couldn't stop.

Brax saw the transponder on one prisoner's wrist as she worked the controls of her 'dozer. The transponders were the minimum-security facility's main method of keeping track of inmates.

In the oldest areas, Brax knew, exploratory excavation had gotten down to the level of the salt marsh; there, it was slimy primeval gray muck with perhaps the odd bit of building material. Higher up, though—as he was seeing now—there was evidence of the insane folly of pre-Turn times. The ultimate eco-verité theme park.

Men and women were digging up the trash and loading it on conveyor belts where some preliminary sorting was done by other inmates. Most of the refuse went to sorting sheds, where the bulk of the work was wet, sloppy, uncomfortable and vile beyond most people's concept of the word.

And so at last the contaminating medical waste, the toxin-laced cosmetics, the cleaning fluids and latex paint, the used motor oil and cadmium batteries and disposed diapers and ton upon ton of undegraded newspaper—all were painstakingly extracted from the sickened soil, this time to be dealt with honestly. Looking around, Brax thought of estimates that there was enough work here to keep twenty times as many prisoners busy for a hundred years and wondered if those estimates didn't err on the side of optimism.

A few other passengers were let off at a sorting shed to visit with inmates on a brief morning break. As the trolley pulled away, Brax watched the embraces, the tears, the hand-holding while people sat at picnic tables built, so Monella told him, by the prisoners. The last of the other visitors disembarked at an auxiliary power plant that ran off methane generated by decomposition. "A soft gig," Sal Monella smirked.

The trolley passed through the chain-link fences again, out onto a vast stretch of the landfill that was just being opened up: test bores were being made with a bucket auger, a pad prepared for a sorting shed. "Real trusty work," Monella explained.

"What keeps them from running?" Brax wanted to know. There was mostly wetland and highways for miles.

Monella shook his head. "Nothing—except the transponders pick it right up. You see those lines?" He meant yellow tape stretched between temporary marker sticks at waist height. "Con misses a head count or even *steps* outside 'em and that's it, no questions axed: all sentence reduction revoked, penalty time added, immediate transfer to medium- or max-security facility, no second chance."

At the new site they climbed off the trolley and it hummed away, due back in fifteen minutes. Someone must have called a break because inmates had stopped work, lit cigarettes, found a seat, or leaned against machinery to gab. Monella pointed out a man sitting alone on a sorting table and watching them, then started over that way.

A dump truck rumbled across their path, and Brax was taken aback to feel the ground under his feet wobble like Jell-O— Fresh Kills still compacting.

Strakes was tall and WASPy with thinning blond hair and a flat-faced look of mistrust. "Raymundo!" Monella greeted him. "How's the boy, they treatin' you all right?"

Strakes rubbed forefinger and middle finger together rapidly. "Give me a smoke, Sal, the clock's running."

It occurred to Brax that there was a lot of smoking going on for a place that produced so much methane, but he concluded that they must know what they were doing. Monella gave the man what was left of a pack and offered him a light. "Yeah,

yeah; here. Ray Strakes, this is my friend Etaoin Shrdlu I told you about. He wants to talk about Phoenix.''

Instead of extending his hand, Strakes spit out a fleck of clove that had gotten stuck to his tongue. ''No problem; those bastards left me to twist in the wind. But what's in it for me?''

Brax had done some thinking about that since linking up with Monella. Strakes had taken the rap, unfairly or otherwise, for an illegal dumping scheme that got rid of the toxic wastes from Silicon Synapse's chip-manufacturing operation but also repoisoned an aquifer in South Kearney, New Jersey, that had been cleaned up during the Turn. Brax couldn't offer him much money and doubted Strakes would believe there was any chance of Brax's getting him a new trial or parole. But there were a few other possibilities. Damn, if Brax could at least get the EPA and regional prosecutors on Phoenix Enterprises's case, *something* might shake loose.

''What about revenge, Ray? I'd like to help you get the people who let you take the blame and serve the time.''

Strakes laughed and flicked the end of his cigarette, though little ash had accumulated. ''Revenge, huh? As a favor to me? What's your end?''

Monella was quick to intervene. ''He's got a little green, too, Ray; there'll be somethin' in it to make life easier out here. And who knows, maybe he'll dig up somethin' the parole board'll listen to.'' He shot Brax a look that asked for corroboration.

Brax nodded. ''I can try. I—I'm investigating Phoenix Enterprises—for a book.''

Strakes blew smoke out of his lungs thoughtfully. ''So let's hear what you know about them and see whether you're worth my time or not. Do you realize the magnitude of the powers you're dealing with?''

Brax became cautious, not having expected things to get turned around like this. Except for the dubious prospect that was Apterix Muldoon, Strakes was the only willing informant he'd found since talking to the late Bixby Santiago—but, should Strakes prove ignorant of what was Really Going On behind Phoenix Enterprises, he and Monella might write Brax off as a psychotic if Brax revealed too much.

He started slowly. ''I know Phoenix is composed of powerful people who have a secret plan. I know that that plan has to do with exploitation and profiteering on a worldwide basis, and the subversion of all Earth's governments.''

Sal Monella was staring at him goggle-eyed. Strakes was nodding slightly. "So, you're not just some bullshitter. But what's your proof? Where are you in all this?"

Brax balked. "Just a second, Strakes. Who's pumping whom here?"

Monella exploded, "C'mon, we haven't got all day! Show the guy some good faith!"

Brax held his breath. In the heat and light and stink of the landfill everything seemed otherworldly and menacing, but he couldn't simply go silent; if he cut loose from the Strakes lead now he'd in all likelihood lose it for good. He'd give Strakes as much as he dared, and if the man couldn't show insider knowledge of the situation Brax would cut and run.

"For some years now Phoenix has been using its powers and wealth to pave the way for a takeover of the entire world. This takeover is being fronted by their theme-park holdings and the cruise ship *Crystal Harmonic*."

Strakes was nodding. "True, true, Mr. Koddle, but anybody who knows anything about Phoenix Enterprises could make accusations—"

He stopped, interrupted by Monella's monotone obscenities as they both saw the look on Brax's face. *Mr. Koddle!* "A setup," Brax said flatly, backing away from them both.

Monella shrugged. "Might as well stay put, man; it's too late to leave and you don't want to give these people a tough time." But he didn't make any effort to grab Brax.

Looking around, Brax didn't see any guards nearby, and the other prisoners were just staring at what was going on with blank expressions. The trolley was nowhere in sight. Unsure of every step, Brax started walking back toward the administration building. Like the others, Strakes and Monella just watched him go. There were no alarms, of course; he wasn't wearing a transponder.

The sun was beating on his brain now, the humid air almost unbreathable with the rankness of rot and trash. He had to fight the inclination to break into a run. He felt like he was stuck on an endless dirt road in a decaying limbo. Then he caught the turbine hum of the land-yacht power plant.

It was as black and streamlined as an onyx dolphin—one of the new status vehicles, so much bigger than even a stretch limo that in some places they weren't permitted in the interstates' left lanes. This one was more capacious than an old-time RV, he gauged—almost as roomy as a bus but lower and sleeker, with two wide wheels in front and a bogey of four in the rear. It came from somewhere out toward the distant highways, cutting straight for him and throwing up a wake of red dust.

Brax froze, looking one way, then another. Far back the way he'd come, Strakes and Monella were watching him. Brax was too far from the safety—as he saw it now—of the prison fences, too far from any sorting shed or cover. He turned and ran blindly anyway.

Casting a look back over his shoulder, he didn't realize until it was too late that he'd blundered onto a working face—an exposed hillside of garbage. He lost his footing and hurtled down, slewing and thrashing. It was impossible to stop: the working face was too steep and offered no solid purchase. Something jarred his head, a jolt more than a pain. He flailed through stinking mulch and yielding trash—cans and newspapers, coffee grounds, vegetable trimmings, decaying meat, and diaperloads of poop from kids doubtless old enough to vote by now. He bodysurfed through the crud-coated plastic bags and bottles, lawn cuttings and tuna-fish tins, the eggshells, scabby Band-Aids, used tampons, wadded Kleenexes, snotted cotton swabs, molded milk cartons, and polystyrene fast-food containers. He barely missed being sliced open by the broken frame of a tricycle and nearly got necklaced by a fabric-belted radial tire that still had some good tread left on it. He had a sense that he was flushing rats and other things before him but was moving too fast to see just what.

And all the time, his main terror was not death by laceration or concussion but rather that he would lose momentum, would sink, would drown in the garbage of a culture that had nearly itself been drowned in the stuff. Instead, he saw he was plunging straight for a rusted, torn-off chrome fender that looked jagged enough to slash him in two. He thrashed hysterically, praying for a handhold, and felt his arms threaten to wrench from their sockets as he caught something.

His face was scraped but he didn't care as he was slewed around to a halt on a small mound of refuse with flat, marshy ground not far beyond. His palms were bleeding and sore where the skin had been ripped away from them by the handhold that had slowed and saved him: a dead and rotted oak limb someone had sawn down and cast into a dumpster long years before.

As he clawed his way to his knees Brax felt a repulsive

squirming on his lips, spat, and slapped away a smear of hamburger that was—he was sure he'd felt it—writhing with maggots. Too shell-shocked to puke, he fought to flounder his way clear, to run for cover—when he heard the sound of clapping.

It came to him that there was still muck rippling and settling from the land-yacht's sliding stop. He looked over to where a rear door was open in the black-mirror fuselage and a tall, blond, handsome man in a gorgeously cut suit was looking out, applauding politely.

"Excellent run, Mr. Koddle. The professionals would rate that an expert slope, I should think—or advanced intermediate, at the very least. Some nasty moguls."

Brax sat down suddenly in the trash, astounded that the mighty Phipps Hagadorn should know his name.

TWENTY-THREE

LUCKY SECURED HIS hotel room and, carrying the gadget sent to him by Puhn Jahnt secured to his waistband under his snazzic jacket, set off with Hono bringing up the rear. He had a few things to sort out on Zillion, including, for his own peace of mind, squaring away his clients. Then he'd be on his own.

The troupe encountered Dame Snarynxx and Lumber Jack coming in the opposite direction to find Lucky. The giant from Wood Wind looked troubled, but Lucky was in no mood to sympathize. Besides, the idea of assassinating somebody just because of what some old geezers said at a séance was just plain insane.

He took Lumber aside. "Listen, there's not going to be any killing. Your mission's canceled, understand? We'll straighten it all out some other way."

Lumber Jack gazed down at him unblinkingly. "I see."

"Good. Let's go." Lucky went back to the others, Lumber trailing after. "We'll stroll around town a bit," he suggested. The side trips, under escort of local guides, weren't due to start for another two hours.

The Dimdwindles had been in the lobby. Lucky recalled something about questionnaires and Dult, the father of the little family, acknowledged amiably, "Yes, some new Pan-Galactic Consumer Data Bank is soliciting the insights and advice of Trough travelers and we thought, well why not? Gave the boy here a thrill to relate his experiences into the autoterminal."

"Told 'em *everything!*" gushed GoBug.

Lucky thought about reminding them that he'd told them not to interface with strangers or answer unauthorized queries, but decided that wouldn't faze the dumb householders from the smart houses of FoolProof. It just reinforced his enjoyment at the idea of leaving them.

It was difficult to believe the apathetic Mr. Millmixx had even contrived to leave his room on his own, much less venture forth to—as Hono described it—solicit sex from females of his species as Lucky had advised.

"By the way, I never said that," Lucky told Hono.

"But dear, in a manner of speaking you did—" Doola Dimdwindle started to remind him.

"Forget that for now! Oh, and if anybody spots the Rphians, give 'em a yell."

Millmixx having gone, according to Hono, to the nearest outdoor rec reserve, Lucky set a course in that direction. Carbuncle was dotted with such places, a necessary antidote to the urban crush. This one took Lucky's breath away and let him forget, for a few minutes, his problems and perils—let him feel like the paranormal wanderer and witness to miracles he'd like to have been but could never spare time to be. Zen contemplation was too time-consuming and distracting when you were one jump—sometimes less—ahead of the kidnap crews, the mind-wipers, the interstellar hit squads and zombie recruiters and IRS flying dutchmen with talking briefcases.

The rec reserve was five hundred acres or so of open ground palisaded on all sides by the towering rust red boneyard architecture of Carbuncle. From what Lucky understood, it was something more than a nature sanctuary and amusement center and only slightly less than a social free-fire zone. Visually, it suggested Central Park, Copenhagen's Tivoli, and Epcot Center, mixed in with Red Square, Skull Island, and the grounds of Balmoral Castle.

Lucky was spared the decision of which way to proceed when, with happy yips, Hoowe and Arooo came bounding up. Both wore expensive color-coordinated training outfits; their tongues lolled and dripped from exertion. "I *knew* that was your scent!" Hoowe panted. "The old hunting instincts are sharp as ever!"

"I knew it too!" Arooo puffed, ever the competitor.

"Having a howlin' good time, huh?" Lucky grinned. Their olfactory senses really were keen; great.

The fact that the two were still on the loose showed that behavioral strictures in the reserves were as indulgent as Lucky had heard. "We're looking for Mr. Millmixx."

"We saw him earlier." Their nostrils flared as the Rphians tested the air. "He's over that way, by the lake."

They moved out, Hono pointing aud-vids up, down, and everywhere in between. Dame Snarynxx moved along with that surprising speed she could attain, busily sniffing flowers. Lumber Jack was gazing around in unreadable silence.

When Arooo veered off toward some bushes with an investigatory sniff, Lucky whipped a gardening applicator out of his pocket, aimed it midway up the trunk of a nearby tree, and pumped the trigger. The gun spat and a small wet patch appeared on the bark. Arooo and Hoowe both stopped in their tracks and spun around.

"What—?"

"Hu-hhhh?"

But before they could work up a protest their instincts had them loping neck and neck, homing in irresistibly on the tree and its wet spot. "What's the meaning of this?" Arooo growled, manifesting a distinct resemblance to Henry Hull in *The Werewolf of London.*

"I have a right to mark territory too," Lucky explained airily as he sashayed by. The Rphians either decided not to challenge the point or found it irrefutable on some glandular level. In any case they went back to circling the tree, whining.

"Maybe you could cooperate with each other," Lucky suggested. As he strolled on with the others, Arooo and Hoowe exchanged barks and gesticulations. Then Hoowe made a stirrup of his hands and Arooo got a leg up. When he saw the Rph had gotten a handhold on a lower limb and was ready to climb higher, Lucky paused and shot at the top of a huge boulder that sat in the middle of a pool of water-lily-like things.

Hoowe immediately dashed out from under Arooo, who lost his grip and tumbled to the sward with a piercing yelp. Then Arooo leapt to his feet and took up the chase, closing in on his partner and rival. They splashed gingerly through the pond, slapping at tiny swimmers that appeared to be nipping them, and began an assault on the boulder. When they were well into their crazed free climb, Lucky stopped to scent mark a couple of easy spots near the path.

The applicator—he fought the urge to think of it as a *pisstol*—was a delightfully versatile little design. It could mist, spray, and squirt its contents—high-stim-factor synthetic

Rphian urine extract—as well as jetting small quick-dissolving glassine packets of the stuff up to fifty yards, helping him keep the young executives from Rph on the move.

For Lucky and the other travelers it was the pleasantest time since the gondola ride on Root Canal. The place was stocked with fabulous though nonthreatening life-forms botanical and zoological, samples of minerals and eco-settings from all over the planet, and various artistic and historical displays. There were also Zillionites at their leisure, playing odd sports, performing songs or engaging in learned discourse. Lucky savored a precious, enchanted morning.

There were only a few flies in the ointment. Love Handle machines and the occasional Boob-Cube were bothersome reminders of the Trough and Black Hole; and though GoBug couldn't move fast enough to keep up with the Rphians, he managed to be a pest. Lucky recalled that he'd meant to ask the kid something but couldn't bring whatever it was to mind. Still and all, he felt himself in a state of grace.

He also marveled at the doggedness of Hoowe and Arooo. The neurosensory drive to establish territorial dominance must've been fearsome, but that didn't mean a little behavioral mod wasn't in order. He pegged shots hither and yon and the Rphians shagged grimly after. Once or twice one of them managed to overcome all obstacles, drag open his workout pants and mark over the tiny patch of dampness. Inevitably, the other had to keep at it until he did the same. Within fifteen minutes the two were bruised, cut by thorns, soggy, and beginning to foam at the mouth. Puhn Jahnt had more than repayed his investment tip.

"I can do this all day," Lucky assured them pleasantly. He raised the applicator and sighted on a clump of stuff that looked like a rolled-up eight-hundred-pound porcupine.

"No, no!" wheezed Arooo.

"Please" was all Hoowe could manage.

"Suits me, but the next time either of you piddles out of bounds, I start shooting." Lucky put the applicator away, and the Rphians, huffing for breath and watching one another closely to make sure neither cheated, rejoined the group. He heard them growling to each other—something about a "great workout."

Rounding a shifting free-form sculpture of magnetic-bottling effects, they came to a shade-dappled glen where soft Zillionian music played. It was a miniature faerie of decorative pools spanned by arches that looked like they were made of cake frosting; free-floating abstract mobiles; ponderous granite sculptures that were, astoundingly, kinetic art, slowly shifting configurations; holographic dancers doing what appeared to be Zillionian druidic production numbers; and activities Lucky couldn't decipher. Locals were chatting, laughing, sipping drinks, or sampling snacks. Despite their golliwog appearance they were elegantly dressed in flowing, summery clothes and had an air of urbanity.

All except one.

Mr. Millmixx was slumped on a slab of rock near a little fountain. Aside from frequent curious looks he drew no attention whatsoever from his fellow creatures, though the other tourists caused a minor, restrained stir. The group went to gather around Millmixx, and Lucky asked what was wrong.

"I made myself available but the females haven't come to copulate with me and no one has even brought me food."

Lucky threw his hands up. "You want it all handed to you?"

"It always was before," Mr. Millmixx said glumly.

Dame Snarynxx lost patience. "Really, Mr. Waters! Aren't you at all aware of the Dunnage Depopulation campaign?"

"I was out sick the day they taught that. What was it?"

"It was also known as the Sterile Solution," she said with a hint more disapproval, and all at once Lucky's erratic general fund of knowledge kicked in again. The crisis on planet Dunnage had involved accidental release of a shipment of gene-engineered Zillionite clones who promptly went feral and, what with their quick breeding cycle, became a planetary pestilence within two years. Bureaucratic error was officially blamed for the accident, but Black Hole malice was implied by some conspiracy addicts.

Zillionites were horrified at the suggestion of extermination measures; the people of Dunnage were at wits' end. War loomed.

The compromise plan was to release new ferals, lots of them, all male and all sterile though capable of inseminating. They would mate with the feral females—who could only be inseminated once for reproductive purposes though they remained sexually active thereafter—thus acing out fertile male ferals from reproducing. That would shrink the infestation to manageable size or eliminate it altogether in a few years.

Naturally a great many sterile males were needed, and that

was where Mr. Millmixx and others like him entered the picture. Cloning sterile males or reproducing them by artificial
insemination switched on a troublesome genetic side effect. It
was quicker, cheaper, and easier to simply set up a live breeding program—and Mr. Millmixx was the last surviving member of a generation of breeding studs.

Gene-engineered on Dunnage to produce only sterile male
offspring, he'd been surrounded by receptive, sexually active
females, food and drink, and little else to distract him. The
crisis over, he was pensioned off well, as per Dunnage's treaty
with Zillion. So he was on his species' homeworld for the first
time and without a clue as to how things worked there.

"Great zot," Lucky whispered to himself. He'd remembered at last what it was that Millmixx reminded him of.

The Dunnage Depop campaign wasn't so very different from
Earthly efforts to reduce various insect pestilences. The scientists irradiated male fruit flies, say, part way into their breeding
life and released them, intending the steriles to take as many
fertile females as possible out of the mating dance. There was
just one problem.

The irradiated, lab-raised sterile males were unused to doing
anything for themselves. They'd been confined their whole
lives with lots of eager females, plenty of food, and no danger.
When the scientists released them, the sterile fruit flies would
sit around on a branch or a rock, like Millmixx, and wait to be
offered sex and food. No concept of courtship rituals, competition, or the laws of supply and demand.

"I was told my guide would help me," Millmixx was responding to Lucky.

"Aw, Mr. Millmixx, I—I'm sorry. Didn't know I was letting you down."

Dame Snarynxx swung her horns at Lucky. "You are turning out to be a most thoughtless and irresponsible young man."

No doubt the Millmixx backstory and advisory were in with
the other briefing materials that he couldn't access, never having attended guide training. The guy was hopeless, a non-
personality—

"Hold it!" Lucky exclaimed while the thought was still
coming together in his mind. His parents' books and college
course materials and obsolete stuff Ziggy used to go on about—
they were all throwing up images and doctrine in his brain.

His clients were looking at him strangely. Lucky slowly

inhaled. "Awright, I'll do what I can. The rest of you spread out, act casual, talk about anything but Millmixx. Refer all questions to me, understand?"

They obeyed, Lucky sensing in them that enthusiasm and pleasure travelers so often feel when they suddenly have a sense of purpose beyond simply sightseeing. He crossed toward a buffet table where a few Zillionites were gathered and cruised the food. When one female glanced his way he made eye contact and said hello. It didn't take long for a conversation to start and that didn't take long in turning to Millmixx.

"We all noticed him," she said. "I take it he's brain damaged?"

"Vix? No, he's just practicing his new Coolest Medium Life Art. He never, ever breaks character."

"I beg your pardon? I have never heard of Coolest Medium Life Art. Is that Trough?"

"Well, that's where Vix brought it to fruition. It has to do with the Lure of Suddenly Empty Spaces and McLuhanistic media thermodynamics. The audience member has the maximum opportunity to inform nonoccupied places with his or her own perceptions."

"Come again?"

Other Zillionites were listening in now. Lucky tried not to sweat, dredging up every undergrad pomposity and art-scene pickup line he could remember. "It's like the empty spaces of the sculpture being the most important parts, or the silence in poetry, the rests in music. And like that. You fill them in with your own creativity."

She was giving the languid Millmixx a reappraising stare.

"It's really a self-exploration kind of thing," Lucky rattled on. "By creating a minimally responsive interpersonal gravity well, Vix collaborates with the audience. He's the only one who can really explain it—and he won't, of course."

"Of course. Would you pardon me for a moment?" She wandered off in Millmixx's direction. Several eavesdroppers trailed along.

"Just don't expect him to break character," Lucky called after.

For once not a single client was precipitating a crisis. Lucky, brimming with the nectar of interspecies kindness, watched his plan take effect. Millmixx showed no nervousness at being the center of attention; Lucky wondered if he felt like he was back at the breeding project. One of the females laughed, scandalized but not offended, by something Millmixx did or didn't do.

Lucky decided that, when all was said and done, this was a trip *he'd* have paid to come on.

GoBug was laughing, poking around the antigrav anchor under a buffet table. "Easy there," Lucky advised.

"Yessir. Mr. Waters, can I come along when the man from the Agency talks to you?"

Lucky felt as though a cloud had passed across the sun and somebody'd dumped a brick down his esophagus. "What man?"

"The one the hotel questionnaire's being forwarded to. The one who wants to know about anything having to do with Earth."

Lucky had gotten to his feet without realizing it. "I *told* you all not to go blabbing to people! What was the man's name, GoBug? C'mon, think!"

"Oo, it was a funny one. Lun, no, *Lint!* Hey, where're you going? Do we have to leave already?"

That was what had been teasing at him, that questionnaire! Lucky didn't even stop to say good-bye, panning and craning in search of the nearest transport, taxi stand, or whatever served in their place here. He was debating the wisdom of abandoning the 8 Ball and the rest of his belongings at the hotel and going straight for the Adit when, with an explosion of light and a knockover shock wave, a figure appeared between two large trees to his right.

"I knew you had unreported income, Junknowitz!" exulted Zastro Lint. "Your number's up!"

Brax toweled his hair, still wet from the hosing down he'd been given with cold but welcome water from the land-yacht's main tank. He was still mulling over how considerate Hagadorn's people—henchmen? security? entourage?—had been in taking the tool bag and putting it aside before sluicing him down to avoid soaking his belongings. Somehow, running for it again simply didn't enter the picture, especially since the Phoenix über's attendants looked like Olympic athletes turned hit men and women.

Brax was getting a suede captain's chair damp in the saloon area at the rear of the yacht, hands and other injured areas still smarting some from the antiseptic Hagadorn's people had applied. "So you, what, sent that little cockroach Monella to clean up Willy's truck hoping to get close to him?"

Hagadorn guffawed. "The most debilitating effect of paranoia is that it complicates things so. No, Mr. Koddle, use Occam's razor; try the simple explanation." At his gesture one of the other gorillas angled an air-conditioning nozzle at Brax to drive back offensive aromas.

"You—" Brax was still shaking from the fall and the impact of the morning's events, still not sure he wasn't going to go into shock. He tried to picture faces and events, to unroll them backward in his mind like a movie on rewind. "You . . . got Sal to work for you once you knew we had heard about Phoenix? Willy and the rest of us?"

Hagadorn nodded, pleased. "Well, modestly, I have the wherewithal to find out a good deal about anyone I please. And of course Mr. Monella was rather easy to bring aboard, given his own predicament. Strakes actually is an inmate, though he had nothing whatsoever to do with Silicon Synapses, of course. It just happened that he and Monella had worked together in the past. Obviously they're somewhat in need of practice."

Brax had cruised Willy's truck a few times and Hagadorn—or whoever arranged such things for him—had gone to the trouble of throwing an impressive con game together. Well, it impressed Brax, even if it was probably small-time stuff by Hagadorn's standards and even if Brax's interests and vulnerabilities must have been pretty easy to figure out.

"All that, just to find out what I'm doing?"

Hagadorn leaned back, sipping easily at some mango juice over shaved ice. The land-yacht's ride, now that it was back on hardtop, was smooth as baby oil on glass. "Rather more than that. But yes, I must admit, I'm very curious about you—you and your friends in the, the 'loft posse,' isn't that what you people call it? You see, I know more about you than you might suppose."

He motioned to Brax's pack with its all-important roll of manuscript, which had survived the plunge down the working face as miraculously as had its creator. "I *want* you to continue your work; I admire your talent. More importantly, you people have become loci of incredible events and I very much want to understand that phenomenon better. Unfortunately, observing you more or less in situ is out of the question now. Events have taken on a certain velocity overnight; my charade with you wouldn't have lasted long in any event, I suppose."

"The prison authorities will know I disappeared from the site," Brax tried to bluff. "People will be looking for me—"

Hagadorn smiled sympathetically. "Mr. Koddle, I own Inmate Industries and the warden is most beholden to me. I sponsored the director of the Federal Bureau of Prisons for a rather important club and contributed to his son's congressional campaign fund. Why do you think I inserted Fresh Kills in the scenario? It was perfect, especially with Monella knowing Strakes."

Brax examined one of his dressings, forcing aside the thought of what would've happened if he'd careened through a handful of old razor blades or a carton of broken window glass. "But it didn't play so well, did it?"

Hagadorn carefully put the drink into a holder in the arm of his chair. "Too true. That sort of thing doesn't happen to me often, which makes you an even more interesting fellow. But the pace of the game is accelerating, as I said. Pieces are being plucked from the board, so I had to be sure I didn't lose you."

Brax couldn't control the trembling of his hands. "If I cooperate, answer your questions, what then?"

Hagadorn studied him with one eye shut. "For one thing, later on, you and I will take a sea cruise together."

"How'd you like the flash-bang effect, *tax dodger*?" Lint's briefcase taunted as alien tourists and Zillionites screamed and stampeded. "Spoil your little picnic, did we?"

Maybe Lint had some kind of homing instinct but he didn't appear to have brought along any backup. Over near Lucky's side of the glen the path wound around a towering quartz stela and he thought that, if he could break contact and lie low, he stood a chance. His direct route of escape was blocked, though, by a struggling knot of Zillionites, so he turned and took a shortcut, a delicate mother-of-pearl rainbow possibly a handspan wide that bridged a murky orange pool, like a tightrope walker.

"Stop him!" Lint yelled, and an altogether odd beige waveaction effect hit the frosting arc. It shattered like an ice centerpiece smashed by a LAW and Lucky plunged, cawing and propeller-arming, into the pool, whose contents resembled month-old consommé.

The single consolation was that it wasn't deep. When he came up spitting what tasted like XT dishwater, it was to hear Lint screaming at his briefcase, "Take him out, curse you!"

"Recharging!" snarled the briefcase irritably. So, they had their limitations.

Lucky, sitting up to his sternum in primordial chowder, spat out some writhing protoplasmic strands whose nature he did not care to know. "Wait! I haven't done anything wrong!" He swamped to his feet.

"Peddle your alibi in Tax Court!" Lint hollered, coming at Lucky with the unrecharged briefcase raised. Lucky did the only thing he could think of, which was to whip out the garden applicator, flick to autofire, and stitch a heart pattern of synthetic Rphian essence in the center of Lint's chest.

That stopped Lint because he thought, not unreasonably, that he'd been shot. It brought in Hoowe and Arooo from wherever they'd been lurking, to sniff and growl at the Fed and fumble at the flies of their training suits. It made the briefcase go "Plaugh!" and it gave Lucky time to leap and cling to the broken end of the rainbow bridge.

A Hono was still there—the one he'd inadvertently singled out with the ribbon. "Gimme a hand up!"

But the rest of Hono was gathered at the end of the rainbow, entreating the one near Lucky to rejoin them. "We need to talk!"

"We're all Hono!"

"It's not like we're perverts, like other beings!"

The Hono withheld helping brachs and scampered back down the rainbow arc. Lint was beating the Rphs away with his protesting briefcase. Lucky waded to the side of the pool and saw Lumber Jack standing there. "Help me."

The giant only gazed down. Whoever Lumber was fated to kill, the deed would be a lot easier without Lucky around.

"Lum, *help me!*"

But the wooden man only retreated a step. Lucky heard the howls as Lint's briefcase drove the Rphs away with some kind of electroprod bursts. Lint's slow, squeaky, cheap-shoe footfalls came Lucky's way as he hauled himself out of the pool and wormed slimily between Lumber Jack's footlocker-sized feet; at least Lumber didn't try to stomp him.

He knew he could never get to his feet in time to escape.

GoBug, however, chose that moment to dart heedlessly into the IRS man's way. "Mr. Waters, you're not being very coop-*wauuugh!*"

This, because he'd tripped up Lint and the agent went down, the briefcase bellowing "You little maggot!" Pneumatic as he was, GoBug bounced out from between Lint's feet and re-bounded from the turf—but he was making sounds of inartic-ulate shock at the unique experience of having come to harm, albeit minor.

By that time Lucky was under the churning spokes of one of the granite kinetic pieces, up on the other side and on his way with a growing lead. He hurdled a hedge and skidded in a tight turn around the crystal stela. As he came around the monolith, though, he let out a yell of dismay and stopped so short his soles flew out from under him. "Stay away from me! Nooo!"

But, yes, the refulgent Boob-Cube tumbled through the air in his direction like a huge, computer-animated child's block, filling the path between impassable hedges. It shimmered with alluring images of Nu-Topian time-sharing, "Tired of your dull routine?" the siren spiel coaxed. It came rolling through the air at him as Lucky scrambled back until his shoulders came up against the obelisk. "Longing for an escape? Just tell us what you want; just tell us what you want."

Sobbing for breath, Lucky surrendered. "Y-yeah, okay, you win."

Back by the pool, Lint had been delayed only briefly by his stumble over GoBug. He strode briskly around the quartz stela only a moment or two behind Lucky, his thwarted briefcase making gnashing-teeth sounds interspersed with obscenities.

Then he paused in midstep, gaping up at the radiant, image-rich Boob-Cube. The agent's mouth dropped open as he saw Lucky Junknowitz beckoning to him *from the Cube*, his upper torso halfway emerging from it to smirk maddeningly. "Reach out and contact—now-www!" Lucky crooned.

"Hiding in there won't help you!" Lint raged, and grabbed for his quarry's proffered hand, ignoring the briefcase's objec-tions. There was a multihued lightning strike and Lint kind of yodeled. The briefcase ranted, "You *putz!*"

As the field agent rocked back and forth slowly, recovering, a truck-sized pewter egg descended to hang an inch from the pathway. The hatch clanged down and out hopped a vigorous little figure in nacreous suit, cravat, high collar, and blue hat.

Zipping out to hover nearby came his Christmas-star remote. "Hi there; the name's Glooey Tadwallader! Congratulations on your wisdom in signing up for a trial visit to Nu-Topia."

Lint had recovered himself somewhat. "Stand aside, you! There's a fugitive from justice within that Cube and I mean to have him out!"

"Oh, a welsher, eh? Hey, boys!"

Though his image still protruded from the Cube, Lucky himself was watching from concealment around the curve of the monolith. Three mugs in vanity plate armor emerged from the egg with monster cordless-drill handguns, electronet, and energy prod. They looked like the same ones he'd seen on Confabulon, and for that matter so did Glooey Tadwallader. Lucky theorized that they were clones or simulacra working off a common data base.

When the squarefoots grabbed Lint they got a surprise. A strobe of light came from the briefcase and the enforcers were jolted as if they'd been sandbagged. But their armor absorbed the blast, and with Tadwallader screeching "Grab him" they piled on Zastro Lint as if he were carrying a football for the wrong team. The star yanked in its points and tinkerbelled off for safer parts.

Lucky was already easing around the obelisk, retracing his course. When the Cube had asked him to tell it what he wanted, he'd played a longshot. "Me," he'd answered. "I want an exact duplicate of me." The Boob-Cube was ready to pander to any perversity and so the doppelgänger had appeared just in time to decoy Lint.

Now the fight was turning into an Olympian brawl, with Lint somehow giving the three biggies a battle royal. Massive punches were thrown and absorbed on both sides; from the briefcase came plasmic jets of destruction. Defensive and offensive flare-ups intermittently made the struggle too bright to watch.

But weight, numbers and size began to tell, and bit by bit the enforcers dragged Lint toward the egg and the dreaded time-share weekend. Lucky would have liked to stay and watch, but there was such a thing as getting while the getting was good.

As he was tiptoeing away, Lucky heard his name howled. He turned back to find that, in the midst of the melee, Lint had somehow spotted him. Bracing himself in the egg's hatch while the three hulking stooges hammered and dragged and kicked at him, he bawled, "This isn't over, Junknowitz! I'll hunt you around perdition's flames!"

One of the tough guys gnawed Lint's hand loose from the hatch and he was dragged inexorably inside, the briefcase wailing, "Oh, ye tax cheat, ye damnèd tax cheat!"

TWENTY-FOUR

WHEN LUCKY RETURNED the Zillionites had fled the glen but his clients were still there. "Thanks a lot for nothing," he told them.

"Well, he *did* claim to have legal authority," Dame Snarynxx pointed out.

Lucky was so furious he couldn't even answer. Typically, Dult Dimdwindle failed to read the danger signs. "Mr. Waters, I don't understand. My boy there was, was physically damaged."

Lucky grimaced but replied, "That's because you weren't looking after him. What'd you think would happen?"

Dult evinced shock. "Why, someone is supposed to be taking care of these things! Things like that aren't supposed to be allowed to happen."

Lucky studied him a moment. "That's because the veeblefertzer systemry in the pond is broken, see? There's a, a mechanism that shows how things go wrong when you don't take responsibility for your own ass."

While Dult and Doola were bending over the pond Lucky shoved them in. He heard them come up, sputtering and bleating, as he whirled on GoBug. "You ratted me out, kid."

GoBug gulped spasmodically. "But I didn't think—"

"Exactly." Lucky took all the others in by eye. "Anybody follows me when I leave here, I'll call an airstrike on 'em." With that he turned his back on them and left.

If Black Hole backup hadn't nabbed him by now, he had enough breathing time to reclaim his belongings, he reasoned. At the hotel he threw his clothes into the disposal slot, washed down in record time, and donned the gaucho-superhero getup Sheena had gotten him to buy so long ago.

Loo-gout, Black Hole—here comes Earthman, the Zoomin' Human . . .

Nobody at the Zillion Adit gave him any grief about not having his group with him; if a guide wanted to risk being subjected to the punishments of Tyro Assessment, that was the guide's option. Using his tour ticket he reached way station Blits at long last.

Only to discover that the al-Reem Adit had been shut down for the time being, top security investigation teams being the only exception. Casual inquiries got him no solid intel, but there were rumors of anomalous events in the teleportational webwork of the Trough itself, the appearance of phantom Adits, and some tremendous uproar in the interrogation pits of 'Reem. It was said that full service would be restored within the next baseline-day.

All he could do was bide his time. There were a few things he'd need to do before he went nosing around al-Reem anyway; one of the first was figure out how to cover the cost of the fade. His tour ticket wouldn't help him there, but as a guide he had some discretionary funds he wasn't planning on returning or accounting for, and he had a few other ideas as well.

Another priority was to convert his Wise-Guise so that it would show up on the scanners as a new magic-marker ID. No doubt Salty Waters would be a wanted man very soon—if he wasn't already.

The Wise-Guise help menu had taught him how to change identities back on Alas, but it would take a bit of privacy. As he sauntered along Lucky passed, yet again, a rogue's gallery of Wanted-poster holos and saw himself, Ka Shamok, Silvercup—

Asia Boxdale.

The sight of her made him feel faint. His heart was pounding, dream-machine nanite or no, as he leaned forward for a better look, fighting back a thousand vivid fears for her safety.

The first thing he saw was that this was no ordinary Wanted poster. It read:

ASIA BOXDALE
ADIT NAVEL
Earthman, contact Up and Adits
Specialty Tours, way station Sierra

(Proof of this individual's authenticity
and presence available upon request)

That last part told him it probably wasn't some simple sucker's game. Anybody in the Trough could phony up an authentic-looking holograph, along with lifelike audio synths, fingerprints, maybe a fake DNA sample or even a real one. Some kind of lifelike android was no problem for anyone with the right resources, either.

But whoever was posting Asia's likeness was claiming to have convincing proof. Aside from the person herself—whom her purported captors might be inclined to keep sequestered to exert added pressure—that might mean among other things a mindbender recording with graphic memory references. Their game might be anything, from the obvious to the utterly unguessable.

He looked at Asia. His chest and gut felt like a roil of acid. Harley he'd adored and Sheena he'd come to regard as boon companion, friend, and lust object. His feelings for Silvercup he still felt a long way from understanding. But Asia . . . Asia had been his lover; he knew her in ways intimate and inimitable—knew her better than he did the others. He knew too that she'd loved him, in many ways still did. He sure hadn't gotten over loving her, was resigned that he never would, completely; the pain of seeing her image floating ghostly there reminded him of that.

Without further discussion from the floor Lucky's current plan of action was scrapped and a new one set in its place. Al-Reem was inaccessible for now and he couldn't bear to simply wait around way station Blits.

Up and Adits. The company was supposed to be a packager of whimsical getaways, used as a cover by Rashad Tittle—claiming to be a tour promoter named Gaspar de Torque—when he had reappeared on Earth, only to be murdered—a murder for which Lucky had been blamed. Lucky had assumed the company didn't exist. Maybe it was a front for former employees of AzTek Development Consortium who, like Rashad, had survived Black Hole's savage purge of that organization.

Or again, it might be an artistic touch to an elaborate lure.

At least Asia was implied to be on way station Sierra rather than al-Reem; that might be a good sign. Sierra was the only transfer point to Earth.

His discretionary funds didn't amount to enough to get him to Sierra and for once nobody seemed to have heard of the Sphere of Influence's mystical powers. The six-armed, cube-skulled Edrian pawnbroker Lucky found on a little-traveled Blits side concourse wasn't even interested in the Magic 8 Ball as a curio and showed no reaction to the interlocking-rings medallion. But just as Lucky was about to leave, the canny-eyed Ed spotted something under Lucky's clinging cape, pinned to his open-neck Renaissance-style shirt.

All the pawnbroker's world-weariness fell away. "The Edrian Legion of Decency!"

Lucky had stuck the medal there on a whim; it had been awarded to him when he—with Sheena's help—had negotiated an end to the internecine war between the Eds and the Kammese and incidentally saved his own and the guide's neck. A quick scan of the decoration's authenticator confirmed that Lucky was in fact its recipient even though everybody had been insisting on calling him Miles Vanderloop at the time.

The awestruck Edrian was practically kissing the hem of Lucky's cape. Earthman swaggered out of the place with enough gelt to cover his ticket, and the pawnbroker's pledge that there was no time limit on repayment. The medal had been set in a display case behind the counter—not for sale at any time under any circumstances. Twenty minutes later Lucky was back in way station Sierra.

The first thing to do was recon Up and Adits from a safe distance. The company's operation on Sierra was only a branch office—another strange factor. Why else would it have been picked but for its proximity to Earth?

Also, the concourse on which it was located was undergoing major renovation. Somebody's idea of a pleasant decor concept, it developed, was a reefs-and-tidal-pools ocean-walk motif inspired by some marine planet. Rental spaces along that stretch of the concourse had been shuttered, and the middle stretch had the look, from where he stood, of an abandoned mall. Despite that, internal station monitors showed that there was a lot of activity over in the cul-de-sac where Up and Adits and a number of shops, concessions, offices, and other businesses were located; plenty of crowd in which to conceal himself.

Well, his Wanted-poster viz had been face-scrubbed and his Wise-Guise was giving out a new name now: "Orb Ideal," in tribute to the Earth toy that had found him and served him so well.

He'd considered spending the balance of his funds on a mimetic copycoat, some vision-enhancing all-sights, and maybe even a shooting iron if he could find one, but decided that those were more likely to get him noticed, busted, kidnapped—any or all—than to help. Resetting his bag on his shoulder and gathering his cloak about him, he sauntered down the concourse trying not to look like a man on an urgent mission.

It was easy to keep from running, though, what with the unfinished reconstruction providing more obstacles and mini-detours than he was used to seeing on a concourse. There were breaking-surf noises in the distance accompanied by surges of water to and fro through the scenery, artificial salt-sea breezes, and some nice turquoise-sky holo effects. The path wended among salaaming fronds, miniature crags of exposed XT coral—some of which shed diminutive waterfalls—swaying estuarine grasses taller than he was, and a sandbar or two. The breeze ruffled his hair.

In ten steps along the raised wooden nature-trail catwalk he'd lost sight of the concourse proper. In twenty it felt like he'd faded to another world. He started as he thought he saw something move in the turgid water.

Lucky closed his eyes, got a grip on himself, and marched on. Then the walkway dropped open like a trapdoor. He was plunged into a deep pool and something huge, muscular, and sinewy had him in its coils even as he hit the water.

He tried to scream "Don't eat me!" but only swallowed brackish salt water thick with alien tastes. He coughed and more water was drawn into his lungs. He felt himself pulled irresistibly deeper, then bashed his head on something and faded to black.

From tiny DNA strands mighty organisms grow; from infinitesimal quanta of happenstance, transcendent events take shape.

For example: A certain Edrian pawnbroker in way station Blits boasts reverently of the Legion of Decency medal left in his keeping—while he's lunching at a Trough Feed automat whose cyberchef is a Fealty sympathizer. It is one of the few viable leads, and the only timely one to date, in the hunt for Lucky Junknowitz.

Sapper SIs infiltrate data systems throughout Blits and, soon thereafter, many are destroyed by defensive programs and other security or are captured and suicide, but several succeed. The kidnap operation run by Plinisstro's sea serpents in way station Sierra lacks the polish and resources of a Black Hole operation, and very shortly the Fealty verifies Lucky's identity and pieces together what's been done with him.

But all these actions are carried out by disembodied SIs. There's still a scarcity of mobile operatives—situationally mobile, that is; socially mobile in the sense that organics won't throw a fit and open fire when the machine in question is seen moving on its own or shows up unexpectedly somewhere—that the Fealty can bring to bear on this crucial assignment. And there's only one it really trusts and gives significant odds of succeeding.

When word reached her of what had happened to Lucky she had taken on yet another shape—or nowadays *configuration* was, sadly, a better word. At that moment she inhabited a full-track, all-terrain wrecker and was clearing up debris in the wake of a tidal-quake at a six-hundred-square-mile open pit mine on Crankshaft.

In a way she'd become a debased and hobbled counterpart to Sobek, machine version of his infinitely transmutable organic form, both of them capable of remanifesting themselves in exhaustive variety.

But the Probe couldn't take on his *original* shape because he didn't know what it was. And neither could Silvercup, for inescapable interdictions had been implanted in her at Foresite: that she not revert to her true conformation or anything closely resembling it until her mission was complete and she'd brought Lucky Junknowitz back to Sweetspot, into the custody of the Fealty. The Monitor had advocated the measure and put forward various rationales—motivation; insurance that she would follow her other programmed directives—but she'd come to the conclusion that those were all sophistry on the Monitor's part.

In reality the monitor wanted her for himself alone and was too jealous and resentful to let her venture out wearing the body in which she'd been quickened. How this contemptible fixation had taken over the once noble machine, her former mentor, guardian, and friend, she hadn't a clue. He wanted to be sure no one else could gaze on her; he had her body under close guard in Computopia against her personality's return. At that time, she felt with growing certainty, the Monitor would consummate his desire for her at last via the godlike male metal-flesh, the newly forged Masculine Aspect, the Monitor's virile instrument.

The Monitor had further made sure she was strictly enjoined against libidinous acts even in her current bulky, lumbering, power-machinery incarnation. Otherwise she might have spited him and vented her longing in the clandestine orgies of the heavy rigs, taking part in their robust, good-hearted, gimbal-shaking carnal marathons.

She still thought of herself as Silvercup just as humans tried to sustain an identity even after illness, injury, or other misfortune had stolen some or most of what they'd been. All of what had been excised from her, though, was still secreted in the purloined data crystal back at Foresite; how long before it could escape discovery, no entity could predict for certain. If it was found by the Monitor, that part of her would be obliterated forever: all the emotions she'd felt toward Lucky, and all her reasons for feeling them. She would know those feelings had existed, but never what they had been.

She'd put in place subroutines to keep herself from dwelling upon that but still it was hard to put from her mind, especially because rumors of a sighting of Lucky Junknowitz on Crankshaft had proved empty. Then by coded squirt over a little-used freq came word from the Fealty of the Edrian pawnbroker, the medal, and the kidnapping sea serpents.

The good-natured but uncomplicated automata of the vast Crankshaft pits had never seen a machine simply jettison all nonessentials, defy mining-company programming and Traffic Central, and rumble off toward the headquarters complex. By the time pursuit was organized the wrecker had taken refuge in a freight-tube transfer station garage. The wrecker was docile—in fact, inoperable. Its cognitive core, memory stacks, and a number of effectuator modules were gone, vanished.

Phreaking the company's bills of lading and expediter's forms was tougher in her present configuration, but soon the disassembled pieces of Silvercup's essential structure were in transshipment on the mass-transit cargo freight system she'd become so adept at exploiting. She was on her way to Earth, and though none of the Trough's overseers were aware of it yet, so were a number of very special components.

*   *   *

Lucky's body knew, quite a while before his brain came back on duty, where he was.

The certainty came from the subtlest components of odors in the air, from the feel of the gravity, atmospheric pressure, perhaps even the magnetic field of the planet. As his head began to clear with an unreal speed, Lucky muttered, "Earth."

"You could tell that right away, Mr. Junknowitz?" inquired a cultured voice with a perfect mid-America pronunciation but a hint of the foreign nonetheless. "How extraordinary—no, lie still. You're in no danger."

Not that he could move much; he felt as if he were buried in sand. At least he wasn't in the belly of the Loch Sierra Monster, that much he could see for himself as he blinked his eyes open. Fragments of backstory came downloading into his waking brain as he glanced around at a room that looked a bit like an intensive-care ward mixed with a motel room decorated by Nagoya Aerospace. There were windows off to his right, nearly floor to ceiling, their blinds shut tight. On a hospital nightstand nearby were his bag, the 8 Ball, the medallion and his few other belongings, neatly stacked. The only occupants were himself—lying on a powered bed with its pillow end slightly elevated, wearing his swashbuckler suit—and a human male who looked to be in his middle years.

That is, the man and Lucky were the only ones Lucky could confirm; outside of a bit of head-neck range of motion and the ability to speak, breathe, see, and the like, he couldn't move.

"And there's no need to be alarmed about your paralysis," the man told Lucky. He went about five-ten with a squarish, well-chiseled face and dark wavy hair that was only beginning to go gray; he had a steady, easy but sharply discerning presence to him. . . dressed in an impeccable business suit that reeked decorously of twelfth-generation London tailoring. "It'll pass." His voice had an undeniable reassuring quality. "You were held in pseudocoma on Sierra until you could be transferred here and—what with a slight head injury you suffered—a bit of medical treatment's been required. But you're in perfect shape, believe me."

Maybe he was lying about the paralysis; it was a pretty good way to keep a captive manageable. Lucky was aware, too, that he had come to with a lot less pain, disorientation, and other collateral unpleasantness than he would otherwise have expected. They'd been working on him, all right. He had other matters on his mind, though.

"Where's Asia Boxdale, Mr. Tanabe?"

Takuma Tanabe evinced no surprise. Doubtless he was used to being recognized. "She's being transferred here, too. I expect her later today—within six hours. You'll be able to see her as soon as she arrives."

"Where's 'here'?"

Tanabe aimed a remote and the blinds swept aside to admit light, shapes, blue sky, and a crayon box of colors. Lucky might've been excused for anticipating some kind of SPEC-TRE sub pen or Justice League orbital base, but he saw right away that he was back, in several senses, on home turf.

Lucky found the colors too riotous and vivid for those traditional architectural schemes—but then, earth tones didn't have broad-spectrum appeal to ticket buyers. Interestingly, Tanabe had had a whole hill moved so that the HOLLYWOOD sign was visible from more areas of World Nihon.

A theme park, where else? Lucky sighed to himself. If there really was an aura of coincidence and causality surrounding him, no doubt theme parks figured in there someplace prominent. It made sense on a practical level, too; World Nihon was an incorporated municipality and Tanabe's control and security within its precincts was near-feudal, about as absolute as it could get without his seceding from the Union.

"Why not al-Reem, Mr. Tanabe? Or Light Trap?" Not that he couldn't pass on those particular side trips indefinitely.

"Mr. Junknowitz—may I call you Lucky? Lucky, there's a lot I need to explain to you, but first things first. You haven't been captured by Black Hole."

Lucky's jaw dropped and he was pretty sure there was a cartoon of a blazing light bulb in a balloon floating over his head. "A-and that's why whoever or whatever grabbed me did it before I got to Up and Adits."

"To be sure. The Up and Adits trap was set up by Sysops security in an effort to lure you in. Even though my people had safely gotten Miss Boxdale out of danger, the Agency had a mindbender recording taken while she was briefly in captivity, and so they went ahead with the initiative to recapture you. Oh, and let me say the operative who intercepted you sends his regrets that you were injured."

Tanabe gestured with one hand toward that part of *Land of Yamato* that was his private sanctuary. "He's down there now, enjoying a respite and some hundred-year-old goldfish. It's an expensive reward, but Plinisstro's team earned it."

"How'd they know it was me?"

"That refreshing sea breeze blowing through the Ss-sarsassiss eco-walk on the way station concourse? Well, it was engineered to carry all scents to where our agents waited. They have truly astounding olfactory senses, both in and out of water. I'd gotten them some samples for comparison, from forensics and a few personal effects you left behind."

Oh. Innovative—Trough authorities were still relying on their magic-marker readers and such, but Tanabe and his sea-snakes had gone back to basics. "What about Harley and Sheena?"

"We don't know. They were on al-Reem but there're indications that something unforeseen and highly upsetting to Black Hole occurred there—"

"*You're* Black Hole. Or Phoenix, same difference."

"You're wrong. You want to keep Earth from being laid waste and discarded; well, so do I, and so do a lot of other people, and I'm not referring to Phoenix Enterprises."

Lucky had to make himself answer slowly; he wanted so badly to believe what he was hearing. "That a fact? You trying to get in touch with the Trauma Alliance, are you? Or if I phone up that Ka Shamok, will he tell me you're fractal or will he tell me you're fucked?"

Tanabe gave no sign of taking offense. "I've learned in corporate warfare that the so-called white knight rarely turns out to be a saint in armor, Lucky; in the real world, those in distress have to save themselves. The answer to one alien conspiracy isn't more alien conspiracies, although alliances are going to be important. No, we *homo sapiens* are going to have to take on the Black Hole Travel Agency, and your help may well be the critical factor."

No two ways about it, Tanabe was persuasive. He spoke and acted and responded in American fashion to the subtlest degree, knew just what to say. And yet Lucky sensed that the steel inside him remained unalloyed Japanese, sharp and durable as a 10,000-fold sword blade.

"Fine, thaw me out or slip me the antidote or jumpstart my neuromotor and let's get to it." Getting mobile was the first priority in escaping World Nihon; if that took lip service, Lucky had plenty.

"Not necessary. As I said, you'll be up and around shortly. Some of the people in my organization want to ask you some questions but I wanted to speak to you first. I wanted to give

you my word that it is *vital* to the survival of Earth that you
help us, and to ask you as a personal favor and a service to this
planet to help us. Will you?''

It was not the least bizarre experience of his misadventures
that Lucky found himself being beseeched by one of the most
powerful people on Earth. "Yes! In return, you let me up now
and answer a few questions for *me*. Plus, I have some friends
and I want proof they're okay."

"Of course. I shall work all that out as fast as I can. And
you'll be up as soon as the aftereffects of your treatment wear
off.'' Tanabe was turning the Magic 8 Ball over, glancing at
the clear bull's-eye. Lucky couldn't see what answer it gave
him—and would have liked to know what the question was.

"You can get a teleconference rig in here and get my friends
on linkup," Lucky persisted.

"Very well, but we'll have to contact them inconspicuously
and establish a secure channel," Tanabe replied reasonably.

"No. Now."

"We can't play fast and sloppy," Tanabe shot back without
a trace of malice. "I won't risk my people's lives, and I can't
gamble Earth's survival. I realize you've been through a nightmare but you'll have to be patient just a little longer. Now, we
need to do an immediate debriefing with you.''

Lucky didn't know how hard he dared push. Surely Tanabe
had the resources to peel Lucky's brain like an onion. But
maybe Tanabe didn't have the time to spare? Or he needed
Lucky with a full mental inventory.

Lucky decided to play a wild card. "All right then, if my
nanite says you're telling the truth, it's good enough for me.''

Tanabe didn't falter. "We've heard some rumors about an
AzTek ID forger and are very interested in it, but I don't see
how—''

Lucky was shaking his head, as much as he was able. "No,
this one's a sort of lie detector. All you have to do is put your
forehead to my lips and tell me what you want me to believe.''
Lucky knew security cams at Rodeo East had picked up Rashad
Tittle's dying-kiss transfer of the Wise-Guise to Lucky; that
image just might provide Lucky's bluff with the reality hook it
required.

Tanabe betrayed the faintest hint of discomfort. "I have no
objection to this—as soon as I check with my technical staff to
make sure there's no danger. It's a kind of experimental nanite,
after all. In the meantime I'll get to work on a teleconference

link with your friends and you begin talking to my people, what do you say?"

Lucky didn't say what he was thinking because calling Tanabe a liar would only accelerate matters, maybe bring in people with syringes and thumbscrews. Lucky *did* believe Asia would be brought to *Land of Yamato* and, having had it rubbed in his face that he was no E-comic superhero, he had no doubt that he would then tell Tanabe whatever he wanted to know and would do whatever Tanabe demanded. There would simply be no way to resist, and the consequences would have to sort themselves out as they would. Lucky stared blankly ahead, reflecting. *So this is what the end of the trail feels like.*

Suddenly, Lucky let out an involuntary yip that even made Tanabe jump.

"What is it? Are you in pain?"

"N-no. Heh-heh. Just my nerve sensations returning is all. I guess." Lucky could feel himself starting to sweat, because suddenly it was very, very important that he get Tanabe to go away—that he have just a few lousy seconds to himself.

Tanabe was looking at the interlocking-rings medallion. "I suppose that you've already learned the meaning of this symbol—"

"Mr. Tanabe, I'm not feeling so hot. You've been immunized, haven't you?"

Tanabe showed him the best poker face Lucky'd ever seen. "Immunized from what?"

"Nanites. My group visited Fimblesector and I met High Heurist, maybe you heard? And even though I went through decontam I've had this strange little mental flux ever since."

He could see from the man's face that Tanabe was concerned; maybe he *did* know enough about what Lucky had been through to halfway believe him. The tale came rather quickly on the heels of the lie-detecting nanite maneuver but, as Lucky had hoped, the CEO was the kind who preferred to play it safe. He moved toward the door.

As Tanabe left, Lucky began furiously rubbing his right ear against his dead shoulder, grateful one of the few times in his life for his nobly proportioned mudflaps—they'd given good cover to the wadded Collect Call he'd stuck back there. And plainly his captors hadn't detected it—why should they? It was partially organic and completely inert.

Or at least it had been until it buzzed him a few seconds before and made him yelp. Somebody was using one of the subordinate units—somebody on Earth.

Rubbing frantically didn't help; he couldn't get the leverage to scrape the Collect Call loose. The door handle turned and he resigned himself to failure. But the isolation-suited, equipment-draped tech holding the door open paused there, looking into the corridor with respectful attention and kowtowing periodically while somebody—not Tanabe—fired instructions at him in machine-gun Japanese.

It was then that Lucky realized he was shrugging his right shoulder—some slight feeling and control had returned. A second later he'd smeared the Collect Call on his collar; two more and he had it in his mouth, chewing vigorously.

That would activate its automatic tracking and hailing function and identify him. SOP said he had to stick it back behind his ear to open commo with the subordinate unit, but the tech was now looking at him and let out an exclamation, seeing Lucky chewing.

By reflex—and perhaps some primeval learned response from early grammar school surfacing after decades—Lucky swallowed his gum. The flustered tech pointed at him with some kind of wide-bore widget resembling a dry-cell flashlight, and Lucky went black again.

TWENTY-FIVE

"BUT I AM SO BORED!" GoBug whined.

"I do not *care*," Doola replied righteously. "I don't want you playing with that thing. You could put your eye out!"

"With gum?" her husband ventured.

Since they had been shoved in the pool back on Zillion by Lucky Junknowitz and had their own mortality and vulnerability driven home to them, the Dimdwindles had become somewhat cautious about their own actions and their son's, but Doola was more anxious about it than her spouse.

"Or electrocute himself!" She upped the ante, grabbing away the object of contention.

"Then c'n I go play the sensoswitch machine?" whined GoBug.

"Absolutely not! Oh, it was a mistake to try to complete our tour!" Doola gazed out the dining-room windows, disquieted, at the waters of the South China Sea, which were calming after an afternoon monsoon squall. Off in the distance a cargo lighter bore yet more shipping containers ashore from the cruise ship to the Cam Ranh Bay docks.

Doola's anxieties weren't evoking much argument from the rest of the troupe gathered around a table aboard the *Crystal Harmonic* except, perhaps, for Vixlixx Millmixx's noncommittal mew. He'd been one of the prime movers, along with Hono—who were uneasy at the thought of deviating from the contracted plan—in getting the others to resume the journey after Lucky had abandoned them in the Zillion reserve several baseline-days before.

Millmixx's motives stemmed not from a newfound eagerness to see the galaxy but rather from distress at what Lucky's artsy Coolest Medium ploy had made of the Dunnage Depop vet. With his torpor mistaken for the ultimate audience-participatory art, Millmixx had been hounded day and night for one-sided discourse, for zero-input performance pieces, and for some of the most passive sex ever recorded anywhere. He was the sensation of the media, the idol of the intelligentsia, and the darling of the avant-garde.

So naturally he wanted out in the worst way. Travel was inconvenient but at least when he was doing it people didn't expect as much of him. He slumped in his chair watching the chop lift and fall and felt only minimally hectored by existence.

Undeniably, it had been a less interesting, if more structured and organized, tour the group had resumed once Black Hole was apprised of the crisis. Temporal Adjustments, Trauma Advisory, and even Sysops security had shown up, not to mention the darkside characters to whom the tourists were instructed to pay no attention—with this the clients cooperated willingly. Some rather sinister and unsettling players had been glimpsed on the periphery of the investigation: malign and powerful entities difficult to see clearly, lacking in any cheery public-contact skills whatsoever. These the tourists assiduously ignored, as well as chance-heard phrases: *Terminal Abductions*, *Tyro Assessment*, *Transmogrification Auxiliary*.

That was when the group first discovered that Salty Waters was really Lucky Junknowitz. Since then they'd come to call him by his real name. GoBug had pilfered a Wanted-poster holo of Lucky's original face and stuck the projector chip on the wall or bulkhead wherever he slept.

Unexpectedly, somewhere behind the scenes a quick decision had been made that the group resume its tour without delay. The remorselessly jolly and cajoling PR fixers from the Agency's lightside said there was no need to further discommode the group—but some of the wayfarers weren't so sure that that was what the brisk expediting of their journey's resumption was all about. Piercing glances had been turned their way by the nameless darksiders, glances so fulgurantly intense that it was hard to discern the beings behind them.

Lumber Jack, in particular, had the distinct impression that Black Hole's servants were prodding him and the others on their way in the hope that *something would happen*, that the little band would attract or trigger or induce the next in some chain of events they could not and would never comprehend. Like all of them, though, Lumber had his own turmoil to

wrestle with, raised by events and Lucky's departing words to
his charges on Zillion.

The Rphians were subdued, almost mournful, and curiously
deferential to one another in what little territorial marking they
did; the Hono were spending more and more time gazing off
into space in different directions and silently pondering *private*
thoughts; Dame Snarynxx seemed unsure of behavioral abso-
lutes anymore; and even GoBug now looked before he leaped.

The wayfarers had been led onward by a quick succession of
rigorously trained, formidably able, infinitely patient, flawlessly courteous, and unfailingly peppy substitute guides. As a
result, they were bored, restive, hostile, and bewildered about
what it could possibly be that was suddenly missing from their
lives.

Then again, one thing all the travelers' respective cultures
had in common was strong injunctions about obligation toward
one who had done a major service by saving a life, offering
protection or guidance—and they'd come to see that Lucky had
done those.

The Vietnam stop had primarily been made to offload cargo
that had faded aboard via Adit. From Cam Ranh some of it
would go out by South African cargo sub, Kampuchean aerostat, English HOTOL spaceplane, and unmarked Israeli
surface-effect freighter. There hadn't been much chance for
sightseeing: the country's tourism infrastructure was woefully
lacking in the wake of Turn upheavals in which economic and
political reformers had been ruthlessly purged. Moreover, its
current leaders—those who'd thrown in with Phoenix and
Black Hole—were terrified of the idea of the visiting aliens
accidentally being outed.

Still, there'd been one or two limited side trips and the group
had given them a game try, pretending to be Terrans dressed as
XTs or, in the case of Lumber and Dame Snarynxx, jerkily
animated remote-controlled machines. Certainly Earth was
beautiful and Southeast Asia was fascinating, but that hadn't
lifted the group out of its collective funk.

At that moment their latest cheerleader, Wham Hoalsumb,
was in the lounge signing them all up for line-dancing classes.
Their fellow XT shipmates struck them as irritatingly naive,
arrogant, and sheltered. Even the prospect of gawking at unenlightened human cultures along the Ring of Fire didn't appeal to them now that they understood a little better what Black
Hole had in store for Earth.

"There's nothing fun to *do*," GoBug whined.

"I bet you'd eat another slice of that Pesky Pizza," Doola coaxed. "You would, wouldn't you? And tonight we can line dance."

"I don't *wanna* line dance!"

Lumber Jack sighed, rising. "Perhaps it's time to tell Mr. Hoalsumb we'd all like to go home." He hadn't yet worked out an answer to the conflict between his debt to Lucky and the one Lumber owed to his own people and home planet, but he felt that he had to state the obvious. While everybody was glancing Lumber's way, GoBug took advantage of the distraction to suck up the confiscated item again and chew it.

His mother spun on him; she seemed to have developed preternatural instincts and several additional senses since being alerted to the dangers of life by Lucky's immersion therapy. "Did you put that back in your mouth?"

"No, I whoa-ooo!"

With everybody looking at him now, GoBug spat out the Collect Call unit. "It's signaling."

Nobody wasted time pointing out that that was impossible since the master unit to which it was keyed couldn't be on Terra. And although a Collect Call would reach its subordinate units anywhere on a planet, there was no way it could do so from another stellar system.

There was quick chewing and wadding of other Collect Calls—for some reason none of them had been willing to discard the units, or carry the replacements they'd been issued.

"It's a homing signal, beyond any question," Dame Snarynxx announced.

"Then, why isn't Salty—Lucky—opening a talk channel?" Mr. Hoowe wondered.

"Maybe he can't," from Arooo.

That started them all buzzing but it broke off abruptly as handsome, upbeat, fit-for-life Wham Hoalsumb returned. "Music starts at eight sharp, folks, in the main lounge. Oh and, there's a, um, gentleman here from upper management to ask you a few more questions—purely a formality; you understand. He'll meet you in the purser's cabin at six. Hey, let's have a *fantastic* evening, what d'ya say?" He did little Alley Cat steps out the door.

The second Wham was out of sight the group got into motion, and it wasn't to dress for dinner.

They began making their way aft toward the ship's Adit by

sheer force of habit, as though someone there would fade them directly to wherever Lucky was.

The Dimdwindles were the first to call a halt to that. "We must be very cautious and calculating or the staff and crew will stop us," Doola said.

"Moreover we have to get a location fix on Mr. Waters— Lucky, I mean." Dult took up the issue as the others gathered round in an otherwise empty passageway. "And unless he's at the Sumatra installation, or in all probability even if he is, we'll need local transportation of our own."

"We need a *scheme*," GoBug amplified. He'd been doing a lot of reading. Though their smotheringly protective buildings had let them thrive in blithe ignorance, there was nothing wrong with the Dimdwindles' mentation now that they'd had the errors in their previous thinking pointed up to them.

"Have you stopped to consider what you're doing?" Millmixx wheezed. "Committing major felonies and interstellar crimes? Defying Black Hole?"

"What alternative is there if we are not to let Lucky Junknowitz be executed or worse?" Hono challenged.

Millmixx exhaled wearily. "No, I mean, have you considered it and decided? Because if you have, I won't waste my breath pointing it out. As for myself, I'm too put upon to think of an alternative. I have already seen Zillion and anything is better than line dancing."

They all looked at each other and realized that they *had* made a decision. "What we need is access to the ship's coredata system," Lumber Jack mulled. "What we need is information."

"Then we shall just have to avail ourselves of it," commented Dame Snarynxx.

Lumber gazed her way. "That's illegal, ma'am."

"Young man, as a well-known arbiter of manners and propriety I can vouch for the fact that there are times in life when they have to be given the, the heave-ho, as I believe the local euphemism has it."

"Yes, but the core-data access terminals are all guarded," Mr. Arooo growled. "Bridge, Adit compartment, engineering section and all."

"Wrong," said Hoowe. "No offense," he hastily apologized to his fellow Rphian. The one-upsmanship between them was pretty much a thing of the past. "There's one other terminal—in the social director's office, so he can coordinate trips and all without bothering the working crew.''

"Splendid," remarked Dame Snarynxx, and came about like a galleon under full sail to lead the way. The social director was busy getting the line dancing organized; his office was locked. Dame Snarynxx deftly nudged the door with her flank and it crunched open. Everyone managed to squeeze into the office—Lumber Jack and the dowager slug just barely. Lumber closed the door and leaned against it to make sure there'd be no interruptions.

"We believe Hono is best suited for this task," one of the Hono said. The creatures gathered around the data terminal, digging into their pouches and coming up with more interface adapters than any of the others had ever seen before.

"I knew you work with computers," Dult said worriedly, "but are you certain—"

"Believe me, Hono is a super-user," one of them vouched without looking up. With the gadgetry they produced, the Hono connected the terminal's port to cranial contacts they adhered to their own skulls, then wired themselves to one another. The lockouts stymied them for something like seventeen seconds. They accessed the core-data areas and began rummaging around, getting their bearings.

A world map appeared with a DF fix centered in California. The focus narrowed and the scale increased until they were looking at a few acres of Greater Los Angeles. "What's *Land of Yamato*?" GoBug wanted to know, observing from the top of a file cabinet.

"That's where the Collect Call signal is originating," Hono explained. "We used indig satellites to get a general location." Various data-crystal recorders glowed. "We're now downloading everything of use that we can find. We are inquiring as to any data having to do with Lucky Junknowitz. Black Hole is apparently unaware that he is present on Earth."

There was a surging squawk from the speaker meshes and a processed but oddly feminine voice spoke. "Pull back your inquiries and stay away from me, I warn you. Who are you? You're not Black Hole; what do you want?"

Hono was occupied both mentally and physically but one of its members murmured an aside. "There is another intruder in the system, operating from sources both aboard the *Crystal Harmonic* and ashore."

"Why are you raiding files related to Lucky Junknowitz?" the female voice challenged.

Hono's synthesized voice came over the meshes, too. "We see you are a metalflesh who is concealing her identity. The descriptive algorithms of your inquiries suggest that you are a friend of Lucky Junknowitz. We are, too."

The female voice returned, "If you drop your wards we can both be sure of that."

Lumber and the adult Dimdwindles were about to object, but it was already done; in certain ways Hono was insanely brave. After a few moments of machine hyperactivity one of the Honos said, "We are in touch with Silvercup, of the Fealty."

"To save Lucky we have to get to him *now*, at once," her voice came again. "Even seconds count. Circumstances being what they are, I'll need your help."

Dame Snarynxx was for once at a loss, staring at a wall map that showed the thousands of miles between the ship's location and California. "But—how can we get there? We did not come to this planet in any way prepared for such a task!"

"No, but I did," answered Silvercup.

It would've been the envy of any Earthly smuggler: Trough cargo could be offloaded anywhere security and convenience recommended, with no danger of Terran authorities—should any become interested and prove hard to suborn—backtracking shipments to their original source because *the source lay on the other side of a naked singularity*. It was as if the drug runner's powerboat never had to make a run to a mother ship but could just keep making dropoffs.

The ship's Adit could only fade in cargo up to about the dimensions of a medium-sized RV, but that was little obstacle; the majority of portable Trough technology was designed for such frequently encountered limitations. Disassemble-fade-reassemble was a basic procedure. There were a lot of components for the Agency's various technical endeavors—lots of upgrading to do before Earth was raised from tertiary status. In particular, the secret commo and rapid-transport infrastructure would have to be beefed up and suitable aerospace craft brought online. The latter was particularly important in that the need might arise to do some hands-on tinkering with Earth's military and commercial sats and orbital stations. Then, too, a detailed survey update of the Solar system was overdue.

There was so much more flight activity that certain disciplinary measures had already had to be taken; fun-loving aircrews had been entertaining themselves with practical jokes at the expense of the locals. All the classic gags—buzzing airplanes, leaving crop circles, putting on sound and light shows—had been tolerated. The cattle mutes and live appearances got upper management PO'ed, though, and a few object lessons were made.

Although the *Crystal Harmonic* wasn't listed with U.S. Maritime authorities as offloading cargo, there at what had once been the huge American harbor facility at Cam Ranh Bay, quite a bit of faded-in "mass transit" had been taken ashore. Normally the crew would've carried out offloading with the same tractor field the cruise ship had used to pluck Sean Junknowitz's attacking swiftboat out of the water and play spin the bottle with it, but the sprawling, moribund port facility was just a little too public.

Officials of the People's Republic of Vietnam were just as bribable as their counterparts anywhere, but putting every guard and dockworker on the pad would've been a budget buster. Hence, offloading was carried out via cargo lighter, the old-fashioned way. It would have been easier to berth at one of the few Yankee-built piers that was still usable and let cranes do the work, but Phoenix and Black Hole disliked the idea of having hordes of locals, many of them noncooped, so close for so long.

The Vietnamese hadn't known quite what to think of "Alien Themers" in their midst, but it hadn't struck them as any crazier than a lot of other things foreigners, and particularly Westerners, did.

Though the cruise ship was ostensibly a Hagadorn-controlled enterprise, it had been Tanabe's influence that gave the XT tourists access to the country. With post-Castro Cuba nowadays more closely resembling Battista World and the last of China's hardliners having been executed by some of their own former slave laborers, Vietnam was the last austerely Marxist-Leninist state—an ideology notoriously out of sync with the concept of happy camping. Its government, desperate for Tanabe's help in getting its economy and especially its tourism and theme-park industries out of intensive care, had rolled out the crimson carpet and slashed through the scarlet tape—a considerable coup for the Japanese in his maneuvering against Hagadorn, though no one had been unpolitic enough to observe that out loud.

Officials had been delighted, too, with the windfall bribes provided by the ship's cargo transfers. Most of the offloaded containers had already resumed their journey when the last piece of cargo came ashore on a lighter just after five o'clock in the evening; the rest had been stored in a large warehouse of leprous corrugated iron, its vent windowpanes cannibalized of their glass decades before. The enormous space was otherwise almost completely empty, and the big cargo canisters looked like a tiny modular hamlet at one end of it. The workers and their aged forklifts went off duty soon after the last box was set down. When it was quiet within the warehouse, the last module was opened from within.

The Rphians' noses told them no one was around, and that was confirmed by Silvercup; she had been surveilling the place through the eyes of several effectuator drones whom she'd directed to lase holes in their shipping pods. The tourists emerged from the container in which they had been directed to conceal themselves. Even as they did they could hear Silvercup assembling herself. As promised, the falsified shipping orders she'd placed in the ship's data system delivered Lucky's one-time clients to where most of Silvercup already was, in the same consignment that brought the remainder of her.

"Glad you're finally here," she greeted them, a little vexed. "I can use the help."

Constraints of time and resources had obliged her to implement her plan despite a shortage of effectuators and assembler units. That was why she was still in pieces. The tourists threw themselves into the job; Lumber Jack's brawn and Hono's technical skills were especially helpful. Containers were cracked open and the prefab modules she'd caused to be gathered in the warehouse pieced together. A polycontoured fuselage began to take shape on the concrete floor.

Things were moving along briskly until the door to the warehouse office swung open and they heard a panicky shout in Vietnamese. Silvercup had tapped into the base's own central security data system and been relying on it to forewarn her of any intruders; what she hadn't counted on was that the system was so antiquated and glitch-ridden that its reports frequently bore no resemblance to actual conditions. And the Rphians and the others had been so intent on their work that they hadn't detected the guard's presence until it was far too late.

The man in the brown pith helmet, shortpants tropical uniform, and thong sandals recovered from his involuntary squawk of surprise. He slapped an alarm button with one hand and fired from the hip with his ancient Kalashnikov with the other. The assault rifle was of course hard to handle one-handed, and the first burst went wide.

That gave the tourists a split second to react. The Rphians dove for cover and the Honos, each holding a section of hull-plate, crouched together to form an impromptu turtle. Mr. Millmixx simply went limp, sliding down behind a pile of crating.

Doola lurched for her son but Dult pulled her behind a drive unit as the guard got both hands on the AK-47 and opened up again. Lumber Jack snatched up GoBug and shielded the larva with his own hardwood body, the bullets punching into him. More by accident than design, the same burst found Dame Snarynxx and drilled an arc of holes across her side.

The firing cut off unexpectedly; the firing pin had struck a dud round and the Kally had hung fire. The People's Republic's centralized planning with its poor quality control and hopeless inventory disorganization had put old, badly manufactured ammunition in the guard's clip.

"Cover your eyes!" Silvercup yelled through the speakers Hono had connected to her mentation center. They did, even Dame Snarynxx, who retracted her upper, eyebearing set of horns. The tremendous burst of light Silvercup put forth shone through eyelids, hands, and layers of nictating membrane. The guard, blinded, dropped his weapon and clapped both hands to his eyes.

Even though he couldn't see, he dropped to all fours and groped for his gun, bravely determined to do his duty. Before he could recover the assaultomatic, though, Hoowe and Arooo were on him, pinning him to the floor and holding his neck and hand in their jaws.

"Are you all right?" Doola asked both her son and Lumber Jack. They were; even parabellum bullets didn't get very far in tough-grained Jack. As for Dame Snarynxx, little clicking sounds made everyone turn to watch as her amoebic flesh pushed the undeformed slugs back out of her and they dropped to the floor.

"There're reinforcements on the way!" Silvercup snapped. "Hurry, get me closed up—we've got to get out of here!"

Hono gestured to the remaining pieces of systemry. "But we have yet to install the—"

"There's no time! Close me up, grab what you can and leave

the rest!'' Hono and the others scrambled to do just that, joined
by the Rphians—who'd trussed up the guard and left him in the
office. Lumber Jack grunted, hefting a piece of machinery
the weight and general shape of an inboard diesel engine; all
the others rushed to grab whatever they could lay hands on, the
Rphians taking opposite ends of a shipping pod as big as a
coffin. Even GoBug did his best, nudging a hatbox-shaped
canister along with his head. Despite the effort there were
hunks of technology big and small left behind, some still in
crates.

No chance to go back for them, either, because just then one
end of the billboard-sized rolling door was bashed open and a
Bao Giap light tank came ramming through, treads chewing up
the cracked and aging concrete, a coaxial chaingun on its turret
already firing. Luckily, the tourists were already protected by
Silvercup's hull.

The tank commander took one look at what was stirring on
the warehouse floor and opened fire with the *Giap*'s main
armament, a 125mm smoothbore gun. It was loaded with an
HE round, the tank's main duty having been to watch over the
foreign ship offshore. The shell should've been more than
enough, under the circumstances, for the job at hand.

Except that Silvercup wasn't where she'd been when the TC
squeezed off the firing grip. The round hit the far side of the
warehouse and blew it wide open, making that whole side of
the rickety roof sag alarmingly.

The guard and the tank crew could be forgiven for subsequently reporting that they'd seen a flying saucer, but the shape
of Silvercup's airframe looked more like a cross between a
manta ray with a goiter and a tentacle-less squid swallowing a
bowling ball. The squid comparison would be particularly apt
in that Silvercup's smart fuselage was running a kind of light
show as she tried to bring her phototropic stealth systems online.

She'd taken off sideways to the right at a steep angle, like a
frog yawing off a hot griddle; the tankers couldn't even follow
her movements visually, much less track her with their weapons. She would rather have undertaken the mission as a fully
automated, asteroid-sized battlewagon complete with remote-
controlled strike wing and ground-assault elements, but this
was the best she'd been able to come up with: a nimble little
general-purpose aerospace truck, sixty feet nose to tail—now
bereft of considerable, possibly critical, systemry.

She'd debated knocking out the tank and setting down again so the tourists could recover the rest of her, but gaps and glitches in some of her control gear meant she was in effect unarmed for the time being. And not cannonproof.

Instead she juked to port, the tourists clinging to whatever they could grab and trying to fend off sliding cargo—the internal grav system being inoperative. Then she hurdled the tank and zipped out through the hole it had made in the rolling door. She hung an immediate right so as not to collide with the open five-ton full of astounded militiamen and -women coming straight for her, angled her pert nose back, and did a high-gee climb, leaving them only sonic booms to shoot at.

In moments Silvercup was acquired by indig radar; in milliseconds she'd vanished from the local screens again. Even if they'd fired a missile she could've outrun it. She was a lot more worried about being picked up by the *Crystal Harmonic* but successfully eluded detection—for the time being. If any Troughtech adversary was alerted and ran a full-dress search for her they'd likely spot her.

Time enough to worry about that later. At 65,000 feet she leveled off and her passengers and cargo, until now jammed into the aft end of the cabinspace, began settling down on a broader area of deck. She ignored the tourists' questions and objections as they sorted themselves out; she'd been at pains to see that no harm came to them, and, aside from a few dents and scrapes, she'd been successful. What was more, they struck her as a fairly resilient lot.

She cut through their jabber. "Stop distracting me and wasting time! Get that gear lashed down then square yourselves away for a high-speed flight under constant maneuver forces. If we don't rescue Lucky Junknowitz in the very near future it'll be too late to help him at all."

That quieted them down fast. With Silvercup providing guidance, they broke out cargo netting and lashing gear—the most primitive kind of backup tackle, necessitated by her lack of artificial gravity. She put herself on course for California, climbing for thinner air, her thermal shields already absorbing a heavy flow of air-friction heat.

"The plan I had to break Lucky out of *Land of Yamato* won't work now," she told them meanwhile, "because the remotes and other equipment I was going to use are back in that warehouse." And with *Crystal Harmonic* at anchor she didn't dare go back. "So you're going to have to do it.

Hono, please rig up neurointerfaces for everyone and prepare to access the data I've compiled. Then everybody'd better buckle down and cram; you're got a lot to learn and a very short time until your test.''

In throwing together her rescue mission to Earth on the fly, as it were, Silvercup had naturally allotted even more emphasis to data than she had to instrumentality. It was certainly useful to have the aerospacer body, and the tourists' help would be crucial now that so many components had been abandoned at Cam Ranh Bay, but as a true denizen of the Trough she knew that information was the first and foremost implement in her breakout plan.

Given more time and the right data, she felt confident, she could've pulled off the whole rescue from a comsat, bodiless. But time was a constraint even Black Hole hadn't conquered.

Many details concerning World Nihon—its day-to-day routine as well as its secrets, its minutiae as well as its most highly classified info—were, although Tanabe didn't know it, in Black Hole's immense data ocean. The Agency wasn't machinating against Tanabe in particular; it simply had a reflexive and voracious appetite for information.

Indeed, the confidentiality of Tanabe's organization was far better than most, including enterprises on secondary and primary worlds, but information was something over which the Agency's gravity exerted particular attraction. It seldom did much good to render tributes of money or luxury items to Black Hole—though bribes to middle and lower management had been known to go a long way toward solving narrow-focus problems; its resources were too vast for it to feel any gratitude. Those seeking to curry favor or assuage the company sometimes did well to offer up the most precious and hard-won *secrets* they had. The upshot of it all was that Silvercup knew more about World Nihon than Tanabe would credit anyone outside his own organization with knowing.

The question was whether or not that would be enough.

During the screamingly fast flight around the planet in suborbit, the tourists were immersed in the information she'd amassed. Even with Trough biodownload techniques they'd be able to get only a portion of what was there. Meanwhile Silvercup reviewed her options and decided on her best fallback plan.

By innate and acquired attitudes and values she felt distaste for violence, especially unnecessary violence. It was wasteful, inelegant, and cruel. Be that as it may, she was sorry the tourists hadn't happened to grab the ELF-EMP pulse unit with which she could've knocked out unshielded humans and circuitry for a half mile around, or the compact multimission weapons emplacement that was supposed to go in her chin turret.

She wasted no time in regrets; there was too much else to do. It would have to be innovation and speed against established security and power now, improvisation and luck against foresight and planning.

Even if she won it didn't bode well. By the dictates programmed into her when the Monitor wrought her transformation, she had to turn Lucky over to the Fealty. And she knew that, with the Monitor's influence increasing, Sweetspot would not be safe for Lucky.

Charlie Cola, too much in turmoil to concentrate on periodicals, mutazines, or the promotional loops running on the waiting area screens, gazed out at World Nihon and tried to pass time by figuring out just what had been there before Tanabe took over so much of the greater Los Angeles area. Charlie hadn't been in that part of the country in ages, and it was tough to reconstruct his memories. In any case, Tanabe had refashioned the landscape. From where he sat, ground floor of the corporate headquarters, he could just about see the HOLLYWOOD sign.

Charlie sighed and caught the glance of the eye-popping Bengali receptionist when she looked up at the sound. He did his best embarrassed smile, conspiratorial wink. "I guess his plate's really full today."

She made a moue and gave him a pitying nod, then pretended she'd gone back to work. Yes, Mr. Tanabe's plate was always full. It had been so for the past day and a half while Charlie cooled his heels hoping to see the great man. He'd been told when he called from New York for an appointment that Tanabe-san was very pressed for time.

Charlie had flown out anyway, in the vain hope that the Quick Fix connection would get him two minutes, just two minutes, with Tanabe. The man had been so warm and amiable back there when it looked like Charlie's star was headed for the zenith; Charlie couldn't believe he wouldn't help out now, if only Charlie could get his attention.

He'd been able to persuade himself of that sufficiently to unpocket for a full-fare ticket and hop a flight to California. In the wake of Asia Boxdale's disappearance—Molly Riddle's car had never been found; what did that say about the hopelessly outmatched Boxdale's chances of ever being seen again?—Charlie had felt the walls closing in. Not one for prayer—what Black Hole employee was?—he'd nevertheless exhaled fervent, wordless thanks up toward the Quick Fix ceiling upon hearing that his adopted sons Labib and Jesus had come out of the kidnapping with nothing worse than mercilessly pounding Crowd Control hangovers.

Then he'd taken the most direct action he could think of. He hadn't been stupid enough to try to sneak a tanto knife into Tanabe's kingdom, but he was prepared to plead for the use of one; chop off a finger to show loyalty, if that was what it took to save himself from going under.

There hadn't been much point in sticking around Quick Fix. Molly had been plunged into a strange silence by word of Willy Ninja's disappearance and, right on its heels, Boxdale's kidnapping. She'd refused to argue with him about her decision not to blow the whistle on Junknowitz back when she let him fade.

As for the possibility she'd broached that night after Boxdale left, he'd shut her up about that straight away. Playing politics with various factions and power cliques in Phoenix Enterprises and even the Agency was one thing, but the concept of working *against* the Black Hole Travel Agency, of betraying it, was connected in his mind by an equal sign to suffering and death too ghastly to imagine.

Nevertheless, Molly had brooded about the news concerning Willy Ninja and the rest, completely unlike her—and then dropped out of sight. Charlie could only hope she'd gone to ground.

Didi had taken off for parts unknown—and, truth to tell, Charlie didn't want to be privy to her destination. That way no one could drag it out of him, in case Black Hole or Bhang or someone else decided to do a clean sweep on him. His sons and Sanpol Amsat were doing their best to hold things together at the store, but he'd given them strict instructions to cut and run unless they got a stand-fast signal from him very soon.

It was looking less and less as if he'd be making that call. As his wait dragged on his imagination had fleshed out a vision of Tanabe, laughing sardonically somewhere many stories overhead, enjoying Charlie's squirming before squashing him like a roach. But somehow all the waiting had put Charlie in mental neutral gear, almost deprived him of the use of his limbs. He'd run out of all energy and momentum; some new force was going to have to exert itself upon him.

TWENTY-SIX

SOMETHING WAS OFF schedule in *Land of Yamato* and that was enough to bring cold sweat everywhere. The Ghost-Fox Train was on the move.

In the center of the historical area a replay of the epic "*Me* Brigade Riot" of 1805 was being refought outside the all-purpose Shinto shrine, which was in this instance standing in for Shimmei in the Shiba district of Edo. Roughneck *Me* Brigade firemen renowned for their daring, their esprit and their in-your-face attitude had shown up to drink sake and heckle the sumo wrestlers' matches and feats of strength. An all-out brawl was under way, a riot that made other theme parks' saloon fights and kung-fu melees look like contredanses.

In a reenactment meticulously copied from Yoshitoski's woodblock depiction, the mighty wrestler Yotsuguruma Daihachi was squaring off with brigade leader Kotengu Heisuke and the crowd was going batshit. Classic speed-versus-size face-off here, though American onlookers weren't sure how that ladder the sumo was swinging would stack up against the aggressive fire captain's long-handled pick.

The visitors loved it, though; *gaijin* who resolutely avoided sushi and would sooner have died than tune in to a Kurasawa retrospective were rooting at the top of their lungs, about to pop blood vessels in throat and forehead, "GET 'IM!" . . .

When all of a sudden there was noise from nearby *Tengu Mountain* and the Ghost-Fox Train appeared, the replica nineteenth-century British engine pushing clouds of EPA-approved demonic black smoke and geysers of sparks into the air. Strange figures clung to the hell-train or gesticulated from its cab and caboose roof; the chugging dirge of the locomotive cut through all other sounds.

Back at the riot and all through that part of *Land of Yamato*, cast members glanced around and at one another in confusion, doing their earnest best not to break character. Unwillingly, blood-'n'-guts fans were losing concentration and craning around toward the train.

In 1889, with Meiji Japan in the upheaval of joining the modern world after centuries of isolation, a tale circulated in which were met traditional terrors and fears of technological change. As reported by Basil Hall Chamberlain, rumor had it that a phantom train was doing infernal midnight milk runs on the Tokyo-Yokohama line. Pursued by a mortal engineer in a real train, the spectral one vanished—leaving the ground-up remains of a fox on the engine's wheels.

In *Land of Yamato* the legend had been resurrected and enhanced a good deal, the train itself becoming a kind of ghoulie-jamboree themer attraction and ride. However, due to technical problems—some misunderstandings between park teamster shop stewards and the local Mafia franchisers—it wasn't scheduled to roll until the next day.

Security people, talent-control, and event-coordination personnel were stepping all over each other's transmissions on the commo nets. Central Control was completely nonplussed because the computers were suddenly saying the train had clearance to go and the route-switching devices and warning signals were clearing the way for it and not responding to CC's commands. The train engineer's freq was a snake's nest of static. The Ghost-Fox Train was giving all the right failsafe responses and authorization signals; apparently people who knew what they were doing were running it. But no one in management could back-trace its clearance to roll.

The Ghost-Fox Train didn't run on steel track despite its rotating driving wheels and pumping main and connecting rods. To build in variety of route and versatility against future changes in the park's setup, it ran on camouflaged solid-fill tires along a network of miniroads laid out behind and among other features and attractions, and was driven by power packs that could be recharged from roadway strips. All this meant that the train would be difficult to force to a stop. Park managers sweated, working out emergency responses, each of them silently wondering how many more seconds they dared let slip by before they informed Tanabe of the crisis.

*   *   *

"Has anyone even bothered to tell you what it is that's happened to you, Lucky, what's brought all these cosmic intrigues down around your head?"

Tanabe had neatly shifted gears in the wake of Lucky's ruse and the sonic KO the tech had administered upon seeing Lucky swallow the Collect Call—the tech fearing Lucky had somehow contrived to gulp a suicide pill. They'd brought Lucky around again after what Lucky took—hoped—to be hours, but it was impossible to be sure. Tanabe's people, detecting no toxin or other lethal infusion, had refrained from cutting Lucky open but had pumped his stomach. The Collect Call hadn't come up—because it was designed not to, Lucky concluded. Whether or not Tanabe believed Lucky's story about absentmindedly chewing some piece of stuff his tongue had found lodged in his teeth, the CEO had wasted no more time on the subject.

Having detected no stowaway nanites on Lucky, Tanabe proceeded on his new tack. There was no more mention of conference calls or when Lucky's paralysis might leave him. "Did any of your acquaintances in the Trough, these Trauma Alliance people or whoever, so much as let you in on the meta-energies controlling your fate? No? Because I'm prepared to. I'm not asking you to like me or even trust me at this point, just to make a fair exchange of information."

A nice gambit, Lucky had to admit. Without being effusive or ingratiating or doing any of that let's-be-friends song and dance, Tanabe was still a kind of natural force of persuasion—something to do with his intent and unswerving focus on the person to whom he was speaking. And offering to reveal insights on some of the forces that had been flinging Lucky back and forth was a near-irresistible enticement.

"Sure," Lucky temporized. "You first." He was playing a waiting game now, and had very few cards.

"If you like. I'm told you've already concluded that something very unusual happened to you some months ago outside the Click Fist convenience store in Sumatra."

GoBug pulled the cord again and the steam whistle blew a lamenting wail like a tortured banshee, a random jumble of agonized longs and shorts. Human faces, astounded, afraid, or delighted, looked up as the train belched by.

Aside from the larva Arooo and Hoowe were probably having the best time, both manning the locomotive cab. Silvercup's quick-study data had given them a passable knowledge of operating procedures and there was joy now in applying it, steering the train, waving and just plain baying. They were gotten up as acceptable-from-a-distance *tanuki* badger-demons, costumes they'd hijacked along with the train inside *Tengu Mountain*. The Rphian executives were ecstatic, pounding their authentic scrotum-drums, howling at the crowd, and giving GoBug the occasional hand yanking the whistle cord.

Standing grandly astride a wood tender whose gruesome fuel was convincingly gory human heads, Lumber Jack was wowing the throng in the person of O-Fudo-sama, the avenging Buddhist deity, waving a flaming sword and a plaited thong with which he was charged to bind the wicked and bear them off to their punishment. Lumber had been sprayed with blue paint and fitted with an improvised, outsized wig and other accoutrements but his own face was undisguised and his fearsome mugging convinced a lot of onlookers that they'd gotten their money's worth.

Further to the rear, on a flatcar that had been set as a scary wasteland, Dame Snarynxx writhed and wriggled under the biggest and most concealing dragon-dancers' costume the tourists had been able to locate in the storerooms of *Tengu Mountain*. She was doing her best to emulate the serpentine movements of half a dozen dancers who would normally line up under the costume; she paid particular attention to the quirky, whimsical moves of the horned and bearded slit-eyed headdress. In some ways she outdid anything the visitors or the real park cast had ever seen before.

On the scenery's high ground behind her, goggle-eyed Millmixx posed as the dreaded Hag of Adachigahara, preparing to slay a cowering pregnant-woman animatron and drink the blood of her unborn child. Luckily, all that was required of the vet was a certain amount of knife honing and Millmixx's normal range of facial expressions, turned on people along the right-of-way.

Dult and Doola Dimdwindle as *tengu*, and the Hono gotten up as misshapen *oni* imps, half in red costumes and half in blue, capered and cavorted all over the two coach cars and caboose. The *oni* had been given different costumes and personalities by the park's creative team and the Hono did their best to come up with original bits, gestures and dance movements.

The engine's twin spotlights shone an evil, slitted red, and the smokestack blasted; a red and white fox's tail fluttered from the caboose. With savage baying the Rphians threw imitation heads into the fake firebox.

The Ghost-Fox Train wended its way through a stunned *Land of Yamato* at top speed, barely five miles an hour. People were running to keep up or at least not let it out of their sight. There was some dismay when it didn't stop at the designated "Platforms to Hell" to take on passengers, but not much; it wasn't too surprising that the train would do a few victory laps upon its triumphant appearance.

The train bellowed as it slipped behind the Noh theater and the *Budokan*. When it reemerged some onlookers noticed that there were fewer themers in view and so supposed that some delightful new assault on their sensibilities was being prepared inside the cars.

A new force did exert itself on Charlie Cola as he sat in the waiting area, but in this case it was only hunger. His stomach growled so loudly that the receptionist looked up again, alarmed. "Would you like some more juice, Mr. Cola? Some ahipas chips?"

"No, thanks." He craved something more substantial—he hadn't eaten a decent meal in days—but was also scared he'd miss some fluke chance to see Tanabe.

She took pity on him; maybe she'd been told to? "The CEO will be in a staff meeting for at least the next hour, I'm sure. Perhaps you'd like to get something at the staff cafeteria?"

When he hesitated she smiled. "It's just across the quadrangle. If a scheduling window opens up I'll page you."

He surrendered. She emphasized that he mustn't wander off route or his visitor's pass would trigger a security-staff response. Failure to have any badge at all, he knew, would win an intruder the same kind of hospitality the Native Americans gave Custer.

He went, unable to work up much energy in his stride now. Maybe he'd feel better if he got something to eat. The landscaping in the quad raised his spirits a bit, though; he hated to think what it had cost. He wondered what the cafeteria was serving—anything but amusement-park food, he hoped. A little teriyaki would be nice.

He was still thinking that, and admiring an arrangement of

perfectly contoured raked white gravel, when alarms went off everywhere and suddenly a lot of guns were pointing his way.

Charlie Cola had just about worked up the spit to object when somebody yelled, "No, no, not him! He's a verified friendly!"

HQ security response-team troops were clearly ready to sacrifice any visitor's peace of mind for their mission. Here, away from the theme park proper, the helmets, riot gear, and anti-tank and other heavy weapons were out. He didn't have any time to ask what was going on because a pair of officers in filter masks, helmets, and flexible body armor, pistols holstered but hands on the grips, hustled him back inside the HQ foyer.

Very soon he was sitting there with all the other visitors and three times as many admin personnel, all crowded into the visitor waiting area and its environs and guarded by the two troops. Nobody would talk about what was going on, leaving Charlie to imagine a thousand scenarios—many of which made him wish he were in another hemisphere. Not surprisingly, his renewed demands to speak to Tanabe were ignored. And over and over he asked himself a single, brain-throbbing question:

Cut and run or *carpe diem*?

"So you see," Tanabe finished, "by sheer accident you've become a probability node, rather important in the scheme of things."

Lucky didn't know what to think. There was every reason to suspect Tanabe would color the story, slant it to his advantage, or even mix in plenty of sheer deception. But so much of the incredible tale of the toxic probability spill meshed with things Lucky knew to be true that he couldn't help feeling Tanabe was in great measure leveling with him.

"Now it's your turn, Lucky. First I'd like to know who—"

"No, hold on. You can check out my answers, but, lying here like this, I can't go out and verify yours."

Tanabe gazed down on him and Lucky thought to see impersonal, wholly dispassionate strategic decision making going on behind the handsome face. "I don't seem to be able to convince you, Lucky. Perhaps it's time to show you what I'm *not* doing to you, that I could if I so desired."

Without looking aside he made a tiny finger gesture. A man in a disposable white clinician's suit came into view, readying two temple contacts. *Mindbender*—if they got it on him they'd likely find out about the Collect Call. Lucky could do little more than tuck his chin into his neck. "What about Asia?"

"She'll certainly bear on our conversations when she arrives, but in the meantime I need some information; events are unfolding even more rapidly here on Earth than they are in the Trough.

"Unless you'll change your mind? Lucky, my organization is the best hope Earth has of resisting takeover by Black Hole. I like you and I'm going to try not to hurt you but I can't let you bring down annihilation on my country and our whole planet."

Goddamn if Lucky didn't find himself believing that one part of what Tanabe was saying so fiercely and earnestly. Surely what the man had done so far wasn't a patch on what that Ka Shamok and people like him were doing elsewhere to fight Black Hole; those other enemies of Black Hole made Tanabe look ultrarestrained. It was on the tip of Lucky's tongue to say yes, that he'd cooperate a little anyway for the time being, but the med was bending closer with the contacts. Helpless to avoid them, he shouted, "No-oo!"

Tanabe was already raising his hand to intervene, to motion the med back and make peace and common cause with Lucky, when the door caved in, taking with it the frame and a certain amount of the surrounding wall. Something hulking filled the space where it had been, something demonic and unearthly, waving a flaming sword and swinging a plaited binding thong. A guard ran toward it, firing a spitting pneumogun; Lumber Jack carefully swatted the gun aside and hit the guard's chest with the heel of his hand a lot less forcefully than he might have. The guard lofted back with the wind knocked out of him and curled up on the floor, moaning. For once even Takuma Tanabe couldn't find words.

"I think you better stand back," Lucky hinted. Tanabe did, as far as the walls would permit. With him clustered the med and the other guard, who wisely dropped his sidearm.

Hono swarmed into the room, almost unrecognizable in their *oni* outfits. A couple of them recovered the weapons, including the tech's sonic device. " 'Fraid I done gone lame, coach," said Lucky, frowning.

More Hono worked at something at the head of Lucky's bed with some gizmos they'd brought, one saying, "That is only because your sleeping furniture has been provided with a kind of modified anesthetizing field. We will disable it."

Lucky preferred that to letting the medtech play around with it. His eyes cut back to Lumber. "Hey there, lignum vitae. Thanks for coming, man."

Lumber bent close to him worriedly. "They didn't damage you?"

"Nah, no problem." Lucky thought of the things Tanabe had revealed to him. It occurred to him that Tanabe and the others were listening but he was feeling life was too short to put off important words. "Look, Lum, I guess we both know I'm probably the one you're supposed to kill, right?"

"I kill no one," Lumber declared with the steadfastness of an old-growth tree, "same as you. The rest will have to sort itself out as fate dictates."

"There," announced one of the Hono. Lucky rose without restraint or pain. He didn't hear any alarms, and most assuredly Tanabe had had no forewarning, so Lucky figured he had some maneuvering room. With Lumber at his shoulder and the Hono pointing pneumos, he told Tanabe, "Asia. Here. Unharmed. *Now.*"

Tanabe wasn't hiding the fact that he was apprehensive, but he answered without turning a hair. "I'm sorry; it's simply impossible. The aircraft carrying her won't arrive for another—"

"If that's the case, you're coming with us. Lum, if this man right here tries to get away would you be capable of crushing his kneecaps into *picante* dip and then carrying him?"

"Why, in view of the circumstances, that I'll gladly do."

For want of a better move, Tanabe froze. Lumber threw around him one loop of the outsized O-Fudo-sama binding cord, clamping Tanabe's arms firmly to his sides.

Lucky turned to the med, indicating the downed guard. "Give him a hand and the both of you lie down over here. Uh-huh, c'mere, snuggle up."

When he'd gotten the two bedded down and Hono had switched the immobilizing field back on, Lucky turned to Lumber. "How do we get out of here?"

But it was Hono who answered. "The same method we used to gain entry would seem optimal. Come."

"No, wait," Lumber interjected. "Prudence dictates that you wear a disguise." He began unlimbering a lashed bundle from his belt.

" 'Prudence,' " Lucky muttered, accepting the armload of

clothes. Events had been blindsiding him in such rapid succession that it came as little surprise to see his rescuers had brought him a Goofy suit.

"From the *Crystal Harmonic*'s very extensive wardrobe," Lumber Jack supplied. "Silvercup selected it because—"

"*Silvercup?*"

"Emphatically. She is, ah, driving the getaway vehicle and planned this endeavor."

"Fractal!" He began climbing into the suit; it felt like a homecoming. Exchange-themers were common among most major parks on the theory that they synergized park attendance in general. Their appearances were normally confined to a few least-thematic, general-tourism areas.

Lumber clarified. "Silver's research indicated that this themer identity is the one with which you've had extensive experience in portrayal."

True enough, and Lucky had to admit this suit was state-of-the-art, with self-ventilation system, wide-vision one-way optical inserts, plus camouflaged quick-relief crotch closures for fast latrine calls and a rehydration beverage reservoir with nipple-mouthpiece drinking tube. A Rolls Royce among themer suits. *I just might not come out for a while*, Lucky thought.

All at once there were alarms sounding everywhere. Lucky pulled his head together and beckoned Tanabe with a bulbous white forefinger. "Let's go." His floppy black ears swept his shoulders as he followed one of the Hono out of the room. He noticed another Hono scooping up his belongings. Seeing they were headed for the elevator, Lucky objected. "We should take the stairwell."

The impish *oni* Hono looked up at him. "From this floor the elevator is the only access to the tunnels." Goofy always smiled anyway but now he was grinning on the inside. Of course: the tunnels!

Lucky hadn't the faintest idea how Hono had rigged the elevator, but it was waiting for them with doors wide and didn't stop at any other floors on the way down.

Something was going on over at *Tengu Mountain*—Charlie Cola could see that much from the monitors that regularly swept *Land of Yamato* and sent the images back to the waiting area over wall-mounted monitors numbered 1, 2, and 3. The other Nihon domains appeared tranquil by comparison. But events at *Tengu* had been transpiring for some time, while alarms in the HQ area had only gone off moments ago.

Security people were gathered at the base of the artificial mountain, trying to force an entry—without much success, from what Charlie could observe. Elsewhere some kind of old-time train attraction appeared to have strayed from its course, and park security guards were hard-pressed to keep the crowds away from it and maintain order, much less stop it. And in the fancy shrubbery outside the corporate HQ, he could see security park SWAT and WAP—War And Parabellum— teams taking up positions.

While the office workers and lower-management types were gawking up at the overhead screens and out the windows, Charlie edged over to the desktop monitor abandoned by the Bengali receptionist. He prodded the selector buttons until he was over into the security channels. Framed by brightly decorated concrete, Disney character Goofy piled off an elevator along with Takuma Tanabe and what had to be, Charlie's practiced Adit-operator's eye told him, a bunch of XTs.

"I'll be damned." It didn't look as if anybody outside was aware of what was going on within the HQ; he couldn't tell why. Charlie switched the channel rather than sound the alarm. If he raised a hue and cry in the waiting area, chances were that Charlie Cola would be forgotten or ignored even if Tanabe *were* rescued alive, and Charlie had his sights set much higher than that.

The two guards posted by the waiting area were distracted just like everybody else. Charlie backed up to a fire door, held his breath, and leaned gingerly on its bar. He let out possibly the best exhalation of his life when it opened without setting off another alarm. Slipping through into a fire stairwell, he headed down, as the elevator had.

Faced with the loss of everything and everyone he cared about, Charlie Cola was ready to risk all.

The elevator was freight-sized because it had to accommodate HQ equipment and freight as well as business and other delegations on tour. Hono led Lucky, along with Lumber Jack and Tanabe, off it and into the tunnels.

By necessity the place had an industrial look, concrete with readily accessible infrastructure systemry—plumbing, wiring, cooling, and more. But an effort had been made to keep the underground maze somewhat cheerful for the sake of cast-member and other-employee morale: the place was painted in soft, light pastels and well lit, decorated with framed, upbeat themer slogans and displays of general information on conditions around the park. The usual emergency phones and escape hatches were there, too, along with emergency equipment. There was no graffiti whatsoever. Perky theme-related music played, mall stuff.

There were special sanitary facilities for those constrained by costumes; drinking fountains and sports-ade beverage dispensers specially constructed to serve people inside various themer suits; and fast-transaction media terminals for the personal memos, e-mail, and other items of private business that would otherwise have distracted people from optimal character identification. The system granted thirty seconds' service per themer per day, nonaccruable, with exceptions requiring supervisory permission.

Lucky saw from various monitors that a lot was happening up above, but it was quiet in the tunnels—not even any alarms. "The system isn't yet complete," Hono explained as they led the way, Lumber herding cord-bound Tanabe along in the rear. "We'll have to go above ground at Attraction J-73, where the Ghost-Fox Train will rendezvous with us for pickup."

About that Ghost-Fox Train, Lucky refrained from asking. He considered making Tanabe leave a ransom note via one of the convenience commo terminals but feared that it would draw park security. The Hono were apparently linked not only to some sort of direction-finding system but to Silvercup as well; he followed their lead.

A few moments later, Lumber and the Hono were giving Lucky bits and pieces of backstory as the band sallied through the tunnels. He was too much in their debt to tell them to shut up, that he couldn't absorb it all and that they weren't answering the questions he most wanted to ask anyway. They were covering concrete fast, though, toward Attraction J-73. Lucky didn't know whether it was good fortune or Silvercup's interdictions, but they encountered nobody else in their underground exfiltration.

They rounded a corner and passed a bay full of tools, equipment, and parts as well as a flatbed dolly; ahead lay another elevator. There was also an electric tunnel runabout, but Lucky

didn't bother seeing if it was operable since Hono said the
group had reached the place where it was to ascend. At the
elevator an illuminated map showed the J-73 attraction among
other *Land of Yamato* features aboveground nearby; the shaft
itself was in the staging building where various *matsuri* festival
performers prepared. Hono studied the map while Lucky, his
Goofy headgear flipped back, pressed for the car. Lumber Jack
was glancing back the way the party had come, straining as if
to catch a smell or sound. "I think there may be someone—"

In a sequence of movements as fluid as if he'd rehearsed it
for days, Tanabe loosened the keeper on the binding thong,
threw off the loop that had been holding him, and jumped
back, drawing something from beneath his jacket. At the same
time he warned, "Everyone stay where you are!" Lucky
glanced to him, saw what the CEO held, and got the automatic,
quirky translation from his nanites: *lightning rod.* An almost
archaic handgun by Trough standards but a terrific hole card for
a Phoenix Enterprise member—against unshielded targets at
close range, a Jovian derringer.

Lucky wondered fleetingly why Tanabe hadn't used it when
the rescuers had first burst in. Perhaps he'd thought they were
armed and had the drop on him, or were shielded—he'd plainly
seen right away that they were XTs. Given the CEO's intelligence and Hono's talkativeness, it hadn't taken Tanabe long to
revise his assessment of the circumstances, decide on a plan of
action, spot his chance, and take it. It had been a desperate one
prompted, maybe, by the fear that he wouldn't get another.

Tanabe had positioned himself so that Lumber Jack's bulk
shielded him from the Hono's commandeered weapons and
was covering both Lumber and Lucky at close range. Lucky
didn't want to see Earth turned into World Tanabe any more
than he wanted to see Black Hole take over, but he'd seen what
weapons like the lightning rod could do, and so he stood still
rather than throwing his life away in ill-advised heroics. Tanabe was saying to the Hono, "Put your weapons down slowly
and careful—"

That, as Lumber Jack came at Tanabe like a falling sequoia
even though Lucky screamed at the giant not to. On Wood
Wind, Lumber had told Lucky, one was expected to repair the
damage caused by one's mistakes.

But Tanabe had put some distance between himself and the
others, and so got off a shot with the flat little pistol as Lumber

charged. Thrashing pythons of electricity crackled around the
giant; the air became hot and Lucky's hair was floating. A
surge of current made Lumber keel over like a wooden Indian.
As he did, though, he somehow managed to lash out, sending
Tanabe reeling even though Lumber's fist had barely grazed
him. But as Tanabe fell back there was someone there to catch
him and bear him up, to take the lightning rod from Tanabe's
faltering grasp.

"Stay back, stay back!" Charlie Cola yelled, sweating and
wild-eyed, waving the pistol. Tanabe, sagging against him,
looked at Charlie as if he were the strangest XT of all.

The Hono were raising their unfamiliar trank guns and the
sonic unit uncertainly, and Charlie looked ready to cook everybody. Lucky yelled, "No, lower your guns!" to the Hono and
made palms-down motions with his white-gloved Goofy hands.
Charlie Cola backed away, supporting Tanabe, to the little
electric runabout; the CEO looked like he had something to say
but couldn't get it out. Charlie flopped Tanabe onto the bench
seat and he slumped over, unconscious.

When Charlie turned back to them, Lucky and the Hono
were kneeling around Lumber's stiffened body, the Hono
with weapons only halfway lowered. The lightning rod was
shaking in Charlie's grip. There was what seemed to Lucky
like a very long while during which nobody spoke and nobody moved.

"Fuck it," Charlie declared. "This big a hero, I don't need
to be." He slid into the seat behind the runabout's steering
yoke. "Junknowitz, don't say I never did you a favor." The
runabout leapt from its parking place, rounding the tunnel corner on two wheels as it disappeared.

"He's alive."

Lucky, gazing at the spot where Charlie Cola had vanished,
couldn't believe his ears. The Hono bending over Lumber
Jack's body with a little indicator widget repeated, "He's
alive."

Maybe so, but he was as stiff as a mainmast and scorched
over a quarter of his body. Some of the O-fudo-sama costume
was smoldering and the blue paint was blackened.

"The train will meet us up above," another Hono added.
"All we have to do is get Lumber Jack across the street."

Oh, that was all? Lucky felt himself starting to hyperventi-
late, made himself stop. There had to be a way to get a giant

wooded stiff through a crowd of Japanese themers and theme-park visitors—

He spun around to the map so fast that he almost wrenched his neck. *"Yes!"* He glanced at the utility bay. *"Gimme a hand! Hurry!"*

TWENTY-SEVEN

ATTRACTION J-73 WAS one of the most storied events in Japanese history: the getting-acquainted bout between the mighty warrior-monk Benkei and girlish-looking *Tengu*-trained superswordsman Yoshitsune on the Gojo bridge. It was an episode as well known in Japan as Robin and Little John knocking quarterstaves was in England. With the Ghost-Fox Train off somewhere else on the spacious World Nihon grounds, the cast members at J-73 had their concentration back and were attracting a good crowd.

At the moment in question, big and burly Benkei had had about enough lip out of little Yoshitsune—who, disguised by the shawl over his head, had been sauntering along playing a flute. Benkei's collection of captured swords stood at 999, and he was out to round off the number with the beautiful blade Yoshitsune was hauling around. Only the big guy was getting quite a surprise because the diminutive youth was faster than a mongoose on speed.

The performance was interrupted, however, by the appearance of another pack of themers from behind the ersatz armory in which the elevator was located. It was a strange-looking group whose singing and choreography were clearly *way* off, capering and dancing around and throwing to the crowd rice cakes, imitation-ivory *netsuke* carvings, and colorful fans—items that were ordinarily sold, not given away.

It was *supposed* to be some kind of *matsuri* celebration, that much was clear. Throughout Japan, local groups got together—sometimes bearing outsized sexual icons of wood or stone: dildos the size of battering rams and vulvas big as VW beetles—to cavort through the streets and rejoice in elemental creative energy and good spirits. This particular group was odd not only in that it included *oni* demons and was wheeling a very burnt-looking and oddly shaped wooden figurine-phallus, but also because it was led by a rather agitated Goofy.

In a real *matsuri* the icon would have been carried along on the shoulders of celebrants or maybe hauled by great hawsers; Lucky hoped nobody would get too inquisitive about the high, flatbed dolly on which he and Hono were trundling Lumber Jack's rigid form. To add to the illusion that Lumber was a virility symbol, Lucky had hastily chopped a shallow crevice down the middle of his rounded pate. Now Lumber was *Lignum Vitae* indeed, Lucky thought—Wood of Life, another euphemism for a penis.

The Hono were hopping and dancing up a storm, each developing a personal repertoire; people were engrossed in looking from one to the other. That couldn't come easily to the Hono, whose inclinations would probably run more in the vein of Rockettes-style precision dancing, but they gave it their most energetic shot and so did Lucky. Having been to a *matsuri* or two he recalled what he'd seen and emulated it.

And it was working. Where the mere appearance of the Hono and Lumber's body would have invited a crowd to close in and perhaps impede or compromise the escape—especially if the group had to wait very long for the train—the magic aura of theater kept onlookers at a distance and put them in an accepting mood. The Hono, who were in only intermittent contact with the Ghost-Fox Train thanks to freq clutter and static, reported that it would meet them on the other side of the open area by the bridge.

It was about the time Lucky thought they were home free that the other *matsuri* showed up.

This one wasn't very authentic, either, being composed mostly of brawny young *gaijin* high school football players from Plexus, Arkansas. They were part of a local full-court press to get a subsidiary of Nagoya Aerospace—on whose board Takuma Tanabe exerted much influence—to build a cardboard-recycling center there.

The flower of Plexus manhood was decked out in calligraphy-decorated headbands and *fundoshi* loincloths and led by a young man named Chikamatsu Kirokku, whose folks had moved to Plexus when his father was made president of a small Japanese-controlled firm there three months earlier. Plexus had not been notably kind to Chick-Keek, as his name had been Southernized, until he demonstrated his resourcefulness in organizing the PR *matsuri*.

He'd given great thought to the icon and, with the giggling help of the cheerleaders and the school's We Are the World club, constructed one that he hoped would convey proper veneration and old-country spirit. It was an oval plywood replica of the fertility symbol treasured by Tanabe's own hometown —a fertility symbol over four hundred years old.

There'd been a minor war about that, assorted Plexus fundamentalists registering righteous anger. Since it was a question of some fifty skilled and one hundred and eighty semi- and unskilled jobs, however, biblical constraints had been shelved.

Many of the robust young gridiron stars were a tad vague on just what it was they were doing, especially the defensive linemen—particularly since they'd been up partying on the sly all night, getting acquainted with Kirin beer and sake. But they knew they owed Chick-Keek for a bitchin' junket to World Nihon and the chance to be shouldering a giant vulva along, drunk before noon, dressed in Oriental jockstraps—thus, his stock was high.

Chikamatsu Kirokku, himself slightly wasted, rode the bier like a conquering hero wearing, in addition to his *fundoshi* and headband, a varsity sweater ten sizes too big for him. He didn't realize his cortege had strayed off course, and so much was amiss at the park that no one else did, either.

From his vantage point Chick-Keek spied Lumber Jack's prone and phallic body and roared to his vassal lettermen. It was not uncommom for *matsuri* groups to joust in symbolic megacopulation, and this looked like the time for it. The pride of Plexus put their shoulders to their icon as though they were hitting tackling dummies and drove the plywood yoni straight at the furrowed crown of Lumber Jack's head.

Lucky didn't see the contingent from Plexus until it was too late. The cleft plywood lozenge and its bier smashed into Lumber; there was a rending, splintering impact. In moments Lucky, the Hono, Chikamatsu Kirokku, and a metric ton or so of Plexus football players were crawling around trying to figure out what had happened. From the crowd there was a light, almost timid pattering of applause which built and built, people whistling and shouting, some a little glassy-eyed and wistful.

Lucky spotted park security people closing in on the periphery of the crowd. A wheel had been knocked off the dolly, and he and the Hono couldn't have gotten Lumber away even if the opposition hadn't shown up. End of trail.

He was looking straight at a woman who was speaking into a dermal patch mike and unholstering a compact trank shooter from her belt when the whole world began to vibrate. Everybody glanced around and one by one, visitor and staff, they realized *Tengu Mountain* was erupting. Flame and smoke shot out of the volcanic summit as well as from various holes, caves, and apertures on its side. Landscape features and assorted animated monsters and other figures were on fire. Secondary explosions came from inside, showers of sparks shot from short-circuiting electrical wiring, and cracks and melted-out holes appeared in the sides of the mountain. Unidentifiable debris skyrocketed out of the attraction's top, leaving fireworks wakes.

Some audience members cheered, supposing it a climax to the performance they thought they'd just seen. But Lucky could only bow his head, knowing Tanabe had somehow managed to take out Silvercup where she'd lain concealed in the mountain. If they put Lucky in a mindbender, his only request would be that they take away all his memories.

A gasp from the crowd made him look up. Something big and sleek and dark had launched out of the top of the exploding *Tengu Mountain* like a ballistic missile. It changed vector under power even though there were no exhaust gases or fires visible and dove straight at him—at where he, personally, stood.

People made sheep sounds and threw themselves aside or down. Security fell back, a few of them firing at the spaceship to no avail. There was some barfing and praying from the boys of Plexus but only a happy howl from Chikamatsu Kirokku, who purely adored any kind of extravaganza. Lucky stood up shakily as a sleek airframe came down to align itself with its nose pointed directly between his eyes from four feet away. A hatch deployed, its lowest step only inches off the ground. "Get aboard," a voice said, and he recognized it.

"Hi Metallica. Or should I say Silvercup?"

"Lucky . . . don't look at me. All right? Just get aboard. And hurry."

There was such tremendous pain, such humiliation in the voice that he averted his eyes from her, not sure why he felt ashamed. "Hono? Bear a hand, here."

But even their best united efforts couldn't extricate Lumber;

they'd only gotten him onto the dolly with a hoist in the first place. Onlookers were getting to their feet and security was regrouping. "Silver!"

"I know, Lucky. Stand back."

She'd gotten control of more of her components while she lay doggo inside *Tengu Mountain*; now a rounded enclosure on her nose opened and gleaming, articulated alloy tentacles deployed. They extruded side branches and sub-sub-branches, like a living armored root system, and swooped toward Lucky and the others. He felt himself seized and saw that the same was happening to Lumber's body and the Hono.

"Get seats and hang on!" Silvercup cautioned.

He found himself inside the cabinspace, being jounced like salt in a shaker. Things looked unexpectedly makeshift in there, especially the acceleration seats biffed together from crating and padding and netting. Only the pilot and copilot chairs smacked of factory specs. Lucky dragged himself to the pilot's seat—unless Silvercup functioned on the English model—and was whipped sideways at the waist by maneuver forces.

"Yowch! Hey!"

"I *warned* you to hang on!" Silvercup righted again, and this time it was the Rphians, Dame Snarynxx, and the others who came stumbling in or were flung in by the alloy tentacles. It was suddenly very crowded. There was a pile of squirming Hono in one corner and GoBug had landed on his father's head. "I need some quiet time!" Mr. Millmixx cried. The hatch powered shut and everybody's conversation was stifled as gees began stacking up on them. Lucky stared into a screen as L.A. slid by underneath and Silvercup arrowed out over the Pacific.

He was pressed deep into his seat's upholstery. "Silver, bank right; head north—"

"Lucky, I'm sorry." It sounded like a crystalline bell shattering. "I can't do that. I'm programmed to take you back to the Fealty, and that means using the Adit at Click Fist in Sumatra or, failing that, the one aboard the *Crystal Harmonic*—somehow."

"Yeah? Then how come it looks like we're banking?"

"*What?*" He was right; she'd complied with his request without even realizing she had. "I don't understand." The gee forces slackened.

"Ah," vocalized several of the Hono at the same time, untangling themselves. "We can perhaps be of service there.

When we interfaced with Silvercup we noticed the programming implant compelling her to take Lucky Junknowitz back to Sweetspot and expunged it—leaving only the thought that it was there, in case some internal diagnostic came checking for it.''

Lucky and Silver stepped on each other's lines for a bit, thanking the Hono. When the tourists were distracted sorting themselves out, Lucky turned to the instrument panels and the optical pickups that looked back at him. "Listen, I heard about this probability business and all. The spill that hit me.''

"Oh? Lucky, I feel very strange. All courses are open to me now. Which way should I go?''

"I have a sister in San Francisco; maybe she has a hangar in her backyard.''

"Very well.'' She gained altitude. "I had to come to you. The same way I had to let you see the contents of that data crystal back on the Staph spacewheel. There's some kind of tie binding you and me to each other, Lucky. It came over me when I met you.''

Lucky hunched forward and spoke softly. "Look, Silver, it's this probability bath I took! It's a function of the spill—''

"I don't care what the cause was on the quantum level.''

"But—''

"What happened to me was real, even though the feeling has been stolen from me. Whatever the genesis was, what I experienced was real and gave me feelings I've never had before and it happened to *me*, it's *mine!* It was powerful and it made me think of things in a new and different way; I don't remember how but my peripheral memories tell me that's true. I want that part of myself back.''

He sank his head in his hands. "Okay, then, we'll get it back.'' Might as well be hung for a sheep as a lamb.

"And thanks.'' He slid cautiously from his chair. "You're a peach.'' Figuring it was wired for feedback, he planted a symbolic kiss in the middle of the seat cushion.

"Lucky!"

"Can't help it, I love your well-rounded contemporary styling and elegantly contoured lines.''

"I can't imagine what I ever saw in you.'' She sounded happier, though.

He hiked himself back into the seat feeling a lot closer to it. But there were troubling images whirling behind his eyeballs:

Harley, Sheena, Asia; Sean and the posse; the deaths of Bullets Strayhand and Rashad Tittle.

"Where are we going?" Silvercup asked.

"Huh? I told you: San Francisco."

"No." She activated her stealth suite and split the air northward. "I meant, what address?"

The break in contact with Silvercup came through to the Monitor graphically, as if a nerve ending had been seared, then severed. Rearing on its suspension jacks, the blocky, sphinx-like machine overseer let out a cybernetic burst of distress and fury that set subordinates scurrying for cover.

The surveillance telemetry that had been coming in from her, piggybacked on routine Trough telecast traffic via a technique resembling that used by Ka Shamok, had ceased. Though the data up to that point was somewhat spotty due to events and technical difficulties, the Monitor knew Hono had rooted out and expunged its implanted controls over the transformed gleamer. Its towering pulses of anger had machines all around it cringing and fearing its wrath—all but one.

The Monitor's silent summons had brought the Virile Construct, gleaming and impossibly heroic on his floating platform. A near-instantaneous transfer of data explained what had happened. The Virile Construct was shocked, infuriated—*scandalized*. "Do you mean to say she's malfunctioning so badly that she *accepted* this unauthorized modification? That she actually *allows herself* to remain with that cretinous primate?"

"That is my assessment," the Monitor seethed, gazing down on the vessel it had meant to use to fulfill its desire. Elsewhere in its domain was stored Silvercup's actual body, the one from which her essential self had been removed for her mission to find and fetch Lucky Junknowitz; her body the Monitor could take and use however and whenever it pleased. But where was the point in that? What the Monitor lusted for from her no mere shell of metalflesh could provide.

"But—then, she will be denied access to *me*." The Virile Construct sounded more bewildered than distressed.

"Inconceivable as it sounds," the Monitor told him, "in her current state, Silvercup *prefers* Junknowitz to you."

The Virile Construct's expression showed dumbfoundment, then dawning comprehension, then indescribable rage. *"I'll kill him!"*

He whirled, emitting orders both cybernetic and verbal, calling for resources to be marshaled, preparations to be carried out, transit arrangements to be made—all with the highest priority. "I'll find that simpering retard and tear him to bleeding shreds!"

"Good," the Monitor approved, gazing down. "I knew you'd see things logically."

There are only so many ways the atoms can accrue, the molecules clump together. Patterns and motifs repeat; variations on themes occur galaxy-wide.

The Blight had been the name of a region of the planet Echevar where merciless clear-cut logging and slash-and-burn agriculture had denuded and depleted the land, rendering countless species extinct. The locals dealt with the problem—cheered on by the ramrods of a local Black Hole subsidiary, Mow Money, Inc., and profiteers of their own race—by moving on, attacking new tracts of virgin timber. The consumer toys, novelties and baubles shipped in from the Trough were avidly received.

The protests of a few brave environmentalists made them that much easier to identify and neutralize.

The miraculous wood of Echevar was tremendously valuable for its medicinal properties as well as reputed aphrodisiac and psi-enhancing attributes; uncountable megatons of it were mass-transited offworld via special freight Adits. Mow Money's profits well pleased the Sysops. To replace fruits and other foods the trees had provided, subsistence crops were sown in slash-and-burn zones, but deprived of the nutrients that had been locked up in the trees the ground would only yield one or two harvests before becoming barren, so still more land was slashed and burned.

Nowadays most folks called the whole planet Blight, and with good reason. Its climate, biosphere, and ecosystems mortally wounded, it would be uninhabitable within another three baseline-years—though nobody was letting the Echevarian populace in on that. A Mow Money, Inc. sideline had made a considerable fortune selling cheap respirators, UV-protection products, and processed-cellulose nutrient gruel—the latter to replace the edible fruits, vegetables, and animals that no longer reproduced on Blight. In order to buy these things the Blighters had to clear-cut their ancient forests at an ever-increasing rate.

One knee-slapper Black Hole was keeping to itself was that

though the local profiteers planned to flee into the Trough when their planet became untenable, there were so many hidden costs and add-ons in their accounts with Mow Money's company store that none of them would be able to afford it.

Among the offworld functionaries working at the headquarters area were a number of Chasen-nur. As he faded in, provided with the most thoroughgoing cover his organization had been able to come up with in the time available, Ka Shamok appreciated his informant's thoughtfulness: there was, at least, some hope of blending in. He recognized none of the Chasen-nur and ignored them, as they did him and one another.

Avoiding the eyes of others of his species was more than a habit; as with all Chasen-nur, it was in Ka Shamok a survival reflex. Long ago, for reasons generally attributed to sadistic curiosity, the Sysops had infected the telepathically gifted natives of the planet Tiiphu, the Chasen-nur, with an appalling plague. "The killing thought," as it came to be called, was transmitted by the meeting of eyes, carrying madness and death. Many died of it or suicided upon being infected; the surviving Chasen-nur fled their homeworld and avoided each other's glance. Beings whose central joy had been their optically maintained mental linkage, its multilevel and harmonious intimacy, were forced to shun one another and live lives of wretched spiritual loneliness.

Ka Shamok had often wondered if the Sysops had been so unthinking that they didn't realize the likelihood of creating a terrible enemy—or if, on the other hand, the Lords of Black Hole simply didn't care.

Looking out across the hazy, sun-scorched barrenness of Blight, the lifeless and cementlike red clay that lay underfoot, he thought how good a representation it was of his own soul. As instructed, he set out across the parched, eroded landscape on foot. As part of his cover he carried a portable sampling kit and a data relay. He wore a respirator mask even though, tough as a boulder, he could have managed without one; the concealment of his features was a welcome effect.

He'd been told to come alone and would have in any event. He owed his unseen comrade many times over and would not risk having his most valuable asset's identity compromised—especially after the informant's long and troubling silence.

The rutted heavy-equipment road led him from the Adit facility in the direction of current logging operations, and he paralleled it from a distance to avoid the choking dust of an endless stream of gigantic lumber carriers. Off near the horizon, immense machines rumbled and scythed in a perpetual twilight of grit and dust.

At one marker he veered away, toward a high point of ground where the remains of some titanic bonfire still lay—mounds of ash and the blackened remains of trunks and limbs, like the bones in a funeral pyre of gods. A worker had explained that this was where the last Echevarian shaman had tried to work a transformation spell and exorcise the aliens—magically bring the forest back into existence.

As Ka Shamok approached the pile a young adult Chasen-nur male came into view around one end of the cremated remains of the great trees. Slightly taller and less burly, he averted his eyes, acknowledging Ka Shamok's status as elder. "I have been sent to lead you."

So, the informant had subordinates. Ka Shamok fell in behind, knowing the other would be keeping track of him with ears and subtle sidelong or darting glances exactingly calculated to run no risk of a meeting of the eyes.

The way was a difficult one, up through the blackened, jumbled remains of the forest holocaust. Most of it followed the natural paths of fallen trunks and skewed limbs, though here and there a notch appeared to have been cut with an energy ax. There were steep inclines of slippery bark ash, hand traverses, narrow spans over dark pits of broken branches like sharpened stakes, and gaps that had to be leapt on the first try, without error. It demanded tremendous surefootedness, balance, strength, and an unswerving sense of purpose but Ka Shamok was more than up to it. His young guide was a splendid athlete, quick and powerful.

They emerged three-quarters of the way up the pile onto a natural balcony formed by a limb stump some fifteen feet in diameter. From there they could gaze out over ransacked and moribund Blight. His eyes trained respectfully on Ka Shamok's feet, the young Chasen-nur said, "You will please wait here, Your Honor?"

"Very well. How long must I wait?" He'd known going in that he would be vulnerable but was feeling acutely so now. However, he did not regret coming.

"How long are you *willing* to wait?" the guide parried. He had edged around so that Ka Shamok now stood with his back to a long and deadly drop.

Ka Shamok considered the question. "As long as it takes."

"You are that patient, sir?"

"I am."

"I am not!" With that the young Chasen-nur seized Ka Shamok's brawny wrists with a grip of amazing strength and, holding him fast, *lifted his head suddenly, blazing eyes boring directly into Ka Shamok's.*

Such was his fear of the killing thought that Ka Shamok would have torn himself loose and cast himself off the limb if he'd been able, but he couldn't break that terrible hold. A shriek built in him as he fought to drag the guide from his feet, hurl them both to their deaths. His dread gave him hysterical strength, and he was beginning to win—when he realized that no killing thought had entered him.

The one who held him *looked* a Chasen-nur in every particular, but the eyes had proved he wasn't. There was no telepathic contact, no breaking of the mental isolation Ka Shamok had endured for so long. Ka Shamok stopped struggling; his guide opened one hand to show eight interlocking rings limned in his palm.

"You!"

"Yes." With Ka Shamok no longer trying to destroy himself, Yoo Sobek released his other hand, stepped back a pace. "Me."

Still meeting the rebel leader's gaze, Sobek reconjugated, going back to the human form he'd assumed when he'd spoken to Charlie Cola on the Westhampton beach—humans having come to be a matter of great preoccupation to him lately. The male manifestation had the pallor of someone raised in a cave, standing a very fit-looking six feet and appearing to be in early middle age. Wavy black hair was brushed back from a prominent brow that suggested high intelligence; long-lashed blue eyes conveyed a sense of melancholy and an air of purpose. The eight rings had disappeared from his palm.

"Are you so surprised?" Sobek added. "You must have realized your informant was high in the Agency."

"You misunderstand," Ka Shamok responded with a bleak grin. "From the information you provided, the things you knew, I thought your rank would be *higher*, Probe—no offense intended."

That actually drew a smile from Sobek in return—a rare thing. "I *was* of higher status, once. A great deal of my memory is missing but there is much I can tell, though I must depart Blight before nightfall. But the most important matters should come first. I want vengeance against the Sysops as much as you do, perhaps more; in me you have the ideal confederate and counterpart. But as I said, I am less willing to wait than you—in part because I don't think we need to much longer.

"I propose that we ready an assault on Light Trap itself and make an end to the Sysops and the Black Hole Travel Agency."

Ka Shamok might have been machined from purple steel for all the reaction the words drew. The rumble of the distant logging and the moan of the parched winds were the only sounds. Then at last he responded. "Many have tried before."

Many and great ones had tried, in efforts that ranged from apocalyptic frontal assault to wraithlike infiltration through other continua. The list had become long, down through the ages, and never a success or even near-miss. And the catalogue of Black Hole's retribution was enough to sap anyone's fighting spirit.

Yoo Sobek showed animation enough for both of them. "But none of those others had the advantages that lie within our grasp now! You know what's abroad in the Trough as well as I. In these last months all the old equations have been made obsolete. But Black Hole is already on the move; we have to strike soon, as soon as we can."

It was a decision to daunt even the great Ka Shamok. But faced with it, he had to admit that Sobek was right. The unique conditions that made Light Trap vulnerable might vanish at any time, and would almost certainly never occur again. If that happened, he and his rebels could look forward to a fruitless life of fleeing and hiding, perhaps a few minor victories—and Black Hole would outlive them all.

"Agreed," he told Yoo Sobek. "Provided that the other things you have to say to me quell all doubts."

Where Ka Shamok might have expected elation from him, Sobek grew grave now, even tremulous. "Then there is one thing I have to tell you first. From it springs most of the others you'll need to know from me. Change places with me."

Ka Shamok guardedly did as he was asked. With his back to the sky, Yoo Sobek held his arms away from his body, as if offering himself up for sacrifice.

"I know almost nothing about who I was before. I'm like a newborn. I know that once I was a Sysop and . . . I was the one who shaped the killing thought and visited it on the Chasennur."

That was the great wrong the luminous green needle had

shown him, along with his glimpse of the transcendent meaning of the eight rings, as he perched there looking down on Light Trap. He'd had to unburden himself of it; whatever happened now, he was prepared to accept.

The very air seemed to stand still for a moment. Then a sound began to build deep in the chest of Ka Shamok. As it became a howl that filled the sky, he plucked the unresisting Yoo Sobek off his feet and made to hurl him down to his death.

But the rebel stopped, poised, Sobek raised high. It wasn't the thought that in killing Sobek he'd be literally throwing away any chance of stopping Black Hole; it wasn't the fact that his irreplaceable informant would be gone forever, and it was not gratitude.

What gave him pause was that Sobek hadn't conjugated in an effort to save himself. Ka Shamok somehow sensed that he wasn't going to, either—that Sobek wouldn't take wing or develop high-impact resistance or otherwise metamorphose to survive. Sobek had come prepared to die if Ka Shamok chose to slay him.

Ka Shamok could have personal, racial revenge; the price was that Black Hole would endure.

Three times Ka Shamok leaned forward, muscles bunched, to cast down the Probe. Three times he stopped himself by main force of will. At last he dropped the man to the bark under his feet and went to lean against the seared trunk of the tree, gasping for breath.

Recalling the victories Yoo Sobek's secret communication had brought him, Ka Shamok took out the little recorder and stood looking at its cover. "You never told me what the interlocking rings mean," he grated.

Sobek had risen to his feet behind Ka Shamok. "It's a symbol used with reference to Adit Navel—to Earth," he answered quietly, "though it doesn't represent the planet per se. Rather, it refers to that world's special status as idiot savant of the galaxy. It has another connotation as well, one I knew once but had ripped from me.

"Whatever the true meaning of that symbol is, it broke my sanity but also drove me to rebel against Black Hole. That was why I adopted it as the secret emblem of my private war. Whatever it is, this symbol is about a great deal more than just Earth."

"Earth," Ka Shamok reflected. "Over and over, that benighted place."

"And it's not over."

Ka Shamok turned back to Yoo Sobek. "Where do we begin?"

"Come, I'll tell you."

They began the climb back down the jumble of sacrificial timber, off to bring down the Black Hole Travel Agency or die trying.

About the Author

Jack McKinney has been a psychiatric aide, fusion-rock guitarist and session man, worldwide wilderness guide, and "consultant" to the U.S. military in Southeast Asia (although they had to draft him for that).

His numerous other works of mainstream and science fiction—novels, radio and television scripts—have been written under various pseudonyms.

A self-described "ambulatory schizophrenic," he is currently dividing his time between New York and Annapolis, Maryland.

ROBOTECH

by
JACK McKINNEY

The ROBOTECH saga follows the lives and events, battles, victories and setbacks of this small group of Earth heroes from generation to generation.